Soblar
Concealed Revelations
Vol.1

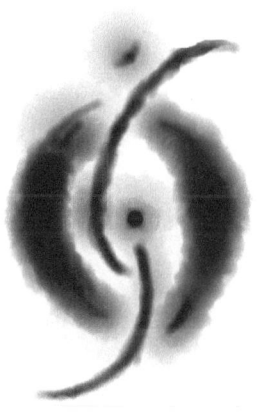

Soblar
Concealed Revelations
Vol.1

A. E. Pasker

This book is dedicated to the compassionate conscience in us all: past, present and in the future.

PREFACE

Y ears before *The Interview of the Century...*

"The exact time of his beginning is still uncertain, but it must not have been recent. It must have taken him some time to decide how he was going to do what he's done. Where to go, on what occasions... Who to approach and when. How to initiate those he had chosen and how to motivate them in the way that he intended. Finding what troubled their souls, what triggered their actions, what inspired their desires... What made them tick..." Avraham began to speak in front of his audience, as he swept away the wavy salt and pepper hair from the front of his eyes.

"He showed up one day out of nowhere," Avraham said, looking into the eyes of those in front of him as he continued, "and began wandering around the world, possibly exploring all the continents. And during this wandering, he was interacting with people from all walks of life. People of different physical, social, spiritual and economic conditions. He mingled with some very dangerous people. And it seems he also traveled with international volunteer workers bringing aid to some of the poorest and most abandoned places around the world.

"It seems impossible, but he seemed to be everywhere at once. Simultaneously, he conducted lucrative deals with some of the most powerful and richest people. He also debated with some of the most critically acclaimed scientific minds of our times- philosophers, influential religious leaders, political advisors.

"It has come to our attention that there are traces left of his communications, with his chosen few. There may still be many others who are unaccounted for. During his nomadic pilgrimage, I believe that he came to see something that may have enlightened or perhaps disturbed him. We believe that this drove him to the conclusion that perhaps many of the people he met along his travels, had embarked on a journey, which would lead them away from their 'true path.' The path that destiny had set out for them. He believed that at one point, they had gone left instead of right. They may have said yes, instead of no, they may have stayed still, instead of in motion. Or maybe they were asleep and not yet awoken.

"We believe that based on these self-acquired conclusions, he decided to align those individuals with the path he believed they had been destined to follow, in order to achieve what the very aspect of their true persona was supposed to conquer. That is, to become who they were supposed to be. They needed to relinquish who they were, right from where they were, at that very moment and transcend into who they were supposed to become.

"In order to achieve this, he crafted what we believe to be, a hypnotic mirror image sub-reality, in which he was able to bring each of those he had chosen, to experience a different existence. One that they had created over the lives of others, whether directly or indirectly, whether they knew it or not. By doing this, he caused dramatic and unexpected changes to the chosen subjects, of what we can best describe as, the analysis of his experiment. Thus, he turned good and noble people into villains. Villains and dangerous individuals, into kind and gentle-hearted people. Pious people, into incredulous thrill-seekers.

"His influence caused certain wealthy people to give up their wealth by choice, embracing a life we would call 'average poverty.' Poor people began turning into wealthy characters. Others yet were confused and remained how they were. They searched for a gray line to figure things out the best they could. This situation was initiated in a calm and unassuming manner, but soon and before anyone became wary of it, it had turned into a wildfire which began affecting the lives of everyone. It affected institutions, it affected people. It affected the very fabric of society. The news of what was occurring did not move as fast as the deeds.

"But in time, word began to spread. And some became aware of what he had done by the word of mouth stories that circulated. And according to whatever interaction or indirect relation one would have with this man, he would be recognized by a nickname. Amongst them, the most popular nickname is the *Prophet*, some others refer to him as the *Vigilante*, and some simply call him *Teacher*.

"As of now, he has become the most wanted man in the world, and yet his face is missing from the most wanted list! Because... the rest of the world does not need to know this yet. Many wish to find him for nefarious reasons. Others are curious as to how he managed to do what he's done. And some just want to thank him, to embrace the person who supposedly opened their eyes.

"Regardless of everything else, the actions of this man, however he is recognized: Prophet, Vigilante, or Teacher, his actions have affected places at the highest levels of civilized and uncivilized power.

"Change is taking place all over the world. For many, change can be unwelcome news. For those searching for hope, for signs of better days to come, change is a positive forecast. For those already established in the world as it has been for the last millennia, change is a disruptive force, which needs to be dealt with fast and swiftly.

"A global movement has been conceived to find and capture this Prophet character. Even the President of the United States has been affected by the actions provoked by this disruptive individual! President Smith blames the disappearance of his top adviser and close friend on this man. He has personally ordered all major law enforcement agencies under his power, to go after the so-called Prophet. FBI, CIA, NSA, Secret Service, the President's allies abroad and others as well, have been commanded to track the individual down in any way possible.

"And gentlemen, this is where we all stand at this moment. But before I continue, I would like to say that it is my privilege to have the honor of working with such an eclectic and unorthodox group of highly regarded individuals, such as yourselves. During my years of operating with Mossad, I never had an opportunity such as this! Here we have envoys from the Queen, represented by MI6, CIA officials sent by President Smith himself, well-respected members of the Bratva. Members from the powerful Yakuza, the influential Triads, one of the most powerful drug cartels of South America, and a representative from our friends at the Vatican. Collaborators from La Camorra. And let us not forget *the Kingdom*." Avraham said as he pointed to the back of the room. A Saudi Arabian man with a short neat beard, dressed in a business suit, was sitting alone near a corner. He sat quietly as he smoked a cigarette and listened intently.

"We have all been gathered together for the sole purpose of hunting down this Prophet, Vigilante, or whatever he likes to be called." Avraham's tone had changed slightly. His voice began to sound more restless as he continued. "And those who made it possible for this union of our minds to take place, are expecting a definitive measure of success from us. But before we set out to achieve, what could arguably be, the most important mission of our lives, we need to cover a couple of minor obstacles, which need addressing." Avraham looked at everyone gathered in the grand room.

"You've said it yourself, Mr. Azra," The man who spoke was Vladimir Chekov, the Russian mob envoy. He was tall and slim, with black hair and piercing green eyes. "This is the 90's, we're nearing a new century and with the power that we represent in our unions, nothing is impossible. We can find and eliminate our target in no time."

"What are the problems you are concerned with, Mr. Azra?" The envoy from the Yakuza asked. He was a short and muscular man, who was well-mannered and eloquent in the way he spoke. He wore a dark gray suit that hid most of his tattoos, with the exception of those on his hands which still showed, as he sat with his hands folded in front of him.

"Look at all of us here," Chekov again spoke. "We are here because we all know and understand how we balance each other. Each of us represents a branch which in one way or another interconnect with others around the world."

"Gentlemen, I understand and share your perspective," Avraham said, sensing the anxiety of those gathered. "But regardless, there are important hurdles that need to be covered before we undertake this mission." At that moment, Avraham opened his right hand in front of himself and to the view of those in the room. The man representing the Kingdom brought the cigarette away from his lips and without releasing the smoke from his mouth, he was listening to what Avraham was about to say.

"Number one," Avraham commenced counting down using the fingers of his right hand. "We do not know where he came from. We know nothing about his past. Number two, we do not know his name. No one does, which is why he's always given a nickname depending on his deeds at whatever given place. Number three, we do not know what he looks like. Eyewitness reports are completely contradictory and cannot be trusted. All we know is that most likely, the Prophet is a male. And number four, as important as the others, we do not know where he's going to show up next. And this is the worst challenge yet, as there is an entire network I believe, out there somewhere, working to cover his tracks. If he didn't have such an effective network, we would have at the very least a description. We are chasing a ghost, gentlemen. There is no way we can conduct a successful hunt, without knowing the principle fundamentals of who it is we are hunting."

They all looked at each other. For a short time, silence had taken over the room, having realized how little they actually knew about their target. Avraham remained on his feet, staring at all of them around the round table. Nevertheless, they were all resolute in their desire for taking this man down, however they could, and at whatever the price.

Chekov spoke up once again. "Mr. Azra, what does the last one represent?"

Avraham looked at Chekov before looking at his hand. The thumb was still left. "Uncertainty, Mr. Chekov. Everything else which I'm not aware of, I understand. But this, this represents what we are up against. Uncertainty." At that moment, the representative of the Kingdom released the smoke he had been holding, while gazing up at the hundred-foot ceiling.

"We have to find this man at once Mr. Azra." A voice sounded from the back of the salon. Avraham turned to look at the man with the cigarette in his hand. There was a massive window, floor to ceiling, partially covered by a shimmery curtain. The view of the desert was seen at the far distance through the fabric of the curtain.

"His ideal is to systematically and methodically end the way of life that we have crafted together for our world, through many generations of hard work. And this cannot be allowed." The same man continued. "The people of our nations do not know what they want, until we tell them. They will not even know if they want it, unless we guide them towards it. They need us to keep things together for them, to keep their lives balanced. This so-called Prophet and what he's doing will cripple the lives of those who know nothing about the way the world works, as well as those who control everything - our lives. We can't live without each other; this is how the balance of power is distributed. But we can do well live without him."

∞

Several months later...

Within the walls of a black sight, at an undisclosed location in the Middle East, the shadow of a tall and muscular man is cast walking near the wall of a short hallway. There were only a few lightbulbs on, while others seemed to have been purposely knocked out. Individuals dressed in military fatigue are seen entering and leaving a room at the end of the same hallway. Voices and murmuring are heard. Then suddenly, shouting, cursing, and banging sounds followed by a burst of maniacal laughter.

"Tell me now, or I will kill you right where you are!" The laughter continued, as the voice of a threatening man overshadowed him.

At the same time, a military truck had just pulled up outside, in front of a wire gate. Heavily armed military men stood guard all around. A man with an injured left arm, wrapped in bandages, stepped out of the vehicle. An AK-47 hung over his right shoulder. He was medium built, with a short dark beard. He wore a dark green military cap that covered half of his face and his long gray hair was tied back into a ponytail. He heard the shouting as he walked towards the hallway and into the back room. Those who saw him saluted him with respect.

"Captain Sullivan, I'm very glad you made it sir." A soldier walked by him, making sure he shook his hand if only for a moment.

"Thank you, son," Sullivan replied. He kept his head down and kept it that way while walking towards the door at the end of the hallway. A young soldier stared at him momentarily. There was something on his mind, but his face did not display any emotions.

Sullivan arrived at the room but did not immediately enter. He remained right outside the door, just listening to the questions someone was asking.

"Where was he? Was he there when we got in? Which one was he? Was he one of those who got killed, or did he get away?" The man asking the questions was a marine seated on a chair across the table. He appeared to be Hispanic with dark hair and a long dark beard that gave him a youthful look. His tank top displaying his broad shoulders was soaked by sweat. His marine corps tattoos and the veins of his forearms were displayed as he held a black cable between his hands.

There was a badly beaten man with handcuffs on, seated across from him.

"He may not have been there," Sullivan spoke from outside the room, before walking in. His words made everyone silent inside the room. The man in handcuffs looked up at him, with his eyes wide open and mouth agape. An American from the mid-west, he had a wide bald spot on the top of his head, while the rest of his hair was short and disheveled. A Hawaiian shirt with blue and red flowers appeared as if someone had been trying to rip it off him.

"What makes you think he wasn't there?" The marine stood up from his chair as he stared at the man in handcuffs. He held the black cable in one hand while swinging it from side to side while asking Sullivan the question. "And you Cunningham," the Marine continued. "Now you happen to know about his whereabouts?"

Sullivan looked up at the other two Marines in the room. They were standing behind Cunningham, wearing clean uniforms. Standing, waiting for orders.

"Son, will you hold on this for me?" Sullivan handed his weapon to the Marine standing to the left side of Cunningham.

"Sir." The Marine quickly hung the AK-47 over his right shoulder and took several steps to position himself right back to where he was before.

"Maybe he was in South America and not the North Pole?" Cunningham laughed and stared at the Marine holding the cable while speculating to Sullivan. "I heard the news on the radio. The soldiers had been listening to music on their way back to this base, I don't know what they were listening to. They had me on the floor, in the back of the truck. My head and my eyes were covered but my ears were wide open. I heard it over their radio. The explosion of the prototype electric plant. Those things don't just happen..." Cunningham's laughter once again echoed throughout the room.

Sullivan stared at him without making anything of it. The Marine holding the cable was not so patient. He jumped behind Cunningham and wrapped the cable around his neck. He then turned him around to look at his face, it did not take long for Cunningham to turn bright red, losing his breath. He tried to remove the cable from around his neck. Sullivan allowed the scenario to play out for a moment, before deactivating it.

"Sanchez. Let him go."

Sanchez looked at Sullivan. The soft-spoken tone of his superior did not make him let of Cunningham's neck.

"Captain, just give me a couple of more seconds with this piece of garbage." Sanchez looked at Cunningham's eyes. They looked like the eyes of someone whose life was quickly abandoning him. "He will begin to take this more seriously Sir."

"Sanchez, enough I said!"

This time Sanchez's hands snapped away from his prisoner's neck, releasing the grip of the cable. It took a minute for Cunningham to stop coughing and regain his normal breathing. He brought his hand up to his neck to feel the skin around it.

"You really wanted to kill me this time, didn't you?" He looked at Sanchez with both animosity and sarcasm. Sanchez walked away from him and placed his right hand over the left shoulder of the Marine standing to the left side of Cunningham. The Marine walked away, and he took his place, breathing hard and wiping the sweat away from his face.

"Avraham has been after you for some time now." Sullivan remained on his feet.

He spoke to Cunningham but did not look directly at him. "Do you want to tell me what happened? If you can help me with anything you may know, I might be able to help you." Cunningham was staring at his hand over the table. A light bulb above him was slowly swaying left and right, the handcuffs had left his wrists scratched and bloody. A smile was displayed over his mouth. Heavy breathing followed, before fanatical laughter. He reclined himself back, almost to the point of falling off the chair. Sanchez held him up and straightened the chair for him.

"If you do this again, I will let you fall, and stomp on your head while you're on the floor." Sanchez's warnings before had come with circumstantial action. Cunningham looked at him, fully aware he meant what he said, and smiled at him before looking back at Sullivan's direction.

"Regardless of how or when you leave this place," Sullivan pulled up a chair and placed it near the table, right across from Cunningham. "Eventually you're going to get bored, and you're going to have to spill it. Why don't you just make it easy on yourself and the young blood behind you? They don't show it. You will never see it on their faces because they are all the best of the best. They will not show fear, fatigue or worry. But they feel it when they think about their loved ones. Neither of them, want to be here one minute longer than they have to. Don't make it any longer Cunningham. Spill it. Then we can all get the hell out of this place and go home." Sullivan brought his face up for just an instant and looked at Cunningham right in his eyes. Cunningham displayed a different reaction than what he had shown everyone else so far. He was attentive to Sullivan's words, to every single one of them.

"I mentioned to you about the explosion," Cunningham began speaking, but he seemed different somehow. He spoke in a manner to which Sanchez and the other Marine, felt compelled to listen. "He was here before it happened," Cunningham continued. "For all any of you know, he was with you, all along. You may have thought you didn't see him, but you all did. He was there before you found me, and he remained there afterward. Sullivan?"

Sullivan was staring at Cunningham, analyzing every single word he had said and in the *way* he had said it. There was also the understanding in Sullivan's mind, that he was listening to a man who was once one of the closest advisors to the President of the United States. A man whose intellect had never been doubted by anyone. A man who knew the innermost deepest secrets of the President and other very powerful individuals in the country, whom he had served for almost four decades.

"Yes Sullivan," Cunningham leaned closer while staring at his face. "Think about it, Sullivan. You know exactly what I'm talking about. You know I'm not crazy, and you are well aware of what I'm telling you is a description of the scenario in which you have been dwelling in all of this time. You are all lost in a dark tunnel, without an exit." Cunningham laughed. He paused while shaking his head from side to side. "For all you know, you may be him." Sullivan shivered but did not dare to lift his head again. He did not want to look into Cunningham's eyes, he did not want Cunningham to look into his.

Sanchez took a few steps forward, staring at Cunningham while gazing at Sullivan from the corner of his eyes.

"What the hell is he talking about sir?" Sanchez asked. The other Marine seemed confused too. At that moment, Cunningham turned his head, looked at Sanchez and smiled.

"Oh! You are not there yet my good fellow." He told Sanchez.

"There? Where? What are you saying?" Sanchez grabbed Cunningham by the collars of his shirt and turned him around, body and chair, to face him directly. Sullivan remained thinking, motionless. As did the Marine standing guard.

"What is this bastard talking about, sir?" Sanchez looked very confused and angry, demanding immediate answers to clear his head.

"He will not have the answers," Cunningham said. "He knows very well that no one does. You have all gotten this far. *The Z initiative*. You actually found me! But this moment, right here, right where we are all together. This very moment is as far as anyone will ever get to him. As a matter of fact, Sanchez," Cunningham slowly turned his face to look at Sullivan, who was still facing the table motionless. He then turned his face to look at the Marine behind Sanchez, the shadow of the Marine standing outside in the hallway, before looking at Sullivan once again. "Who knows Sanchez, there is a chance that you are the only one obliviously sleeping as we speak."

"What?" Sanchez took two steps away from Cunningham while staring at Sullivan. He then turned away from the Marine behind him.

"As ease, Sanchez." Sullivan noticed Sanchez's demeanor was becoming unstable. "Cunningham has learned a trick or two from his spiritual captor, but..."

Sanchez was still gravitating away from everyone and towards the hallway, only pausing as he saw five other Marines heading towards the room, accompanied by the mission Commander. It was General Timothy R. Silver, a man in his early seventies, in great physical shape, who towered over the rest of his soldiers.

"Did you hear about the explosion General?" Cunningham asked as everyone saluted their superior. Cunningham again went back to his maniacal laughter. "He will change the world whether you want to accept it or not!" He shouted while laughing even louder. "There is nothing anyone can do about it. He will change it all!" He continued screaming over and over again, under the watchful eyes of his captive audience.

Chapter I:

Uninformed Casualties

Elsewhere in the world...

"I want you to bring me more morphine and additional sheets, bring the used ones as well, we need them all right now!"

A nurse was heard saying as she and another nurse gathered together the kits needed, from a very narrow supply room. They both wore white bio-hazard suits with special masks. It did not take them long to exit the supply room onto a chaotic scene. It was the hallway of an advanced military vessel, where armed soldiers suited up in highly advanced black military gear, could be seen rushing in every direction.

Nurse Smith, as the rectangular tag over the upper left side of her uniform read, was a strong looking, blue-eyed, dark-haired woman in her early 30's. She walked into one of the rooms where there were several doctors and other nurses attending to a man. The man had been acting irrational since awaking from a coma not long ago and his body has been rejecting all the medication he had been given so far. The doctors and the additional nurses were dressed in the same bio-hazard suits that nurse Smith was wearing except theirs were gray with four red stripes on their left shoulder, indicating a higher rank.

Hours later, Nurse Smith walked back into the same room. She was now wearing her regular uniform which was plain white scrubs. Her hair was tied up into a neat bun, and this time the patient was quietly sleeping. The light in the room was very low and the illumination of the devices connected to the man was dimmed as well. She looked at him for a moment seeing that he was missing his right leg, his right arm and had burns covering most of his body. There was sadness in her gaze as she looked upon him. She went ahead to change his IV fluid bag. He appeared to be a man in his mid to late twenties, with fair skin darkened by the sun, curly dark hair that grew past his ears and thick eyebrows that were partially burned. Burn marks were visible from under his neck to the top left side of his face. She thought about how different and challenging his life is going to be after this.

"Poor soul..." Nurse Smith said quietly to herself while cleaning the man's wounds and changing the bandages around them.

When she was done, she gently tapped the man's left arm reassuringly, one of the few places he was not wounded, before turning to leave the room. She was startled when she saw there were two men there, dressed in dark blue suits, seated behind her in the shadows on the left side of the door.

"Poor soul indeed..." One of the men whispered. Nurse Smith walked out of the room without saying anything to them.

The next day, Nurse Smith was going to begin her usual rounds, along with Nurse Roche. As they entered the room where the man with the badly burned body was being kept, she saw that he was awake and was accompanied by a doctor and the same two men she had seen the night before.

"You may go now and assist in the care of the other." The doctor instructed. She hesitated a moment, but she then took a step back and allowed the sliding door to close automatically in front of her and went ahead to the next room with Nurse Roche.

"Now I will leave you with these men and they will do everything in their power to help you, Mr. Douglas." The doctor said to the patient. "Don't worry, you will be fine."

The doctor then excused himself and only the other two men remained with Douglas. One of the men made sure the door was completely locked by scanning his wrist band over a keypad by the door. He then spoke an order into the wrist band for the door to remain locked. As he came back closer to the bed, the other man sat in a chair by the side of Douglas's head and pulled out a very thin small recording device. He placed it near Douglas's pillow in an inconspicuous manner.

"Clarence Douglas. Please confirm that is your name, correct?" The man by the other side of the bed asked while researching information about the patient in the bed through the lenses of the thin-framed glasses he was wearing.

"Yes," Clarence replied. His voice sounded very fragile and he was still under the effects of the medication he had been given, but his presence of mind was enough to understand and answer questions.

"Who are you?" Clarence asked the man by the side of his pillow.

"At this moment, that is not important Mr. Douglas. What is important is your recollection of the events which brought you to this place and the condition in which you find yourself in right now." The man replied. He looked at his partner standing at the other side of the bed. He then looked again at Clarence and got closer to him without taking his eyes away from his face.

"God, what's happened to me?" Clarence asked while taking a quick glimpse at himself in the hospital bed.

"You are one of the few survivors, Mr. Douglas." The man standing by the left side of the bed answered.

"Survivors...?" Clarence asked slowly.

"Do you remember what happened to you? What caused all of this damage to your body? Do you remember anything at all?" His tone of voice was becoming demanding and impatient.

"Stop! Stop please!" Clarence cried out for a moment while the two men observed in silence. He looked at them and he saw no mercy or compassion on their faces, only determination. After a moment, Clarence finally pulled himself together and asked the man to his left for a glass of water. The man looked at his partner and his partner agreed. Clarence used his left hand with the help of the man in glasses, to drink from a plastic cup. He took several sips and afterward, reclined himself back while looking at the ceiling.

"Who am I talking to?" Clarence finally asked.

"That is not important at the moment." The man in glasses replied.

"What are your names? You know my name, and you seem to know who I am. I don't know anything about you. I need to know who I am talking to!" Clarence insisted.

"You may call me Mr. Burton and the gentleman over there is Mr. Vaughn." The man near Clarence replied. As Clarence began to cough again, Burton gave him more water. Burton let out a soft sigh as he went on to carefully place his glasses into his jacket pocket.

"We need you to tell us everything you can Mr. Douglas. It is very important for our investigation to figure out how and when, things began to get so out of control, that the consequences of what exactly took place, brought us all to this very point." Vaughn said, carefully measuring his words, while Burton placed the cup back on the table near the bed.

Clarence began to think and search in his mind. He again coughed momentarily, as tears were automatically coming down his eyes. He paused for a while as he composed himself.

"There were... Demons." Clarence began hesitantly.

"What? Speak louder, what did you say?" Burton asked Clarence.

"I saw demons..." Clarence again said, now, looking at both men in the eyes as he spoke to them, while still searching within his own mind, to sift through all the chaotic images he was beginning to recall.

"Please continue..." Vaughn said.

"I... I was never supposed to be at that place. Luck or, maybe the lack of it perhaps, had brought me there. I felt as if it was going to be the start of a new beginning for me, and it turned out to be nearly my end." Clarence said, speaking while looking at what was left of his body.

"Tell us about those demons you said you saw Mr. Douglas. How did they look, what did they do?" Burton asked. Clarence looked at him for an instant, then looked at himself and stared at the place where his right leg should have been. He then closed his eyes tightly.

"The demons, they moved in the air," Clarence said. "First, there was the one who wanted to get the woman. It seemed to me like, he had been taunting her to the point of driving her mad. Then, others showed up. I am not sure whether one of them wanted to protect her or kill her." Clarence paused momentarily, shaking his head from side to side.

"Please continue Mr. Douglas." Vaughn implored him while taking a quick look at one of his notes, within the very thin compact black device in his left hand. In it, Vaughn had several pictures, including one of the badly burned and dismembered body of a woman near the entrance of a sewer tunnel.

"They began attacking each other... their voices seemed to be chanting, they made sign languages with their hands and as they did, some kind of evil magic came to life." Clarence paused to take a breath. "That magic killed everyone who was nearby, the police and the Gypsies, those trying to flee, everyone. They all dropped to the ground as if they could not handle their own weight, as if a house had fallen on their backs... Blood, fire, bodies...all over... Everything happened so fast, no one had a chance. They couldn't even move."

Clarence became quiet and Burton again asked him to continue speaking. He looked at Burton with tearful eyes. His body trembled and shivered, as he held on to the left side of the bed with a tight grip. His eyes closed shut and his mouth opened as if he wanted to yell out very loud, but his voice had disappeared inside him. Suddenly, Clarence remembered something. His eyes opened wide, immediately looking at Burton.

"Where's the little girl?" Clarence asked.

"Little girl?" Vaughn asked, looking puzzled. Burton looked at him, ordered the door to open and exited the room in a hurry. He was looking at his notes in his thin black, u-shaped, device.

As he walked outside, he placed a call through his wrist band.

"Yes, Burton..." A woman answered.

"Have you come across the body of a little girl, Lennon?" Burton asked the woman.

"Negative, we have covered almost the entire God-forsaken site and we haven't found any more bodies." Lennon quickly replied. "The other team is trying to track down the sarcophagus, but we have not heard from them yet."

"Revisit the field again and keep me posted if you find the little girl or anything else." Burton requested.

"I doubt there is anything else to find here Burton. We blew it. We blew it all up, almost the entire town. This is just a pile of fire, debris, and death. If they did not make it out, what makes you think a little girl would?" Lennon responded.

"Search again," Burton said, before ending the communication.

"What little girl are you talking about?" Vaughn asked Clarence. At that moment, Burton entered the room again while reading the device in his hand and gave a negative signal to Vaughn.

"The little girl that... I carried through the sewer." Clarence replied.

"The sewer? What was her name?" Burton asked.

"Her name...?" Clarence seemed puzzled by his own thoughts.

"What was her name?" Vaughn demanded from Clarence, speaking in an increasingly aggressive tone of voice.

"I don't remember, she was very little, maybe six or seven years old, and she was very scared...and..."

Suddenly, Vaughn got closer to Clarence and grabbed him by the collar of his hospital gown. "What's her God damn name? What did she look like, and what was she doing with you?"

Burton ran to Clarence's aid and removed his partner away from his side, telling Vaughn to stay calm.

"Speak! Speak now!" Vaughn demanded. His loud voice prompted one of the doctors passing by to attempt to get near the door, but he was stopped by one of the armed guards outside.

"Mr. Douglas, it is very important for you to tell us everything you know, anything you can remember at this point can help us save lives. The lives of those others who are unaccounted for and who may still be out there in danger, including the little girl you just mentioned." Burton understood Clarence was in a tough predicament, but there was an impending need for information which was necessary to piece together the missing links in his investigation.

"I can't... I can't remember." Clarence told him. "Everything in my mind is blurry and disturbed."

Burton then asked his agitated partner to leave the room. Vaughn walked out the door under the watchful eyes of some of the nurses and a doctor, who happened to be walking outside. The door closed behind him. The agitated nature of his personality prompted him to conduct persistent research with the device in his hand. He did not notice Nurse Smith and another nurse walking past him.

Smith looked at the door and saw a red light on the keypad, which indicated it was locked from the inside. She turned around and followed Vaughn to where he stood by and analyzed visuals from a satellite feed. His eyes rose up from his device and met Nurse Smith's eyes. They stared at one another briefly, neither one lowered their gaze.

"What drives a man to lose compassion for those of his own kind, who live in constant peril? Especially under the circumstances where we find ourselves." Nurse Smith asked Vaughn, speaking to him while looking away from his face.

"The same reason the gravely abandoned have landed into the tender care of your hands," Vaughn responded while placing his device into his jacket pocket. "IF the question asked came from someone who has experienced, what the world out there has forced many others to confront, without guarantee of success. Then to survive, it is not a question, but a misinterpreted perception of reality. The very ugliness of reality reached out and landed you here."

"My reality is vivid with hope," Smith replied. "What I have gone through will never tarnish the resolve I have found through the eyes of others. And hope is the reason I have rejected what my fate would have been and remain where my feet have driven me, where we both stand together. This is to remind you of what your duties and oath are based upon."

"Our oath?" Vaughn replied. "This oath does not reflect upon you, what has been forced upon me. Yes, we are both a part of this because of similar circumstances, but we are not looking at life through the same lenses, you should open your eyes to this reality."

"What reality?" Smith asked.

"The reality that the world out there will not be for our children anymore. Whatever that remains of this world when it ends, will not be for mankind. You are here due to that reason. And the sooner your eyes are open to this reality, the better your sight will be and the better prepared you will become to fight at the end, when it arrives."

"Vaughn." Smith looked at him but at the same time, avoided his eyes. "They say our eyes are the windows into the truth of our soul." Vaughn stared at Smith's face. "I agree with your statement, indeed, the same circumstances landed us both where we are, in different ways perhaps. At the same time, it was your decision to make when you were given the choice. You chose to serve, fight and help and do whatever you could to keep the preservation of this world for those who will be here, after we are gone. If we don't bring compassion to those who will land where we are, for the reasons we have, then, it's just as if we are doing the devil's bidding. We may as well go out there and keep blowing it all up until we destroy the world ourselves, along with everyone in it."

Smith's eyes now remained deep within Vaughn's. His mind has traveled farther away from what Smith would have anticipated. She walked away to continue with her duties. He remained where he was, returning to the analysis of the information in his device, while his partner spoke with Clarence.

"Mr. Douglas, try to go back, I need you to remember what happened." Burton took out a small silver container out of his jacket pocket while walking closer to Clarence. "Start from the beginning. I will give you this pill, it is not medication, it is to relax your mind. I believe this will help your mind to ease into the rest of your memories and maybe in that way, you will be able to dig deeper and come up with more detailed memories of what happened, and how you were able to survive. Maybe you can remember what happened to the little girl and if she's still out there, we may be able to save her life. But I need you to tell me everything to figure this out."

It took a long while, but after the effects of the pill began to work, Clarence became more relaxed and began to feel numb to the pain. He again closed his eyes. He went searching and looking into the deepest parts of his mind and he then began telling his story to Burton based on the fragments he was beginning to remember.

"I was just down on my luck, and Jeffery was my last hope at that moment."

Clarence began telling his story to Burton, through the fragments which began to resurface slowly in his mind.

"who's Jeffery?" Burton asked.

"Someone I knew back from Chicago. A good guy, always in search of what others weren't." Clarence explained, this time with a calmer tone of voice. "And so, I followed him when he told me this trip could be the beginning of a new occupation for me. Something more adventurous and fulfilling.

"I needed something new in my life, an escape, and at this particular moment, I thought this was the opportunity I'd been waiting for. Everything seemed to be as he promised, and I felt it the moment we arrived at the shipyard of La Cruz, a small coastal town to the north of Costa Rica. I began to feel alive as soon as the ocean breeze flowed into my lungs. And then I saw her... She was everything any man could possibly want, and then some. I saw her talking to a man twice her age, whom she later told me was the main inspector of the local fishermen union.

"I was already getting off the small vessel that transported us to that part of the country. Jeff had told me that he met a man on the south side of Chicago, who told him that for the right price, he could put him in contact with one of the most powerful crime lords in charge of the drug smuggling and human trafficking businesses in the region. A man who also happened to be one of the most wanted criminals by the United States government. How? It turned out this was a plan crafted by the drug lord himself, to bring out his own side of the story, ready to be revealed to the American people.

"Jeff was obsessed with those types of stories, he told me that if he was ever going to win a Pulitzer, it would be due to a story like that, and he would not rest until he got the right one.

"The shipyard was very busy on that day. I don't know what she was doing talking to that inspector, but it seemed more like she was in control of everything that needed to happen. She later told me the inspector was a relative from the far side of her family. I didn't believe her, but I didn't care either. Everyone's got their own secrets, and I was no exception, you know?

"I hung around as Jeff went to contact the person we needed to meet. I kept the bag with my belongings close to me on the floor while some of the merchants traveling in the boat began to carry their things out. They all walked by, pushing me around and telling me to get out of the way. But I ignored them all, I wasn't going to move from where I was standing, and I didn't care if they pushed or shoved me.

"I could see how she gave the inspector an envelope, which to me seemed like some sort of payment. The inspector didn't even look inside the envelope and quickly stuffed it in his pants pocket while not taking his eyes away from her beautiful face, without appearing disrespectful. She looked like a goddess. Her hair was long and dark brown and at moments floated in the air, pushed by the sea breeze. Her eyes were the color of honey, her skin lightly tan, soft and shiny. Her lips were full and inviting and as she spoke, she never allowed her smile to vanish. She was wearing very short denim shorts, which I believe she shortened herself and a silky blouse that danced over her skinny waistline and her beautiful figure.

"I couldn't believe I was staring at such a perfect woman in this part of the world, whereas, it was hard for me to even feel comfortable with the ones in my own country. I saw her give a signal to three little boys who appeared to be waiting for her. They looked about nine to twelve years old. They walked away from where they were, running playfully, and she then gave a tap-kiss on the cheek to the man she was talking to before walking towards my direction. And as she did, the man she had been talking to, immediately turned the other way, while rubbing his hair with both hands. As she walked closer to me, I swear I felt like doing the same.

"Then one of the merchants pushed me with a sack of something heavy he was carrying over his shoulder and I stumbled against my own bag and dragged myself a few inches until I fell right in front of her feet. I almost caused her to fall as well but I was able to catch her just in time.

"She smiled at me and said something in Spanish. I believe she said I was a little clumsy or something like that. I was quickly back on my feet and told her that I was very sorry and pointed at the idiot who had pushed me. I quickly realized that I was still speaking in English to her and rapidly attempted to express it in her language, which I had learned somewhat on previous jobs.

"Her eyes gazed at me for a moment and as she smiled, she asked me if I was a tourist from America. I answered yes, and she smiled even more.

"I noticed she looked around as if she was looking for someone, just before she continued talking to me. She asked me for my name, and I told her my name was Clarence before I asked for her name. She told me her name was Helena. She said her mother gave it to her and told her it was like a Goddess's name or something like that. In my mind, I said she couldn't have been more right about that.

"She then asked me what I was doing in her country and she told me she didn't see many young Americans around these parts anymore. Only old men looking for sex and gambling vacations. I asked her if she understood English and she told me, in her very cute accent that she spoke only a little, that she had learned it in school because it was the second language of the country.

"I don't know how or why but in a matter of seconds I think I told her a partial version of my life's story and she kept smiling at me and actually trying to understand what I was telling her. I have always been a very shy person, but this woman was making me feel like I have never felt before in front of anyone and I loved every second of it, and I wanted more. We had walked a few yards away from where we were before, and I found the courage to ask her if it was possible that she could make time to show me around and she said yes. She said yes. I was not expecting such a quick answer, but I definitely liked the one I got."

Burton asked Clarence about the relevance of that woman with what had happened in the town, what he said he saw and his present condition. Clarence told him that she had everything to do with his condition, for it was only because of coming back for her that he ended up where he was and in his present condition.

Clarence then continued telling Burton his tale as the man sat with patience and took notes from time to time, with the help of a device like Vaughn's but thinner and wider.

"She told me that she would try to make time to show me some areas of her town but not all," Clarence continued. "I told her that I wanted for her to show me everything: the good and the bad, the nice and the ugly. I told her I wanted to spend as much time as I could with her, that is if she was okay with that. She smiled while looking at the ground... At that moment the smile I was displaying parted from my face and I just stared at her and... I knew. I knew at that moment that, if she would ask me to stay with her, I was never going back to where I came from.

"Little did I know my story in that place was just beginning and not only there at the shipyard. One of the boys she had signaled before she saw me, came back for her. He had been hiding behind a corner, saw her talking to me and for some reason, did not like what he was looking at. But elsewhere, miles away from that part of town, I believe something dark and very sinister had been brewing since before I was even set up by my destiny to end up where I had..."

Clarence closed his eyes and, slowly, everything began to come back from within the deepest parts of his mind. As he continued telling Burton his story as best as he could recall, Burton began to place other details together. Details that were unknown to Clarence but were just unraveling at the same time his saga was beginning to take shape into words. At that moment, as Clarence told his story and Burton went through the secret records he had in his possession, the story took a life of its own...

∞

Weeks earlier...

"Ah! Mommy!" The terrified crying of seven-year-old Lora awoke her mother who was sleeping in a bed across the room. Her big brother David, who was eight, fell from the bed scared by the sudden sound of his sister crying. Their mother, Susan, was quick to get to her side. Susan embraced her tightly and stroke her silky dark hair gently. She attempted to console her daughter, but Lora could not stop crying, nor erase the look of fear from her eyes.

David looked at his mother and little sister for a moment and slowly trenched himself against a corner of the room and placed his arms above his head. He was shivering and afraid. His arms were covered with goosebumps. Susan noticed it and approached him while carrying Lora in her arms. She lightly touched his arm to get his attention, but she had to remove her hand quickly.

"My goodness David, you are freezing!" Susan said. She quickly went to get the blanket from the bed and as she did, David lifted his head slowly. He looked at the dark corner of the wall behind his and his sister's bed. As his mother came back to cover him with the blanket, his head was under his arms again.

"David, are you feeling okay? Why are you so cold?" Susan asked, after placing the blanket over David's shoulders.
She caressed Lora's back.

"Mommy... Can I sleep in your bed?" The little girl whispered.

"Yes, my dear," Susan replied, removing her from her shoulder and placing her on the bed to look at her face. David quickly stood up and also asked to be taken to his mother's bed. Susan complied with both children and as they all walked towards the mother's bed, which was only two steps away from theirs. Lora looked over her mother's shoulder at the wall behind her brother's bed for a moment. She saw something in the shadows in the corner of the wall that bothered her. She buried her face into her mother's neck and hugged her tightly.

At that moment, as Susan placed both children in her bed, she waited and watched as they both fell asleep again. She saw them shivering and then tossing and turning. She covered them both with her blanket until she saw the sun rising through the shutters of her bedroom window.

It was still early in the morning and those people, not yet enjoying the partial economic boom the country was beginning to experience, could be seen gathering by the areas of a lake where some washed their clothing and others picked up water to take back to their homes. A different group of people was seen on the other side of the lake, men, women and other children. They looked a bit strange and unfamiliar to those who were already used to practicing their daily routine in that part of town.

∞

Elsewhere, near the center of the city, a man in his early twenties named Ramon, had just pulled up in his pick-up truck right in front of a newly developed plaza. There were new modernized apartment buildings, for those who could afford them, a new supermarket, a hardware store, a new and fancy looking hotel, a doctor's office, as well as other, well-appointed variety stores and restaurants.

Ramon had brought several boxes out from the back of the truck and began placing them at the entrance of the Doctor's office, which was located on the second floor of one of the new buildings. A young man named Luis came down from the doctor's office. He was short and skinny. He offered Ramon a hand, after telling him that he needed a haircut soon. Ramon looked at himself against the glass window of his truck and indeed, noticed that his hair had gotten much longer than what he was used to. Luis quickly took a dose from his inhaler for his asthma before he began picking up one of the boxes. Ramon knew Luis through past odd jobs that they had done together at the shipyard.

They were quickly done with the task and as Ramon was on his way downstairs, he took a misstep and fell backward on the floor, hitting the back of his head very hard. Luis and one of the Doctor's assistants who was having her morning coffee at the time rushed over to Ramon and helped him up. Luis asked Ramon if he was okay as the nurse went and got him a glass of water and called the doctor to come over quickly and have a look.

Later that morning, Ramon was back on his feet. After splashing the last bit of water over his face, he started to head downstairs and although he did not want to admit it, he was still not feeling well. His head was still throbbing and hurting, and he was having some trouble breathing but he was a stubborn young man. He could not bring himself to admit to others that he hit himself hard as he fell, because he did not want anyone to fuss over him.

As he walked outside the door, the glare of the sunlight bothered his eyes. He saw sparkles, bright strings and flashes of light in the air all around him and it was all making him dizzy. He had to cover his eyes for a moment before being able to see clearly enough to step out onto the sidewalk. He was feeling light-headed and had shortness of breath. These symptoms amounted to a moment of weakness, prompting him to lean against the wall for support while looking everywhere to make sure no one saw him in this condition.

He looked across the street and as he did, he saw the blurry image of a man he had not seen around before. For a moment he lost sight of him. Ramon then rubbed his right eye with his hand, and right afterward he regained a partial image of the individual walking back and forth across the street.

The man appeared to be a homeless person by the appearance of his dirty long hair and tattered clothes, his unshaven face and his overall unkempt look. Ramon observed as the man walked after some of the people who walked by him. He stared as the homeless man followed some of the people who walked past him. He panhandled and even touched some of them and said things to them, but everyone was ignoring the man. Not one person acknowledged what he was saying, ignoring the poor man as if he was not even there.

Ramon put his left hand into the left side pocket of his pants and pulled out the money he had just been paid for delivering the supplies to the doctor's office but then he quickly put the money back, while still staring at the man across the street.

He looked at several people coming out of the grocery store next door and others coming his way from across the street. Ramon put his right hand into the right-side pocket of his pants, where he kept his black hair comb, a piece of paper with several phone numbers, as well as a little cash. He pulled out three notes and decided to walk across the street towards the stranger.

At the same time, Susan was walking across the street with her children Lora and David. Ramon spotted them and recognized the children's mother from the last time she was at the doctor's office. He looked at her and smiled at her and the children as they walked by him, just before refocusing his sight on the direction where the homeless man was stumbling around.

For a moment Ramon could not see where the man was and looked around to try to locate him again. His head was still hurting, and he took several steps back towards the sidewalk to close his eyes and catch his breath. He then looked across the street one more time, where he spotted the homeless man standing near the corner, and after two seconds, he decided to go back towards him, walking across the street.

Ramon noticed that the man was looking in his direction, and he continued walking towards him. But then, Ramon saw something strange. Ramon soon realized that the man was not looking at him and as he got closer to him, to Ramon's surprise, the man did not smell bad like he thought he would. He did not smell like anything at all in fact.

"Hey!" Ramon greeted the homeless man. The homeless man looked at Ramon very surprised for some reason. He appeared almost shocked that Ramon was addressing him.

"Here, this is for you," Ramon told the homeless man, extending his hand towards him with the money in it. The man stared at Ramon in the eyes without even paying attention to the money he was being offered, then he quickly set his sight towards the doctor's office before looking back at Ramon. Ramon was looking at the man's face but for some reason, his eyes became blurry momentarily and he could not clearly describe his appearance.

"Who...?" The homeless man whispered while staring at Ramon curiously.

"Here, take this. It's for you." Ramon again said to the homeless man, who did not appear interested in the money at all but only seemed rather surprised that Ramon was trying to talk to him.

After a moment, the homeless man snatched the money away from Ramon's hand and took a step back, looking again towards the medical office. He then attempted to approach someone else to ask something but as with the others, he was being ignored. Ramon looked at the homeless man for a moment noticing that there was something very odd about him, but he couldn't quite put his finger on what it was, besides the fact that he was not from the area and his appearance was both strange, and uneasy.

"Ah!" A very loud horn blasted right next to Ramon's face as a truck rolled right past him, just barely missing him by an inch of his hair. Ramon cried out startled as he looked towards the sidewalk.

"Oh, God!" Ramon exclaimed. He looked around himself and saw other cars approaching, realizing at that moment he was standing in the middle of the busy street.

"Where, what, but how...?" Ramon wondered how he had gotten to the middle of the street. He ran quickly to the sidewalk and as he looked in the opposite direction, he noticed the homeless man walking away from him.

"What the hell? How did I end up there?" Ramon did not know what had occurred, but he quickly walked over to his truck. He looked again at the homeless man almost hoping to see if he turned to look at him, but he did not, as he continued walking away.

"Ramon!"

"What?" Ramon responded, somewhat surprised to see Luis calling him with some urgency. Luis waved at Ramon as he was placing his inhaler back into his mouth. Ramon looked at him for a second but there was something of concern in his mind. Luis placed the inhaler back inside his pocket while staring at Ramon oddly.

"Are you okay?" Luis asked, approaching Ramon. "What were you thinking man? You almost got hit by that truck."

Ramon was surprised at what he was hearing since he himself could not remember how he ended up in the middle of the street and in the path of the truck.

"That stupid idiot didn't see me. That's what happened!" Ramon quickly defended himself.

"Whatever you say man, but that was close!" Luis added with a nervous laugh. "Do you need me to come with you tomorrow?" Luis asked Ramon.

"You can if you like. Sure."

Luis was very happy to hear that. This would allow him to earn some extra cash. He then asked Ramon, "What was it that you went to get across the street? And who was that person you were pointing at?" He asked Ramon.

Ramon found it very strange that he did not remember even having called anyone.

"No one told me anything Luis, what are you talking about?" Ramon replied.

"What do you mean no one told you anything?" Luis asked, surprised.

"No one did." Ramon reiterated.

"Yes, but what did that man say to you?" Luis asked, feeling confused. "'Cause after you shouted at him, you went back walking across the street, and he followed you and got close to you. That's why I asked you because he appeared to have been telling you something in your ear. Then he walked away from you, I turned my eyes away, and when I looked again, I see you almost getting hit by a truck."

At that moment Ramon did not know what to think. He quickly looked at the other side of the street and as he walked into his truck, he looked at his rearview mirror but there were no sightings of the homeless man anymore. "Luis, go home, I will see you tomorrow..." Ramon said, while still trying to see if the homeless man was around.

"Okay man, see you tomorrow." Luis waved goodbye, as he walked away, while again placing the inhaler in his mouth.

Ramon stared at his friend and thought about what he had just said. He attempted to remember the timeline from when he walked up to the homeless man and the time Luis was talking about, but he could not remember anything in between.

So how can it be? Ramon thought. *How did Luis see something that I can't remember doing a few minutes ago? And how did I end up almost hit by a truck in the middle of the street? What's wrong with me?*

"What the hell did Luis just tell me...?"

As Ramon decided to continue on his way, Clarence and Helena were making their way off a very crowded minibus, which made a stop at a corner away from where the doctor's office was. Helena had brought Clarence to show him one of her favorite parts of town. A place she would only come to visit on her own. It took them a moment to make it out of the vehicle, with Clarence walking behind Helena. He was covering her rear from all of the undesirable stares and catcalls from many of the men in the minibus. This included the driver and his assistant, who got reprimanded, for his inappropriate comment, by a couple of women traveling in the back of the minibus.

"Helena, does this happen to you everywhere you go?" Clarence asked, in a cautious and curious tone of voice. Helena smiled and took hold of his hand to speed up his steps. Clarence smiled back at her while taking notice of the change in the atmosphere and people's demographics in this part of town in comparison to where he was staying. And as they paced together, they soon became part of the blend of the atmosphere of that part of town.

"This is what I mentioned to you about the men here," Helena said, attempting to convey her speech in English as well as she could, while still walking two steps ahead of Clarence. "I don't believe I am the only woman in it, but the way these men attempt to capture the heart of women is very, very undesirable. I believe that all women want the same things. We want someone to treat us nice and with respect and make us feel loved. We don't want to feel like momentary objects, and that is the way all of the men here act."

"But you must already be aware of how beautiful you are," Clarence commented. "And you probably get more catcalls and proposals than many others. You do handle it very well though, but what if some of these men try to cross the line and go beyond a catcall, and…" Helena did not fully understand where Clarence was going with his words, but she had an idea. Playfully and suddenly, she spun around with a small knife in her hand pointing it at Clarence in a very decisive way.

"Woah, Woah…" Clarence was shocked to see this aspect of Helena. He paused and put his hands forward, allowing some distance between the two of them. Helena saw how surprised he was and after a short smile, she began laughing uncontrollably, placing the knife in Clarence's hand.

"You are so cute," Helena whispered in Spanish.

"What was that?" Clarence quickly asked, while inspecting the short knife, as Helena turned to point at the place they were going to.

"Here we are." She said, pointing at the main entrance of the newly built plaza where most of the new businesses were being sponsored and handled by foreign investors pouring millions into the local economy of that part of the country.

"Hey, I said I really wanted to see where the truly native people live," Clarence said to Helena. "I want to know how they eat, where their children play and how they all exist together, not this nice shopping area most of the people in this country cannot even afford to enjoy right now. Look around, everyone around here looks foreign."

"Including you!" Helena quickly replied, with a big smile on her face. "I said I will show you everything, but at the right time." Helena gave Clarence a little wink and grabbed his hand. "I want to get to know you better. Doing that while being in a nice and beautiful environment is not bad either, right? Plus, I have been wanting to come to this part of town. I haven't been here in a while."

"Why not? You can come any time you like." Clarence said.

"I didn't have the right person to do it with," Helena replied. She turned her face and her eyes stared right into Clarence's. For him, this gave more and more meaning to wanting to know what Helena and her life was all about. He knew that he had to be somewhere with Jeff but his new interest in life now, was no longer journalism. Discovering what the local drug lords had for brunch in the afternoon when they woke up, would have to wait. Something else sparked his new desire for life and that something just happened to have dangerous curves and a hypnotizing smile.

∞

At the pediatrician's waiting room, Lora looked very much drained as she and her family waited for their turn to be seen by the doctor.

"Would you like to be carried?" Susan asked her daughter.

"Yes, mommy," Lora replied.

"David, can you please hold these for a while?" Susan asked David to hold on to their bags which contained snacks and extra clothing for both he and his sister. The waiting room was not big enough and it was very crowded at the time. Susan did not want to misplace the children's things.

Susan picked up Lora in her arms as Lora rested her head on her mother's shoulder. One of the doctor's assistants saw the family from the window at her desk. She walked back to one of the exam rooms to tell the doctor that Lora was back.

"I'm tired mommy," Lora whispered. Lora's voice sounded fragile and her skin looked very pale. There were dark circles under her innocent eyes.

"Mom, are you okay?" David asked looking up at his mother.

"It's alright honey, I'm okay." Susan quickly replied but Susan struggled for a moment carrying Lora. She hadn't been able to sleep the night before and it had been the fourth night in a row that she could not sleep because of Lora's nightmares.

Lora had already fallen asleep as Susan spoke to the doctor's assistant. Susan was able to find an empty seat nearby and sat down with Lora in her lap fast asleep. The person Susan had been talking to went back to help the doctor and the head assistant came out to talk to Susan.

"Hello, Susan." The doctor's assistant said.

"Hi Margo, how are you?" Susan said and smiled. Margo told her she was going to be back with the papers she needed to fill out for this visit.

"Is she showing any improvement?" Margo asked Susan, handing her the forms.

"She really hasn't been eating and is experiencing more and more nightmares lately," Susan replied. "I'm really worried about her Margo."

Margo had noticed that Susan herself looked extremely tired and had dark circles around her once beautiful eyes. "Are *you* well? Have you been sleeping normally?" Margo asked in a kind voice. Susan just smiled and nodded.

David was playing with a toy he found along the side of some books at the bottom of a small cabinet. Susan and David looked up at the entrance door when they saw it closing back on its own. They did not remember it being open. Susan continued to fill out the forms she was given. David went back to playing with the toy, as Lora slept.

"Here, drink this," Margo said handing a glass of water to Susan. She then looked at Lora again.

Fifth time in one month, this cannot be good... Margo thought.

Susan took a sip of the water. "She had a really bad episode last night. I hope Dr. Marco will see her soon." She said.

As they spoke about Lora, an elderly woman was exiting one of the rooms. Susan noticed that she looked a bit upset and was trying to be discreet about her feelings. One of the doctor's assistants followed the lady out of the room and walked with her to help her down the steps.

The doctor then walked out of the room and another assistant followed him. He waved hello to Susan as he made his way into his private office. Dr. Marco was in his late thirties. He was fairly tall and slim, with dark hair combed forward. He had a thriving business where his patients ranged from young to old and he was well trusted and well respected in his community. Susan noticed a preoccupation on his face. One of the assistants, a lady in her early fifties named Carla, approached Susan and asked her if Lora was feeling sick again. Susan quickly responded by telling her about the tumultuous night her daughter had.

As Susan continued conversing with the assistant, she failed to notice the elderly lady being escorted out, was profoundly staring at Lora. Lora opened her eyes and looked right into the lady's eyes. At that moment the elderly woman felt a strange sensation, which Lora reciprocated. The lady looked around the room momentarily, as if looking for something in it. She seemed to have wanted to say something but then decided to keep it to herself, and calmly turned her face away from the little girl.

"Let's get going, Mrs. Fontaine. Your taxi is waiting downstairs." The assistant escorted the lady down the stairs as Lora continued to watch her walk away.

"Is there anything wrong Mrs. Fontaine?" The assistant asked.

"No. But you can let my arm go. I am okay on my own." Mrs. Fontaine replied.

The assistant noticed that she was shaking and hesitated to let go of Mrs. Fontaine's arm, but she gently pulled her arm away from the assistant anyway. She walked out of the building and took one last look back, remembering the look in Lora's eyes. For some reason, it reminded her of something disturbing, a memory from long ago that she had intentionally buried away.

Sometime later, Lora and David walked out of the doctor's office towards the sidewalk, followed by Susan and Dr. Marco. "I do not believe it is prudent for you to overreact my dear." Dr. Marco said to Susan, as they both watched Lora and David playing only a few feet away from them.

"Little Lora is just overcoming a mild case of allergies and we shall allow more time for the treatment we started two weeks ago to start baring results with her migraine situation. She is just too young to be prescribed any other treatment method for the time being. It is best to allow her body to develop more strength on its own and we will continue observing her to see how she assimilates to this new approach."

Susan had her doubts about the cause of Lora's nightmares and sudden sickness but at the same time, there was nothing she could do but continue with the treatment and pray for the best.

"I understand you have enough on your plate, but you also need to pay close attention to David. His weight has dropped since his last visit." Dr. Marco added.

Susan explained to the doctor that David was very used to doing things with his father and eating was one of those things. But now that her husband was away for work, it had become more of a challenge for her to be able to make David eat appropriately, especially with Lora's problems getting worse.

"Don't hesitate to contact our office if you have any questions or if anything unusual should arise with the children." The doctor reminded her to get the new prescription for Lora while advising her to give the children warm milk just before bedtime to help them sleep better. Susan thanked the doctor for his help one more time before she told the children to say goodbye to their doctor.

The doctor waved goodbye to the children as the family made their way to the bus stop. The doctor remained where he was, his hands inside his lab coat pockets and his eyes continued studying Lora as the family walked away. He was very concerned about the little girl and emerged deep in thought. His experience was signaling to his better judgment that there was probably an underlying problem with Lora, to which conventional medicine would not be the solution. It was something which he could not yet figure out but needed and wanted to continue investigating.

Chapter II:

Ephemeral Legacy

Susan sped up her steps towards the bus stop, which was still under renovation and was currently being served by a privatized group of drivers. The groups knew their time was almost up, due to the new regulations ready to be implemented by the new government. Thus, prompting them to operate their vehicles to more than their full capacity to maximize their profits without much regard for the safety of their passengers. Susan caught a glimpse of one of the minivans about to leave the stop, it was completely overcrowded with people.

Another one had just departed and passed right by her and her children at a fast speed. Susan grabbed her children's hands and asked them to walk a little faster so that they could make it to the stop before the next minivan arrived, which she saw was now three blocks away. As Susan and the children got to the stop, there were already many others waiting for the next van to arrive.

"Mom..." Lora whispered nervously, as she got closer to her mother. Susan glanced over at David with worry and then she looked at Lora before picking her up in her arms. The van got to the stop very abruptly and people did not wait for it to make a full stop when they began to jump on to it from every direction and through any opening. Two men were working with the driver and they were in charge of collecting the fares from each passenger.

There were momentary commotion and even some punches thrown. Susan hesitated to even attempt to get to the side door of the van when she saw how a young teenager was pushed so hard, he fell to the ground headfirst. One man paid his fare to one of the men in charge and quickly got himself on top of the van and secured himself to the part where cargo normally gets fastened.

Susan looked at David and attempted to take a few steps forward while still carrying Lora, who was already asleep. She tried to get to the passenger front door of the van but was pushed back by the moving crowd. She was about to fall backward with Lora slipping from her arms, but Clarence happened to be behind her and was able to catch her in the nick of time and made sure she was balanced.

"Are you okay?" Clarence asked Susan, speaking Spanish with an American accent. Helena remained near, looking around while stroking David's hair.

"Yes, oh my God, thank you! If not for you, I would have fallen for sure, and my little girl... Anyway, thank you so much!" At that moment Lora opened her eyes and saw Clarence. Clarence looked at Lora and felt something, which went very deep into an unknown part of his soul.

"Hi, are you okay there?" Clarence asked Lora. But her eyes were heavy, and she closed them again as she replied, "yes, I'm okay."

"She is really tired. She hasn't slept the past four nights." Susan explained. Clarence asked her if she and the children needed help getting somewhere but Susan told him that the only way of getting home was getting in a van.

"Now we'll have to wait for another van," Susan said. "This one was a lost cause."

Helena held Clarence's hand tight, pulling him to walk with her. Clarence waved goodbye to them and walked away, but he could not help looking back again at Lora. He had a strange feeling about that family. He took one last look back at them before turning the corner of the street with Helena.

Clarence and Helena walked three blocks to a place she decided she wanted to show him. She told him she did not know anyone that would want to go there with her. It was a tea house that opened not too long ago by an Indian woman.

"I have never told this to anyone." Helena began confessing to Clarence. "I am a tea addict, thanks to my mother and my aunt. They used to drink tea whenever they ran out of coffee and I used to go behind their backs and drink the leftover from the pot, with a little bit of sugar. And ever since then, I have always loved drinking tea, at least once every day."

They both laughed together at Helena's story. It had been a beautiful day. Clarence had never been so interested in anyone his entire life. He and Helena spoke about everything, without leaving any details of their lives out to question, or so Clarence made her believe. For Clarence, it was an incredible experience and the beginning of a very special chapter in his life.

A few corners away from there, another van had arrived.

"Mom, I don't want to get to the house when it's dark again, it's scary. Can we go somewhere else that is not the house?" David said. Indeed, it was getting late and Susan did not want to entertain the thought of arriving in her very dangerous neighborhood, with the daylight already spent. During the mess to get into the second to last van leaving that part of town, one of the men collecting the fares shouted out.

"There is no more room left, we are ready to leave!"

When David heard the announcement, he started crying and telling his mother that he wanted to get home already. Susan attempted to take another step towards the van but the announcement of the van ready to depart caused even more commotion among those who were still not able to board the vehicle. The van was already filled to capacity.

The driver was writing down the fares collected on this trip onto his notebook when something distracted him momentarily. He put his notebook down and the reflection of someone passing right by his window got his attention. He looked out through the rearview mirror, he thought he saw a little boy but when he took a good look, there was no one like that out there.

"Camaron! (Shrimp)" The driver barked, calling out to one of the fare collectors to get over to his window. Camaron was a very skinny individual with an aggressive attitude and the second in command when it came to the route. The driver whispered something to his ear. Camaron asked him if he was sure and the driver moved his head positively without saying anything else to him. At that moment, the other collector began pushing back the rest of the people who wanted to get inside the van, and they attempted to bargain with him. As they saw Camaron approaching, they all quickly backed away from the van.

"You there…" Camaron said, pointing to Susan with his finger. Susan turned her head to see if there was someone behind her. The fare collector could not possibly be talking to her, she thought. A man behind her was quick to walk towards Camaron, thinking it was him who was being called. But Camaron quickly shook his head.

"No! Not you, *gordito* (chubby)." Camaron then pulled Susan by the hand, out of the crowd. After forcing some of the passengers already inside the van to open a very narrow gap, he was able to push Susan and her children into a small space the driver usually kept for allowing distance between him and the rest of the passengers. Lora sat on her lap as David squeezed in close to his mother.

"Thank you so much!" Susan said to the driver. She was so relieved that she could barely contain how happy she was. She could not believe her luck.

"Hmm…?" The driver looked at Susan with a puzzled look on his face but then ignored her and began to drive away from the bus stop.

As the van pulled away from the curb, a passenger gripping onto the side ladder and the cargo basket on top of the van, dropped to the floor onto his back. The guy stood right back up and ran after the van and was able to climb on top of the rear bumper. A man already on top of the van grabbed hold of his hand and helped him from falling backward again. Camaron noticed what happened but ignored the situation when the other collector signaled to him that his fare had already been collected earlier.

The trip was very uncomfortable for Susan and her children. The curvy and bumpy road didn't help the situation for anyone inside the van. Several other people almost fell out from the van again but Susan, holding both of her children very tight, was just relieved that she was able to make it inside the van where it was safe.

Almost an hour later, it was already dark, and the van approached Susan's stop. Camaron was quick to get a small knife out from the side of his high-top sneakers. He stood nervously on guard while allowing the departing passengers to get off the van. He looked around in every direction to see if anyone weird tried to approach the van, as did the other fare collector.

Susan and the children got out of the van and David begged his mother to get him his favorite candy before they went to their house. Susan was about to say no but Lora asked her for a cupcake. Lora had not eaten much during the day and Susan decided to venture towards the grocery store, which she knew would be closing very soon. She took a second look at the direction to her house and she noticed that the road was already getting darker.

"Hey!" Susan called out, getting the attention of the man inside the very well gated grocery store. "Please, can you attend me?" Susan asked hurriedly. The man looked at Susan and then looked around in a very rushed manner.

"Okay, quickly, what do you want?"

"Just one of those chocolate candies, a guava cupcake, medium-sized milk, bread, half a dozen eggs and two pounds of chicken." Susan got what she needed and began making her way to her house. David took a moment to look around as Lora held hands with him and her mother. It was very dark and there was no electricity throughout the neighborhood since early in the afternoon.

The people walking about in the streets seemed like shadows swerving from side to side. David was very afraid of the dark and even more afraid of what took place in their neighborhood at night.

"Mom…" David mumbled. He tried to get close to his mother, but he knew he had to hold his little sister's hand instead and be brave for her.

"It's okay David, let's just walk as fast as we can and let's stay very close together and we will make it to the house in no time at all." Susan tried to reassure the children. As she and the children walked very close to the edge of the street, they passed some parked vehicles that looked like they've seen much better days perhaps twenty years ago.

"But it's dark," David replied.

"Mommy…" Lora then spoke, her voice trembling.

"Why don't you close your eyes as you walk dear? Your brave big brother and I are holding your hands, so nothing can happen to you. Does that sound okay?" They were about to pass a corner where some dangerous looking individuals were talking in hushed tones. They became quiet and looked up at the family. Susan deviated from walking by that corner and went across the street to avoid them, just as a car with only one headlight passed by them a little too closely, followed by a line of motorcycles driving too fast.

David looked back at the strangers after making it to the other side of the street and saw them walking away from where they were standing. They were disappearing into the shadows of the night, as Susan accelerated her steps.

"I'm scared." David's teeth chattered as he spoke. He knew he had to be brave, but he felt like crying.

"We are almost there," Susan told David. "Just hold on. When we get home, you can have that yummy chocolate and Lora, you can have your cupcake. Doesn't that sound good?" Susan tried to do her best to quiet the children's fears.

David kept looking back and seeing shadows moving all around as if they were following them. He could hear in his mother's voice, no matter what she was saying, that she too was afraid. His skin was covered in goosebumps. He was starting to feel cold again and as he looked behind and ahead, everything was becoming darker and darker. The number of passersby became less and less.

Susan continued walking and pulling the kids to keep up with her. She also wanted to make it to the house as soon as possible because she knew how dangerous the area became at night. She wished she hadn't bought so many groceries, so she could've carried Lora and walk a little faster. David looked back again and saw what appeared to be three people walking not too far behind them, slipping back and forth between some parked vehicles.

David felt a very strange sensation, causing him to look up at his mom. He then looked over to a window of a house to the right side of the street. He saw someone move the candlestick that was by the window while watching the family. He attempted to say something to his mother but then decided not to. He looked down to the ground as he continued walking, but this time, the children were effortlessly keeping up with Susan.

Susan was able to peek at David while holding Lora's hand and continued walking, now only a block away from the house. David was now more relaxed and kept looking over at his right hand from time to time as he was now walking with more ease.

"Mommy…" Lora whispered while her eyes slightly opened for a moment as they were already turning onto the narrow street where their house was located.

"Yes, dear?" Susan replied.

"Who is that?" Lora asked. Susan looked at David and looked around as she walked faster seeing her house was only steps away.

"Who baby?" Susan asked Lora.

"Who is that mommy?" Lora again asked.

"Baby, who?" Susan let go of the children's hands, so she could get her keys out before getting close to the door.

Susan asked David to hold onto Lora's hand tightly as they walked towards the door. Susan looked around. She did not see anyone near them. She could see only the shapes of a few people who lived nearby walking around with their flashlights in hand. She quickly opened one of the three locks of a fence protecting the front door of their house.

Lora rubbed her eyes with her right hand and attempted to make out something behind them in the darkness. She looked worried as she did. She then turned to look at her brother. David kept looking back at the street and saw someone walking towards them, from a half block's distance. The person was walking very slowly and appeared to be walking while holding onto the tall walls that separated the other properties in the area.

David stared at the person approaching their direction.

"Let's go in," Susan said. They rushed inside the house and Susan locked all the locks of her front door in a flash. It was pitch black. They could not see anything, but it didn't matter to them since they were inside and felt safe.

"Get the candles, David," Susan said while she reached for a box of matches inside the drawer of a cabinet against the wall in the front room of the house.

"Found it," David said handing over the box of candles.

She then struck a match and reached for a candle. She noticed there were only two candles left inside the box David handed to her. One of the two had been halfway melted from the last power outage.

BOOM! BOOM! BOOM!

Someone began banging on her door hard. Susan looked up startled. Lora hugged her brother tightly. David led Lora to hide with him under the table. Susan had dropped the match and the candle on the floor and attempted to find them, but she couldn't see anything in front of her.

Oh, God! She thought, as her heart pounded frantically to escape from her chest.

David and Lora were crawling towards where Susan was.

"It's okay darlings, it's going to be fine," Susan told the children as she moved around the floor searching for them. Just outside the door, someone was yelling out, calling someone's name. They started banging against the door and the front windows and it sounded as though they would break in at any moment.

"Come here," Susan whispered to David. She searched the floor and finally found the matches. She lit one of them and David could now see her frightened face. Susan looked at Lora and the little girl was quiet and stood completely still next to the table. Her eyes were wide open, petrified but she was very aware of what was happening. Susan asked her to come over to where she was, but Lora stayed staring ahead into nothing. Susan crawled over towards Lora while holding David's hand and she held them both. She got them under the table again where they remained quiet.

The noise and the banging sounds ceased. Susan and the children had fallen asleep under the table, they were exhausted. Susan opened her eyes and as she realized her children were sound asleep, she embraced them tightly and remained right where she was throughout the rest of the night. She hadn't noticed the fading glow emanating from the back of Lora's head, nor a shadow vanishing away from it.

∞

Two days later, it was 7 am at an abandoned property outside a town near Abuja, Nigeria. Herman Sokolov, who was in his late twenties, was busy gathering soil samples and taking notes. He was a slender Russian man with dark brown hair and athletic build. Herman walked towards a dumping sight, near a lake and collected water samples as well as samples of the vegetation.

There was a small bus waiting for him and the others, who had been brought to Nigeria as part of a research group from UCLA. The group was to document the rehabilitation of a very polluted area of the country. Millions of dollars were being invested by a giant pharmaceutical company, in conjunction with some of the local clinics in the area, to gain permission from the local government to conduct drug trials.

The rest of the people were already boarding the bus and Herman was the last one to get on.

"What took you so long?" Herman was questioned by one of the men in charge of bringing the researchers from place to place on the bus.

"I was taking pictures of birds." Herman showed the man his camera, which hung from his neck. The man looked at one of the pictures Herman said he took.

"This is a Samuro." Herman told the man, as he showed him the picture of a black bird, that looked similar to a crow.

An hour later, the bus arrived at the headquarters of the main pharmaceutical company in the country, Mozambican, Inc. The students were brought there to hear a speech given by four of the pharmacists in charge of the development and testing of some of the most effective drugs. These drugs were being used regularly by the people of Nigeria and their neighboring countries.

The conference began and the first one to speak was Edosio Efemuaye, the lead pharmacist who gave a brief introduction to his partners. He then quickly went on to explain the benefits and the vast success achieved by the expansion of the main drug distribution program of Mozambican, Inc. and their partners throughout the neighboring countries.

The rest of the pharmacists also had their chance to speak and each of them talked about their respective positions and branches within Mozambican, Inc. and upon conclusion of each of their speeches, those gathered listening had a chance to ask a few questions. Herman had a chance and decided to ask a question to Dr. Efemuaye about the sale of a drug, which stage three trial, had been postponed by the Food and Drug Administration in the United States, due to uncertain results given by two of their main labs.

Dr. Efemuaye was taken by surprise and could not immediately decide if he was allowed to answer it. Resourcing instead, for explaining to Herman the benefits of a previous drug, from where the new drug in question was being modeled after. But Herman insisted on asking about the new drug and the reason it was already being sold in certain sections of Nigeria, even after the FDA's findings.

One of the company's attorneys took it upon himself to put out a confusing, but distancing answer to bring an end to Herman's time, but not before others began to comment about the question and the lack of concrete answers by Dr. Efemuaye about the drug. Herman looked at his notes and while at it, he could see Claire, one of the researchers with the tour looking at him with a smile on her face. He smiled back at her. She was an attractive twenty-three-year-old girl from California, with light blue eyes and short dirty blonde hair. They had shared a brief conversation earlier while checking in at their hotel.

An hour later, Herman and the rest of the researchers and students were back at their hotel, in the center of the city. Herman got along well with Claire and her friend Leonard. They sat down to share beers at the hotel lobby. Leonard insisted for Herman to teach him some words in Russian, his native language so that he could impress some of his Russian friends back at UCLA, where he was working on a master's degree in pharmacology. Herman agreed, and they practiced a few easy words. Claire also participated, up until several men from the department of health walked towards them and asked Herman to accompany them. Leonard and Claire asked what the reason was that Herman was being taken away, but they were told it did not concern them.

An hour later, Herman knocked on Leonard's room. He was happy to see that Herman was okay. Herman asked if he could hang out for a drink and Leonard was more than welcoming.

"What did those men want with you?" Leonard asked.

"They wanted to know how I got the information about the trial's postponement," Herman said. "I told them I saw it on the news in the States."

"Did they believe you?" Leonard asked. Herman had a glass of water and Leonard tossed a beer bottle in his direction, which Herman caught with his left hand.

"I don't know if they did or didn't." Herman opened the beer and took a long sip. "They insisted on asking if I knew anyone at the FDA. I don't know why they were so interested in learning if I did. But after a while, they just told me not to say things that I don't know much about, and if I am not sure of the source, I'd heard those things from." Herman had another sip of his beer when a pager he kept inside the left pocket of his pants went off.

"I've got to take this, it's my mom." He told Leonard. Leonard took a walk while lighting up a cigarette. Herman used the phone in Leonard's room to call his mother. He had a very nice conversation with her and his sister. They asked him to come to Russia for her birthday.

Herman thanked Leonard for the beer and the use of his phone. He told him he was going to rest in his room for a while and said goodbye. As Herman entered his room, Claire was there waiting for him. The room door was still half-open.

"What in the world happened to you? I was so worried!" Claire said. "Those men seemed really shady and dangerous." Herman did not have a chance to answer when she began undressing him and kissing him passionately.

45

After making love for some time, they lay under the sheets and Claire confessed to Herman that she belonged to an environmental group, which for some time, had been keeping an eye on the doings of Mozambican, Inc. She asked Herman how he became aware their new drug had been put on standby. Herman did not answer right away. He asked Claire what group she was talking about and how long had she been a part of it.

"Seven months ago," Claire said. "I began hanging out with three of my friends from college who were members of PETA. I got hooked on their idealism and I began campaigning with them. Two months later, I met a man named Paul Linwood, who was part of the environment protection organization known as Clear Horizon."

"Yes, I've heard of them," Herman said. "They singlehandedly dismantled an illegal dumping operation of biohazardous material in the waters off the coast of Alaska, thanks to a whistleblower from the Vanguard Corporation. They discovered this was affecting the fish and wildlife in the area and getting the locals sick. Vanguard had to spend millions cleaning their mess and lost a lot more from their shareholders. But I heard Linwood was found dead of an accidental drug overdose in Vietnam not too long ago."

"Yes," Claire said sadly. "And ever since his death, some of the other members of the organization have been under scrutiny from everyone. The media, politicians, other environmentalists, you name it. We believe this was a Vanguard operation, to retaliate against Clear Horizon for unmasking them."

Claire stood up from the bed. She was still undressed as she walked close to a window. She had left her purse under a lamp, on top of a small table.

"Do you?" She asked Herman, displaying a pack of cigarettes in her right hand.

"Sure," Herman said while walking towards her.

Claire tilted the windowpane towards the left side, opening it enough for their smoke to blow out of the room.

"Vanguard is a very powerful multinational corporation." Claire continued. "Whatever they said they lost in the market and in the cost of cleaning their mess, is absolutely nothing compared to how much they are earning in a single week, thanks to their pharmaceutical sales all over the globe. There is nothing these people don't manufacture, all the way from bandages and aspirin, to even cancer treatment medication. They have their hands in everything and even worse, they operate without rules or scrutiny. They have every politician who matters in their operating field, right in their pockets. That is, until Clear Horizon called them out. We strongly believe they had a hand in Linwood's death, but we just haven't been able to find any evidence to prove it."

Herman looked at Claire from the corner of his eyes. She stared at him with an uncertain look, which Herman had seen before in others.

"How did you come up with that conclusion?" Herman asked her, the cigarette tilting from his lips as he spoke.

"Samuel Walberg, the founder of Clear Horizon is being accused of having and distributing child pornography."

"Walberg?" Herman seemed surprised. "That is impossible." He murmured while extinguishing what remained of his cigarette over the table. "I don't know the man personally, but for what I've heard, he has never gotten so much as gotten a parking ticket."

"We believe they are after us," Claire added, she seemed nervous and kept staring out the window as if looking for something or someone.

"You believe Vanguard is trying to destroy Horizon's credibility," Herman asked while getting dressed near the bed.

"They are not only tarnishing our credibility Herman, but they are also taking us out, one by one. Melissa joined Horizon just about the same time I did, probably three weeks before me. I spoke to Sac and John and they have not heard from her since last Sunday. She was supposed to join them in Haiti before coming here and they haven't been able to get in touch with her, nor have her parents. This morning, at the conference, I saw two men staring right at me from the right corner of the salon. I tried to move away from their sight and then I lost them, and I have not seen them since. I'm scared, and I don't know what to do or who to talk to, Herman. When I heard you talking the way you did, it gave me the impression that you were one of us, and I wanted to get closer to you to tell you what we believe is happening and, maybe, to hear from your perspective."

Herman walked closer to Claire and handed her, her clothing. He was thinking about what she had just told him, and it did not seem farfetched. But he did not know if it was prudent for him to become involved in this particular situation. He did not know what would come of it, or if it would affect his own current investigation on the pharmaceutical company Mozambican, Inc. Not to mention, he did not really know Claire.

"Besides the people you've mentioned, who else is involved in this?" Herman asked.

Claire informed him that Sac and John have gone into hiding after the last time she spoke with them. She also told him that there were two others, who were in fear for their lives and believed were being followed. They were also supposed to meet her in Nigeria, this was the reason she signed up for the trip to Abuja, but she has no way of knowing if they made it there, and now she felt as if she had been left all alone. She had no one to talk to and she did not want to involve her parents. She feared if she was right, she did not want anything to happen to them.

Herman understood and after they both got dressed, he sat Claire on the bed and made a confession to her.

"I couldn't tell you this before because I did not know if I could trust you. I needed to hear what you had to say, and I needed to make sure what you said made sense with what I know."

"What do you mean?" Claire was confused.

"Vanguard and Mozambican, Inc. are the same," Herman said. "Vanguard operates under different corporation names in various countries around the world. This is how they remain a step ahead of everyone when it comes to what Horizon was trying to do. They also do much more than dumping in the oceans. I believe they have been taking advantage of the needs of people in certain countries to conduct illegal trials of unsafe drugs and other things.

"They have been able to keep their market value by staying out of the eyes of the FDA and international watchdog organizations. If there is no bad news about their future drugs, there is no bad news about their stock. It is a win-win situation for them. But there are other things they have been hiding, which I believe go beyond their drug industry and may be affecting the people they are using as lab mice in an even worse manner." Herman took a couple of steps away from Claire as he continued speaking.

"So far, they have been able to keep everyone from digging deeper into their main work frame, thanks in the most part, by having everyone in their pocket and dismantling anyone who comes after them. You do understand that Horizon has not been the first environmentalist group after Vanguard, right?"

"I know," Claire replied. "But everything happened so fast for me when I joined up with PETA, and then I met the others from Horizon. I went into all of this too fast and with too much passion. I didn't know better and I didn't do any research. I just wanted to do something positive with my life, I wanted to make a real difference. I wasn't an actor or a celebrity trying to put my face out there to become more popular, saying that I believed things just for the exposure. It just so happened that something snapped in me one day, and I woke up thinking that this was my true calling in life. And now, I don't even know if I'm going to be alive for much longer..."

Claire broke down in tears. Herman embraced her while letting her know that she was not alone. He looked out the window and saw the two men she had mentioned before. He remembered he had seen them as well, and he knew there was something not right about them. But he did not mention it to Claire.

"Listen, let's conclude with the rest of this day and let's get out of this place. I know some people who will be able to help you. I have to meet them in an hour. Come with me, you are not alone now."

Claire looked at Herman and felt a sense of comfort she hadn't felt in a while.

"Okay." She said, feeling much better about her odds now.

"What about Leonard?" Herman asked her. "Does he have any involvement in this situation? Did you tell him anything?"

"No, I just met him as part of the group at the conference."

"Okay, let's just get out of here then." Herman looked out the window, as Claire went into the bathroom. The two men were still standing across the street. Herman knew that it would be wise to leave the hotel through the back.

Chapter III:

Ill Advice

It was a clear night, around 11:30 p.m. At the penthouse of one of Japan's most exclusive buildings, Koshitsu No Hasu (The Imperial Lotus,) a very important and clandestine meeting was about to take place. Miyamoto Matsuda was the head of one of the three most powerful crime families of the Asian continent: The Woo family of China, the Hangul family of Korea and the Matsuda family of Japan. The Matsuda family was at the present time held as the center balance between the other two, thanks to an agreement created more than a century ago. An agreement that guaranteed to preserve the essence of pure Asian power in that part of the world, in a manner only experienced during a long-gone era. And this could only be achieved if that power rested solely in the hands of those of pure Hun origin.

Matsuda, who was in fragile health, was in his late sixties. He had at one point developed skin cancer and as a result, he was left with a half-inch scar on the right side of his face. He was being escorted by his personal advisor Riku Hinata, who was a skinny framed man with dark hair. Following close behind were two of his most trusted bodyguards Mori Tadaoki and Hanzo Oda. Both men resembled sumo wrestlers.

They entered a salon decorated in the old style of ancient times. There were dozens of bodyguards, dressed in black suits, in and around the place. Each of the main bosses was all dressed in traditional gofuku kimonos, made of exquisite silk in artistic couture. There was a symbolic round table with an engraving of a golden dragon, at the center of the room. A single velvet pillow was positioned over each place of the floor, where each head of the three families will seat. Two of them were in control of the daily undertakings and global operations of the families, Hangul Gao Ssi of Korea and Woo Cheng Xian sheng of China. If for any reason there was to be a vote on a decisive matter concerning anything associated with the families' welfare, the third man Matsuda San was designated to be the decisive factor.

Three additional pillows remained outside the perimeter of the round table. These were designated for each advisor of the three heads of the family. Over the table, tea was being served for each of the main bosses. Incense smoke billowed from short jars, placed strategically to enhance the Feng Shui of the room and by the entrance of the hallway outside the salon. The entire building was owned by the families and to preserve privacy and security at the top peak, the six floors below the penthouse were never occupied.

In the salon, all were on their feet as Matsuda San entered the room leading. He was closely followed by Hangul Ssi who was a medium built man with short gray hair, wearing his trademark gold watch. He was walking side by side with Woo Chen Xian sheng, who was also in his late sixties. He had a defined short and pointy beard and as usual, was holding his prayer beads in his left hand. Those who were already in the room, respectfully bowed their heads until each of the family heads walked right up to their places and sat down.

"You may be seated." Matsuda San politely bowed. His bodyguards, as well as the others, exited the dimly illuminated room and slowly closed the doors while remaining outside on guard. The entire building was surrounded by private security. Three choppers flew in the air, monitoring communications from outside sources and watching the surrounding terrain below.

"Hangul Ssi, please speak." Matsuda San spoke in Korean, to address the leader head of the Hangul family, who had in fact requested this unscheduled meeting in the first place.

At the same time, north of the very busy Harajuku district, a young Japanese man sat at a very small table unaccompanied. It was a small and quiet restaurant in the subfloor of a building and at that particular time, there was only a handful of people, some of them very drunk, catching a bite to eat at the place. A tired but polite waitress approached the lonesome man to ask if he was ready to order. He shook his head no but quickly recanted what he was about to say, as he looked through a glass window. A young lady with straight platinum blonde hair and a black goth outfit was walking down the steps, which led to the entrance of the restaurant.

The young man stood up to greet the blonde. They both smiled as the young lady sat down across from him. The waitress then approached him again and he requested water for both himself and his companion.

"I'm very happy to see you Aiko." The young man said.

"You too Ryu..." Aiko replied, just before reaching over the table to give him a quick kiss on the lips.

"I want you to tell me everything about your trip and the school and the people and if the girls are crazy for you already," Aiko said excitedly.

"Girls?!" Ryu cried out. "No, no! What do you think I'm doing in America? I'm not there to be a playboy and get drunk every day before my exams. No way Aiko, I barely get out of my dorm room. I stay in studying all day or all night, depending on the time of my classes."

They both laughed gleefully, happy to see each other. The waitress carefully placed the glasses with water in between them.

The couple both decided to try out the ramen noodles the place was well known for. The waitress wrote their orders and gave the two a quick smile before walking away. Aiko continued her conversation with Ryu by asking him about Shinseki, a mutual friend of theirs.

Ryu smiled. "You know, he is still the same. That is, messing around with a bunch of girls, partying hard, amongst his other activities. He is still the same Shin."

Aiko was not surprised. She knew the type of person Shinseki has always been. "Ryu, try not to waste your time trying to help him whenever he gets in trouble."

Ryu stared at Aiko without saying anything. She did not realize it as she continued telling him what to do and not to do around Shinseki, but when she looked at Ryu's face, she quickly stopped talking. Her hands reached for his and she stared at him silently.

"I know..." Aiko whispered.

"Do you?" Ryu asked. "Aiko, you seemed to have forgotten that if it was not because of Shinseki, I might not even be alive. I wouldn't be here holding your hands perhaps."

"I accept that, but for how long should a person have to repay another human being after receiving a favor?" Aiko looked down. "I really love you Ryu, and I know you are a really good person. And an even better friend to have. This is why it is hard for you to see Shin as bad company."

"I know," Ryu replied. "Sometimes I truly believe that is the reason why the universe sent you to me so that you can be my eyes when I cannot see ahead of my own nose." Aiko smiled and held Ryu's hands tightly. She brought them up to her lips and kissed them.

"Let's forget about this bad company stuff for the time being. Let's focus on calculating how much time we are going to spend together and what places you want me to take you to when you begin your internship at the company in America." Ryu said.

"I'm not so worried about the American company. I know I am more qualified for the job than most of the other recruits." Aiko said with some satisfaction. "I know I will be able to make time to take our short trips to visit museums and go to the movies on weekends. I am so excited about that."

"I'm so excited too. I cannot wait to be able to live with you and not constantly be hiding from your family." Ryu said with exasperation. "And it's good that I am going back before you, that way I will have more time to prepare our itinerary." He added.

"Yes, I know," Aiko replied. "But my uncle will be visiting for a week and I will have to be at an event with him. It's only for a day. I'm his favorite niece and I could not even consider saying 'no' to him. Maybe I'll introduce you to him. I love him so much; he is very understanding. Everyone says he's gay because he never got married, you know?" Aiko started laughing and Ryu joined in seeing she wasn't completely serious about the last comment.

"There would not be anything wrong with that Aiko. We're living in a modern era." Ryu added laughing.

"I know," Aiko said. "It is because he is so nice and ... different. I think he is the one person in my entire family more in touch with his humanity above everyone else. That's why I love him so much."

Meanwhile, at the penthouse meeting, Matsuda San had just given the word to Liu, who was one of the commanders of the Woo family, strategically based in south China. Liu was seated behind Woo Xian sheng and as he addressed the bosses, he quickly got to the point and spoke about the concern he also had with some of the members of the Niema group, a primarily Russian criminal organization that served as an outsourcer into the European continent and their underground market.

Liu spoke about the mishandling of a matter that took place in England, during the first quarter transaction of properties. This is when they collected their money and handed over more merchandise.

"Members of our transaction team noticed several inconsistencies in the security when the product that was sent, exchanged hands. The pre-planned protocol was not followed by Niema and when confronted by one of our men, Mr. Niema disregarded the inquiry. This resulted in a situation, which caused the arrest of three of our men and the death of an associate."

This was something which Gao Hangul Ssi had already presented but Liu wanted to put an emphasis on.

Liu mentioned the names of several other members of the extended European branches of the organization who also had concerns about the inappropriate actions of the Niema group. As the conversation extended and Matsuda San heard all the complaints and concerns from the members around the table, he asked for a moment to pause, so that he and the others can come to a decision on the matter. Kito, his personal adviser got closer to his ear and answered a question Matsuda San had asked him under his breath.

"Sato..." Matsuda San said.

"Hai. (Yes)." Sato, a skinny and nefarious looking man, wearing black reading glasses, quickly responded. His three-piece suit and polished look made him look more like a high-end attorney than a gangster. As he stood up from the background, he immediately placed his attention completely towards Matsuda San's face, before bowing his head. Sato was the only other person besides the bosses' personal assistants to be allowed in the salon during this meeting. He was the most influential, of many spies the organization kept throughout the continent. Spies like Sato were necessary so that the organization could keep tabs on some other sub-branches and syndicates, which they secretly backed to enhance the power grip of their criminal enterprise and their outer reach. This ensures the never-ending flow of billions of dollars coming their way, to be placed on the needs of their secret primary objective.

"What is the level of integration we have achieved with Lyubov within the circles of the Ukrainian guard?" Matsuda San asked Sato.

"Fully operational since last year, sir..." Sato replied. "Consumption and international transactions of products and livestock are running at one hundred percent of their full capacity. I have projected that in two years we will develop a much higher demand for our suppliers to grow at forty-five percent every month. We will be making one thousand percent profit on every weapon, every kilo of heroin or cocaine, and every organ we sell, sir. Above all, everyone is completely satisfied with the manner in which we have set out to operate sir. And our scientists are in the process of developing a new substance which will stamp our global dominance in the world of narcotics for generations to come. They will all fall under our dominion and under our control." Sato concluded.

Matsuda San, as well as the other two leaders, were very pleased by the developments Sato described, the information painted a perfect scenario for their future plans. They looked at each other and slowly clapped their hands three times, with one-second intervals. Sato again sat down in the background, and after they all remained silent for a moment, Matsuda San proceeded to ask Gao Ssi to give his opinion about the Niema matter and what action he would consider prudent. Gao Ssi did not hide his thoughts, nor his desire for a better choice in partnership in the region.

"Very well..." Matsuda San said, just before asking Sato to approach him again. "Speak to the Ukrainian guard. Inform them that our deals with Niema will end. Bring our decision to the attention of the Soviets and be clear about the source of our Intel and the reason behind our decision to go in a different direction. Show them the evidence and do not leave any detail untold. Once you get their answer, inform Sao Li."

Sato bowed deeply and departed immediately to complete the task his boss gave him. As the satisfaction was clear on the faces of those who remained behind, Matsuda San then asked that only the other two leaders remain with him so that they can privately talk about the frame of their main agenda for the year ahead.

"Woo Xian sheng ..." Matsuda San said after everyone had walked away from the salon. The lights were off and outside the room, three men activated devices which certified no electronic apparatus could be utilized to spy on what was being said inside the room by the three leaders.

"Mr. Lang has already set things in motion." Woo Xian sheng said, speaking in Japanese, addressing Matsuda san. Hangul Ssi also understood the words being spoken by Woo Xian sheng. "He reassured me that his commitment to our proposal is second to none. He is, above all, a patriot and a true believer in the cause. I believe he deserves our trust. In six months, he will initiate the conversation with the leader of the party. This will give him enough time to use conventionalism in his approach before the election of the new Prime Minister. He used to be one of his trusted advisers, Matsuda San." Woo Xian sheng then gave the word back to Matsuda San.

"In eight months, in accordance with our concealed mediator, I will be granted a meeting with the Emperor's most trusted envoy." Matsuda San said, speaking in Mandarin Chinese. "Agreeing to send the envoy is already a positive gesture by the Emperor. It shows that he is willing to listen and study the initial installment of our proposal. Hangul Ssi, you have the word." Matsuda San then gave the word to Hangul Ssi, addressing him in Korean.

"In five months, I will have a meeting with the Supreme Leader's chief of staff." Hangul Ssi informed the others, speaking in Japanese. "It will take place during the chief of staff's secret trip to Turkey. This is very promising. It may present an actual opportunity to set up a meeting with Supreme Leader himself. Matsuda San you have the word." Hangul Ssi proceeded to give the word back to Matsuda.

They all agreed that the motion of their proposal had been received with decent perceptions by the parties they had attempted to reach, and this made them very optimistic about the future of their movement.

∞

Three days later, Woo Chen Xian sheng was seated on a comfortable stool, contemplating the fish in a man-made lake in the back of his estate. The estate was located in the province of Hangzhou, at the southern end of the Grand Canal of

China. Two little girls ran in his direction, playfully laughing as they got close to him.

"Ah Lam, Cai Hong, come. Come near me." Woo Xian sheng called upon the girls. They played together and stumbled. One trying to outdo the other as they ran towards him.

"Yeye, Yeye! (Grandpa! Grandpa!)" They shouted. Woo Xian sheng was thankful to see his granddaughters so full of happiness. He loved them dearly. He opened his arms as wide as he could, as the two girls tried to tackle him down as they hug him. He almost falls to the wooden floor beneath his feet, laughing heartily.

"Yeye, we want to have ice-cream with you." Al Lam said, she was six years old and was a year older than Cai Hong, who also wanted to have ice cream with grandpa.

"I want ice cream too!" Woo Xian sheng replied in a loud voice to his granddaughters, looking at the girls, before embracing them again. He was trying to hide the sadness in his eyes. With Woo Xian sheng on his feet, and the girls rushing to have their ice cream, they ran back to the inside of the house, which was discreetly surrounded by security personnel.

Later that night, Woo Xian sheng, with his eldest daughter, Ming Nmei, by his side, put Ah Lam and Cai Hong in bed. Their bedroom was lavish and nicely decorated in Asian culture and Disney characters. Woo Xian sheng looked at the girls sound asleep. Little Al Lam had dried ice cream on the left side of her lips. He smiled and looked at Ming Nmei. She looks down to the floor and does not make eye contact with him. She does not want him to see her tears, but he does. He embraces his daughter, knowing exactly what she is thinking.

"I love you so much you cannot even imagine." He said to his daughter.

"Father…"

"Don't say anything." He tells her. "Everything will be okay soon."

A few hours later, Woo Xian sheng's security personnel could be seen smoking outside their vehicles, posted at the back of a private hospital for children. Inside, Woo Xian sheng is seated on a chair near the bedside of Cuifen, his thirteen-year-old granddaughter, who suffers from an incurable disease that was causing her organs to fail. Thus far, doctors had exhausted all avenues of conventional medicine to try and extend her life. The organ transplants she had received were incompatible and unsuccessful.

Woo Xian sheng held her frail hand, while he read a story from one of her favorite books, something which he did as often as he could. He read for as long as he could until he could no longer keep his eyes open.

∞

The next day, three old box trucks with worn-out beige tarp canvases covering the back, were carefully making their way through a narrow and muddy road. They were heading towards a small village in Bangladesh, miles away from the capital, Dhaka. The morning was foggy as usual, but it was cooler today since it had rained the night before. The truck moving at the front of the convoy seemed to be having some problems with the wet soil, but the driver was skillfully maneuvering around the edges of the ground, to prevent the vehicle from getting stuck.

"Are we closer, sir?" Firash, the driver of the last truck asked the person sitting to his left, in between himself and another passenger. Three people can easily sit at the front of each truck. Firash was from Afghanistan and had some family members who were settled in Yugoslavia.

"Not much longer now." The person in the middle responded, in a passive manner. The driver took a moment observing how he looked: pale skin, dark blue eyes and curly brown hair and wearing a hooded coat which seemed big for his size. Right ahead, the driver could now see a glimpse of the entrance of the village and at that moment, the man seated by the passenger door received a signal from one of the riders in the truck ahead of them. He then told the driver to slow down. The truck at the center moved all the way ahead and pulled up only a few feet away from a frail-looking wooden fence, held together to a pole by a simple twine.

The driver of the last truck looked ahead and could see a small group of people. The first were some children who pushed open the fence and were emerging from the village boundaries. He could not make out what they had in their hands but for the person seated on the right side, it appeared they were carrying flowers with them.

Some of the children seemed curious to know who they were bringing flowers for, while others brought handmade baskets of fruits. Some of the elders held items in their hands as well, which they brought as gifts to share with the other people in the trucks.

"Shagotom janai." Gauri, the revered elder of the village, spoke in her native Bangla. She walked towards a person who, with the help of several others, had just gotten off the back of the truck. He was seated on a very old looking wheelchair that creaked. The person suddenly struggled with his breathing and a short outburst of coughing followed. After appropriately adjusting himself in his chair, he spoke to Gauri in the same language.

"My dear Dolly…" The person said to the Gauri, addressing her by a personal nickname.

He was dressed in a wool hooded coat that concealed him from head to toe. Gauri held her hands together and bowed in greeting him. She was a petite lady in her early seventies, with long white hair tied back into a neat bun. She had kind eyes and a warm smile. As the person behind slowly pushed the wheelchair closer to her, he instead gently opened his arms to embrace her. After a short but very meaningful hug, Gauri took over from the person pushing the wheelchair and brought it away from everyone. They were hidden behind a thick ancient tree, where they carried a much-needed conversation.

"Hello again, Dolly." The person said. They embraced each other again and Gauri stared at the face of the person with love in her eyes. The hood of the wool coat covered his head, her back was turned away from the others and the tree covered them both. No one saw what their eyes conveyed, nor hear what they spoke about. Soon after, they both calmly emerged back from behind the tree and headed towards where the others waited.

When they caught a closer sight of their special guest, the curious children suddenly became very playful and happy. They ran, and all gathered around him, but his arms were not big enough to hug and embrace all of them, all at once.

"I was under the assumption this was our first time in this particular village," Firash asked the person next to him.

"Is this your initial visit overall?" The man asked the driver in return.

"This is my first time." Firash went on to tell him that he had just been recruited from an economically ravaged area in Afghanistan, and he volunteered to be part of the truck services.

"Well, what about your family?" The other man asked him.

"I was not doing anything for them where I was. I couldn't. The person who approached me offered to take my family to a safe place and set them up for a better life. What about you? Do you have a family?" Firash then asked.

The man by his side remained silent.

"Let's head out." The man seated by the door said to him after a long pause. The other people were dismounting from the other two trucks.

"I believe it is the first time for many of us coming here to this village, but he has been here many other times before." The man seated at the center told Firash, as they climbed out of the truck.

"What is your name?" Firash asked him.

"You can call me Omar." The man replied.

The special guest took a moment to pause. Slowly, he began to stand up from his wheelchair. He began to walk into the village accompanied by the other elders he had come to greet. Their guest was almost always surrounded by all the children of the village.

The rest of the men who had traveled with him proceeded to unload big wooden boxes from the back of the trucks. They began organizing themselves to bring them into the village, with some help from the villagers. Soon those same people cut through the village, so as not to be seen by anyone other than the villagers. Once they were out of the village boundaries, they walked through a field of tall weeds, carrying the same wooden boxes, away from the village. They eventually entered a cave, which led to a hidden underground tunnel.

Sometime after, the guest of honor sat on the ground at the center of the village council, with Gauri seated by his right side. They spoke about several different topics of importance to the village and their guest addressed all their worries with straight forward answers and proposed some resolutions.

Gauri spoke about a subject, which others in the village were very troubled by. She said they expressed growing concern with the continuation of illegal logging and development, spreading from the cities into the nearing villages. Gauri had spoken with some of the other village elders from several villages to their east and they have told her about the threats they had received to prevent anyone from even attempting to interfere with their work. They said they were also offered monetary compensation to cooperate and to convince others to abandon their lands.

"Those in charge are calling this progress," Gauri said in a solemn tone of voice.

"Teacher, what is there for us to do if this grows till the steps of our very borders? It will be beyond our ability to continue to live here safely." One of the elders asked their guest of honor.

The teacher pondered in silence for a moment and took a slow glimpse around the simple and dimly illuminated room where they had gathered. It was just the walls, carpets made from jute, (a woven dried plant from the region) and different handmade cushions on the floor. A small fire at the center of the room burned, to keep the tea kettle warm. They each held teacups made from clay, and just their pleasant company was all that was needed at the moment.

"For the time being, it will not be something that will reach your homes, uproot you and change how you all live." The teacher said to the elders. They all listened quietly as he continued speaking.

"At least, for now, that is..." He silently observed each and every one of those in the room with him and waited a while before allowing the rest of his words to reach their minds.

"At the same time…" The teacher continued, "…that which seems to be unwelcoming news to the roots of your way of life, may just be a test. A trial of fortitude perhaps, for the foundation of the old ways you have strongly preserved for all these years. You have acquired what few have thought of, even those from adjacent regions have yet to understand with their eyes what you can see from them, not being revealed in you.

"This will not, in other words, affect your method of farming, but the seeds of your future. And they must be planted much deeper than what your own roots are. This must be stressed to the deepest of your cores. Your future seeds will be tested at their own time, for the world in which they will grow is slowly becoming cloudier. That precious illumination, which gives an impulse for the preservation and proliferation of what the farms birth, at a certain time, will no longer be enough. There will be a phase in the future, in which the root of your strength will be put to task by the hands of your seeds."

The teacher spoke, the village elders listened. For Gauri, it was understandable in the way he presented them with a summary for the future: ominous and unclear. She understood his ways. After all, she had been his brightest disciple. As for the others, the foundation of fear and insecurity still lingered in their minds. They were not ready. He knew this, but at that moment he was not yet sure if the time was enough to tell them.

Later that night, Gauri accompanied the teacher on a walk away from the village. They spoke of other times while observing the stars in the clear night sky. Gauri asked if any aspects of the setting within the village council needed to be addressed. She wanted to hear from him, his true perception of those in it. The teacher laughed briefly, just before asking Gauri to stop pushing the wheelchair at a particular spot.

"What do you believe in the setting of the very council you helped to install?" The teacher asked, while Gauri sat down on the grass and gazed up at the stars. She felt the grass beneath the palms of her hands. She closed her eyes for a moment.

"I have known them. And trusted them from their early mental age." Gauri said. "Still, one's own sense of trust does not always fit a true indication of what lays deep within anyone's inner soul. For the true aspect of change of anyone's mental age, and stage remains a mystery. Which is, at last, dictated by the very impact life circumstances and assimilation of experiences, shapes within each of us. As it goes, some may learn faster than others. Some may find *the ways*, sooner than many."

Gauri then became silent.

"Can you hold me, as you do?" The teacher made a request, which Gauri was happy and eager to comply with. She got on her feet and sat near the teacher on the wheelchair and embraced him, just as a mother would to her own child.

"The helios within this astral have taught us so much." The teacher commented. "We have learned many of *the ways* from them. And yet, the true vastness of the knowledge they attempt to offer us, we have yet to even conceive. For still, our age is young, still rebellious, at times impatient. Nevertheless hungry, in need, eager to be guided.

"And this, my beloved, brings one of the truer aspects of trust. For no matter the mental age of anyone, or their inner soul. Trust will be always acquired by who plants it and nurtures it into flourishing. This, you have."

Gauri had tears in her eyes, it was clear to her that she had indeed earned the respect of her beloved teacher, but what was not, was how far into the future she would have the honor to show him she merited it. She did not want to say much more, she above all was his developed disciple, and she knew very well, the ominous reason for his visit.

Chapter IV:

Nearsighted Means

The next day, it was early in the evening in the capital of Sier, Africa. Herman and Claire had traveled through various channels, and different smugglers, to make it there. They had some close encounters against people that Claire suspected had been operatives of Mozambican, Inc. Herman had successfully fended off several attempts made against Claire's life while getting closer and closer to finding the information he needed, to put together the final pieces of the puzzle he was attempting to solve.

They made it to the place of a French American black man named Montel. His dual citizenship had enabled him in the past, to be an international organizer for the Coalition for Ocean Life Preservation. Due to the numerous perils the organization had endured, and the assault against many of their members, Montel was now living in secrecy to escape the same fate the other members of his team had suffered. Montel had gotten information about a clandestine lab secretly set up by one of the branches of Mozambican, Inc. Claire had asked him about the level of trust he had on the source of the information, but Montel did not have a concrete answer about it. He still felt the information was good enough to follow up on.

"Aliya will be back before nightfall," Montel mentioned to Herman and Claire. "I told her we would be out for a drink. She wanted to meet with us, to get to know the two of you, but she has to get up early tomorrow. Anyway, it's better this way. Without her, we'll be much freer to do what we have to do." Montel was very skinny, about six feet tall, with very round dark eyes. He wore his thick hair in short tiny twists.

"I agree," Claire said. "But regardless, I believe we should try to figure out what we came here to and leave as soon as we can. We don't want to stay in this place for too long, I feel we will risk exposing your friend, Montel. The people who are after me can be very resourceful in their searches. They've been tracking my steps faster and faster."

"I also agree with that, Montel." Herman felt certain that this would be the right move. "From what we have seen, Mozambican's people work really fast at finding their targets. We don't want to put your friend in their crosshairs."

"Okay, so then let's get going," Montel said.

Two hours later, Montel, Claire, and Herman were on a busy street, filled with popular restaurants with outdoor tables and people out and about everywhere. Montel was told to be on the lookout for a red bus, where they were supposed to meet with his contact. As they waited, they sat out on a table where they had beers and acted accordingly as if they were one of the regulars. Pop music played from a small radio somewhere nearby.

Soon enough, Montel saw the red bus approaching the station near where they had been waiting. He told Claire and Herman to follow him to get on the bus. Montel spotted his contact as soon as they got on the bus. There was someone with a radio, playing loud music, who greeted them as he danced his way over to them. Montel told Herman and Claire to finish their beers and that he would be buying them another round inside the bus. There was always someone selling cold beer inside buses since this practice was allowed as a legal method of earning additional revenue for the bus owners. The local officials then took advantage of it by collecting extra taxes.

"They are cheaper in here," Montel said. His connection approached them, a young man named Sydney, the same person who was in charge of collecting fares inside the bus. Herman looked at him and mentioned to Claire how much he resembled Montel.

"You are right!" Claire said, "They look like brothers. But Sydney is a bit more handsome though."

"I really wouldn't know about that," Herman replied. Indeed, Montel and Sydney had similar features and were almost the same height. Although Sydney had a small flat-top haircut and bigger ears than Montel.

Montel waited near the front of the bus, Sydney was collecting fares from the back door, and his partner who was selling the beers was collecting from the front door. They switched places and now Sydney was able to talk to Montel.

"My girlfriend does the cleaning at the place next door," Sydney said, speaking with a heavy accent. "They are part of a company from the US. They import soft drinks into this part of the world. The lab is next door and it's easy to get to, from where she works."

"What time are we going there?" Montel asked.

"I finish in an hour," Sydney said. "You will get off in two stops and will wait for me near the park."

"What park?" Herman asked.

"You will see it when you get off the bus," Sydney said. Two stops later, and indeed, Montel spotted the park Sydney spoke about the moment they got off the bus. The bus kicked off a cloud of dust as it drove off. Montel pointed out the park to Herman. They waited around for an hour while smoking and telling stories until Sydney showed up, driving a small four-door Fiat car.

"They believe no one knows what they are doing here," Sydney said while driving by slowly into a dark alley. "They have only two security guards working there at the place. I guess they keep it simple and unassuming in this manner." They had driven for thirty minutes until they arrived at the location.

"They create less attraction to the place if they make it look unimportant," Montel said agreeing.

Sydney parked the car a block away from where his girlfriend works. They walked through the back door and Sydney's girlfriend was surprised to see him so early. She was short and very skinny with long dark hair. She discreetly handed Sydney a key to the equipment room on the second level and from there, they got into a narrow threshold, where they climbed over a fence up to the rooftop of the second level laboratory. They opened a window and gained entry inside the building.

Sydney stayed outside on guard while Claire, Montel, and Herman went inside. It was dark, and the sound of stray dogs barking could be heard from the distance. They looked around from where they were, at a top-level staircase but did not see anything out of the ordinary. The place was not even well equipped to fit the description of a sophisticated lab where experiments were being conducted. But the group became separated and began searching in different areas.

The sound of a toilet flushing was heard. A security guard stepped out of a restroom and began walking around. All the lights in the building were turned off. The guard had a flashlight in his left hand but did not have it turned on. Montel was about to run into him but ducked down to the floor and hid under a desk as the security guard passed by him. Claire was inside an office and heard the security guard walking in her direction. Herman was standing behind the door. He was planning on following the direction the guard was headed towards, but something else caught his attention. He saw what appeared to be cold steam. It was softly billowing from under a door, a couple of steps away from him. He looked everywhere but did not see Claire and Montel anywhere. The door had a security keypad to the left side of the wall, Herman was determined to enter the room, and the keypad was not going to stop him. He stood there staring at the door. His eyes squinted, his hands raised up, fingers separated and trembling.

The security guard had walked away. Claire and Montel found each other. They walked with their backs against the wall. "Where's Herman?" Montel asked her. He and Claire bent down to whisper.

"Last time I saw him, he was going that way." Claire pointed to where Herman had been hiding before.

"Let's go find him." He and Claire carefully walked up to the door with the keypad, Herman had been curious about. Claire noticed what she thought was smoke, billowing from under the door.

Suddenly, she noticed the door was partially opened. Herman had found a way to open it without activating the alarms.

"Herman," Claire whispered, silently pushing the door to open wider. The cold steam that was coming out from below, was covering the entire room, to the point where Claire could not see her feet. It was very dark inside, but the lights of modern equipment and monitors were visible all around. Claire could see what appeared to be a chamber, where the steam was emanating from. Montel was right by her and saw it as well on the left side of the room.

Someone grabbed Claire's left hand, almost causing her to scream. It was Herman holding on to Claire's hand. Montel had seen him before she did.

"I found something here," Herman told them. Claire and Montel followed him near the chamber, where they immediately found a very sophisticated laboratory setting.

"This is it," Montel said. He brought a small camcorder out from his backpack for Herman and Claire to see. "Let us get as much as we can, from whatever they are working with here. If we find anything detrimental to Mozambican, we can use it later as evidence."

"Montel, you are full of surprises," Claire said, joyful to see they were about to gain some traction. Herman looked at her for a moment, just before he asked Montel for the camera. Montel handed it over without hesitation. Claire was about to say something but did not. Herman looked at the camera, inspecting it briefly.

"Here. Make records of those documents set aside on those tables over there. Put your hand like this over the light of the camera so you only point it to what you are filming." Herman said, handing the camera back to Montel. Herman asked Claire to come inside the lab with him. There were test tubes and blood samples in different settings over metal tables, to the left and to the right side of the room. Herman gazed over at the samples on the right side. Claire was right behind him; Herman could literally feel her breathing. She saw as he paused over a petri dish that was placed under a microscope. Herman approached it and took a closer look at it, bringing his right eye over the eyepiece of the microscope.

"The flu," Herman mumbled to himself.

"Is that what the tray has?" Claire asked him, before looking into it herself. Herman looked at her as she placed her left eye peering into the eyepiece tube. He did not answer her question, allowing her to find out on her own.

"Guys, they have another location to the south," Montel said. He was walking behind Claire, reading a document he held in his right hand. I have a bill here from a delivery company that they've been using to transport equipment."

"Did you capture it on film?" Herman asked.

"Yes, I did," Montel replied.

"Put those papers back exactly as they were," Herman said to him. "And come and take a look at this." He waved his hand at Claire to walk up to him. There was a computer over a desk with two other monitors next to it. Herman had turned on one of them. He found a video that had been recorded three months earlier, at a different location. The person recording the video was also recording the analysis the computer was completing. Claire was stunned, she walked closer to the monitor. Montel had begun recording and asked Claire to move so he could get closer to the monitor.

The three continued to record the video when suddenly Herman heard a sound, that caused Claire to look back and Montel to stop recording. Herman was not bothered by the sound but decided to fast forward the video they were watching. They were shocked by what was on the video. The three of them stood there momentarily to try to understand what they just watched.

Montel's hands were shaking. The light from his camera distracted Claire.

"Careful with the light Montel." She said. Herman was calm, analyzing what he had seen, recording every detail of it in his mind.

"We have to put this out there," Claire said. "We just have to." Herman looked at Montel, who was standing right behind him.

"We have to." He agreed. Just then, the security guard turned the lights on in the hallway outside the room.

"Shit!" Montel exclaimed. He, Claire and Herman ran out of the room, just in time to avoid being locked in by the door with the keypad. Herman was able to throw a chair in its path to prevent it from closing. The noise of the chair and the sound of them running alerted the guards.

There were four security guards now, and they began chasing after them, just steps behind from capturing them. They had their guns out but one of the guards advised against shooting so close to the main lab. The three managed to gain some ground as they zig-zagged, trying to confuse and lose the guards. Herman was able to push Montel up to the window six feet up, where they had gained access to get inside the lab. Montel did not know how Herman was able to do that but, in his rush, he did not have the time to think about it either. He then carried Claire up for Montel to grab her hand. Several shots hit the wall near Herman. He yelled at Montel and Claire to run away. Claire did not want to. But after hearing more shots being fired, Montel grabbed her hand and dragged her away. They were able to make it back to their car and quickly drove away.

Later that morning, Montel and Claire had made it back to Sydney's house. They hadn't heard from Herman yet, but Claire felt happy to hear about her two friends, Steven and Clark. They were two of the people she was supposed to meet before but had gotten separated. Steven and Clark were two free-living hippies she had met during a Clear Horizon meeting in San Francisco. Sydney had informed her that they made it into the country safely.

A day later, Sydney waited till late in the evening and drove Montel and Claire to a restaurant, three miles from the bus stop where they had met two nights before. It did not take long for Sydney to pick them up from a back room where a close mutual friend was hiding them. Claire was ecstatic to see them well. But there was not much time for chatting, time was not on their side and they needed to make as much headway as they could. Sydney told them that he would take them to an underground safehouse away from there. Neither Claire, nor her two friends were very well-acquainted with Sydney, but he knew he could trust them, mostly because of Montel who knew Claire, as well as one of the owners of the safehouse. Montel did not want to say anything but after some thinking, he decided to tell Claire. He did not want to keep her in the dark about anything, as Herman had suggested a day earlier.

"I have something to tell you guys," Montel said. "Aliya heard about a robbery at the laboratory last night."

"What did she hear?" Claire quickly asked, sounding very concerned.

"She told me that someone had been taken into custody." Montel's words and the idea that Herman may have been the one captured set the tone for a very somber mood inside the car. No other words were spoken until they arrived near the safehouse. It was located in a particularly rough area of the city, where the military patrolled the streets constantly. Putting pressures on local street gangs and potential religious radicals, kept a checked stronghold on any would-be terrorist cell attempting to spark out of control. Only one powerful drug lord was left alone. He had managed to keep most of the military inside his pocket. Sydney had warned the others of a potential encounter with the military. He explained to them, what to say and how to act if this were to ever occur.

"Believe it or not, this is the safest location for all of you," Sydney said. "Those who are after you, would not consider trying to find you in this part of the city." Sydney's words were a small breath of fresh air for Claire and her friends. After hearing what happened to Herman, they were shaken up. Montel was not familiar with the logistics, but he trusted Sydney blindly.

"Here, we are already oppressed by the military." Sydney continued. "They have everyone in check. Other places will offer more of an opportunity for people like us to hide and find a safe place. This is why we are better here than anywhere else. The eyes of the enemy will be put there, where everyone is a radical of some sort. Here, they assume everyone is under control, therefore we will be hiding in plain sight."

As they arrived at a location less than half a mile from the safe house, Sydney parked the car inside a garage. Other vehicles were being repaired there. There were motorcycles, old cars and burnt and busted up vehicles from accidents. One of the rear tires of Sydney's car was taken out, to make it look as if the vehicle was being worked on.

Four men dressed as mechanics told them to wait ten minutes before leaving to where they were headed. Claire and her friends wore hooded tunics and kept their hands inside their pockets, to prevent anyone from seeing they were foreigners and avoid unnecessary curiosity towards them. After ten minutes passed, they exited the garage through a back door and walked the rest of the way.

After a short time, they arrived at a one-room dwelling in the middle of a slum with narrow, muddy streets. Only motorcycles would be able to travel in and out, the military SUV's would not be able to go through. To Montel's surprise, he was being welcomed inside by Herman, who had opened the door for him. Claire could not contain her happiness when she saw him and jumped over to hug him.

"How did you make it out?" She asked him right away.

"Long story." Herman replied while shaking Sydney's hand, before being introduced to Claire's friends. They were all offered tea and homemade bread by Zain and her husband Kali, the owners of the property. The couple was Muslim and offered a prayer for their guests before they sat on a large and worn out carpet. Only two feet away, a dark green curtain divided their sleeping quarters from the rest of the room. Herman gave a brief narration of what took place at the lab after Montel and Claire escaped. Claire's friends were very impressed by his courage, telling him that they felt much better now, knowing that Claire had been in his care. For some reason, they felt Herman gave them a renewed sense of hope.

"There is no telling how much damage we're going to be able to inflict on Mozambican, with the video that we'd been able to collect." Claire was already crafting a retaliation against the drug company. Sydney, Montel, and the others saw potential in what they might be able to achieve if they utilize the new information they'd acquired in the right way. Zain and Kali were seasoned activists and they wanted to advise Montel's young crew to look in a different direction and be patient if they wanted to be successful utilizing what they found against the drug company. Steven and Clarke agreed with Zain and Kali, but they also believed the information and evidence they had in possession could be used to help themselves and others being pursued. Herman did not give an immediate opinion, opting for keeping his own thoughts to himself. He wanted to hear what Zain and Kali could give him in strategy and advice.

Later that night, the men planned what their next course of action will be, while Zain and Claire went for a walk outside. They had walked several meters away from the hideout. There was a large portion of unoccupied terrain in the back of the slum, where people dumped their garbage. From where they were standing, they could see candle lights in some of the rooms, while others shared electricity, stolen from nearby towns. Zain had noticed the desire for action in Claire's intentions and she wanted to have a talk with her privately to ease her stress.

"It seems you have gone through a great deal of suffering because of those men pursuing you and your friends," Zain spoke softly and placed her hand on Claire's shoulder. "But if you allow the suffering to become the eventuality of hatred, you will be falling into the never-ending circle of malice. It is true that those men working for the drug company are not good people. They have decided to utilize the power entrusted to them in the worst of manners. But you should not fall into the same pitfall they've thrown themselves into in the pursuit of their goals, whatever those goals may be. For that is the path to their perdition, and yours as well."

Claire remained quiet, listening to what Zain was saying. She listened and thought about her words. Zain had asked her to walk with her along a narrow trail of sewer water, which had run off behind the grounds of her neighborhood. They saw others taking a nightly stroll by the other side of the water trail. Two men and two women of old age greeted them in the Muslim way. The night was offering its ambient sounds. Dogs could be heard barking, crickets chirping, and trees waved their branches from side to side with the wind. The half-moon over the sky offered a light blue veil over the lands.

"You are an activist," Claire spoke while looking down at the ground.

"For many years now," Zain said.

"You know what it is to feel that you are doing something wrong," Claire said while bending down to pick up pebbles from the ground. She then began to throw them into the sewer water. It created tiny ripples distorting the reflection of the moon on it. They continued to walk for a while without saying anything. As the moonlight became more prevalent in the sky, Zain listened to Claire, she looked at her own shadow cast next to a tree where they decided to pause.

"When you know deep inside your heart that you are right, and they are not, it's only because of their money and power that they make themselves to be righteous in the eyes of those brainwashed by their power and prestige, painting all of us as the villains and they, as the victims of the crazy. We are the crazies; we are the troublemakers and the anti-socials. The law is put against us, and yet, that is all we ever wanted; For the law to be upheld. When the world turns out in this way, and we risk our lives to try to make a difference. To try to reveal what these people are really after, for more money, more power, more control. Can we just stand by when we finally have the chance to turn the tables and show the world who they really are and what they are really after?" Claire continued.

Zain looked up to the sky, she was only able to see a handful of stars. She then bent down and grabbed soil from the ground. She held on to it for a moment, only to let it fall again slowly through her fingers.

"The difference between them and you," Zain began to explain, "their cause and yours, what they are after and what you are after. It is only the balance of power. Their power sits on the ill-gained money and influence they've acquired through what they do. What they do, is what gives you the courage to become who you are. All of us are a product of what they are doing. Of what they have done to hurt others. It is this way because some of us in the world have the foresight to see through their lies and their wicked deeds. And this is why we have decided to take action of our own, where others have decided to stay still. That puts us in the minority, even as we may outnumber them. Their power makes them more than us."

"Exactly! Their power!" Claire interrupted Zain. "Their power makes them more correct than us, even when they are not. This is why, when the opportunity is given to us, and we find the power to level the playing field, we should use it to put them down and make them suffer. To show the rest of the world who they truly are and what they are doing to the rest of us."

"Yes Claire," Zain interrupted, "but there is a right way and a wrong way to go about this. Above all, you must remember that you are not like them. And if given the chance, you come across power that you know for certain you can use against them, you must never allow yourself to use this power in a manner that would be similar to what they do with theirs. It would only be detrimental to your own cause. And it will only perpetuate a never-ending circle of negativity in which only the innocent will suffer the consequences of our war against them if we begin to act as they do. If we do, they will win. And those we have been trying to protect, they will continue suffering. Think of this as the tale of the young boy, the friend, and the bully... The young boy who gets bullied at school by the big tough kid. He gets bullied until the friend tells him a secret about the bully." Zain closed her eyes and tilted her head down. Claire listened to her story while carefully analyzing how it compared to her own.

"The young boy now knows the bully wets his bed at night," Zain continued, "now he is waiting for an opportunity to confront the bully and humiliate him in front of his friends and everyone else at school. The friend advises the boy not to spill the secret in front of everyone else, because it will not have the same effect as if he lets the bully know that only he knows his secret. The young boy did it in the way his friend advised him, and it worked. And now the bully has been staying away from the young boy, afraid he may tell others what he knows about him. And the story should end there.

"However, now it is the young boy who appears to have a change of attitude. Now he feels empowered thanks to the safety net the bully's secret has provided for him. The friend warns him about how he has been acting, but the young boy ignores the warnings of the person whose advice helped save him from his misery. He feels he has power now and his power had freed him from needing the help of his friend any longer. But power, in any way, shape or form may always turn out to be partial or temporary. And it might even turn against its wielder. Especially when used recklessly.

"Soon after, the bully is now frustrated being bullied around himself, so he enlists the help of his older brother's friends who attended a different school. They began taunting the young boy after school hours, chased and harassed him, and the young boy has no idea who these new kids are and why they are harassing him. He had nothing to protect himself with from them. Now, once again he had gone back to the same suffering which did not let him have the freedom of peace. The friend who once helped him, disappointed after seeing how he had behaved after having power over his bully, left him alone to teach him a lesson."

"I don't know what to do, to be honest with you." Claire said, "Is this what you're trying to tell me? To lay low? Instead of leveling the playing field with Mozambican? But this is what we have been after. We needed something to show what these people are doing. And we finally found it. Maybe now we can protect ourselves against them. If we use what we have and put it out in the open, it will cripple them. They will have to leave us alone."

"Yes, like the bully did the young boy?" Zain asked Claire, making a point about the lesson she was trying to teach her.

"I don't know what to do..." Claire seemed hopeless, now she truly did not know what needed to be done to escape from her troubles. She was confused, and she felt Zain was trying to steer her in the right direction, but that direction was not going to protect her and her friends.

"Why is that, no matter how we try to go against these people, who are clearly doing something very wrong and putting the innocent and vulnerable at risk, why is it that we always end up looking like the crazies and the troublemakers? Even as we are being hurt and hunted... why?"

Zain moved closer to her and placed her hand over her shoulder again. "Because this is how the world has been shaped into my dear," she said. "Those wolves prey on the sheep while appearing as noble shepherds guiding them. And for those who see the truth and want to warn the sheep of the impending danger, they are made to look like lunatics. But anyway, I would like to see this video for myself before a decision is made."

"Okay, let's go back. I want you to see it. And I want everyone to see it. Maybe you will understand why I'm feeling the way that I am."

Herman watched as the two women began to make their way back to the safe house. He had been listening to them seated on a branch near the top of the tree. He made his way down and followed them silently without them seeing him. As he walked into the room, he could see in the way everyone was staring at them, that a decision had been made. Everyone had decided to watch the video together before deciding what to do with it.

They gathered around as Sydney brought out his camcorder and hooked it up to the small television set in the room. He rewinded it back to when they first entered the room with the keypad. Everyone listened as the voices of Claire and Sydney were heard in the background of the video. Footage of papers with names, locations, and equipment that was ordered was being shown. Sydney's voice narrated what he thought they may be and what they were looking at. The camera then pans out and zooms in on Claire's face. She and Herman say that they may have found something as Herman is seen opening a file inside one of the computers and a video starts playing.

The video showed ten men, laying on their beds facing up, in what looked like a big hospital room. Herman was not looking at the men, but for any clues around the room, which may determine the whereabouts of that location. The men in the beds were only partially dressed, with sheets covering the midsection of their bodies. They were all of African descent and appeared to be in poor health. Claire had a clear visual of the intravenous therapy they were being given. It was a copper color liquid of a thick consistency and the person recording the video made sure that it was clearly captured on film. The intravenous bag had an eight-digit number on it. The patients all had numeric clocks next to their heads, counting days, hours, minutes and seconds.

"Look at this." Claire pointed to Herman, showing how a monitor was displaying the activities within each of the men's internal organs. A group of scientists entered the room dressed in bio-hazard suits. They took their time and chatted amongst themselves before eventually attending to the progress each of the men were displaying in their physical appearance. They checked the pupils of their eyes, under their tongues, checked their pulses and blood pressures. The scientists began reading some notes inside the patient files and a brief conversation later, the scientists agreed on accelerating the speed of the strange intravenous liquid on three of the men, while decreasing it on the remaining seven.

The video reached a point when it was four days later. The clock displayed the date and time when the scientists returned to the room once again. Montel began recording again. The effects of the intravenous liquid on the three men whose dosage had been accelerated were devastating. Their bodies had begun to decompose, in the same manner, an old fruit exposed to the hot sun for hours will decay.

The scientists were confused and believed the men were dead. But the effects did not stop there. The men in the worst shape suddenly began behaving strangely. As their bodies began to tremble radically while still on the beds, the scientists became aware that it was quickly turning into an impending emergency. The men appeared to be suffering greatly, writhing in pain. Eventually, they stood up from their beds and their eyes became vacant. The scientists tried to get them to lay down again, but the patients soon began to attack the scientists nearest to them with terrifying strength, eventually dismembering them. Once the scientists were on the floor, unable to move, the patients began to chew on their flesh like wild animals. The shouting and the screaming woke up two of the other men, who were being treated with the slower dosage.

The person recording the video was able to make it out of the room and continued to record from behind a glass wall. The three men continued to devour four of the scientists who could not escape in time. As the scientists lay on the floor, bleeding to death, the patients began attacking the other men in the beds in the same way. The patients were clearly unaware of what they were doing. As it appeared, they were no longer in control of their own bodies.

Zain and the others couldn't believe what they were watching. It seemed like something out of a horror film, but it was happening right there at a Mozambican lab. Herman noted the data the person recording pointed the camera at. Then something happened so suddenly, that it caused the video to go dark. The way everyone was staring at Herman, made him realize that everyone had made up their minds about the video.

"I see, and so it shall be done," Herman said while revealing a set of documents he had not shared with them earlier. "Before we put this thing out, I think we should follow one more link." He continued. "I was able to see a word in one of the charts the scientists were holding before the security guards came after us. I had seen a similar looking chart over one of the drawers against the wall at the end of the room. After you and Montel were out," Herman looked at both Claire and Montel. "I hid and went back to the lab and took a look at the chart. I was able to take a couple of pages with me. These are it." Herman showed the pages to the rest of the group. He placed them over the carpet and Kali brought a candle, so they could see what Herman wanted to show them. They were records of the origins of many of the men they had utilized to conduct experiments on, at many other locations. Herman turned to the last page to show everyone where the next possible source of guinea pigs may be coming from. It was from an impoverished area in Costa Rica.

∞

A week has passed, and it was late in the afternoon at a neighborhood an hour away from the port of Bin Qasim, in the city of Karachi, Pakistan. It was an hour before prayer time. A Muslim woman, wearing a traditional Hijab over her head and over her nose, walked among the crowd of a very busy street, carrying a mid-size, protuberant fabric bag. There was a small group of young boys, with very dirty clothing, hustling and panhandling in the streets. The woman took notice of this as she walked near them. She noticed one boy in particular, eleven-year-old Tofiq, being very persistent and aggressive in his panhandling techniques. He was playfully distracting people while placing his hands in their pockets and smoothly stealing from them.

Two of the boys approached the woman as she walked by them and quickly offered to help carry her bag. When she swatted their hands away from her bag, they reacted by quickly asking her for some money. She asked them to stay away from her as she walked forward. Tofiq was right ahead of the woman and attempted to succeed where the others had failed. He was attempting to be charming to her, but the woman quickly dismissed him and told him to go away. Her eyes caught him by surprise. They were deep blue and pierced through his when she looked down at him, scaring him into walking away from her without persisting with any other requests. Tofiq stared at her wondering as she walked on ahead, away from him. His friends called him to go somewhere else and as he marched away, he could not prevent himself from looking back to search for the woman, amid the crowd in the street, but she was already long gone.

The woman stopped at a spice market, where she purchased a small portion of street made food as well as fresh vegetables and spices, which she put inside her bag to take with her into a back-alley way. There were many doors, belonging to different properties which were built very close to each other. She looked up and saw a young woman and an old lady picking up several colorful sheets from a clothesline outside their window. Shadows cast by the higher walls, as the sun was slowly setting, the woman walked to a door halfway across the alley and opened it without hesitation.

"Red Ireland." She said in Ukrainian, as she walked in.

There were two dozen heavily armed men dressed all in black military gear, pointing machine guns at the door. It was dark, and the fog of cigarette smoke expanded all over.

"It's clear! It's clear!" One of the men shouted out, also speaking in Ukrainian.

"Vitaly, I didn't see anyone covering the main access of this place from the top." The woman spoke with a strong and commanding male voice while addressing the man who shouted out to the others.

She removed the Hijab from over her head, and it was no woman. A 6 foot 3, blonde-haired, blue-eyed Ukrainian man named Victor Niema, who controlled a large underground international crime operation, with small outlets all over the world, stood in front of everyone in the middle of the room. He was sharp, strong and solid built from years of fighting and conflict. Other than Vitaly, the contract on his head was unknown to the rest of his men, till just that moment.

"Bora is at the top of the last apartment, boss." Vitaly instantly replied. "We have also three men near the market and one across the street, inside the eatery."

Vitaly, who had very black hair and an equally black short beard, had thought about the very small eatery and the man seated in a corner with a good view of the entrance to the alleyway, as he placed his weapon down and assisted Niema in taking off his disguise.

"I saw him," Niema said. He was dressed in dark combat gear and black combat boots, which were not visible thanks in part, to the length of the attire he had been wearing outside. He picked up several guns to arm himself and positioned a combat knife inside a strap around his belt.

"Have you learned anything new?" Niema asked.

"It appears to be as you heard, boss," Vitaly said. "They gave the order not too long ago, after the problem in London. My contact told me they may have offered the assignment to Li, from the..."

"Hangul family..." Niema said, finishing Vitaly's sentence. "I see... Favorable odds." Niema thought out loud as he began walking around the area where his men were positioned, all strong and intimidating looking. Some with very short hair and grown out beards and others with completely clean-shaven heads and faces. Niema knew they were just finding out the sudden change in circumstances, but he saw no deviations from their resolve and their desire of working for him.

"This will be a short-lived engagement, gentlemen..." Niema spoke to his men. He grabbed an open bottle of vodka that had been sitting over a small table near a narrow window, where one of his men was looking out to the street. Niema drank the vodka straight from the open bottle.

"It seems that one of the members of our Asian partners have decided that our services... No, *my* services are no longer needed for the continuation of their Eastern European and North American operations. I presume that a vote was requested for the termination of my partnership and I believe that it culminated in acceptance.

"Since the process of partnership-termination will conclude with the head of the leadership being executed, I have made arrangements for each of you to receive double the full payment for the sum of three years' worth. I also added a bonus for the trouble you are about to confront on my behalf. By this time, each of your chosen family members has already been provided with account numbers containing your payment. They have also been instructed to retrieve their funds at once.

"Each of you in this room with me, and those outside, have been part of my operation for many years. I have learned to know each of you, and I have learned to trust each of you. The risk you are about to take will not be prolonged. I have already made arrangements to cover my steps after a point which I have already set up. I will only need your services for less than a month. Afterward, each of you can go and start a new life."

Vitaly looked at the men. The rest of them looked at each other. For them, there was no question. They all agreed to stay with their boss for as long as he needed them. Niema was not surprised. Without any further words or hesitation, he put his next move in motion by placing a call from a cellphone he took out of a metal box. A person answered the call speaking in Greek. Niema stated his name and the person at the other end of the line asked him what his need was, this time speaking to him in Ukrainian.

"Has everything been arranged as I requested?" Niema asked.

"Half of the gold has been transferred to our pre-arranged location." The person on the other line responded.

"The rest will be delivered by sundown tomorrow," Niema said.

"Alive?" The person asked.

"Yes," Niema replied, he then ended the call and looked at his men. "Let's move."

Two hours later, Niema and his men traveled in four small minivans, away from the crowded city and up to a food processing plant. They were welcomed by a small army of heavily armed men outside the plant. Vitaly went ahead and asked for a man who called himself Afzal. Afzal walked forward accompanied by eight others. Vitaly instructed him to get in the back of the van where Niema was waiting. The rest of Niema's men dismounted from the other vans and assumed their positions guarding the surroundings.

Afzal and Niema had a brief conversation where they established the rest of the steps which needed to be taken to conclude their temporary relationship. Afzal exited the van with Niema by his side. Vitaly followed close behind with four others. Niema gave the signal for another van, which was left at a safe distance, to be brought in.

"Don't worry Mr. Niema," Afzal said, guiding Niema and his men inside. "At this point, you can tell your men to relax, for you as well as they are under our full protection. I must say, my leader, is very pleased with the product you have been providing us with thus far. Our sales have exceeded expectations, far beyond our predictions. It is most sad that you are retiring from this business, which you have managed with the greatest dignity, and that is why he wanted to thank you personally."

"I do appreciate the gesture, Mr. Afzal..." Niema replied. "It pleases me to know you have corroborated my words with the success of your business." Afzal smiled.

Niema looked back at Vitaly, just as he was about to follow Afzal towards a well-guarded door. At that moment, Niema turned his head to look at Vitaly but stumbled on something with his left foot. Afzal was about to open a door for Niema but instead, a bullet shot right through Afzal's head and struck the door. It did not take long for all hell to break loose. Shots were being fired from every direction and bullets rained down as if a sudden storm had descended upon them.

Niema's men took fast cover but the Pakistanis were dropping like stones all over the place. Vitaly and Niema, together with three other men ripped through the door running over Afzal's body, as well as the bodies of those who had been guarding the door. Niema and his men were being shot at by Afzal's boss's security personnel inside the warehouse. But they were no match for Vitaly and the others with Niema.

One of Afzal's men shouted out at comrades not to fire at them. After a short-lived conversation, Niema, his men, and Afzal's men made their way through the middle of the warehouse. They quickly took cover behind cardboard barrels and factory equipment.

"Red Ireland, Red Ireland!" Shouted three more of Niema's men, running into the warehouse under a rain of bullets. Two of them did not make it, as one was struck on his head and dropped right in front of the door and the other was hit all over his body as he ran to look for cover inside.

"Boss!" Vitaly shouted out. Niema was five steps away from him standing right next to five very scared looking men and a lady in her sixties, pointing their weapons at him. The five men seemed to be protecting a heavy-set looking man in his fifties. The man had gray hair and a gray beard and seemed to be very upset about what was taking place. The lady was hunkered down near a heavy piece of machinery, covering her ears in panic. Niema became aware of her, she seemed to be only a second away from crying. Niema could see how the bearded man continued talking to his subordinates, ordering them to keep moving forward. All the while analyzing how the situation was being handled as the sound of gunfire grew louder and closer to them.

"Are you Allam?" Niema asked, his voice was calm and sound, unparalleled to the surrounding sounds of bullets, crying and shouting. The heavy-set man was about to respond but Niema slowly lifted his right hand to prevent him from talking and turned his sights towards the frightened lady. She seemed to have missed the question and did not answer, nor look at Niema. Two of the five men took several steps forward while helping the lady up. The other three guarded the bearded man to offer him better protection as they moved forward and deeper into the factory.

"I am not here to bring harm to you," Niema said. He did not take his eyes off the frightened lady as she was being dragged forward three steps ahead of him. The two men by her side speaking in Urdu told Niema not to pressure the lady as she was already too frazzled. The bearded man walked closer to Niema and informed him that he was in fact, Allam.

"Allam." Niema took one step closer to the lady. The two men with her brought their weapons up, pointing them at Niema.

"Keep back!" One of the men shouted to Niema. The other three men reacted by leaving the bearded man and surrounded the lady.

"What do I do?" Vitaly asked. He and the others with Niema took quick measures pointing their weapons at the Pakistanis. Shouting and yelling ensued, the Pakistanis were very nervous and agitated. Every one of them was within a hair's distance away from pulling their triggers and firing their weapons.

Niema did not waver. He kept his composure. As did the bearded man, while observing Niema.

"I am here to honor the end of a deal, to a well-deserving business associate," Niema said, his eyes locked on the lady, who still refused to lift her head while appearing very frightened. Vitaly was nervous, and he too kept his weapon up while remaining close behind Niema. A loud explosion was heard, everyone was shaken, then, the lady placed her hand over the shoulder of the man closest to her. She straightened herself up slowly while arranging the very cheap quality traditional dress she wore and the scarf over her head. She did not seem hesitant anymore while moving closer to Niema.

"You are as perceptive as I presumed you would be, Mr. Niema," Allam said.

Niema bowed his head in respect. Vitaly again asked about what to do, as the sounds of gunfire drew nearer.

"The respect you inspire does not do you justice, Madame," Niema replied. "I just wish these minor complications, which had followed me to your country, does not bring any more inconveniences or affect the way you do things around here."

Niema walked closer to Vitaly without moving his eyes away from Allam.

"Ask if they have it." He said to Vitaly. Vitaly quickly brought a two-way radio close to his lips, while Allam and her men guided the way to move deeper into the confines of the place. The men protecting Allam looked at each other from time to time before giving quick looks at their leader, as if searching for answers from her on what to do next.

"Do you have it now?" Vitaly asked. There was lots of noise over the airways but Vitaly could hear someone telling him to wait. Niema looked at Vitaly and then turned his face to look at each of the men protecting Allam, including the bearded man who was now holding an AKM assault rifle. He saw their determination and their readiness to die for her if necessary. Niema then looked at his men, Vitaly, and the two others, who made it in. Allam did as well before she looked at her men.

"We got it." Vitaly heard the voice over the radio.

"Boss, they got it." He informed Niema. The sounds of bullets and the gun battle continued moving closer to them. Niema looked at Allam and his stare gave her a sense of relief, for she knew this man was more than ready to overcome that which to anyone else, would have been a death sentence.

"Take him," Niema ordered Vitaly to say.

"Take him," Vitaly shouted, holding the radio close to his mouth. Each second that passed, the bullets, the crying, and the shouting, resounded faster and louder all around them.

Niema, Vitaly, as well as Allam and her men looked at each other, while a reassuring sound of silence suddenly fell over them. But the silence was quickly broken by the sound of men running fast towards their location. Allam's men brought their weapons up and guarded Allam closely. Allam silently looked over at Niema. Vitaly put the radio down and brought up his weapon, the others with him were already prepared. Niema put his weapon down and walked forward, away from their hideaway.

"Red Ireland!" Someone shouted out. The steps ceased, Vitaly recognized the voice and Niema did as well, as he continued walking.

"Sergei, you son of a bitch, what took you so fucking long!" Vitaly shouted out.

"The operators requested one extra minute, for security reasons, they said," Sergei explained while walking closer to Niema, after patting Vitaly over his shoulder.

Vitaly went ahead and met with the rest of the men who survived the attack. One by one, Vitaly counted them by saying their names. In the meantime, Allam and

Niema remained speaking in private.

"Thank you for your patience Madame," Niema told Allam. "And again, my apologies, for this inconvenience, and for the death of your men."

"I know you mean well, Mr. Niema," Allam said. "I can better understand now the reason behind your decision of terminating our endeavor. Rest assured, I have not been insulted in any way. I am thankful that you took this risk to conduct this deal under your own supervision. But, do I have to be worried now, would those after you come after me in retaliation for their failure to eliminate you tonight?"

"I do not believe they will, but I prepared instructions for your people to follow just in case such a scenario was to ever take place.

Allam remained in silence. She stared right into Niema's eyes momentarily. Niema did not blink once.

"As I said before Mr. Niema, I believe you are a man I can trust, please go ahead," Allam said.

"Thank you," Niema replied. "Now let me explain to you what you have in your hands. This particular merchandise is ten times more potent than anything you have seen before. This was my personal reserve, which I was intending to use one day in the distant future, to seal my full retirement. Those plans have suddenly changed. But as they say, one man's misfortune is another man's blessing. In this case, it is a lady's."

"Very well, let us hope my blessing and your misfortunes serve their purpose as dictated by the cosmos which brought us together, Mr. Niema," Allam commented.

"Let us hope." Niema countered. "Every three kilograms will be enough for you to develop six months' worth of supplies for your client's consumers." Niema continued. "Those tourists from the Netherlands, Amsterdam and the rest of your international clientele will not want to go back to their countries when they get hooked on this. You have about three hundred kilograms in your possession now and they will be enough to sustain a fifty-six-year operation if you proceed as I will indicate."

Niema took his time, and for thirty minutes he provided Allam with complete details about everything that needed to be done and how. He also provided her with a plan that was simple enough, which will keep her organization and herself away from the prying eyes of those after him. After everything was said and done, Allam departed from the area in a secure armored vehicle. A small convoy followed close behind.

Before they left, the rest of Allam's men picked up all of the weapons used in the short-lived battle, and she had given instructions for Niema to blow up the warehouse and the adjacent processing plant, along with all of the dead bodies inside. It would come out in the news as a sad and devastating accident in the factory.

Niema, along with Vitaly and Sergei were flown via helicopter to a nearby location, while the rest of his surviving men went elsewhere, following Niema's instructions according to the plan.

As the chopper landed, Niema could see more than one hundred armed men, dressed in dark brown military uniform and gear, with camouflaged faces guarding the area. As Niema exited the chopper, he was greeted by a man covered by a hooded veil, walking from amongst the others. Niema noticed that the man was walking with a limp on his left leg.

"Mr. Niema…" The hooded man said.

"You are..?" Niema asked. He could not see his face and could not make out his accent, nor recognize his very eloquent and mysterious sounding voice.

"You do not need to know my name, or any of us, for this matter." The hooded man replied. "You were privileged enough to be able to afford a service, granted only for kings, and you have received this service. Walk with me please."

Vitaly and Sergei stayed put, as Niema followed the hooded man fifty yards away. There were about twenty men surrounding something and they all opened the way as the hooded man walked and Niema followed. Niema looked as the man pointed ahead with his left hand while allowing him to step forward.

"Sao Li…" Niema said, staring down at the Korean man who was commanded with the assignment of killing him, as he sat on the dirt with a gag over his mouth and his hands and feet bound together. He looked at Niema without displaying any emotions or fears. He continued to stare at him motionless.

"I understand," Niema said. "You moved up in the ranks of the Imperial Lotus. This is why you were given the contract on my head. But this is the thing Sao Li… You have gotten to your position by taking out a bunch of street thugs. You were hungry before and were out there doing anything you had to. You did it the right way, I give you that. You achieved success. But this success caused you to become arrogant, and this arrogance caused you to make a major mistake in your judgment about me, Sao Li. I am not a street thug, the likes of which you are used to dealing with. I am a villain. I have idealisms as my mantra. Ideals are what separates the pros from the rookies." Sao Li stared up at Niema, only displaying what he was feeling at that moment through the fury in his eyes.

"You will live to try to come back and kill me another day, Sao Li," Niema spoke looking down on an enemy who was now too insulted to look back at him again.

"But not before the news of your failure gets to your boss's ears. Now they will know that I'm not just a pawn which they can just remove from the game at will. I never have been, and I never will be. If it serves as any consolation for you, or for them, I will not be in this game any longer, but I will be out there. If you want to try your luck again, you are welcome to do so. If they want to try another approach, let them know I'll be waiting. But know this! The more you or they come after me, the closer you will all be bringing yourselves to me, and to your certain demise."

Niema looked at the men around Sao Li and the hooded man as well. He turned around and was ready to walk away but stopped. After the second step he took away from Sao Li, he turned around slowly.

"What I said was not a warning or a threat. It was definitive." He said to Sao Li, just as the men surrounding him and the hooded man began to walk away, leaving Sao Li, and a couple of his men, right where they were and how they were, in the middle of nowhere. Niema was sure his message would be heard loud and clear. He also knew this was not the end of it, but to the others, he seemed to be more than ready to embrace what was coming. He was actually waiting for it, content with wherever his destiny would take him.

∞

The next day, back in South America, it was early in the afternoon. The sun was shining brightly, but dark clouds could be seen approaching from the east. A young teenage girl sat alone on a rock, at the edge of a river. A volcano's peak could be seen far in the distance. She was looking down into the waters with a melancholy expression. The clothes she was wearing looked old and dirty. She wore pants that stopped at her ankles, and a baggy light brown shirt which may not have belonged to her. She was submerged deeply in her thoughts while keeping her right hand extended forward. The edge where the waters touched the shore, reflected someone approaching. Before the person walking toward her was able to get any closer, she closed her eyes in a very gentle manner. As she opened them again in the same way, her sight reflected a place just behind the person approaching. It was a man dressed in old tattered trousers and a shirt, just like the young woman. His ashy brown hair was long and curly.

"Do not come any closer Iterdo." The man approaching, heard the young woman talking to him. Hearing her voice as if she was standing behind him, and yet, he could see that she was still sitting in the same place ahead of him, within his sight. This made him pause.

"Lytha, I just wanted to apologize for what happened. And for what I did not tell you." Iterdo said to the young woman, speaking in Ovi'ntia in a gentle voice while looking ahead to where she appeared to be. He paused for a slight second in order to term what he would say next. But before he had a chance to say another word,

Lytha had disappeared.

Iterdo was not surprised and stared at the waters of the river for a moment before turning around to walk back to where he had come from. He slowly turned his head looking east. A sense of calmness and at the same time, mild preoccupation reflected on his face.

"I am sorry Lytha..." He whispered into the wind, hoping that his words would reach her.

Some time had passed. Iterdo had walked for miles, taking deep breaths, touching the tree leaves with the very tips of his fingers and sometimes, pausing to listen to the sounds of the wilderness- the air, the birds, the sounds of the water, the wind and the trees that swayed from side to side in the breeze. He walked past a small waterfall. He also stared into the clouds of the sky as they change shapes and watched them go by.

After walking many miles, he reached the opening of a cave near the bottom of a sleeping volcano. He stopped short of entering, contemplating a moment of inner search. He turned his face to look back and attempted to connect with Lytha telepathically. He had to do this without Lytha becoming aware of him.

Lytha was walking by a park and became interested in watching a group of children that were playing with a soccer ball. In the midst of unawareness, she realized she had let her guard down when she sensed Iterdo turning his face in searching for her. "I've been careless." She said. She closed her eyes gently for a couple of seconds. A gentle blue glow calmly wrapped around her body, shielding her from anyone who attempted to find her location. Iterdo could not sense where Lytha was, no matter how hard he tried.

He then walked for miles deep into the cave. It was pitch dark; tunnels formed a labyrinth. When he finally reached the darkest part of it, there were two young women- Genaro and Emiri, as well as three young men- Ogdam, Bakr, and Elvah. They were seated deep in meditation, levitating two inches above the water in the cave. A circle made with silver-colored dust encircled each of them. He looked at the one empty space next to Genaro, where Lytha should have been.

"Ayis." Iterdo said. A calm wave of clear energy exerted from his body and expanded all throughout the cave, and all above those in it. The eyes of those meditating opened slowly and Iterdo was standing just three steps away from the empty spot. Genaro saw him and the empty spot next to her. She did not say anything but immediately thought about Lytha, noticing she was not where she was supposed to be.

At that particular moment, Lytha had arrived at a town far from where Iterdo had last seen her. She was curious about the scenery, the people and the different energies she felt and decided to remain there a while longer. She did not remember being allowed to have much contact with people who were not like her. She was hungry as well and this caused her to venture into a local grocery store/restaurant and look around. She soon realized she did not have any money to buy food with. Some of the patrons were busy buying groceries and others eating were sitting at small tables set out in a narrow space within the store. She stared hungrily at them. Some of the people stared back at her. She was about to walk out of the place, but the growling of her stomach made her stop.

"When was the last time I had a meal? So much training…" She wondered to herself.

After serving a plate of food for patrons on one of the tables, a chubby man named Norman walked by her. Lytha looked at him and thought about something but she felt conflicted and decided to walk out of the place. But a couple walked by her, after picking up a sandwich from the counter and it smelled deliciously tempting. Lytha looked at Norman again, and this time decided to approach him.

This is wrong. She thought to herself.

"Hi, how are you, I'm Lytha." She approached Norman in a very polite and pleasant manner and extended her hand to shake his. Norman extended his hand without hesitation, as she sweetly smiled up at him.

Moments later, Lytha was sitting on the ground, by the outskirts of the park, eating a plate full of food as if she had not eaten in months. When she had finished with her plate, she reached for a can of soda next to her, which she gulped down all at once.

"This is so bad. I will not do it again." She said to herself, after placing the empty plastic plate and the soda can into a paper bag and leaving it under a stool next to her. Sometime later, she had walked near a tree where she found herself again submerged in her thoughts. Her thoughts were momentarily interrupted by a loud belch. She soon closed her eyes again and just as she was beginning to locate what she was searching for within her thoughts, placing her head under her arms and on top of her knees, a ball rolled over to where she was. One of the children playing with it ran up to her.

"Are you crying? Are you sad?" He had noticed she had her head down.

"No, and I'm not sad either. Don't worry." Lytha replied to the nine-year-old boy, as she handed him the ball. She noticed he was barefoot, wearing a dirty blue tank top and a brown pair of shorts covered in mud.

"Okay then." The boy said, as he quickly ran back to play with his friends. He took a quick look back at her and Lytha again smiled at him. For the moment, she had forgotten about what was troubling her as she looked around at the people walking and going about their day. This allowed her to get a sense of different energies, during a brief moment of soul searching. She decided to embrace this with her eyes.

For seven days and seven nights, Lytha hung around that part of town. There were a few rainy nights during which time she took cover between alleyways, sheltering herself with whatever she found. Her nights were filled with vivid dreams. Some were recollections of past memories, mixed together with images that confused her. They kept her from sleeping soundly. They usually began the same way where a young person opened their eyes, but their vision was a little hazy, seeing only shapes and shadows. There would be others around. The voices and movements of people could be heard.

The eyes of the person would close once more but they remained hearing the voices inside the place. The echoing sound of the voice of a man was momentarily heard speaking of black horses and a dark carriage in a strange language that she was somehow able to understand.

Then there was the sound of a woman's voice. The young person's eyes opened once again. The vision was clearer now, a woman was down on one knee. A man with a shaven head, wearing a dark purple tunic, extended his left hand over the kneeling woman's forehead, as she bowed her head. There were others just arriving and kneeling down. Some others dressed in the purple tunics were walking side by side. One of the men extended a hand over the opened eyes, there was an engraving at the center of the hand, which resembled a cross with an oval shape on the top, the ancient symbol of the ankh. The eyes were once again closed but this time, silence took over.

Later in the vision, a man was standing at the edge of a rooftop looking out at the horizon. He was of slender build with long, dark and silky hair brushed back. A black turtleneck sweater and a fitted black jacket accentuated his well-toned physique.

"S'ykel, what is it that you want to talk to me about?" The voice of a young woman behind him got his attention. He recognized the voice and turned around to face her.

"Conceal your kium." S'ykel said while gazing at the shadowy silhouette of the young woman standing in the dark.

"Why would concealing my kium be necessary where we stand?" The young woman posed a curious question, which S'ykel did not hesitate to answer.

"Because of what I'm about to reveal to you, Lytha," S'ykel said. "About what *really* happened to your parents."

"What?!" There was anguish and uncertainty in the young woman's voice. S'ykel stared at her, fully aware of it. Embracing it.

Lytha awoke drenched in sweat. Even though the nights were cool, her lucid dreams continued to haunt her and caused her to wake in a frenzied state.

It has been a strange sort of new beginning for Lytha, a departure from what she had experienced so far in her young life. In a few days, she had become very good friends with the boys from the park. She was able to get food for them, something surprising for the street kids. They were very grateful. In return, they showed her places she could sleep safely. One of those places was the attic of a house still under construction. The boys had made the shed in the back of that house their temporary headquarters. Lytha was slowly bringing them into an aspect of the teachings she had received from those above her. Thanks to this, their minds took a sudden leap and advanced in their ability to understand knowledge. They were becoming more organized and less reckless.

Lytha also decided to give each of them a nickname based on their personalities. Big Foot was the younger one. He did not like wearing shoes. Paper Boy was the oldest in the group. He was eleven years old and always had napkins in his pockets to clean his face with. Gabi was a girl, two years younger than Paper Boy. She wore tom-boyish clothing and was very tough. She kept her hair in a ponytail, which Lytha thought made her look cute. Tin Tin, Keen, and Runner were the same age: nine years old. And although they were not, they looked like brothers. Tin Tin was slim and always walked with his shoulders shrugged, making him look like a robot. Keen had clear eyes and was very perceptive. Runner, who was the first one Lytha became acquittanced with, was the fastest and the strongest of them all.

She soon became their leader, and each morning the boys gathered together to wait for her at the back of the house. Lytha would meet them for breakfast, before making their way to the park and their other hanging out activities. Three meals a day and snacks were becoming a very welcoming routine for the boys, although Lytha knew she would not be around for much longer. She knew she needed to teach them self-sufficiency, by teaching them discipline, how to study, how to work together and how to defend themselves. She told them they were young and strong and if they worked together as a team, they could become a productive unit, which would benefit them all.

Lytha also made sure to keep her kium concealed most of the time. She avoided using any of her powers around them. This was important in order to keep any remnants of it away from the children. She wanted to keep them isolated and safe, away from anyone trying to find her.

One a particular day, not long after the boys crew had become more organized, they had attracted the attention of an older group of kids days earlier near Norman's restaurant. There were seven in total. They moved around from neighborhood to neighborhood, according to how hot they became with the community or the local policemen patrolling the streets.

Keen and Gabi had purchased groceries with money Lytha had given them. They were only a block away from their hangout spot at the back of the house, when they were spotted by the older kids. Keen saw their intentions and asked Gabi to run away. She did not want to but Keen screamed at her to leave. Gabi ran away but Keen could not run fast enough. He was captured by the older kids. They kicked and punched him and took the groceries and the remaining money he had in his pocket. They laughed and then taunted him as they walked away, leaving him beaten up on the ground.

But before they could make their getaway, Lytha, Paper Boy, Tin Tin, and Gabi stood in their way. The older kids did not remember who she was. Lytha attempted to talk to them. It was important not to use her powers. She told them she was willing to share the food with them, but they were not willing to return what they stole from Keen. Lytha pleaded with the older kids for a second time. Paper Boy, Gabi and Tin Tin wanted to fight them, even if they were at a disadvantage. But Lytha knew she would soon part ways from that area and she did not want to leave them behind with any problems lingering.

"You, what is your name?" Lytha asked the oldest boy. She saw he was the one holding the money they had stolen from Keen, in his hands. Lytha figured he was the leader. His attitude, his hat turned backward, the bicyclist gloves he had on his hands, his high-top sneakers; the others were not as well put together as he was.

"Why do you want to know?" The kid replied, ordering the others to continue walking away. Lytha looked at Keen, who was just standing up from the ground. She then looked at Tin Tin and Paper Boy behind her.

"I will not repeat myself again," Lytha said, directing her words to the older one of the boys. "What is your name?" She again asked him. The boy stopped walking and thought about it, before turning around to face Lytha. He took three steps forward with a mean look on his face. The other kids stayed put.

"I am not telling you." He finally answered Lytha. "What? You want to go and tell my father or something?" Lytha was listening to the sound in the boy's voice as he addressed her. "I wouldn't care if you did." He continued. "I don't care about him or anyone else. My family does not care about me either. Even if you get my name from someone, no one would come after me!"

"So that's it then." Lytha took stepped towards the older kids. They did not move an inch. Tin Tin and Paper Boy did not know what to do, and it took them a moment to decide to walk after Lytha. Lytha extended her right hand to the side signaling them to not walk after her. Keen stood up on his feet, to the left side of the older kids. He stared as Lytha walked right up to the leader of the older kids and stood right in front of him. He was slightly taller than her, and this made him feel powerful.

"So, you cry, when no one is watching. Don't you?" Lytha asked the leader. He stared at her in the same manner he had been staring at her, without saying anything. "No one knows," Lytha continued. "But you see, I do. I can tell when someone feels sorry for themselves. I can tell when someone is afraid. You are afraid." Lytha looked at the by right into his eyes. He stared into hers.

"And that fear you have inside, which you don't want anyone to know about, is making you very angry. Your emotions are all over the place and you don't know how to express what you are feeling. So, what do you do about those feelings? You boil up and you go and take it out on those who you see as weaker than you. And you do this only to make yourself feel better. But you can't do it alone. Because you will not be able to do it by yourself. So, what do you do? You come out with a group of kids, who think you actually are as mean as you have made them believe, and you find people to abuse.

"No. Actually, you find people to have your little crew there, to abuse others for you. So that you can feel good about yourself by making others feel bad. Listen, all of you..."

Lytha turned her attention towards the rest of the group while walking closer to the boy she was talking to. The other boys had been listening to what she was saying, and it made them think.

"Anibal is not a true leader," Lytha said to the other boys in his group. The leader took three steps back, unable to disguise the surprise in his face.

"How..?" He mumbled. "How do you know my name?" He asked Lytha, looking at her strangely. Lytha took several steps closer to him again and yanked the money away from his hand. Anibal was shocked by what she did, but he did not know how to react to Lytha's actions.

"Do something!" Lytha challenged Anibal, walking right up to him. "Go ahead, tough guy, you are tall and angry, and you can fight. Can't you?" Lytha was all over Anibal. Anibal looked back at the other kids with him, as if waiting for any one of them to come and stand by his side, but they seemed confused and taken back by the way Lytha took control of the situation.

"Oh wait..." Lytha said. "You actually can't fight, can you? You cannot fight for shit. When it comes time for you to do something, you actually can't do shit. You ask the rest of the gang to do it for you, and even if you get to participate in the action, you just do it because you feel safe while you are surrounded by them. You know what that makes you, Anibal? Do you know what that makes him?" Lytha directed her words towards the other boys with Anibal. "That makes him and all of you... That makes you weak. Weak-minded, weak of strength, weak of heart, weak of valor. When a situation develops, you don't have the mind, nor the strength, or the heart, or the guts, to handle it. Because all of you, all of you only feel safe if you can gang up against a weaker opponent to abuse them. There is strength in togetherness when that togetherness is put towards the right cause and to achieve a mutual benefit.

"But there is no strength in what you think you have. What you have is cowardice. Show me you don't!" Lytha looked into Anibal's eyes, challenging him. Tin Tin, Paper Boy, and Keen were all impressed with Lytha as they watched her take the older boy down with just her words. They could not stop staring at her, looking at her with respect, admiration and happy to be her friend.

Anibal was very embarrassed. He was angry at himself, at Lytha and at his own gang. Seeing them all paralyzed and not doing anything to come near him to take on Lytha and seeing Lytha disrespect him in front of his group, gave him no other choice but to go on the attack.

"Aaaaahh!" Anibal lunged towards Lytha with fury and with his fist closed. Lytha simply avoided him, not allowing him to touch her. Anibal was desperately throwing punches and kicks in Lytha's direction, missing each time, until he stumbled against his own feet and fell hard to the ground. He stayed on the ground silently. He was not moving but Lytha noticed his eyes were open. He was about to breakdown and cry, but Lytha bent down and hunkered over him to prevent the rest of the kids from seeing him.

"Don't Anibal, don't cry. Don't do it." Anibal looked at Lytha and Lytha could see the tears pouring down his eyes and his lips quivering. "This day..." Lytha said to Anibal. "This is a day in which you learned something very good about yourself. Today you learned that you can be, what you want to be, without having to hurt or put others down. You may not get this lesson in the full just yet, but I think that if you allow yourself to be at peace with yourself, you will find that the world is not as bad as some of us believe it is. Even when those who we think do not love us and make us feel unsafe. We can always find the love that will make us feel safe if you look for it in the right way and in the right places."

Anibal got on his feet with the help of Lytha. The boys crew and Anibal's crew gathered together so that Lytha could talk to all of them. They spoke for a long time and shared laughter. Unknown to Lytha and the kids, they had been under the eyes of a Gypsy scout from one of the villages, who had watched how the entire episode played out. Lytha's mind which was focused on the short-lived inconvenience with the teenagers, failed to warn her of something else: A very tall and mysterious looking man. He was pushing the Teacher in his wheelchair away from the corner across the street.

Chapter V:

Branded Encounter

A day later, two of the boys, Keen and Paper Boy found jobs helping a local store owner carry his goods to the local outdoor markets. It had been a very good day for Lytha. She had already gotten food for the others and while they went and studied from the various books she had brought them, she decided to go and venture to the other part of town. There, she found a small park, not as big as her temporary home base, but charming enough. She invited herself to sit on an appealing bench from where birds could be watched playfully chirping and jumping around. Lytha sat quietly and closed her eyes, allowing her energy to flow in calmness, setting herself into a meditative state. This allowed her to search for signs in the sky by reading the passing clouds.

A block away from where Lytha was, Ramon had just parked his pickup truck. After making sure the doors were locked and checking both ways and looking everywhere, he then walked across the street. While walking across, he saw someone who seemed very familiar to him.

"Herman! Herman Sokolov!" Ramon shouted out. He had met Herman two years ago. It was from his time working at the harbor on some of the big vessels in need of maintenance after long oceanic trips. He and Herman had become good friends after Herman helped him land a job working for a Russian company that he had worked for in the past. They needed someone who spoke Spanish, Ramon showed up and became the perfect candidate. Herman wasted no time in introducing him to the company.

Ramon's mother even cooked for them from time to time and Herman would bring her presents when he was in town during work trips. He used to visit her quite regularly before she passed away. Herman was just getting into a four-door dark blue Datsun with three other men and Claire when he heard someone calling his name. He acted as if it took him a few seconds to recognize Ramon, as he was in actuality, attempting to ignore him. But Ramon was persistent and ran up to him.

"How are you, what are you doing here?" Ramon asked as he walked closer to the car to greet Herman.

"Hey, how are you...?" Herman asked, just to be polite, and speaking with less of a Russian accent than Ramon remembered. Ramon also noticed that Herman did not have a clear memory about him.

"What is wrong with you man? Don't tell me you forgot my mom's cooking. It's me, Ramon! How've you been?" Ramon embraced Herman, as he got out of the car and the men sitting inside engaged in another conversation with Claire, but one of them looked at Ramon momentarily, in a curious sort of way.

"Yes, Ramon, of course, I remember you, man." Herman said. "Hey man, how have you been? You never went back to the shipyard after your mother passed. Sure, I know who you are, and I definitely remember your mom's cooking man. I'm sorry Ramon, I have been so consumed by work, especially these past few months, that my memory has begun to betray me at times. Sometimes I even forget who I am. Tell me, how is your life? Do you have a family of your own now? How are you?"

Herman acted as if he was very pleased to have remembered Ramon. Ramon was happy to see an old familiar face. It was the first one he had seen in quite a while and it brought back memories of happier times for him.

Ramon and Herman had a short but pleasant, and undisturbed conversation. But even though Ramon had asked Herman more than once if he was working in the country or if he was going to be around for a while, Herman evaded those questions and quickly changed the direction of the conversation every time.

Ramon became aware of one of the men inside the car staring at him, who gave him a strange feeling, but he decided not to make anything of it.

Herman gave Ramon a phone number where he could get in contact with him and told him to call him the next day if he could. Ramon was more than okay with the idea and told Herman that he would call him in three days after he came back from a job he needed to do out of town.

"Perfect," Herman said. Just at that moment, Ramon noticed that there was a drastic change in Herman's facial expressions. He turned to look towards his left to see what Herman saw.

There stood Lytha, staring at Herman in the most profound way.

Who is she? I have never seen her around here before. Ramon pondered. Herman looked at Lytha for a moment but then thought it would be best to ignore her.

Then, a silver SUV pulled up right next to the vehicle Herman and Ramon were standing by. Ramon recognized the man in the right rear passenger seat as the window went down. Herman noticed the person staring at him, before addressing Ramon.

"And how have you been Ramon?" The man in the SUV called out in a very cheerful tone of voice, "I haven't seen you around this neck of the woods in quite some time."

"Hello, Mr. Salvador." Ramon said, as he approached the window to shake the man's hand. "Yes, you are right, I haven't been around here in a while. After my mother died, I became disoriented and wanted to be by myself for some time."

"I had no idea your mother passed, I'm very sorry to hear that. Are you working? Are you doing anything now?" Salvador said.

Herman remained silent, discreetly looking at Lytha, as Ramon and Salvador carried their conversation. Salvador was one of the most feared crime lords of the entire region. Gabriel Angel Montero, the one most knew as *El Salvador* (The Savior.) Salvador had a keen eye for certain situations. Checking on Herman, the three men, and the woman in the car with foreign looks was nothing of concern for him, but intriguing, nonetheless.

"I'm doing some deliveries and some other things Mr. Salvador." Ramon replied.

"Do you remember the number Arnold gave you before?" Salvador asked him.

"Yes, Mr. Salvador, I still have the card with me." Ramon quickly answered.

At that moment, someone seated in the back seat of the SUV with Salvador handed him another card.

"Dispose of it. Take this new one." Salvador handed Ramon the card. "Call Arnold if you need anything. You are a good guy Ramon, keep in touch." Arnold was Salvador's right-hand man and all-around handler. He was in his thirties, tall and very slim, light-skinned with dirty blonde hair. He was always dressed in business suits and wore a pair of reading glasses with a serious look on his face like an accessory. In a way, he appeared as the very opposite of Salvador who was in his late forties, always tanned and dressed in black, with dark black hair. Salvador always wore a broad smile when meeting people, often to mask whatever he was really thinking. Even though Salvador was one of the richest men in the country, in his mind, he was just another businessman doing whatever he had to do to survive.

The driver of the SUV looked across the street and saw Lytha staring at them. She did not move nor look anywhere else. The driver did not consider her as anything but just another homeless teen who was curious.

"Yes, of course, Mr. Salvador, thank you!" Ramon was very humbled by Salvador's gesture. "Thank you very much for those kind words."

"You bet," Salvador replied. As his SUV drove away, Salvador rolled his window back up, while keeping an eye on Herman and those inside the car. Two other SUV's followed Salvador, as Herman watched them drive away.

"Well, I guess I will hear from you then. You take care of yourself, Ramon." Herman bid Ramon farewell with a firm handshake and a smile.

As he opened the door to get inside the car, Herman quickly turned to look at Lytha one more time. She was about to cross the street. With a very discreet movement of his face, he indicated to her not to approach him. Lytha remained motionless, standing right where she was. As the driver of the car drove away, she turned and looked at Ramon and saw that Ramon was staring at her, in nearly the same manner she had been staring at Herman.

Ramon looked at Lytha, trying to figure out if he had seen her before. Lytha appeared to have read the thoughts around his aura. What she saw was a flash vision of when Ramon had encountered the homeless man. This bit of information made her very curious about Ramon, for what she saw had a rare disturbance, which she could not yet describe. Ramon had left, already dismissing her as just another crazy person in this crazy town. But Lytha was not done with him.

Lytha decided to follow Ramon and see where he leads her. She followed him six blocks, towards the poorest area of that part of town. Ramon walked through a narrow passage, where puddles of sewer water stood still near the sidewalks as children played, completely unbothered by the sight or the smell.

Ramon arrived at a very clustered, eight-unit complex, where typically twenty families inhabited it at a time. He approached a second-floor apartment, where there was a rocking chair outside the door. He knocked on it and a seventeen-year-old man, named Pascal, answered.

"It's Ramon, Pascal. Is Barbara home?" Ramon asked.

Pascal opened the door and told Ramon that he could come inside. Pascal had a fine layer of dirt all over him. He was dressed in soccer shorts and a wool sweater and was walking about the apartment barefoot. Ramon walked inside the place and saw that it was very messy and disorganized, as always.

There were others seated around on the floor, on an old couch, and on some chairs, waiting to see Barbara as well. He heard Barbara screaming at someone in the room with her, about giving her more money for the winning lottery numbers she gave the person the night before. Ramon positioned himself on a corner near the kitchen. He saw a small rectangular gas stove on top of a counter. Pascal was making tea using the water he had been boiling in a tin cup and pouring it through a strainer, where he then added some instant creamer powder.

There were three clear glasses, with brown tea stains inside, turned upside down on top of a white plate, forming a neat triangle, and Ramon was served his tea in a coffee mug. He took four sips of the tea and gave the mug back to the young man. Pascal then splashed Ramon's tea inside another clear glass cup and held it upside down on top of a very low flame of the stove. He allowed it to warm up for a few seconds before picking it up to cover it with a brown cloth. The cup remained still for a short time before he placed it in line near the other cups. Ramon's cup was to be the last one Barbara would consult today.

Ramon looked up after a while, at the three people still ahead of him and began looking around. He saw an empty bucket, which he picked up from the floor and placed it upside down to sit on it.

Lytha was outside the apartment complex and her eyes darted around in different directions, as she appeared momentarily confused by something. She then walked inside the place. A few young men approached her asking if she knew where she was. They also asked if she needed anything to get high on, not realizing, Lytha had already touched all of them with the tips of her fingers when she had passed them by.

"Go back to what you were doing," Lytha told them, stopping for a moment but ignoring them as she walked towards Barbara's home. The young men who approached her were not surprised by her attitude. They went back to play a card game on the floor near the hallway of the staircase as if they had not even seen her. Lytha was almost at the floor of the apartment where Ramon was. She saw a woman in her fifties, walking down the stairs carrying a black bag in her hand. A sensation took over her skin as the woman walked away. She knew the woman had come out from a place where there was an unusual gathering of spiritual energy.

It was Ramon's turn to see Barbara, and everyone else had left. Pascal brought his cup in ahead of him and after going under a curtain, he walked back out. "You can go ahead." Pascal held the curtain up for Ramon to enter inside the very dark room.

"Who are you? Who opened the door for you?" Pascal asked Lytha, as he walked back towards the kitchen and saw her standing right where Ramon had been, while with the tips of her fingers touching the bucket Ramon had been sitting on earlier.

Inside the bedroom, Barbara asked Ramon to take a seat. He already knew where the chair usually was and so he pulled it over near him, without any trouble finding it in the dark.

Barbara was seated in front of a round table with three legs, a white tablecloth, three candles and several framed pictures of saints, angels and sacred divinities. She also had her favorite picture of The Virgin Mary inside a glass frame that hung on the left side of the wall right in front of her.

Barbara had a thick brown cigar in the right side of her mouth and a dark blue scarf covering her head, with a black cloth over her shoulders. She was a heavy-set woman but if one did not know her, she looked almost like a man at that moment.

"It is not the man. You are not a problem for him." Barbara whispered to Ramon. Her voice was strong and sounded almost masculine as she spoke before moving the cigar to the other side of her mouth.

"What is wrong with him… What is he after…?" Barbara whispered to herself, before addressing Ramon again. She looked into the cup he had drunk tea from. "But you have caught the attention of a woman, I see her not far from you. It was not in you that she saw what she wanted to see, but... She is feeling something through you that is going to keep her near you. I see an ominous shadow that will not let you be in peace if this woman stays near you, Ramon."

"What woman are you talking about? Annabel?" Ramon asked. "She is not with me anymore. She always said how handsome I was, but then she found herself a better man. So now she has everything I couldn't provide for her."

"No, not her." Barbara reacted and then paused. "She is right here, look at her," Barbara said to Ramon while bringing the cup up and closer to him and away from the candle that had been illuminating the clear glass.

"Hmm..?" Ramon noticed something unusual, Barbara began acting strangely, as if something was bothering her. He has never seen her like this before. She kept looking to the side of the wall behind him, but she also acted at moments, as if she thought someone was walking towards her or was behind her.

"Is, everything okay Old Lady?" Ramon asked affectionately.

"Yes, yes, everything is okay with me," Barbara replied with agitation. "You are the one who's worrying me now. Where have you been since the last time I saw you? Did you go anywhere foreign?"

Ramon was confused with the question and the way Barbara was asking him.

"What do you mean foreign, like away to another country?" He asked.

"I see things that were not supposed to be around you here." Barbara went on to say while looking inside the cup. Ramon leaned forward trying to see what Barbara was talking about. No matter how hard he squinted his eyes, he could not decipher what she was seeing.

"I don't understand…" Ramon finally admitted. "You don't …"

Suddenly, Barbara jumped up from her chair and ran over to the wall behind Ramon, screaming and swinging her hands in front of her eyes.

Ramon was startled and jumped out of his seat. "Barbara! Barbara! What's going on?" Ramon was trying to figure out what was happening with her. He was scared and did not really know what to do. He then attempted to hold Barbara by her shoulders to try to tell her that everything was okay, but she continued screaming and shook herself way from Ramon, trying to run away.

"Leave me alone! Leave me alone!" Barbara screamed out into the air around her.

"Barbara there is no one here, it's just me," Ramon said while walking after Barbara. At that very moment, something caused Ramon to fall backward very hard onto the floor as if he was pushed down by a sudden and powerful gust of wind.

"Shit!" Ramon screamed out. "What the hell was that? What happened?"

Barbara did not say anything as Ramon was getting back on his feet. He looked at her and again asked her what was wrong with her, but Barbara became mute. She was looking out right behind him and at that moment a big shadowy hand with dark pointy fingertips was about to reach over Ramon's shoulder. Barbara screamed out at the top of her lungs in terror, while scuffling backward on her feet.

Suddenly, Barbara and Ramon dropped to the ground in pain. It was as if something really heavy had fallen over their backs and the weight of it was not allowing them to even move a finger.

"Aaaaaaaaaah…!" They both screamed out in pain, but their voices could not produce the sounds.

Everything in the room became chaotic and blurry in their eyes. It appeared to them as if a tornado was spiraling out of control inside the small room, but there was no wind blowing and everything, except for what Barbara knocked around during the scuffle, was right in its place.

"Oh my God…" Ramon said, but his voice still could not be heard. Barbara stared in horror as a big, obscure and shadowy entity engulfed in a dark mist, with incandescent eyes, walked closer to Ramon. It reached out its hand for Ramon's head while staring towards the hallway that led to the living room.

"Who are you…?!" Lytha shouted at the mysterious shadow standing by Ramon's head. She continued exerting her kium which made the apparition visible to the others. Ramon could not see its feet but saw moisture where the shadowy figure was standing. Then, as the shadowy figure extended its left hand forward towards Lytha, an explosive energy broke a hole right by the wall where Barbara had her table. The only thing that was left on the wall was a dangling picture frame, tilting sideways and about to fall.

The hole gave way to the rear of the complex and Lytha could see as the shadowy figure blew out through it as smoke being blown away by a strong wind. Some of the neighbors were running scared after hearing the explosion and seeing the hole in the wall. Lytha was about to burst out of the room and run after the shadow but as she was just ready to go through the hole, she saw that Barbara was badly beaten by the strength of the exertion of her kium that she had unleashed inside the apartment. Ramon was also in pain and was moaning, asking for help.

"I cannot leave them here like this," Lytha said to herself while observing their condition. She then picked up Barbara from the floor almost as if she was weightless and placed her on the sofa in the living room. Pascal was hiding behind it and screamed out loud as he caught sight of Lytha and ran out the front door. Lytha quickly extended her right hand and closed her eyes and the young man fell backward as if someone had pushed him hard on his chest.

"Oh my God, what the hell is happening?" He shouted out while his body was being dragged back into Barbara's place. As he was inside, the door slammed shut and he saw Lytha, effortlessly carrying Ramon as if he was a small child. Lytha placed Ramon on the floor, while he was still moaning in pain. The young man stared at what she was doing, with his mouth open and his eyes capturing everything in disbelief.

"You...!" Lytha said. Pascal jumped from the floor and attempted to open the door to run away again but he could not do it.

"What do you want from me? You're a witch, a real one!" Pascal exclaimed. "I didn't do anything, and I just help Barbara. Deal with her if you want, I didn't do anything, I don't know anything!"

"Be quiet now," Lytha instructed him in a very calm demeanor. "You need to take her away from here." Lytha continued. "She will be fine; they both will be. Their bodies will hurt, and they will have a very strong headache, but it will go away after a day or two, depending on their own strength."

Lytha paused and looked at Barbara. "She will feel better sooner than he will. Give him lots of water, no food, only water. His body will require it for his blood to flow normally and bring oxygen normally to his brain again. Do not forget this."

Pascal looked baffled and did not know what Lytha meant with anything she was saying but he continued hearing her voice repeating everything she had said inside his head and the voice would not go away.

"She cannot come back to this place ever again if she wants to remain alive. Tell her that." Lytha then ran out the back room and exited through the hole without looking back, leaving chaos and confusion around those she left behind. Especially Pascal.

∞

In the meantime...

A few miles from the neighborhood where Ramon just had a life-altering experience, Susan had just finished reading a telegram her husband sent to her and the children. She had taken the time to go and pick it up from her local post office which was a few miles away from her house. Lora and David were very excited that their dad had sent a message. They were excited to find out when he was coming back to them.

Susan was worried after she finished reading the telegram. Lora noticed it on her mother's face but didn't say anything. She was still too young to understand why her mother might be worried, but she was able to sense it.

"Mommy, when is daddy coming back?" David asked.

"Very soon my dear... And he sends his love to both of you. He said he misses us terribly." Susan said. "Dad's bringing back lots of presents for you two, but he said he will not give them to you unless you both behave yourselves and eat all your meals and brush your teeth at night. Especially you David."

The children were thrilled. And after they made their way back home, they began happily hopping around the living room and playing together. Susan decided to hide the truth from them for now. Her husband, Marcus, was going to be delayed yet again due to some last-minute mechanical problem the cargo ship he worked on, developed at the beginning of the trip back home. At one point, they had been stranded in the middle of the ocean.

Susan did not want to disappoint the children yet again. She resorted to telling them a small lie, she knew that in this way, they would not be further saddened by the absence of their father. Susan told the children to gather and organize their things as she prepared their school uniforms for the next day. She would take them to Summer school, which was nearing the final days.

The next day, Susan dropped David and Lora to the school which was located a mile away from their home. The school was well gated, conformed by two small buildings, each with six classrooms. There was a very pleasant lady by the entrance welcoming the children and greeting the parents.

"Hello Susan, Lora, David." The lady greeted everyone with a smile.

"How are you, Ms. Eloisa?" Susan replied, walking into the school.

Laura walked ahead of David after saying goodbye to her mother. Miranda, a girl about Lora's age, was already on the line, waiting outside the door to get into the classroom on the ground floor. David saw Miranda and three other girls with her staring at Lora. He was very aware of the animosity Miranda had towards Lora, although he did not know why Miranda disliked his sister so much.

"Miranda's looking at you," David said to Lora, before walking away from her to make the line to walk into his classroom.

"I know," Lora said. She was not looking at the other little girl but felt her stare. There was not much to do in the classes, the teachers had allowed the children to play freely in the school playground for the rest of the day. Lora was by herself, eating the sandwich lunch her mother had prepared for her. Miranda walked by and knocked the sandwich out of her hands and began teasing her.

Not long after, Miranda and her friends ran into the classroom where the teachers were gathered. The girls were crying inconsolably. Miranda could hardly speak. Sophia, one of her friends, told the teachers that Lora scared them and had been menacing them in the playground.

Three of the teachers went out into the playground and searched for Lora, but they could not find her. Instead, they saw a group of the children hunkered down inside a room that was used as the cafeteria. The teachers asked what the cause of their misbehavior was. They shouted that they had not been misbehaving. That in fact, it had been Lora who attempted to attack them. The teachers were confused. One of them was questioning the motive.

"Lora? Lora?" Ms. Eloisa asked. "But how? That girl... She hardly even speaks. Why would she do that?" The other teachers agreed but at the same time, they needed to find Lora. And her brother David as well, for that matter.

One of the students pointed into the direction they believed Lora had run towards. At this point, the teachers had a sense of urgency for finding Lora and David. Miranda and her friends walked out of the classroom. David's teacher, Mr. Alejandro, asked her what was is it that Lora did to her.

"She spoke like the Cuco," Miranda said to the teacher, still visibly shaken.

"What do you mean by that?" Mr. Alejandro asked Miranda.

"She said that she will come and get her from under her bed." Miranda's friend Sophia responded.

"Yes, yes," Miranda added. "And she spoke like the Cuco. I heard her voice and the way she looked at me. My mother told me that girls like Lora are the daughters of witches. She told me that because she heard about weird things happening in Lora's house with her and her brother and her mother. People hear weird voices and crying in her house. And now, I know it's true! I heard her! She speaks like the Cuco! I don't want to be around her anymore, she's a witch. I want to go home!" Miranda started to sob.

At the same time, Ms. Eloisa along with three other teachers heard strange sounds in one of the restrooms behind the building where David's classroom was located. They saw David standing outside of the girl's restroom. He appeared sad and was looking down to the floor.

"David, where's Lora? What did she do to Miranda?" Ms. Eloisa asked. David looked at the restroom door, Ms. Eloisa walked in and found Lora sitting on the floor with her head down.

"Lora, what happened?" Ms. Eloisa asked. Lora looked at her and then looked behind her. Ms. Eloisa saw moisture on the floor next to Lora. "Are you ok? Do you need to use the toilet?" Ms. Eloisa asked while bending down to Lora's face level. Lora didn't speak, she shook her head no. Ms. Eloisa kept on asking what was wrong. Lora looked behind her again.

"There's nothing wrong." Ms. Eloisa heard someone say behind her. She turned around to see who was behind her, but there was no one there. She turned to look at Lora, but Lora had vanished.

"What?" Ms. Eloisa said. "Lora, where are you?" She stood up, looking for Lora inside the restroom.

"Just leave." Ms. Eloise heard a voice.

"Who are you? Where are you?" Ms. Eloisa asked. All of a sudden, someone had just grabbed her left hand from behind her. Her knees felt like jelly, like she would fall any second, not knowing what just happened. It was Lora.

"What is wrong with you?" Ms. Eloisa screamed at Lora. "You almost gave me a heart attack!" Lora just stared at her in silence, while taking slow steps towards her. Ms. Eloisa developed a sudden and strange sensation. She felt really uncomfortable where she was. She was suddenly in a rush, running out of that restroom. David saw her and so did the rest of the teachers who immediately asked her if something was wrong. But Ms. Eloisa just continued running without saying anything.

Hours later, Susan was confronted by Miranda's and the other children's parents.

They were gathered together with the teachers and the school's principal. Ms. Eloisa was not there. Susan was given the news about what had occurred, and she was told by the principle that it would be best if Lora did not come back to the school because this was the fifth time there has been mentioning, in situations out of the ordinary, where she had been involved, that had resulted in injury to other children.

Lora was seated in a chair next to Susan. David was seated on a bench outside of the principal's office. Susan held Lora's hand as they walked out. They both looked at David. David shook his head and embraced his little sister. The principal walked out of his office to bring a set of documents Susan had left behind on his desk. And as Susan and her children walked away, the other parents looked down at them in a way that made Susan feel ashamed.

Upon arriving home, Susan was quick to let Lora know how embarrassed and disappointed she felt about her behavior in school. Lora insisted in telling her that she had nothing to do with what happened to Miranda.

"Mommy, it was not me," Lora said. David decided to keep to himself and sat by the dinner table with his face over his bookbag.

"Lora, this happened before," Susan said.

"Mom, Miranda said you were a witch. Why would she say that about you?" Lora was seated on Susan's bed, while Susan paced the floor in front of her.

"I don't know," Susan said.

"She said people hear weird noises in this house at night," David added.

"Who said that to her?" Susan asked him.

"Mom, she said a neighbor told her mom and dad," Lora said.

"That was not enough for you to have to scare her," Susan replied. "What did you say to her? How did you scare her? They said you sounded like the Cuco."

"But I did not say anything to her. It was not me who scared her." Lora replied.

"Then who? Who was it that scared her?" Susan stood right in front of her, stared right into her face. David walked into the room and stared at his mother. Lora looked at David, then looked back at her mother. But neither she nor David said anything to answer their mother's question.

"We will talk about this when your father comes home," Susan said to both of her children. "In the meantime, no more candies or treats for either of you."

∞

Inside an opulent mansion at a secluded location, far from the town, two men sat around a small table surrounded by a perfectly manicured garden, with a view of an Olympic sized swimming pool nearby. Both men had placed their briefcases near their chairs and spoke together in French in hushed tones, as they waited for their host Mr. Salvador.

Salvador approached them, walking with calm steps. He was accompanied by three other men and two women bringing trays filled with fresh fruits, pastries, and coffee.

"My deepest apologies gentlemen." Salvador expressed to the two men waiting at the table, speaking to them in English. The men stood up and greeted Salvador, with strong handshakes, as he came close to them.

"Not to worry. We just arrived. And we are being treated very pleasantly by your house service, thank you."

Salvador was very pleased to hear that and ordered the service ladies to arrange the coffee and the food for his guests. Salvador sat across the two men as those that worked for him, waited for his orders from a decent distance.

"I am very happy to see you both again Mr. Gaston, Mr. Lamer," Salvador said to his guests and they quickly reciprocated their feelings as well. They shared a short story about the last time they all met in Cartagena, Colombia, not too long ago. They reminisced about a night of great fun at a high-end casino, which was appropriately located within close distance to a well-regarded pleasure house operated by an acquaintance of Salvador. They shared a few laughs and sipped coffee afterward.

"So, gentlemen, what is the reason behind your unannounced visit? Is this visit due to some discomfort from the side of your employer?" Salvador went straight to the point. The two men looked at each other and finally, Gaston, the older looking of the two, took the initiative and proceeded to explain what prompted the visit.

"Mr. Salvador." Gaston began. "Mr. Danton has a good deal of appreciation for you. The business model you constructed for him was magnificent. He believes you are a man with a good mind for business. He believes you are progressive and an idealist as well. That is why he took the initiative to introduce you to the people you wanted to get in contact with, regarding your future status in the old continent. This was to show you that he is always a man of his word, at all times and for all matters.

"But you see, he is somewhat concerned about the lack of progress with the last steps necessary to take over the location needed to initiate the project his benefactors wanted to work on. The politicians who recommended you to Mr.

Danton said only you can get this done for us. Relocating this amount of people without major conflicts of interests from our part and their part, was not a task your government wanted to undertake. These 'low-class citizens,' as your officials called them, will only adhere to listening to someone of your stature and power. As you understand, this will be a very big project. We are talking about a mini nuclear energy plant. Which will be a first of its kind and a pioneering development for this part of the world, Mr. Salvador.

"And the people I work for, they are people like you, people who set out to do something and it must get done when they want it done. The diplomatic, as well as social, ecological implications for the people of this part of the country, will be unheard of. Many will benefit in unimaginable ways. Mr. Danton also asked us to remind you of the great amount of capital in sight. He understands you are very aware that your contribution will be very well rewarded. Not monetarily of course. Mr. Danton knows money is no object for you. But socially; he knows this is what pleases your intellect."

"And I am very honored by the trust Mr. Danton has placed in me," Salvador replied in a very mild tone of voice and behavior. "I want you to tell him as of this point, it is only a matter of a very short time now for me to deliver what I promised to him. I believe within the next few weeks everything will be taken care of and by the beginning of the month, he will be able to start preparations for this project. I understand that some equipment and parts have already been delivered to nearby sites."

"Some small parts have indeed been delivered," Gaston replied. "But I have to be very honest with you, Mr. Salvador. The beginning of the month is an eternity away. The project is already in motion."

"Then it shall be done sooner. You have my word." Salvador replied simply. "I will immediately rearrange all of my intellectual resources and I will do my best to satisfy Mr. Danton's request sooner than expected. Leave it in my hands to pave the road, so that he could ensure the satisfaction of his benefactors, as it should be."

With the meeting concluded, Lamer and Gaston made their way out of Salvador's mansion escorted by a small entourage of his men. As soon as Salvador knew the two men were out of sight, he furiously began to delegate orders to those he had put in charge of relocating the population of the lower-class neighborhoods in question.

"Do whatever it takes! I don't want to hear any more excuses. I need this done now! Don't any of you make me look like a fool! I have a lot to lose! But, you have that much more to gain when we are done with this! This is what I pay you for." Salvador's men were very determined, and they wasted no time in leaving the mansion to go ahead and get their job done.

Hours later, Lamer and Gaston were on a private plane on their way to an island near Greece. Gaston had a satellite phone in his hand, which he had just taken out from his briefcase. Lamer's satellite phone was ringing and Gaston told him to answer quickly.

"Yes, Mr. Danton," Lamer answered in French.

"Is Salvador closer to getting it done?" Danton asked.

"I believe he will try, Mr. Danton," Gaston added himself in the conversation. "He said he will have it done. A man of his vast resources should have no problem moving a few people away from unwanted lands."

"I will consider this when I see the results. In the meantime, I will meet with you in two days." Danton ended the call. He was traveling on a private plane as well. The pilot was heard advising they were approaching the Bermuda triangle. Danton was reviewing logistical information on a rectangular computing device, as he was being briefed by a very well-dressed man and a woman seated across from him.

An assistant walked up to Danton and brought him a set of wireless headphones, which he placed over his ears. A green light could be seen by the top side of the headphones and Danton heard a short beeping sound.

"Clear sir…" Danton said.

"The geothermal graphics have not given us anything else." Danton heard a man speaking with an English accent.

"I understand RJ," Danton replied to the person, speaking in English.

"There are two possibilities to this," RJ said. "It could have been as Doctor Parker said before, a geographical tectonic situation, or simple movement of the oceanic rocks by the southern underground peninsula of the region."

"Indeed, I saw the graphics earlier this morning and I'm looking at them now again." Danton corroborated.

"Either way, we are not taking any chances with this situation," RJ informed Danton. "The last two times these types of seismic signals were gathered, we ended up at the losing end of the catastrophic outcome, and we were also left empty-handed. This may be the opportunity we have been waiting for, to get the son of a bitch or destroy him. Let's not move ahead with doubt, but with our eyes on the target."

"Yes sir," Danton responded to RJ. "We will not lose sight of the situation and as soon as we land, we will further inspect whatever else the satellite picked up and we will compare the information we gathered at the site, with the information you had sent. As we speak, our team is going back through the rest of the data which had been gathered since the query began, sir. I will personally assist in comparing it with anything else we have recorded from the past."

"Very well Danton," RJ said. "A Rapid Response Alpha team will be nearby in two days, to assist in any logistical operations if they are needed. I am praying we actually do. They will remain away from the coastline, due to the military operations being in effect in the region, but I'm sure we will be able to work something out and persuade the government to end these drills sooner than what they have anticipated. Our people at the Pentagon are already working on it.

"Do tell your personnel to remain in contact with Salvador and make sure he can clear the site for us to set up the rest of the equipment. If luck is not with us, and the worst-case scenario takes place once again, we will not be blamed for as many casualties this time around. This could be the opportunity we have been waiting for. Nevertheless, we still have to proceed with extreme caution."

"I know sir. I will make sure my people puts the pressure on Salvador. I have a feeling he can get it done, sir. His own personal ambitions and strategic self-exile are on the line. With all the money in the world this man has, he still needs connections in the right places to pull it off." Danton reassured RJ.

"Carry on then," RJ said before ending the call.

Chapter VI:

Searched Soul

Two days later, north of El Salvador, three old box trucks traveled through a treacherous road within the mountainous terrain. They slowly approached a military checkpoint near a secluded area predominantly used as a backdoor for smuggling by the regional drug cartels. The checkpoint was an improvised military strategy conceived by a new commander with vast experience combatting against drug smugglers and traffickers. The military men were heavily armed, and their appearance was unfriendly.

"¿Qué tenemos aquí? What do we have here?" Asked one of five soldiers walking near the last truck, while pointing his flashlight to the canvas tarp covered back. They carefully approached the vehicles, while three more soldiers approached from the back of the first truck and they methodically began their inspection. Other soldiers kept guard as they waited for further orders.

"We are members of an international humanitarian alliance." The driver of the first truck said. "And we are bringing medical assistance, supplies, and food to those in need, at the town ten miles from here."

The soldier looked at the driver straight to his face for a moment. He then began questioning him what type of medicine and what kind of food he was talking about.

"You are welcome to check the cargo." The driver replied. The soldier then ordered three more of his men to go and look at the back of the trucks.

"Wait!" The man in charge of the soldiers shouted out. He was a feared military leader disliked and hated by criminals all across the borders. He was seated inside one of the military jeeps, observing from a safe distance, while lighting up a cigar.

"Si, Comandante." The soldier speaking to the driver of the first truck quickly replied, acknowledging his superior. The Comandante then got off his jeep and took several steps towards where his men were. Cigar in mouth, rugged-looking beard and a mean stare, the Comandante ordered everyone to get out of the trucks so the trucks could be inspected.

But before he was even done giving his order, someone was standing right behind him casting a shadow next to his. The Comandante's reaction was one of sudden surprise and strangely enough, fear. The cigar in his mouth quickly lost its fire, suffocated by the same cold breeze that brought chills to his skin.

"Buena voluntad... The Merciful." The Comandante murmured, his voice was a bit shaky.

"You know who I am." The person was behind him, speaking with a low and steady tone of voice, as he addressed the Comandante with the moonlight behind him and their shadows remaining side by side. The rest of the soldiers calmly put their weapons down and their attitudes became at ease.

"Yes, Buena voluntad... Yes, I know." The Comandante then offered his men to escort the Merciful, and his convoy, but the offer was politely declined. The trucks again headed on the road, towards their destination undisturbed.

At that moment, the Comandante's memory brought him back to a day in his past, nearly twenty years ago when he was a younger man. A day in which he and six others with him, were on their way to rob a bank in Panama.

He was a clever thug back then, to whom other delinquents came for ideas and advice that came to him as a natural gift. At some point, he decided that he was not making as much money as those who he gave his criminalistic ideas to. He decided to go into the crime business for himself and quickly developed a loyal fan base among those who knew him. Many of the criminals he knew, committed petty crimes for which they paid a hefty price inside jails, instead of enjoying the fruits of their labor.

He was not one of those, his ideas were well thought out and carefully crafted. When he put them into motion, everyone around him did very well. This went on for about five years. There was someone in particular who always stayed close to him. He remembered this because the person earned his trust. He felt he remembered him from his school days, and every time he planned the next heist, his former schoolmate was there, adding to the details and asking the right questions that helped him out ultimately.

He gave the person the nickname 'Buena voluntad' (The Merciful,) because there had come a day in which they were about to make their getaway from the scene of a robbery when someone had walked in on them. Not until the very end when they thought the coast was clear, they removed their masks. A man who would normally not be there walked in on them. He had come to do a paint job and entered the place walking backwards while carrying his supplies and pushing the door in with his back. The Comandante quickly held up his ski mask to cover half his face and shouted at the man to get on the ground. The man was just about to turn his head when one of the members of the group pistol-whipped the back of his head, causing him to lose consciousness.

The others advised the Comandante to kill the painter since he might have seen their faces. The former schoolmate was the only one who advised him not to do it. It had been a good day, and no one needed to die unnecessarily. From that day forward, the Comandante began calling his old classmate Buena voluntad.

One day, the former schoolmate asked him if the Comandante had ever considered the thought of himself being at the receiving end of one of his crimes. It was a night when he and his crew had killed three men and a woman who lived in a luxurious mansion during a robbery job that went awry, and they needed to eliminate the witnesses.

He told the person, "My plans are so good and meticulously planned, I will never have to worry about me being at the other end of them."

But just like that, as if a prophecy was coming to a culmination, one of the men of his crew had gotten extremely drunk during a night of celebration. His feelings of jealousy got the best of him. This caused him to react brutally, following a joke a woman made about him. They had only been dating a short while. She had in fact, broken up with her longtime boyfriend in order to date him. He did not make it far when he was captured by the police. His angry tirade landed him in jail and in a very bad place with the police once one of the investigators discovered that he had just murdered his ex-girlfriend. The officer now had the opportunity to get rid of the man his girlfriend left him for. In a moment of desperation, the killer decided to offer up information on the Comandante and the rest of his crew.

He gave the police investigators information about a job they had planned to start in a few days. They will rob the mansion of a jewelry business owner, and if things were to get complicated, everyone at the house would be killed. As it turned out, the investigators had been after this highly publicized and infamous crew for a long time. In fact, they were itching to get their hands on them. And they had just been given carte blanche to put a stop to them by whatever means necessary.

On the night of the robbery, everything was going according to plan. As usual, the Comandante's plan was perfect to the last detail, or so he thought. Inside the house, a full squad of heavily armed officers was waiting, pointing their weapons ready to fire at the first sign of the crew. The man who had given the police all the information on the plan had crafted a proposal that landed him as the getaway driver for the night. Accordingly, he was told to leave the moment the criminals went into the house, leaving the robbers with no escape route and at the mercy of the police.

Just as everyone got out of the car, each of them moved as planned. The Comandante said, "Here, you will earn it tonight," as he handed one of his cigars to one of the members of his crew. Buena voluntad had previously hinted to him that the person would have been very happy receiving one of his cigars. Indeed, the person took the cigar and placed it inside his shirt pocket, as he left the car smiling. The Comandante always stayed last, he wanted to look at the scenario, get a feel for the air and the ambiance. Everything appeared to be perfect, the business owner had gone inside the house with his wife. His children were away at college. The plan went into motion, and as the Comandante was about to get out of the backseat of the car, he tapped the driver over the shoulder.

"Wait right where I told you to, not an inch further. Got it?" As he spoke to the driver, he noticed the driver did not look at him while answering, but he continued on his way anyway. He also noticed that the driver turned and looked at him when he was already out of the car, but he did not make much of it. As he saw the car drive away, he went ahead with his good luck ritual. He pulled out a cigar from his shirt pocket and looked at his shadow as he went on to light it. Then he extinguished the match, just as he normally would, to celebrate success ahead of time.

But this time, as he watched his shadow while extinguishing the match, there was another shadow that appeared next to his. It was Buena voluntad.

"You supposed to be going by the back. What are you doing here?" The Comandante asked, but he then noticed that the flame of his cigar went out as he also felt a cold chill.

"Remember when I asked you if you had ever considered being at the receiving end of one of your crimes?" Buena voluntad asked him. He did not answer. At that moment, chills ran down his spine while looking ahead towards the house.

"Remember when you said you had a gifted mind and saw things in the way others did not?" The person asked him again. "What is your gift telling you now? Do you feel it saying something to you, which others may have not seen or heard? Do you feel yourself being at the receiving end of your own greed? What would be your reaction if you were at this particular moment..."

His words had not ended when shots rang out. His entire crew was killed the moment they entered the house. The Comandante calmly walked away, shivering, looking to the ground at the shadow walking only one step behind his. His mind took him to the driver's face and he immediately knew he did them in.

However, the driver too had been killed. The officer whose ex-girlfriend the driver had murdered, killed him in retaliation. None of the crew members had survived. The investigators were very assertive when they spoke to the media afterward. They informed the public that none of the members of the infamous crew had survived. They announced that everyone had been killed in a shootout, including the leader, who was recognized because of the cigar that he was known to keep in his shirt pocket. "All seven of the dangerous crew members are gone." The investigator in charge of public relations for the police department commented. Everyone in the public, press and the police department were pleased to know that the case was finally closed and none of the notorious criminals had survived.

No one, but the Comandante; and this thanks only to Buena voluntad. From that day on, the Comandante decided to use his gift of being a criminal mastermind to keep others safe from being at the receiving end of something he never wanted to be brought upon him...

"Who was the person you spoke to, sir?" One of the soldiers asked the Comandante.

"Are they part of special forces, sir?" Another soldier asked.

"No." The Comandante said, while once again setting up the cigar in between his lips while quietly walking away from them.

The trucks finally made it to their destination twenty-five miles away from the checkpoint and in the opposite direction of where they had claimed they were heading. There were people anxiously waiting for them. An elderly man named Felipe was front and center, accompanied by four others. He was leading the large crowd of men, women, and children from different ethnic backgrounds, who were happily waiting for the arrival of their benefactor.

Seth was the driver of the third truck. "We have arrived." He said as the other trucks ahead of his were pulling into the main entrance of the secluded location.

"Come, everyone, let's help them!" Felipe said to the others. Quickly, every able man and woman gathered near the trucks and waited until those who arrived in them dismounted. The Merciful was already out and his wheelchair was brought close to Felipe. He was being pushed by a very large, pale-skinned man in a black coat.

"Teacher..." Felipe said while receiving the embrace of his benefactor. "We are immensely happy and honored to have you with us. Some have been worried because they had not seen you in a long time."

"I know Felipe. For that, I apologize." The Merciful responded. "But now that we are here, let us just rejoice in our duties and continue preparing the road ahead for the generations that I see, are soon to take over your place at the leadership..." The Merciful joked with Felipe, as he saw some of the young men, he once saw as small children, helping unload the trucks.

"Yes, as you can see, thanks to you," Felipe told the Merciful. "Thanks to you, we have saved many of them. They would have not made it if it was not for your protection, your help, and the guidance that you provided to all of us." Tears began to fall from Felipe's eyes as he again embraced the Merciful as if embracing his own father. Seth could see them from far while helping others.

"We would have been lost. I would have been lost, without you." Felipe added.

"No…" The Merciful said to himself, "It would have been me, the lost one; if it was not for the few of you…" He silently stared at Felipe and the others, while the rest of the people could be seen bringing very large wooden boxes, some big enough to fit a car and loading them onto carts being drawn by horses. These carts and other things were going towards the ingress of a hidden tunnel, miles away from the village.

∞

Raffa drove Salvador's SUV into the garage of another of his mansions. He signaled the other drivers of three additional vehicles behind him to go park.

"You're mine tonight Raffa!" A man shouted, walking on the rooftop of the mansion with an assault rifle hanging by a leather strap over his left shoulder.

"This is the third night in a row you say that!" Raffa shouted back. "When you can admit that you're still a rookie, then I'll teach you how to play dominos."

"Don't tell him that!" Someone else shouted, "Let's keep snatching his salary out of his hands. We don't need to teach him shit!"

Laughter ensued momentarily by more than a dozen men. Raffa told everyone to quiet down so the boss doesn't get disturbed by their noise.

Salvador heard some of the noise, but he did not care. Hearing the men's voices made him feel safe, silence worried him. As he walked inside his bedroom, he walked over to a nightstand and placed a black satchel he had been carrying, carefully over it. He was carrying something fragile and important inside it. He looked around, then turned the light off on that side of the room. It was a very large space with marble floors, tall walls, black floor to ceiling curtains and a bed that could sleep five people comfortably.

Salvador looked at the sheets, it looked like someone had been in his bed. One of the housemaids walked up to the door and knocked on it softly.

"The bath is ready Mr. Salvador." The maid informed him.

Salvador walked into the master bathroom, only steps away from the bed. A woman was waiting for him inside the bath. White marble and gold were the preferred décors for the luxurious bathroom. The woman was covered in foam up to her breasts. Her hair and makeup had been freshly done.

"I thought you weren't going to make it, again." The woman said. "Three nights in a row you kept me waiting for you. Why do you do this when you know how short my time is these days?"

"Mary, you did your bangs again," Salvador said approaching her and smiling.

"I only do it for you. It's so difficult to maintain." Mary said, pretending to sulk. Salvador looked over to the towel holder to his right. There was a two-way radio next to it on a stand. He needed to know the radio was there before he continued with what he was about to do.

"Come in here with me." Mary invited Salvador while extending her hand to him.

Salvador accepted the invitation and joined Mary inside the tub. Sometime later, Mary was sleeping in the bed when Salvador decided to take a walk around his property in his lounge robe.

"Are you planning to have children with anyone?" Mary whispered to Salvador, adjusting her body under the sheets. Her eyes were still closed, and Salvador was halfway out the door. He thought about the question for a moment.

"This world is cruel and uncertain." He said with his back towards Mary. "And it is about to get even worse. There are people in this world, whose sole purpose in life is to make it hell for everyone else, for the satisfaction of their selfish interests and egos. I would not want to have a son or daughter of mine to have to experience half of what I'd seen, nor what's to come." Salvador looked back; Mary's eyes were still closed. But she spoke again to him and Salvador walked back to the bed as she did.

"But you are so wealthy." Mary said, "What are you going to do with it all after you've died? You can't take it with you. You need to have children; it will give you a completely different purpose for the rest of your life. You will have someone to teach everything you've learned, someone to carry on your legacy, whatever you want for it to be."

"My dear Mary," Salvador interrupted Mary, "I have to be honest with you. No. I *want* to be honest with you. What you see in me, how your eyes look at me, this is the person I would like for you to embrace. This is the person I want you to be attracted to, for you to desire. But the reality of it all is very different. The truth is that for a long time, I stopped considering myself a human being. This is my truth: I am a monster. I would not want to teach anyone what I've seen, learned and everything I've had to do to survive this life.

"Some people are meant to have children, to teach them the roads, enjoy life watching them grow, to suffer emotional pain as they are growing up. You are one of those blessed, to enjoy that aspect of life. You have a husband, a nice house, three children and two dogs. Everything your mother told you to aim for. You are by far, the perfect example of what a successful life can be. I am not. I am what makes that achievement difficult to believe in."

"Everything is not as it appears from the outside. My husband does not love me. I am like a piece of furniture, or like a painting hanging on the wall. My husband is content knowing I'm more beautiful than the wives of his friends and business associates. That is all."

Salvador picked up his satchel and hung it over his shoulder as he left the room. Some of his men saw him walking outside. They asked him if he needed anything. Salvador told them to disregard him and act as if they didn't see him. He walked up to the shed near the garage where Raffa and some of the other men were playing dominos and drinking rum.

"Boss." Raffa was the first one to see Salvador walking into the shed. Salvador did not mind the men drinking and having fun during work hours, so long as they could hold their liquor. He allowed them to relax from time to time. The men were getting ready to put everything away and get back to walking around the property, guarding the house.

"Who's out there besides Felix and Javier?" Salvador asked Raffa.

Raffa gave the names of five additional men guarding the house at the moment. Salvador decided to join the dominos game and asked for a bottle of Dewar's.

"Tell Minerva to wake the woman in the bed and ask Sergio to drive her back to her house." He was seated in a chair facing the door, being someone who never gave his back to an entrance. It was Salvador's turn to play, the second game was in progress and Raffa was playing against Salvador. The dominos were set on the table in the shape of the letter "L." Salvador was staring into the outside. Raffa asked if he had seen anything. Salvador did not answer.

"Boss." Raffa tapped Salvador on the shoulder just as Sergio walked up to them.

"Boss, she said she's not going to be able to see you till the end of the month," Sergio said.

"Tell her she will see me sooner than that," Salvador replied. Sergio walked away, and the game continued, but not before Raffa asked Salvador if he needed anything.

"Don't worry about my blackouts Raffa," Salvador said. "Sometimes I like staring deep into the dark."

"Why do you do that boss, are you developing eye problems?" Raffa asked.

"Don't be a fool," Salvador replied, sparking a moment of laughter. "I want to see what I can see in it. And now, Domino!" Salvador had just won the game and the guy playing as his partner stood up and celebrated loudly. It was the same man Raffa had been taunting before.

"Who's snatching money from who's hands now?" The Rookie said, making fun of Raffa as Salvador lit up a cigar with a smile on his face.

∞

The next day, it was thirty minutes past noon. Cesar Orejuelas was traveling back to the city, accompanying Vice President Orlando M. Rivera Carillo in the back of his SUV, which was one of a convoy of three. Carillo was the choice of the newly elected President of Costa Rica, Archon Romalyn. Cesar was talking to Carillo about all the potential to be grasped from this achievement. The potential having been acquired, thanks in the most part by the funding of hundreds of thousands of dollars that was injected into Romalyn's campaign, from the drug money produced by Salvador. This was something which neither Carillo nor Romalyn wanted to have to pay for in the future. And neither man wanted, nor was interested in that information coming out and into the public's ears.

"The first thing you and Romalyn need to make a move on is cleaning out the coast," Orejuelas said to Carillo while sipping from a bottle of imported beer. "If we are to bring the country into the future with the international coalition that Romalyn will be bringing together, the first thing we need to show them is that we will not be allowing hoodlum drug dealers and murderers to be part of our business society."

"It is easier to say than to do, Cesar." Carillo retorted. "Drug money is everywhere in South America. We have been lucky enough to keep our hands away from it, by conducting the small deals we had the opportunity to take advantage of, with the help of third-party handlers. You know, as well as I, that cleaning out the coast, is not something we can accomplish from night to the next day."

"I know." Orejuelas replied, "But it is definitely something which has to get done. People like Salvador and Verdes, and the rest of the uneducated dirtbags sharing ownership of the beachfront hotels and casinos." Orejuelas took another sip of his beer. "These types of lowlife criminals will not help to attract the right dynamic we are planning for. We want to turn this part of the country into a fiscal paradise for those who we will allow to bring in their wealth and let us safe keep it for them. We want to build a second Monaco in this part of the world. And we don't want to spend decades trying to accomplish it.

"The only way the type of people we want bringing their clean cash to us, will do so, is if they feel their money will never be at risk of being taxed or mixed up with the currency of drug dealers and guerilla fighters. We need to make them feel safe. To do that, they need to see that we cleaned the coastline of all the dirt that's now covering it. The coastline is our face, we need to bring good tourism back to our country. Not the crowd of old farts looking for prostitution and cheap thrills – we need to get rid of that! We want families to come vacation here and buy up properties and invest."

"It will be done, Cesar!" Carillo said while sipping his beer and looking outside his window. "But before we get it done, we need to have the American signature in our hand. And by what Romalyn told me last night, they are coming to hand it to us. Once we are secure with their full backup, Salvador's head will be the first one to roll. I can see you smiling, even as you are visualizing, Cesar." Carillo looked at Orejuelas, who at that moment had a smile on his face.

"Oh, ho! ho! I will definitely want to be there for that." Orejuelas said, indeed with a broad smile on his face.

∞

Later that night, it was eleven past midnight. The sky was heavy with clouds, making it an especially dark night and a misty rain was slowly falling over the town. Ramon had just come home from work and he was very tired. His head was still hurting and as he opened the door of the new place he rented, he dropped his work bag on the floor. He threw himself on the clustered sheets and blankets, on top of a mattress he had arranged in the middle of the room, along the side of boxes and pots and pans, as well as other things.

Ramon could hear the soft sound of the footsteps and voices of the people who lived on the floor above his room, but he attempted to ignore the noise and closed his eyes before placing his right arm above his forehead. He hadn't noticed that Lytha was seated on the edge of one of the windows by the side of the door. Lytha stared at him in silence and allowed him to fall into a deep sleep, which happened faster than she anticipated.

She quietly jumped off the window and walked up to Ramon. She bent over very close to him. Ramon tilted his body and rested over his right arm. Lytha gently placed her left hand over his forehead and slowly separated her fingers. She then placed the index finger in the middle of Ramon's forehead, the middle finger and her thumb rested on the two sides of his temples. She stared at Ramon as if she was studying him and after calmly closing her eyes, the tips of her fingers pressed on Ramon's forehead and temples. His body jolted for a second, as if a sudden electric charge went through it, without waking him up.

Lytha's eyes opened and she brought her face even closer to his face and brought her lips close to his left ear.

"Can you hear me…?" Lytha whispered to Ramon, as he was still asleep. His eyelids fidgeted momentarily, but he did not wake up.

"Hmmm…" Ramon moved his body but remained in the same position.

"Can you hear my voice...?" Lytha again whispered.

"Yes..." Ramon answered peacefully, while still submerged in a deep sleep.

"Open your eyes..." Lytha said. Ramon's eyes slowly opened and when they did, he saw Lytha seated on the floor to his left, with her legs crossed in a meditation position, staring at him very calmly.

"It is you..." Ramon said recognizing Lytha. He was calm and collected, and he then assumed the same position as Lytha.

"What is it that you want from me?" Ramon asked her, speaking softly. He did not know but he was still sleeping in the same position he had been and Lytha still had her fingers over his forehead. She had created an illusion so that she could have a subconscious conversation with him without affecting his common mind.

"I need to know the reason why you have acquired a spiritual connection with the Ojin you saw the other day," Lytha told Ramon. "I know that was not the first time you had contact with it - at the Hekaba's home."

"Ojin? Hekaba...?" Ramon was confused by Lytha's words.

"Barbara," Lytha replied. "Her energy waves become magnetic around the energies surrounding the realms of mortal and spirits. She captures what she is able to and transmits it into words or signs. Where I'm from, people who can do this are known as Hekabas. You also know them as witchdoctors or mediums. The Ojin, you know it as a demon. People have given them different names in your world."

"Okay... I understand now..." Ramon said.

Lytha knew at that moment she had made the right choice by tapping into his subconscious and not his physical being. His subconscious adapted easier than his normal self to the information Lytha was giving him and this made it easier for her to properly communicate with him what she needed to, and in the way, she needed to.

"Tell me, when did you first make contact with the demon?" Lytha again asked.

"I am not sure, it must have been a few weeks ago..." Ramon began telling her. "I don't remember ever experiencing anything strange like that, before that time." Ramon then became silent and thought of something. "The only thing I can think of..."

"Go ahead, keep thinking... What is it?" Lytha urged him to dig inside his mind and search for the answer she knew he already had.

"I remember, I was doing some work at a doctor's office, dropping some stuff they needed, it was one of my usual routes. I remember seeing someone who I've never seen around there before. He looked like a homeless person and when I saw him, he was panhandling across the street from where I was."

"How did you see him?" Lytha asked.

"He was across the street, overdressed for the tropical heat. So, he just stood out from everyone else. He just looked weird, plain and simple." Ramon replied.

"No." Lytha quickly interrupted. "How were you able to see him, you, your mind…? Ojins are not usually seen by people unless they want to be seen. They do this to appear normal, to be able to interact as a regular person within the *quabis* of men."

"I don't understand. How do you know that homeless person was what you were talking about? And what is quabis?" Ramon said.

"It is here, the dome where man dwells and…" Lytha replied instantly. She was about to say something else but paused, and in a very composed demeanor, she decided to bring Ramon even further into what he needed to know. She closed her eyes and continued communicating to him other things he needed to learn. In order for Ramon to acquire a better understanding of the answers Lytha needed from him, she needed to push him even further into his subconscious mind.

"I have to be honest with you Ramon." Lytha said. Ramon's body jolted again, and his eyes fidgeted but he was still sleeping in the same position and Lytha was still in control of his mind, and temporarily, of his subconscious.

"You have come across something, for which your mind, nor your body have been prepared to handle." Lytha continued. "That homeless man you saw near where you work and the entity at Barbara's house, is a demon. They are one and the same. I wanted to make sure we have established this. But what is troubling, is not only that it has followed you, but also the reason why it is still lingering around this place. Those demons belong to a very dangerous sect of evil. Where I come from, they are known as *The Legions of the Lord*. They lurk in the darkest realm of the underworld. It is called *Soumdus*, a place festered with evil energies and things that are much worse. You may also know this place as *hell*.

"Sometimes, sects of the demons become unraveled and they fight amongst themselves. We don't know why, but it occurs more often than not. This causes some of those very demons to break out of their nest and dwell elsewhere, even seeking refuge in the world of man. These demons, we know them as *Obstreperous*, defectors, and they become renegades, inhabiting your world with power and influence over all of you, in the palm of their hands.

"When such events take precedent, the high order of the legions sends out *Somitlas*.

In your world, they would be known as Hunters, which we know to be part of something known as the *Methisthanian Order*. My elders had known them by a different name, which I am yet to learn. They are dangerous, powerful, merciless, and nothing that stands in their way remains alive once it crosses their path.

"If they are captured by the Somitlas, the defectors will suffer a horrific end and in order to save themselves from capture, they seek out the one thing that can help them escape the reach of their hunters, a *Concealer*."

"A concealer?" Ramon asked, wanting to know more.

"Some of us are born with certain abilities Ramon," Lytha continued to explain. "Which we must embrace and foster from an early mental age and nurture them to grow within our inner entity, which will help us learn and understand all that exists around us, and in terms, to learn and understand what we call *Meorafes*. These are the Arts of the universe. Only by understanding these arts, one can acquire spiritual strength, or Kium, to be able to fight against the Legions of the Lord. Within those abilities, some have a rare power to conceal the energies of others so that their energy cannot be traced by anyone, for instance, the Ojins. They can also conceal their own energy and many others if they have to. They can prevent their energy from being tracked by anyone, even the Ojin. This makes them invisible to the untrained human eye and the eyes of demons. They are called *Rojidoms*. But the Ojin cannot conceal from the Methisthanian Order, for they have something from which no Ojin can hide. In your world, for those who do not possess the ability to conceal, it's very normal that a trace of the energy belonging to others lingers around theirs.

"This is why certain people feel affected by the problems or emotional situations of others. That is why a person lingering around the negative trace of a bad friend begins showing signs and resemblances equal to that friend, after a while. This is part of the nature of the universe in which we all exist. It is called 'Ba', which is a different specification of what you call the vibration of the soul. The soul remains inside of you but its image, the reflection of it, can be perceived outside the body, as the reflection of an aura, and it can display both, positivity and negativity. Good or bad.

"Where I come from, we are trained to understand and master these arts and elements from a very young mental age, and when we reach the first pinnacle of our training, we are then allowed to be sent back into the world you know. We do in a dormant stage, many times without memory or recollections of our abilities, until the time in which we need them to arise. This is so that our minds are able to reconnect with the normality of your nature to make us understand who we were and to prevent us from allowing our egos to see you as inferior, for we too, are still human.

"The reason I am revealing all this to you is because you are in great danger. From the moment you came into contact with that demon, his energy has been lingering over yours. That is how he was able to find you again. That is how I was able to find you as well Ramon, but I did not find you to hurt you. And till this point, I don't know what the demon's intentions are towards you."

"What can I do now?" Ramon asked fearfully. "I have no idea how to deal with anything of what you just explained to me. I don't know how to fight, and I certainly will not be able to fight against a demon. You are just a young girl and look at what you did to me and Barbara, who is actually an experienced witch."

"It's not that simple…" Lytha responded. "There is something else against you Ramon. When I traced your energy, I was also able to perceive the energy of a Concealer, which I believe is the reason the demon is dwelling around this city. He is absorbing the kium of that concealer to protect himself against those hunting him. I do not believe the demon knows exactly what he's doing. I was able to perceive the Concealer's kium through the exertion of his energy. He may be unknowingly leaving a trail."

"Kium…?" Ramon asked.

"Kium is the very strength of the entity you are. It is the spiritual strength that every living being possesses. A power that surrounds you and your aura and it can only be controlled by learning the path of *Meorafes*. I cannot get into the details of all at this very moment, but we have to find a way of getting you as far away from here as possible. If the Somitlas can trace even the feeblest of traces of the Concealer's aura together with the defector's, you will never make it. Once they lock on your presence, you will never escape them. Never…"

Lytha then projected images from her own memory into Ramon's mind. He saw horrific visions of dismembered bodies of young and old people, death and destruction – the victims of the Somitlas. Ramon was filled with terror. His body and mind wanted to break away from the connection with Lytha. But his subconscious also wanted to know if he had any chance of survival, and how.

"Following what I sensed from that defector, the reckless manner in which he unleashed his *wretched asba*, a demon's kium, at the Hekaba's house, the way in which he followed you, I feel there is only a matter of a very short time before the Somitlas find him or finds you." Lytha stared at Ramon, his body jolted one more time. Lytha closed her eyes and decided that it was time to wake him.

"What can you do to help me? I don't think I will be able to protect myself against what you just told me. Are you some kind of a superhero?" Ramon said to Lytha.

"There are no superheroes. There are only those who are versed in the Meorofes and those who are still asleep. You and I are the same. Wake up now Ramon…" Lytha whispered in Ramon's ears. He then woke up in a very peaceful manner and as he moved his body around, he saw Lytha standing right by his side.

"Oh my God…" Ramon said. "It was not a dream…" He couldn't stop staring at Lytha, curious, surprised and scared. "Oh my God, what a headache!"

Lytha told him that it would go away in a few hours and that was the reason why she spoke to him subconsciously so that her kium wouldn't affect him again in the way it did before.

"I will have to go for some help Ramon, but you have to stay moving. Don't sleep in the same place twice. I will find you when I come back." Lytha then opened the window and closed her eyes for an instant, while facing outside.

"You are safe tonight, but don't stay here tomorrow. My kium will linger here for some time." Lytha warned Ramon, just before jumping out through the window. Ramon got on his feet and ran towards the window. It was still drizzling outside.

"Ramon," Lytha said. Her voice filled the entire room where he stood. Ramon jumped backward in fear, he heard her voice, but she was no longer there.

"Oh my God, please don't do this." He said.

"Did something happen to you before you first saw the demon, Ramon?" Lytha's voice asked him.

"What do you mean?" He asked.

"Do you remember…?" Lytha was about to ask him again.

"I fell and hit the back of my head," Ramon commented. "There were bright lights and different colored strings floating all over the air. I was feeling dizzy and strange. That was what I remember happening to me before I saw the homeless guy."

"I see now." Lytha analyzed. "The impact to the back of the head must have set off the conscious self-aware mechanism over your cerebellum and your aura acquired a sense of instant subconscious awareness, thus, exerting a reflection of your… Kium." Lytha reflected in her mind. "And you were able to use your sense of sight!"
She did not say anything else to Ramon

"I am sorry. I thought you were part of this problem I'm involved in. I apologize to you." Ramon realized that the young girl was actually trying to help him. His words were mumbled but he hoped for them to reach Lytha's ears.

"I am part of your answer. Don't worry, I will help you." Lytha said, but Ramon did not hear those words. He remained where he was, standing still and afraid, waiting for any other word from Lytha. A few minutes went by.

"Hello?" Ramon asked hesitantly. "Are you there still...?" He realized that he was alone now and slowly walked closer to the window to close it shut.

"Shit... What the hell am I going to do now?" Ramon could not believe the mess he had gotten himself in, but at the same time, he did know it was real.

∞

Lytha decided it was time she sought the help of Iterdo. She had not completed her training when she decided to run away. She had wondered if all the training was just an excuse to keep her there and away from others like her new friends, who did not have any special abilities. But things have changed very quickly, and she realized she needed her elder.

She transported herself back to where she had seen Iterdo last, by the big rock next to the river. She vanished from the rock and an hour later, she emerged out of the river, her clothes and hair still dry. Things did not look the same, however. It was raining but the rain did not seem to touch her at all. She stood by a riverbed, surrounded by dense jungle. Everything looked different than when she was last there. She could not tell which direction the cave was, where Iterdo and the others spent days at a time in meditation. She stood still and held out her left hand. She sensed nothing.

She looked around and decided to try harder. She held out her left hand out again, with her right hand down and began creating symbols and signs with the fingers of her left hand. She clasped her hands together and brought them up to her forehead. Still nothing. She began to get worried.

Have they moved on? She wondered to herself. She went back to bring her left hand forward and her right hand down and back. She began creating more signs and even bigger symbols in the air. Her arms and hands moved furiously while pulsating waves of light began to come together and create nearly imperceptible symbols all around her. She clapped her hands together twice and held the palms together in a prayer position. She tried to hold the symbols together in the air for as long as possible, but they quickly dissipated.

He set up a blinding shield. That's why I cannot find any trace of them. Lytha thought about Herman, Barbara, Pascal and her encounter with the demon and the imminent threat of Methisthanians. It was a situation that required the help of several elders and she could not even find her one elder, Iterdo. She realized she would be alone in this battle. She had not completed her training and she lacked the experience needed for something of this gravity.

Fine. I will deal with this on my own. I will have to fight in my own way. Instead of feeling defeated, Lytha walked away with new determination. She walked over to the river and walked out into the water. When she was ready, she held her hands together again in a prayer position and let herself sink into it.

Chapter VII:

Bait of a Foreign Tale

A day later, it was still early in the morning. Helena and Clarence met at Helena's aunt's house. She asked him if he wanted to come and have breakfast with her and meet her only remaining family member, as they arrived at the small modest house in a lower working-class neighborhood.

Helena's aunt was out of town and had left a note with instructions for Helena wrapped around the door handle. Helena saw the note and immediately knew where her aunt had placed the spare key. She casually picked it up from underneath a box to the left side of the door. Clarence carefully looked around at the adjacent houses as she did.

"Don't worry, most of the neighborhood is already at work at this time." She said, calming his preoccupation.

Her aunt asked her if she could clean up the house for her while she was away. Helena wanted to do it on her own, but Clarence insisted upon helping her. It was a spur of the moment activity they enjoyed doing while getting to know one another better.

"So, how close are you to finishing with what you came to do in this country?" Helena asked Clarence while mopping the floor behind him. He was carrying a bucket with dirty water out towards the backyard. The house was small, with a wire fence around the property. Long pieces of wood covered the back area, barbwire covered the top. Clarence could see neighbor's backyard from where he stood. He could see chickens and two goats walking around. An old brown dog slept near a shed. He was about to walk back towards the house but turned around to look into the neighbor's backyard one more time. He thought he saw someone.

Strange... He thought before answering Helena's question.

"What happened?" Helena asked.

"Nothing," He replied. "I thought I saw a boy looking at me from the house next door."

"No…" Helena said. "The people in that house don't have children. They are old and go into town early in the morning. They have a stand that they attend over there. Maybe you just saw their dog. Now, tell me the answer to what I asked you before."

"Jeff is the one handling that," Clarence replied, as he walked back into the house with a broom in his hand. "Once he puts his thing together with the interviews we have to do, then…"

Helena stared at him. He stared at her. He placed the broom in a corner and walked up to her and embraced her. He held her waist as he kissed her deeply. She took half a step back and looked up into his eyes.

"Do you like it here?" Helena asked him. "I mean, what do you think about the life here? Like the places you have seen?"

"The few you have decided to share with me?" Clarence asked her. "Or in general?" He walked back to take hold of the broom again.

"In general," Helena said half-smiling, walking closer to him while still staring at his face. She took the broom away from his hands and handed him the mop.

"It is a different experience," Clarence replied, calmly setting the mop on a corner near the back door, before walking back outside to pick up the bucket he had left near a set of short steps. "It is not that different from everywhere else in other countries. I guess the growth and the different people moving into these parts."

"Do you see yourself living in a place like this?" Helena asked him while arranging a houseplant to place it near the sunlight.

"You mean, in the long run?" Clarence asked.

"What do you mean with that, 'the long run?'" Helena asked.

"It means like, for a long time," Clarence said to her. "I haven't decided that far ahead about the country. I feel that a decision like that is more based, not in the place itself but more on, what it is that the country has, that keeps you there. Do you see yourself living here for the rest of your life?"

"No." Helena's answer was quicker than what he expected. He was moving an old rocking chair out of the way for Helena to clean the floor underneath it. Her assertive answer caught him by surprise.

"I can understand that," Clarence said. "Where would you go if you decide to go somewhere else?" He paused, this time waiting for Helena's answer.

"My life is here. It has always been." Helena said. "I grew up here, and in the way that I am seeing things now, I believe life, in general, will start to get much better than what it used to be, for all of us. Where would you like to take me, if you could?"

Helena's answer and question to his question, was not one Clarence was expecting to hear just yet. But at the same time, the idea had floated around his mind. Helena stared at him as if not only waiting for words, in the form of his words. Clarence remained where he was standing, three steps away from where she was, without revealing his thoughts. He stared at her in the same way she was staring at him, but Clarence's eyes were less revealing than hers.

"If I can only get inside your head and know what you are really thinking," Helena said to him.

Later that evening, the sun began to sink behind the mountains. It has been a nice day that Helena and Clarence took full advantage of. It was a time in which they shared more of their thoughts and ideas together, which led them to realize how much more they had in common than what they knew.

The room was dark and only the fading flame of a nearly melted candle offered a dimmed illumination. Helena's skin was moist and the sweat drops trickling down the back of her neck sparkled while Clarence kissed her back all the way down to her thighs. The electricity suddenly came back, lighting up all of the light fixtures in the room. Clarence was quick to turn off lamps next to the bed, which was not supposed to be on. He and Helena laughed as Clarence jumped back on the bed and Helena quickly put her never ending energy to work once again. They made love for the third time and Clarence was curious to find out if he could keep up with Helena's desires.

"It will be very difficult not to fall in love with you," Clarence said to Helena while gazing into her eyes. She was sitting on his lap as she kissed him. Helena told him that she loved him as well and before Clarence was able to say anything else, she gently placed the index finger of her right hand over his lips. Clarence kept silent as she began kissing him in a smooth sensual manner.

Bang! Bang! Bang!

Someone was knocking on the door hard. Helena jumped up nervously. She quickly grabbed the sheets and ran towards the bathroom. Clarence was somewhat annoyed but walked towards the door.

"Don't! Don't! Don't…!" Helena was telling him, hushing her words from the bathroom door.

"Who is it?" Clarence stood to the side of the door as he asked. Helena did not want him to go towards the door and motioned with her right hand for him to come back.

"It's me. Open the door." Clarence realized it was Jeff calling him. Clarence opened the door to a little crack to talk to him.

"Have you forgotten about the meeting we had with the contact?" Jeff asked. Clarence did not want to go, and he attempted to make excuses not to go along with Jeff.

"You know, I'm not feeling well. I'm having major stomach issues today. You know man, I'm still not acclimated to the street foods of this country. And I haven't even prepared the camera. Do you want to leave it for a little later, maybe?" Clarence was feeling guilty about ignoring his friend several times before and eventually, Jeff convinced him to go with him.

"I'm going to be in my room, it's at the end of the hallway." Jeff wanted to give him some privacy. He assumed his friend was fooling around with some local girls, so he arranged for the extra room so that Clarence could have his own space. Clarence went into the bathroom to let Helena know that he really had to go with his friend this time.

"I need to leave also," Helena replied. As she got dressed, Clarence stared at her in silence. He had something on his mind, and he could not hold in any longer. He walked closer to Helena and asked her to tell him what was is that she was keeping from him. He did not doubt her feelings for him but knew there was an underlying situation that she was keeping him in the dark about. He wanted to know what she was involved with. Helena turned around to face him. She embraced him tightly.

"I understand how you feel," Helena said. "But you have to understand me, we have just met. I need you to be patient and wait a little bit longer. I want to be able to trust you. This is why I confided in you that I've been hurt before. I don't want you to be one more person who I offer my whole self and my mind to, for you to end up betraying me."

She explained to Clarence that her heart had been broken several times when she gave herself completely to the men of her past and she did not want to experience the pain she experienced ever again by being left behind and forgotten. She cried and fell into his arms. Clarence held her tightly and promised her that he would never leave her behind.

"You did honor that promise, didn't you?" Burton said to Clarence, sitting next to the bed. Clarence had reached for the cup of water and held it over his chest, as he stared at Burton in silence.

"I did..." Clarence said, as his mind remembered more details from that night.

Helena looked into his eyes. "If I open my heart to you," Helena said, "when that moment comes knocking on your door, you have to promise me that you will never leave me behind and be forgotten."

Clarence promised on his own life that he would take her with him wherever he went if she decided to give him her true love. After all, that was what he had been wanting all along.

"I don't believe I have ever felt for anyone like I do for you." He told her while staring into her eyes. At that moment, while looking into Clarence's eyes, she could truly see the love he had for her and she succumbed into that love and allowed him to embrace her in his arms. She embraced him with all of her passion in return.

"Please..." Helena murmured. "Please don't ever leave me...I love you..."

That sealed the deal for Clarence. He had asked her several times before to reveal to him what her business affairs were with those men usually waiting for her at the shipyard. She had always gone around the question, not giving a straight answer. This made him uncomfortable at times but after hearing her words and how deeply he felt she loved him, he knew he did not need to know anything else about her past and he would be everything she needed in her future.

Clarence ignored the timeline proposed by Jeff and stayed with Helena for much longer. They sat on the floor embracing each other and talked for a very long time. She told him about her family, about the way she was raised and the way she grew up, and even the experience of her first kiss. Clarence asked everything he wanted to know about her and in return, she allowed him to take a glimpse into her genuine self.

∞

At the same time, Washington DC NW, President Smith was taking his nightly stroll along the narrow trail of the well-manicured garden, his wife Madeline had created at the back of the east wing of the White House. His secret service detail was, as usual, comprised of the men he referred to as his "squad." A group of six former navy seals, all around 5'11"- 6 feet tall. Two African Americans, Michael McDaniel, with a clean-shaven head and face, was in his early thirties. Dennis James was in his mid-thirties and wore his curly hair short, with well-trimmed edges and a trimmed mustache.

Fernando Ojeda was a Hispanic man in his late thirties, who styled his short hair combed forward, and the rest of the three other men were West Virginian natives, like the President. Philip Roseland was in his mid-thirties with fair skin and a shaved head. Ash Murray was in late twenties, fair skinned with some receding hair on the crown of his head and was clean shaven. Scotty Foxworth, early thirties, wore his short dark hair combed back.

They had all been under the President's command since they were Marines. The President himself, capitulated their fast transition from the military and into the secret service establishment when he was the Senate majority leader. He wanted them to be ready to serve him when the time came. And ever since he became the leader of the country, President Smith has had them around him. He knew there were no secrets that he could speak about in front of these men, that they were not willing to take to the grave with them.

"Ash, remind me to tell Madeline to widen this pathway." The President said to Murray, while measuring his steps, as he walked near the final trail of the well-crafted and carefully arranged colorful flower garden, the pride of the First Lady.

"Yes Mr. President, I believe you are supposed to mention it to her over breakfast." Murray was the one secret service agent always the closest to the President. He had proven himself to be one of the most loyal men, to him and to his agenda. And President Smith had mentioned to him on several occasions, that he had plans for his future.

"Mr. President." James walked closer to the President, with his left hand over his left ear, as he was receiving information through his earpiece. He was usually to the right side of the President's rear, teaming up with Foxworth to the left and Roseland at the center. Ojeda and Murray walked the front, with Murry to the right and Ojeda to the left side of the President.

"Yes, Dennis?" The President asked.

"He is here," James replied.

"Where is he? Have him come meet me here." President Smith instructed.

"No need to James, I'm already here."

The secret service men pulled out their weapons instantly, upon hearing the voice only steps ahead of the President, who had been walking only three steps ahead of Murray.

"Avraham?" Murray was quick to put himself in front of the President, with Ojeda right ahead of him. Both men pointed their weapons forward, in the same direction.

"It is me, Ash." Avraham walked out of the shadows while lighting up a cigarette. His silver lighter illuminated half of his face as he brought the flame close to the cigarette. The lights of vehicles driving back and forth could be seen in his background from the distance.

"One of these days, you're going to get yourself shot," Ojeda said.

"Well, at least it would have been for a good cause," Avraham replied, displaying a smile on his face while releasing smoke away from his lips.

"Tell me," President Smith began, "have you learned anything new about his disappearance?"

Avraham looked at the rest of the security detail and waved hello to them. They were all well-acquainted with him, regarding him as a very necessary ally of the President.
 "I second what Fernando said," Foxworth shouted at him. "You're putting yourself at risk, Mr. Avraham. It's time for a different entrance style. One of these days, one of us will have a trigger-happy day and you above everyone else knows how it feels to have one of those days." Foxworth took a couple of steps away from his position in order to give the President the space he desired when conversing with Avraham. The others did the same.

"Let him be, Scott." The President said.

Avraham continued smiling, while keeping his cigarette in between his lips. "I will only allow myself to see one of you in action if the opportunity was the right one, Scotty." Avraham spoke after taking the cigarette away from his lips with his left hand. He looked at it, dropped it to the ground only to step on it with his left foot.

"Do you have anything new?" President Smith asked him again, walking closer to him as he did.

"He sent a letter to his daughter," Avraham said, he stared at the headlights driving away from Pennsylvania Avenue, circling the edges of the White House.

"Did he write anything that could give us a clue?" The President then asked him.

"The letter was written one month before his disappearance." Avraham continued, this time turning his face toward the President, who looked at him very concerned.

"This gives us a brief insight into the potential of his desire to do what he was about to do, against his own will." President Smith did not clearly understand what Avraham was conveying to him.

"Did he say anything in the letter, specifying his plans?" The President asked.

"He did and he did not," Avraham replied, with the President still staring at him.

"During the same time before the letter was sent," Avraham continued, "several events took place within his close circle of associates. You were not part of these events, Mr. President. This was one of the reasons you were disregarded from our list of inquiries. However, someone close to you was."

"Who?!" President Smith asked bewildered.

"As of this moment, I cannot tell you." Avraham instantly replied. "You, as well as your men, have a clear understanding of what we are working against. This is the only reason you have all taken the precaution we have all taken, in order to keep ourselves in the clear. It is a must, for all of us to exercise the same pre-established procedures the Initiative had built, to handle this matter. This is the only reason we are only talking about this, at this moment. Because of what has been selected for our knowledge, has been strategically filtered to prevent the worst-case scenario, from jeopardizing our success. Selected and misplaced awareness and information are at this point in time, our best safeguards against the Prophet. We all must get more awareness about what we have been allowed to learn, according to timing. This is the only way to ensure our ability to protect ourselves against any one of us becoming compromised.

"That being said, we are, at this very moment, following what could be a potential development to the south of the Middle East." Avraham looked the President and then at his men.

"You are talking about Iraq, correct?" The President asked.

"Not sure yet," Avraham responded.

"How?" The President asked. "How are you not sure yet? How can we become aware if any situation developing, has anything to do with this psychopath? We have been after him for quite some time now. And no one that we know, has found anything conclusive about him." The President took some steps away from Avraham, his hands behind his back, his eyes lowered down to the ground.

"We have found a couple of ways," Avraham said, noticing how the President's men did not take their eyes away from him.

"What are we doing about what you just told me?" The President asked.

"Watching, waiting and listening, Mr. President," Avraham said, looking at President Smith directly in the eyes.

"For what?"

"Listening to every word being whispered. Everywhere." He answered. "Waiting to see what comes out to play… And waiting for the right tiger to hunt, Mr. President."

∞

That same night in Costa Rica, Salvador was being driven in one of his armored SUV's, with Arnold seated beside him. Three other SUV's with the rest of his security detail followed close behind, as usual. It was Thursday night and Salvador felt like celebrating something. There were many things on his mind that night, and he believed they were all going to align for his benefit. He had asked Raffa to drive him to a high-end salsa dance club at the center of the city.

Zapatos Locos was one of the most happening places in the entire city. It was frequented by some of the richest people in the country. Movie and television stars, famous singers and wealthy entrepreneurs alike, all flocked to this place. It was the place to be seen at. If your name was not a recognizable one, a very costly membership was required to be allowed inside. Salvador's vehicle pulled right up to the front. There were three men standing outside, very tall and dressed in black suits and ties. There was never anyone waiting in line to get in. The patrons inside were either VIP or members, there was no other way in. The walls outside were dark granite and the entrance door was dark glass, even the sidewalk was elegantly polished. The name of the place was written in simple four-inch, red colored roman style letters to the right side of the door.

Raffa opened the rear passenger door for Salvador, Arnold stepped out and walked up to the security, who already knew who he was. Salvador stayed behind for a moment, giving Raffa a couple of last-minute orders. As usual, Salvador was dressed all in black, in an Italian tailor-made black suit, a black fitted designer t-shirt underneath, and very expensive black suede shoes. He then walked in a nonchalant manner, as always, carrying his satchel over his left shoulder, already approaching the open door, ready to walk inside. The bouncers already knew him and were happy to see him. They knew Salvador was the best tipper in town and asked why he hadn't been around in so long.

"Business keeps me busier than women," Salvador answered, sparking laughter amongst the bouncers.

Salvador and Arnold walked through a hallway surrounded by mirrors; the acoustic sound of the music made the walls vibrate. There was another glass door at the end of the hallway, with a female host standing behind a short counter with her hands over a blacklist of guests. She pleasantly greeted Salvador and Arnold as they walked by. Two men opened the door allowing the way in. The place was filled up to capacity on this night. Beautiful people could be seen dancing on the seventies inspired glass dance floor, at the center of the setting. Salsa music was favored by those who frequented the club.

There was already a table set up with several bottles of Dom Pérignon waiting for Salvador and Arnold. A very sexy woman dressed all in white, walked a few steps ahead of them, ushering them towards their table. There were no special areas in the place, the entire location itself was VIP, whether someone wanted to hang out at one of the luxurious bars or sit around a table, it was all the same to anyone there.

Salvador stopped walking, allowing Arnold and the lady in white to walk on ahead. Something caught his attention at the other side of the dance floor. Arnold turned around and saw as Salvador was already walking through dozens of people, walking over the flashing colored lights of the dance floor that lit up with his every step.

Salvador was a known fixture by some of the party goers. He shook hands and received hugs as he made his way to a spot a few feet away from the dance floor. He calmly walked towards the counter of the bar and placed himself near a stunning looking woman. He looked at her long black hair, lightly tanned skin, seductive curves, inviting cleavage and mysterious eyes. All complimented by a nearly skintight, low cut, red dress, and open toe six-inch stiletto heels. Salvador had seen her dancing from across the floor, he was mesmerized. Her moves were natural and spontaneous, inspiring a small group of men, without the true courage to ask her for a dance, to only stand by and appreciate her seductive beauty. The silhouette of her body floated and came together with each beat of the music. She sang and danced to the tunes being played, exuding happiness, confidence, freedom, and sensuality all together in one explosive package.

Salvador waited for an opportunity and extended his left hand towards her while she spun sensually towards his direction. She looked at the hand reaching out for her, before looking at the man inviting her for a dance. She did not reject him and allowed her right hand to be taken. They began dancing very naturally. If one did not know, they would appear to be dance partners with moves that appeared made for each other. They danced to the tune of two songs non-stop, they smiled and celebrated each other's dance styles. Salvador noticed she may have needed a little break; they were both feeling a little hot after dancing with such passion. He calmly distanced himself from her and offered her his handkerchief. She took it and used it pat her neck while singing and dancing to a song which appeared to be one of her favorites.

"Who are you?" Salvador casually asked the woman, smiling. He could not help it. She looked at him and smiled, while neither losing the momentum of her rhythm nor the tune of her singing.

"I've have never seen you around here before." Salvador continued, "And I always make it a point to know everyone in this country." Again, the woman gave him a quick look without taking a break from her dancing.

"I'm not here for you." She said to Salvador with a smile on her face. He noticed an exotic accent as she spoke. Salvador signaled the bartender without taking his eyes away from her. The bartender, with his blonde hair in a ponytail, already had a Dewar's straight, ready for Salvador.

"Tell me your name," Salvador said. "We can be judges of the rest, at a later time." He instantly gulped down his drink.

"What would we be judging?" The woman asked, bringing her face closer to Salvador's face.

"You just told me that you are not the woman for me," Salvador said. "I say, you can't know that until I have a chance to show you, that you've never in your life had a man who will only act on fulfilling your needs, and not mine."

"And what makes you think you know what needs I have that need to be satisfied? What makes you think I do not have the men who would do those things for me?" She said not missing a beat of the music.

"The fire in your moves," Salvador replied, "The sense of freedom I see in the way you are singing and expressing yourself, you are free and strong, yes, but you want to be dominated. And you want that in your own terms."

The woman stopped dancing and stared at Salvador, who had just signaled for a refill. She looked at him from head to toe while displaying a partial smile. She then looked behind him. Salvador did not turn but he could see the reflection of someone standing behind him by the mirrored wall behind the bartender. There was a man in a black suit and white shirt standing behind him as if waiting for him to move, so he could occupy his spot.

The woman did not wait for Salvador to move, he was not going to. After taking a glass of champagne from the bar's counter, she walked around Salvador towards the man behind him while looking at Salvador from the corner of her eyes.

"Let's get out of here." Salvador heard the man telling her. He turned around to get a better look at the man standing behind him. He recognized that the man was the son of a multi-millionaire businessman from Panama. He stared as he and the woman walked towards the exit. He took his refill but did not take his eyes away from her, watching as she walked further and further away.

A man named Fermin walked up to Salvador from within the dance floor. He was the go-to guy between politicians and businesspeople. He was speaking to Salvador, but Salvador never took his eyes away from the woman. Staring right until the exit door was opened for her and her companion, and right until he saw her turning her head to look back directly at him, one last time.

"The people you asked me about ..." Fermin began saying to Salvador.

"What did you hear?" Salvador replied.

"They will be there," Fermin said.

"Thank you, as always Fermin." Salvador gave Fermin a hefty envelope filled with money. "I do not have to..."

"You don't, Mr. Salvador," Fermin reassured Salvador that he did not have to worry about Fermin giving away the information he had just received.

A couple of minutes after that, Salvador walked up to his table where Arnold had been socializing with some of the people he and Salvador was acquainted with. Salvador was welcomed with much excitement. He greeted everyone warmly. But instead of taking a seat, he signaled Arnold to get on the move.

"Where are we going, sir?" Arnold asked as they exited the place.

"I just accepted an invitation to a party at the vacation home of the Brazilian Ambassador."

The party was in honor of the Canadian Ambassador's birthday. The Canadian and the Brazilian ambassadors were very good friends, business partners and each other's godfathers to their children. Salvador was a mutual associate of both men, but neither of them had the appetite for flaunting that particular friendship in public. The event was going to bring together a decent assembly of very important people. Salvador wanted to take the opportunity to have an important conversation with a British diplomat he believed would be a good factor in his future plans. But after new developments came to his attention, he decided to take a partially different approach to his initial objective.

There were also several, well connected American businessmen invited to the party, as well as some power players connected to the United States government, both local and North American.

Salvador arrived at the place right on time. He had taken the time to change his look before arriving to the party. Allowing his hair to look more playful and dynamic, as well as going from a black t-shirt to a dressy black button-down shirt and gray tie, to give himself a more approachable vibe for the eyes he was going to be under. He could see the opulent mansion from his vehicle, as they waited to be allowed in by the security personnel assessing the guest list.

"There is a situation with three of the girls, sir. They have them at the warehouse." Arnold informed Salvador, while he was on the phone with the people in charge of the prostitution operation at a high-end hotel and casino Salvador co-owned, near one of the most popular water-side resorts in the country.

"What is it?" Salvador asked while looking impatiently at the line of vehicles ahead of his.

"Two of the young girls tested positive for HIV. They were part of the group returning from the assignment in Taiwan five days ago. Also… the doctor beat up another girl again. This time, over her face."

"What is that fucking guy's problem?" Salvador was furious. "That's my business he's messing with. She could be out of commission for two weeks, till her face heals. Have a serious talk with that asshole. He will have to pay four times her normal rate. And tell him that when he wants to beat someone up, to do his wife, she should get it from him for free."

"Yes sir," Arnold replied. At that moment one of the men in charge of security approached the vehicle holding a list in his right hand. Salvador recognized the big-sized looking man as he walked near the rear right side passenger window.

"Isn't this Thomas?" He asked Arnold. Arnold looked at the man Salvador pointed out.

Salvador suddenly thought he saw someone he used to know standing next to his window. His reaction was not seen by Arnold, but he was shaken by what he thought he saw. His hand almost reached for his satchel.

"Yes, that's him." Arnold quickly replied, as he also recognized the man who had worked security for them at one of Salvador's locations. An idea came to Salvador.

"Good evening," Thomas said while approaching the rear window. He immediately recognized Salvador and Arnold and greeted them both with great reverence.

"What are you doing here? I thought you worked for me." Salvador said to Thomas.

"Yes sir, I did," Thomas said. "But you shut down the place and I was a temporary low-level worker there at that time. I didn't have any good source of communication with anyone at the top. I had to go and get something else for the time being."

"I see… How much are you pulling doing this?" Salvador asked him.

"Uh, it's just another temp sir, not much." Thomas sounded unenthusiastic about his present position. It was not difficult for Salvador to capture the sentiment.

He stared at Thomas momentarily, while appearing as if he was mulling over something. "You know what, give Arnold a call tomorrow. I believe a man of your size and talent should be in a place where he makes the money his size represents. Okay?" Arnold immediately gave Thomas a card with a number to call.

"Yes sir, Mr. Salvador!" Thomas was very excited about his future prospect, displaying a genuine smile. He was quick to move Salvador's vehicle ahead of the rest, while the rest of his security detail remained parked outside.

As he entered the mansion with Arnold still by his side, Salvador felt right at home. He had visited a few times before and he knew the place was fit for a collective gathering of highly important people, at any given day. Salvador was always certain he could work his persuasive magic to continue acquiring and securing the right connections to put into use when he needed to. Connections he knew would be pivotal for the last phase of his retirement plan.

"Arnold, get on the move. You know the rest." Salvador said.

"Yes sir," Arnold said, before separating from his boss.

"Mr. Salvador." A man called upon Salvador's attention. Salvador recognized his voice but did not look right at him. His sight was on Mary, whose husband was keeping her talking to people she did not want to be around. She looked just as he liked to see her. Her dark brown hair, which rested over the shiny skin of right shoulder, her long legs were crossed one behind the other and her physique was very well-toned, under an accentuating white dress with a long slit on the side.

"Mr. Montoya," Salvador said to the man, acting as if he was happy to see him there, but he wasn't. Montoya was one of the corrupt politicians he had in his pocket, a remnant of the former government, which was soon to be extinct. Montoya knew Salvador was someone who could help him maintain a decent lifestyle. He knew his government perks would soon be taken away and he knew this was right around the corner.

"I am extremely glad you were able to make it Mr. Salvador. I was not even told you were coming. I have some people here I know you will be pleased to meet." Montoya placed his right arm over Salvador's back after handing him a glass of Champagne and guided him through the crowd of elegantly dressed women and what Montoya commented were, "old boring men."

As they walked towards the rear of the property, Salvador saw the man who sent Fermin to give him the invitation for tonight's event, a man named Bareli. Bareli was a connection between the Brazilian government and the Italian government in the country. They shared mutual interests in the money to be made, with the continued re-development and modernization initiated by the new government. Tourism and amusement exploitation were Bareli's main areas of expertise. Areas, in which he and Salvador had mutual interests and benefits which they planned to continue exploiting in the present and in the foreseeable future.

"Come talk to me when you have a minute." Bareli discreetly said to Salvador as he walked by him and Salvador agreed, as he continued walking with Montoya, who also knew Bareli but did not have a mutual connection with.

Montoya brought Salvador to a private salon where some of the most important people at the party were gathered. It was Salvador's natural habitat. Everyone was smoking cigars and talking about money, politics, drugs, illicit deals and eccentric sex. Salvador knew he could control every single man in the room with only a few words out of his mouth. The only thing he needed to do was choose who and what words to use.

"Montoya!" It was one of the Americans from a group of investors invited to the party by the birthday boy himself, on behalf of the new president. The man was shouting and calling out to Montoya, like a teenager at a frat party. Salvador did not like the way they looked. They looked old on the outside but were acting like kids. Rowdy and arrogant, disrespectful and were too drunk, too soon. He already knew what they were all about, and this further cemented his decision of making them his next targets.

"Come with me Salvador, let us entertain these investors and see what we can get out of them tonight." Montoya proposed. "Although I've been told that they are fully under the President's protection. You know what that means, right?"

"It means we don't give a fuck about it," Salvador said while studying the room and the people ahead of him.

"Yes, sir!" Montoya said with a big smile on his face. He dragged Salvador with him, knowing full well that Salvador did not like the idea of feeling like a prostitute on the hustle for a potential outcome, especially in his own town, where he controlled everything he wanted. But what Montoya did not know was that Salvador was already ahead of him. Bareli also walked towards the Americans at that moment while looking at Salvador.

"Montoya, come here." One of the Americans said, walking close to Montoya, wrapping his arm around his shoulders, to bring him into his group. Bareli took the opportunity and got near Salvador.

"That is Mathew Bradford." Bareli pointed to the man walking with Montoya. "And those are his college buddies. If you ask me, it would seem they never left college. That is Richard Brenan, Bob Gordon, Dan Miller, and John Kemp. They've been working together since they finished their education and they have kept it like that successfully for years. They do everything together. I would not be surprised if they do each other's wives and mistresses just to keep things simple. Ha!"

"Which is the leader?" Salvador asked. "Is it Bradford?"

"No, Bradford is some sort of fixer for all of them," Bareli replied.

"He sets them up with their victims?" Salvador said jokingly.

"I'm inclined to believe that," Bareli replied, not noticing at that moment that Gordon had turned his head to look at him and Salvador having their conversation. Bareli's hand gestures gave the appearance of him and Salvador talking about the décor of the house.

"Gordon..." Bareli said, after letting out a brief laugh. "He is the one with the most money. His family has been in the real estate and banking businesses since the 80's recession. They made a killing by buying back property from the Japanese and they quadrupled their gains betting against the stock market, just before it hit rock bottom. Everything they bought, they resold at ten times the price and then went back and bought cheaper stuff again. They kept at it for more than a decade, until they began investing in defense technology companies and other things. I don't even believe little Bob there had to even finish college to get his degree in business management, his daddy practically owned the entire fucking school. Even the janitors got contributions from his family."

"And if I was to take on one of them to squeeze, which one would you recommend?" Salvador asked.

"Bradford then. He would be the right target." Bareli asserted. "He is the fixer, so they would follow his advice. Plus, he has a weakness for very exotic and very, very young things. He is also the one with the most influence on everyone else's affairs. Gordon is their leader, but like I said, they would follow whatever Bradford says. They also follow Kemp because he likes to party hard."

"I take it he's the most fun out of them all?" Salvador added.

"Probably, yes!" Bareli replied with a chuckle.

"Where is Lord Brimstone?" Salvador looked around for the British diplomat he had wanted to see.

"He is a different type of fellow, you know, the Brits pride themselves in being complicated and have a need to appear refined above everyone else. They love it when it seems people find it difficult to understand them. They feel this shows a higher level of culture or education for their part. You will find him on the second-floor living room, where everyone there is whispering into everyone else's ears, without any need for it."

"Very well..." Salvador was about to make his way towards the other room, in order to get to the second floor from there, but he was abruptly stopped by Mr. Kemp, who had seemingly exceeded his drinking quota.

"I've heard you are a powerful man in this country, Mr. Salvador, are you?" Kemp offered Salvador a glass of Whisky while standing in his way.

"A modest businessman, with the right connections, would be a better description. Mr. Kemp, am I correct?" Salvador took a moment to entertain Kemp. He had already studied the rest of his associates from first sight and he decided a brief chat would not hurt his cause.

"I see that you are well-informed, you already know my name. I've heard people around here, both, trust you and fear you. Is that true Mr. Salvador?"

"You seem to be very well-informed yourself, Mr. Kemp. You already knew my name before we even spoke." Salvador was quick to reply. "And I will be more inclined to believe the trust part." He continued. "I have spent the better part of my life in this country, I arrived here as a refugee. And I have always been a firm believer in earning people's trust before I earn their business, or their fear for that matter, Mr. Kemp. It is a model that has worked for many others before me, and it has served me well."

"It is a profoundly good model of operating, Mr. Salvador," Kemp said to him. "Would it be applicable in the sense of being able to obtain or do certain things, which others would find more complicated to obtain, or do?" Kemp added with a wink, as Salvador looked over his shoulder. He spotted Mary.

"I see you guys are not wasting any time in getting to the bottom of things around here." Montoya integrated himself in the conversation while bringing along the rest of Mr. Kemp's gang with him, as well as a few others. Bradford seemed to be observing Salvador. Salvador caught a glimpse of him from the corner of his right eye.

Montoya was quick to work on his own behalf by putting an unnecessary extra spoon of good word about Salvador's casinos. At the same time, there was not really much Salvador could bring to the table anymore. He could see that Bradford had a sarcastic smile on his face while listening to Montoya talk about him. Bradford was aware of what was coming. He knew that the new government was taking over everything and a gangster like Salvador would have been instrumental in deals to be done anywhere around the country two years earlier, but Bradford knew Salvador's ruling time was coming to an end, and it was coming sooner than what he expected.

At this point, Montoya was just trying to help his own cause by putting Salvador in a position in which he could come up with something, which could set him up in a good spot. A spot from where Salvador could put something profitable together, with anyone who would like to venture out with him based on his reputation and what was left over from his connections.

Salvador spoke with everyone, and he listened intently to them as well. He was well-versed in politics and international affairs, as well as other more profound topics of conversation. He knew how to keep control over the people in his presence. But as the conversation went on, Salvador understood more and more, that there was not much he could offer any of those men, which the new government and the international coalition could do even better. They were just there watching and listening to him because he was an attraction.

Still, Salvador knew he had the upper hand in the situation, even if he was at a logistical disadvantage. For all the money, resources, influence, and education these men had, he had more. Plus, they all were lacking the principal fundamental aspect of understanding the real world at large, the way it really was – not the one they were accustomed to take advantage of whenever they could. The cruel, brutal, deceiving and real dark world. The world where not the strongest, nor the richest, nor the biggest, but the wisest, only survives.

He looked at them with a discreet smile, knowing they were all just ordinary men with lots of money and only one-sided institutionalized educations. Education absorbed from the filtering of tales passed along from one group to another. Well-conditioned education, suitable for a particular segment of society, to satisfy the individual purpose of keeping themselves above other groups through deceptive capitalistic means.

They did not earn true life's education. They did not have the type of knowledge Salvador groomed himself with. They did not know what he knew, they had not done what he had to do, and they have not seen the likes of what he had seen. They did not have real life experience of what the world was truly about, out in the wilderness, in which the wild animals of the land could eat a man alive in the blink of an eye, without ever giving a reason why.

Salvador's knowledge was the likes of which comes from the bottom of bottoms. To have to deal with every single type of person and personalities that came his way. At times, good people, bad people, those who lied, those who told the truth, those who were ready, those who weren't.

Other times, dealing with the likes of which you need to learn how to read, understand, anticipate and even decipher behaviors, words, body movements, gestures, hand signals, the way someone looks at you or at others, how to read their minds, their motivations and their next move. For his very life depended on anticipating even the smallest and least visible of details. At times, even before they occurred. Hence, Salvador noticed the condescending manner in which Bradford was staring at him from, across the room. He was clean shaven, a diminishing hairline and was wearing a beige linen jacket with a white shirt and dress pants.

My instincts never fail me. Salvador thought to himself.

Salvador knew these men did not need him at all. They were just curious to see what a man like him was. How he spoke, how he behaved, how he might speak with them, how he operated under circumstances. What made him tick. He knew for them he was perhaps a dinosaur or a part of a short list of endangered species. At last, he was an attraction. But he knew better than that, he knew that they knew. And he decided to play their wondering game. But before continuing playing their game, Salvador had business to take care of on the second floor.

"Gentlemen, would you excuse me for, what I believe, will be a short moment?" Salvador again put his sight on Mary, whom he wanted to talk to. She was walking in the direction he was about to take, and he took the opportunity to kill two birds with one stone. He would take a break from his unsuspecting targets and set his claws on another one.

He was able to excuse himself from everyone momentarily and placed Montoya on full-entertaining duty, in order to keep the people he wanted to keep in place, kept in place until he returned. He made his way up to the stairs, which led to second floor. He met Mary halfway near the stairs. They spoke for less than three seconds. But this was enough time for Salvador to assign a rendezvous spot for her, where she agreed to wait for him with a glass of champagne in her hand. Salvador really just wanted to grab her by her waist and kiss her, and she wanted him to kiss her as well, but they both controlled their urges for the time being. Salvador went on to do what he was there to do. There was no shame in his game, ever. He had as much or more money, power and influence than anyone there, but he still operated like the hustler he had been his entire life.

On the second floor, the atmosphere was more like it. The women had more class, the men were more reserved, and he saw the person who he actually wanted to see from the moment he arrived, not Lord Brimstone. Brimstone was at that moment having a seemingly interesting conversation with the Panamanian State Secretary, Mrs. Cristina Minerva and with Lethabo Ngugiso, a very influential and corrupt South African politician. No, Salvador wanted to see Lord Brimstone's trusted and loyal assistant, Harold Stewart, a young man with ambition, needs and a thirst for adventure. The type of man who saw Salvador as the man they wished they could be. Salvador knew that. Where Lord Brimstone was, Harold followed closely. But he was also aware that Harold would be willing to do certain things outside the norm, as long as they did not push the envelope to a place where his status near Brimstone could be jeopardized.

Salvador wasted no time and discreetly signaled Carlos, who worked for the Brazilian ambassador and attended to the needs of his family and his house when the ambassador was out of town. He also had an insatiable gambling habit which Salvador made sure to feed and exploit to every possible extent. Carlos pointed at Harold, drinking whiskey standing at one of the corners of the salon. He seemed very upbeat while carrying a conversation with a man and two women. Salvador went ahead and walked into a rest room which had a door that led to a bedroom. Carlos had signaled for him to enter. Carlos then took hold of Harold, while excusing him from the other guests, who may or may not have known who he was. Harold did not know who Carlos was but followed him into the bedroom where Salvador was waiting. He immediately recognized Salvador from several visits at one of the casinos Salvador had part ownership of.

"Hello again Mr. Salvador, how are you this evening?" Harold was partially surprised but embraced the idea of having a brief chat with Salvador, the man whom he secretly admired and identified himself with most.

"Harold, I'm very happy to see you this evening, and I would like to talk to you about the matter which I mentioned to you at the casino, on the night we met. Remember?" Salvador and Harold walked towards a balcony connected to the bedroom. Salvador drew the curtain to make sure they were not spotted together by any of the other guests. As he did, Salvador noticed two men who looked like they might be Americans, smoking cigars near the back wall of the property's main entrance. He did not remember seeing them before. They looked up at the balcony, not seeing anyone. It did not take them long to walk away. Salvador kept their faces and attire in mind.

"Indeed, I remember Mr. Salvador." Harold was pleasantly available to help Salvador in anything he needed. Salvador had asked him to set up a private meeting with him and Lord Brimstone. He wanted to talk about a deal in which he could ensure having himself a plan B, in the worst-case scenario the American government reached out and created any type of problem for him when he left for Europe, as part of his self-exile plan. But Salvador decided to go in a different direction, knowing Lord Brimstone could pose a threat if he would become susceptible to any future instigation by the American government.

As a former military man, Lord Brimstone had the title, the connections, and some influence which would be helpful to Salvador if he ever needed them. But Brimstone was still under the control of the U.S. government, due to a sexual abuse situation in the United States, which the CIA helped him to contain.

On the other hand, Harold had already enjoyed the pleasantries Salvador's businesses had to offer. In fact, he was a loyal customer. Therefore, he was more than willing to help Salvador with anything he needed, as long as it was within his reach. Salvador needed for Lord Brimstone to set up a meeting between him and Edward Oliver, an influential Australian politician, who used to be the right-hand man of the current Australian Ambassador to the United Nations. Oliver himself was now enjoying a very successful tenure as a diplomat in Panama, where his connections in the United Nations were proving to be indispensable.

It did not take long. Harold left and came back with good news for Salvador. Lord Brimstone would help set up the meeting with Mr. Oliver for the next day. He would, in fact, go to the casino to meet with him in secret. Salvador knew Oliver was a gambler and he also had assets in Macao, China, which made him the perfect candidate for him to enhance his newly developed plan B, which he will craft into his plan A from scratch. He was more than happy to hear the news from Harold. The casino was his best place to conduct high stakes deals, and this one merited it.

"Is Lord Brimstone still looking to locate a good deal in the states?" Salvador asked Harold, as they remained near the balcony.

"Indeed Mr. Salvador," Harold said. "I believe if you can come up with a good solution, it would be most helpful for you and I as well. I get to be the hero who connected Lord Brimstone to the man who helped him get exactly what he has been wanting- a large property to show his mistresses without having to pay the large price tag which goes with it. Lord Brimstone requested for his affairs with you to be under total concealment, if you will Mr. Salvador. I understand why you are taking these precautions, why we are secretly meeting in this room. But I strongly believe it does not matter much if I am seen talking to you. If someone sees you speaking with me and assumes that I am a liaison between you and Lord Brimstone. Our interaction could mean anything or nothing at all."

"Nevertheless, it is best to keep it under wraps, Harold. Eyes can be very damaging when they get to see what they want to hurt."

"I won't mention anything if you don't mention anything," Harold replied.

"Consider it done, Harold," Salvador said. "As long as you and Lord Brimstone refrain from mentioning my name to anyone outside this room, you will both remain safe from the prying eyes I mentioned. Deal?"

"I am a man of my word, Mr. Salvador. And I can say the same about Lord Brimstone. You will never have to worry." Harold said to Salvador. "And I thank you for trusting me, sir."

"Very well then." Salvador shook Harold's hand with satisfaction.

With everything set and arranged on that side, Salvador moved over to the other end he needed to secure. He knew he would not need much effort to get this one done. First, he went after Mary. She was there at the same place, drinking her third glass of champagne, and Salvador loved it. He knew and understood the way she functioned even better than she knew and understood herself. One drink allowed her to mellow out and deal with her surroundings. The second drink she uses just to cope with being around her husband's friends and associates.

But after a third drink, all will be left to the possibilities. With her simply knowing Salvador was around, and they were sharing spaces in a sort of forbidden place, it was just too exciting. The third drink had been just to begin setting up for the fourth drink. She was adjusting her dress, preparing herself for an impulsive action, which will need courage and carelessness.

Salvador knew all of this too well. They had even talked about it during pillow talk. She would ask him, "Why do you do this to me?"

And he would answer, "Because I know it excites you. Because I know the difference. Being attacked and cornered awakes your spirit. The wild beast you have inside, a beast ready to be tamed." She thought about it, even when he was not there. But at this moment, he was. And her legs were trembling from the thoughts racing through her mind.

Salvador spotted a waitress walking by and he calmly walked up to accompany her to where she was going, which happened to be the kitchen. Mary spotted Salvador walking by, but her husband was just walking down the steps. Salvador preformed a gesture with his hand for Mary to follow him, as he sustained a potentially productive conversation with the waitress.

"What are you doing by yourself?" Cesar asked his wife. Mary displayed the glass in her hand.

"I came for some more, as you did your networking up there." She said to him flatly.

"Why down here?" Cesar looked around while putting his left arm around her waist.

"I didn't want to wait for the waitress to bring more upstairs. Plus, I wanted to take a break from the slow talkers up there." Mary replied. Cesar looked at her for a second, then looked around again and waved at someone he knew.

"I'm going to use the restroom, the one upstairs smells like shit. Meet me upstairs. You look too classy to be around the women down here. And listen. I don't want to deal with these dumb people and their chiclet breath either, but if I'm going to be breathing in the same air they are exhaling, I may as well get paid for it." He continued. "I need to convince Letabo to put pressure on his associates into allowing Miguel to invest in his country with minimum obstructions. Now that he is out of the casino business he had with Salvador; Miguel will be fair game for me. And I am planning on making as much as I can with this deal. Speaking of the devil, have you seen that drug dealer around here? Someone told me that they saw him coming in earlier."

"Last time I saw him, he was heading up there. To the second floor." Mary replied.

"The audacity of that son of a bitch." Cesar seethed. "To bring his vulgar stench to the ambassador's party. I guess he has not gotten the memo."

"What memo?" Mary asked.

"No one wants to be around a common thug like him, my precious," Cesar said, walking closer to Mary, touching her lips with his fingers in a soft manner. "That guy is a loser, it's no wonder why women run away from him the moment they realize it. Acting as if he really has money and influence, when it is already becoming a known fact that he just got lucky with a few drug deals in the north.

Big time drug trafficker- that is what he wants everyone to believe. Blackmail and extortion, that is how he made his pennies. He is only influential in his own world of cheap prostitutes and small-time coke fiends. His time is ticking, that guy is an endangered animal. We will all be better off in this country when he's gone! And I'm telling you, there are people working on it as we speak. I'll see you up there, baby."

Cesar kissed his wife on the lips and walked away. As soon as Cesar was out of sight, Mary discreetly walked in the direction Salvador had taken.

"Come with me for a moment," Salvador told her in her ears, just as she walked into the kitchen while holding her by the wrist in a gentle manner.

"Be careful, Cesar is down here. He went to the restroom," Mary said. "Where are you taking me? I hope you are not going to take me somewhere to keep me waiting again. I have to go back upstairs soon."

"No baby, not this time. Remember, what I had said… You'd see me much sooner." Salvador was soft spoken and very gentle, as he walked with Mary towards the back end of the mansion. He had been there several times before and he knew the house like the back of his hand. Salvador and Mary ended up inside a laundry room where he had his way with her, and she had her way with him. One of the house keepers was bringing dirty tablecloths into the room and quickly turned away when she heard the moaning sounds, as well as seeing something was definitely happening inside, which she wanted no part of.

Fifteen minutes later, Salvador walked out of the room in a rush, while adjusting his tie, after straightening his jacket. As he got to the other salon in the house, he was not surprised to find Montoya telling his fishing jokes to the guests. Salvador had a smirk on his face as he walked near the men. They celebrated his return and offered him more champagne. Salvador declined, and instead requested whiskey.

Everything was going as Salvador expected it to go. Now the only thing he needed to do was set the second part of his plan in motion and allow the wheels to roll downhill on their own. It didn't take long, as Mr. Kemp, still attracted by Salvador's mysterious and undecipherable personality, walked closer to him to start a new conversation. Gordon was standing close to Kemp. Kemp was a good candidate, who would help hook the rest of the fish. But Salvador needed Gordon to put the cherry on top of his cake. He knew how to get him on his hook, but he could not be too obvious about putting on the bait for him. Therefore, he would allow him to fall for it on his own.

He looked for Bradford but did not see him around, as he began a conversation with Kemp, which slowly attracted everyone else around them, to become a part of it. Bradford maintained his distance as he continued to observe. It did not take long for Gordon to insert himself into the midst of the conversation, and onto Salvador's hook. Gordon made it his responsibility to elaborate and bring about debate on the most important topic being discussed during the conversation Salvador had introduced: The true aspect of conservatism as a cover-up to impose prejudice, and a certain doctrine over various groups, in order to keep them where desired.

Salvador was more than well educated about the topic, he brought about more than a fair share of his own experiences as a young man trying to survive in a world ruled by institutionalized colonialism, carefully hidden with the very fabric of society. Gordon never had to work hard for anything in his life, and he knew it. Salvador was a South American man, without the world recognized badge of honor from an Ivy League educational background, very unlike the man he was debating against. Everything that Gordon said, Salvador had more than enough to counter, as well as extend the subject to an even deeper level by giving real life examples. Gordon was not only impressed with the surprising debate he was having with Salvador, to the entertainment of everyone else, he was becoming obsessed every minute the conversation went on.

Salvador knew he had him right where he wanted. Gordon wanted more. For him, Salvador's mind was a rare specimen. Someone, the likes of which he thought will be found inside a dark room, discussing esoteric and clandestine subjects, capable of turning the world on its head. Salvador had brought the topic of discussion to places he had never explored before. Gordon was being schooled by Salvador, he knew it, his friends did as well. But he did not care, he wanted more of it. Salvador then did exactly what he had been waiting for the right moment to do.

When he exited the laundry room, after seeing Mary, he had asked Arnold to call his cellphone in exactly thirty-five minutes, which he thought was a decent amount of time to get to where he wanted to get with the people he had in mind. Arnold called his cellphone as planned; he was seated alone, inside one of the SUV's. He turned his head to the backseat when he felt he heard something moving. But there was no one around the vehicle. He went on to continue his conversation with Salvador, not noticing that Salvador's satchel was on the floor, behind the right front passenger seat.

Salvador answered his phone and acted as if he had an emergency and needed to attend to a situation which developed in one of his businesses. He excused himself from the guests, expressing confidence in the fact that he knew Montoya would keep everyone well-entertained with some of his fishing stories, sparking immediate laughter among those near him.

Gordon, along with his friends, approached Salvador as he was walking away.

"Is there any possibility we can conclude our small chat in the near future, Mr. Salvador?" It was as if Salvador had given Gordon a taste of something he had tried before, but this had more potency and lasting effect.

Salvador was dismissing himself from the place, saying goodnight to some of those he knew and knew him. He ignored Gordon for a moment, knowing very well it would build up his anxiety. It was like telling a child he was not allowed to have some of the cake on top of the table, and all the while, the cake had been for him.

Salvador turned around and told him that it would be of bad taste if they didn't finish this, most illuminating type of conversation. Gordon asked him when it would be possible for them to get together again and continue it. Salvador noticed his hand was getting too close to his arm and his eyes stared at his neck and lips at every opportunity available. Salvador recognized that type of behavior, he knew a couple of the men who worked for him, who would look at other men in such a manner. He recognized the behavior as a form of subconscious admiration. It was very simple now, like giving candy to a baby and waiting a few seconds when they asked for more. Now he has the upper hand and command and they will do what he will ask of them, without any second guessing.

"I just got a very good idea, gentlemen." Salvador seemed to have found the solution for the needs of Gordon and his friends. "If you are willing, to allow me the honor to serve as your next host, of course?" Montoya was the first one to laugh and celebrate the idea. He was immediately followed by Kemp and the others. Gordon was right next to him telling him that clearly, it was a no-brainer.

"Very well, it has been decided." Salvador proclaimed. "Leave it all behind and come with me, for the night is young and the day will not come soon enough." Salvador exited the mansion by the rear, some of the men in charge of security stared oddly, as they saw some of the VIP's they had been instructed to guard, walking out of the house with drinks in hands and following Salvador, dancing to his tune.

Salvador ordered his men to bring his other vehicles, to transport his guests. They were all around him, looking excited and very happy to be part of the out-of-protocol new event. At that particular moment, Salvador looked at Gordon, who had remained very close to him the entire time and called upon everyone's attention. Montoya looked at Salvador expecting he would say something phenomenal to further entice his new fans. There were other spectators quietly observing from one of the windows of the mansion, the Canadian and the Brazilian ambassadors, Samuel Logan and Rodrigo Paulo. They both stared at Salvador as he spoke to the others, looking at each other for a moment, revealing nothing but their impending needs in their eyes. They knew Salvador was already a liability for their own agenda, but they also knew he was too dangerous to be treated without proper regard.

"Let me guess, he is making one of his invitational speeches." Someone spoke from behind the two men by the window. It was Archon Romalyn, the new President of Costa Rica. He walked towards the window, standing between his two friends.

"I believe you know this man more than what you have told us, Archon." Mr. Logan said. Romalyn was in his early forties with boyish good looks. At the moment, he had a drink in his right hand and was wearing a suit without a tie. His eyes were covered by designer sunglasses, which complimented his trendy and stylish haircut.

"Yes Archon, how long were you in business with Mr. Salvador?" Mr. Paulo asked. Romalyn remained in silence. He stared as Salvador did what he knew how to do best: coerce, then lead, in order to control.

"Too long, if you ask me…" There was a woman in the room, Rachel Williams, a secret link between President Smith of the United States and President Romalyn. They all looked in her direction. She was smoking while seated on a chair next to a small round table, where Romalyn had been sitting just a moment ago. The fingers of her left hand were caressing the rim of a nearly empty short glass, with only a few sips of rum left in it.

"Salvador prides himself of being a man of the world." She continued. "Well-traveled, a suave speaker, well dressed, nice smell, hard handed, power hungry and has more money than he knows what to do with. And yet, he is still just another drug lord nearing the edge of the cliff, where all of those brutes like him had fallen before.

"The way things were running in this country, with his drug money influence, that is the way of the past. A way which will inevitably only lead to a dead end, a very *dead* end. They are all the same, weather they try to outdo each other by arguing about who has fucked more hookers or killed more men, or who has put more kilos in the states. They are just average, uneducated men, who were lucky to find a gig which allowed them to enjoy a taste of some of the finer things in life. But the only thing about them that's different, are their last names, well, some of them.

"In Salvador's case, it will not be any different than the others. The Colombians being the most recent. I believe Salvador is nothing but a major liability, which has run its course. President Romalyn has not only his golf and diplomatic skills, to thank for his soon to be freedom from his connection to Salvador, but also a bit of luck, which I believe we should all appreciate gentlemen."

"Amen to that," Romalyn added while bringing his glass up and offering a toast.

In the meantime, Salvador addressed his impulsive guests.

"Gentlemen…" Salvador said. "As of this moment, you all belong to me. You will all be in my care as my special guests. But as you well know, I'm a hard-working fella', and as luck will have it, there is the sudden development of a small situation which requires my attention. I will have to part ways with you momentarily, but in the meantime, I will ask all of you… Which country would you like to screw tonight?"

Salvador's words inspired instant cheering and clapping. His guests did not know whether to celebrate out loud, by jumping and shouting like teenagers, or hug Salvador and propel him into the air like a rock star. There was nothing else to be said. Everyone began mounting into Salvador's vehicles, pushing each other, and getting on top of each other as if being driven to the zoo on a school trip. Salvador's men were attentive and helpful with his guests. Arnold stared quietly, only displaying a pleasant smile, as he monitored everything, still not under the full understanding of Salvador's current agenda. One which was also inquiring about Bradford's current whereabouts.

Chapter VIII:

Burned Assets

Later that night, it did not take long for the vehicles to arrive at the Casino El Dorado, at the Dios del Mar hotel. Salvador had called Adriano Verdes in anticipation. He was the general manager of the luxury hotel and casino. Verdes made sure he was at the front to receive Salvador and his guests, who were received like gods at the main entrance by everyone around them. Everyone else was put on standby in order to give them speedy access into the place.

"Adriano, give these men access to everything and more please." Salvador placed his arm around Verdes and introduced him to his guests, while Arnold waited for him inside the SUV. Gordon and Kemp approached Salvador and requested for him to be back soon and join in the action with them. Salvador quickly reassured them that it would not be too long before they pick up where they left off at the ambassador's house. Verdes took over for Salvador in a similar festive manner. He escorted everyone into the casino, where they were greeted by very beautiful women, unlimited alcohol and casino chips on the house.

"Forgive me for asking boss..." Arnold said while sitting next to Salvador in the SUV, as it drove away. Salvador gave him a look which Arnold was all too familiar with.

"My apologies for saying 'boss,' sir..." Arnold said looking down momentarily.

"Yes, Arnold, what's troubling you?" Salvador at that moment had just placed a call, on one of three cellphones Arnold was carrying for him inside a small brown zippered bag.

"You are not the type of person who would, one day, find it in his heart to be entertaining these types of people." Arnold was curious. He had been working for Salvador for several years and had gotten to know a fraction of what he could be like. He knew that for Salvador those men, the very people he was celebrating, befriending and even entertaining, in Salvador's playbook, they represented the identity of the quintessential American imperialist. Those were men who represented the very sources, which Salvador had denominated as the driving force behind the enforced crumble of his own empire, and yet…

"Arnold…" Salvador said while the other line was ringing. "Are you aware that the ancient Egyptians were not very fond of shepherds? In fact, it is said that they deemed them as one of the lowest of the low-class citizens in their lands. Do you want to know why?"

At that moment someone answered the other line.

"Brother, how are you?" It was Salvador's brother, El Pesado, speaking to him on the other line.

"Happy to hear from you," Salvador responded. Arnold, at that moment, let him know that they had just arrived. It was a twelve-unit property located in a middle-class neighborhood. For everyone in the area, the people who frequented the location daily, it was an open secret which no one spoke about. But the true secret lay behind it, within the walls of what appeared to be an abandoned warehouse, surrounded by uninhabited streets. Where the volume of traffic created by the large clientele went nearly unnoticed by the rest of the city.

"Was everything as expected?" Salvador asked his brother.

"Yes." El Pesado replied. "The Mexicans couldn't be happier to see me. They've seen the news of what happened to Garrido in Colombia and for some reason, they thought we were also captured or being hunted by the Army."

"Yes, the thought of them thinking that, crossed my mind," Salvador replied.

"About that…" El Pesado added. "Did you watch the entire report? The son of a bitch made sure to mention us. I didn't like the way he expressed himself."

"I did," Salvador replied. "The Bolivian brotherhood is how they are referring to us. How insulting…"

"Yes, yes, it is." Salvador's brother said. "I am on my way back now. They paid in full. Then, it took me thirty hours to get to the other place undetected, and everything else went just as planned."

"Did you bury them with everything, as I suggested?" Salvador asked.

"As you suggested brother, you were right as always." His brother quickly added.

"The others will meet the same fate."

"Make it so. Are you going on the second leg of the trip now?"

"Yes, I will be dropping in on Jose Lewis." El Pesado replied. "Remember the guns I told you about? I will set it in motion and leave it on remote control. I will make a decision on who will handle it when I get back home."

"Jason?" Salvador asked him.

"Probably." El Pesado said. "I'm also checking on Adriano, his rival. Gave him some stuff to do, to see how he handles himself."

"Good. Be safe, see you soon." Salvador ended the call, just as his vehicle pulled up through one of the gates of the warehouse. There were many heavily armed men near the immediate entrance and others hidden outside the place.

Salvador was welcomed by three older men in their fifties and sixties- Cesar Baraga, Indio Asuncion, and Arturo Consuelo. They were those in charge of the operation being run in the vicinity. Consuelo was the first one to approach Salvador with greetings. Salvador greeted everyone and then went straight to business.

"Show me," Salvador ordered the three men in charge. With Consuelo leading the way, in no time they brought Salvador to the back of the warehouse, to a place where they kept the new arrivals. A good number of young women and girls from different countries and nearby regions. Salvador walked through a room with dozens of beds, with very clean sheets and pillows. The beds were placed close to each other. The girls were seated over the edge of each bed at the moment. Consuelo gave Salvador detailed information about each of them as he walked by.

"Where are the trouble ones, Arturo?" Salvador asked. Consuelo looked at Baraga and he quickly assumed his turn.

"We keep them over here sir, follow me please." Baraga led the way as they walked one floor below. The lower level had a room with the appearance of an infirmary, which indeed was being handled by two nurses. One was an attractive woman in her early 40's and the other, a very inconspicuous woman in her twenties. There were six young women in total were being cared for. Five of them were wearing surgical masks over their mouths. One of them was two months pregnant and Salvador was told they were about to perform an abortion on her. Salvador looked at her for a moment, she seemed very afraid. He then walked closer to her and admired her skin that looked like porcelain. He caressed her face and tried to console her, she did not want to look up.

"You are very beautiful," Salvador told her as he picked up her medical data next to her bed. "What is your name?"

Asuncion, who was in charge of security, was quick to approach Salvador with an answer, but Salvador slightly lifted his left hand to stop him from speaking.

"What's your name?" He again asked her. At that moment she slowly lifted her head and looked at him.

"Kelly." She told him, she looked at his face as she answered softly. Salvador stared at her and then abruptly walked away, wasting no time to ask about the other five. Baraga informed him that they have been brought there because they contracted the flu and they did not want to take any chances with the other girls, for they have been very busy and were almost running short of stock.

"Good, we need to keep a good amount of clean stock this time of the year," Salvador said. "Well thought out Cesar." He told Baraga, walking away from the room, as he took one last look at Kelly.

"Show me the problems," Salvador said to Asuncion.

"Yes sir, follow me this way please." Asuncion led Salvador and the others toward the basement of the place, Arnold looked around, he was surprised that the place was so well-appointed and neat.

"Very good..." He commented to himself while walking only four steps away from Salvador.

"Here we are." Baraga pointed to the glass window of the door of a very clean room. Salvador and the others looked inside but did not attempt to walk in.

"They both look prime and are in impeccable conditions," Salvador commented. Arnold walked closer to the door and looked through the glass window.

"God, anyone would jump into a mistake just by looking at them," Arnold said to Salvador and the others. They all agreed with him without hesitation. Salvador remained in silence, he just stared at the girls in the room, his eyes did not blink once.

"Do they know?" Salvador asked Baraga.

"No, sir," Baraga answered.

"What do they call themselves?" Salvador asked Asuncion.

"The one with the light-colored eyes and brown hair is Amber," Asuncion said. "The one with the blonde hair calls herself Tiffany." Asuncion stared at Salvador, who was still staring through the glass without taking his eyes away from the girls inside the room.

"Where did they get infected with HIV?" Salvador asked Asuncion.

"We believe it was during a private rental sir," Asuncion responded. "It was an important client from the Emirates on vacation in Taiwan. He said his meat had to be fresh and would not have it any other way. They both have been tested according to the protocol, every five days. They were the freshest of the freshest, with an impeccable acceptance and satisfaction record."

"Is the client aware of what he did?" Salvador asked.

"Yes sir, I believe he was aware," Asuncion replied. Salvador sensed a worried undertone in his voice.

"Arnold?" Salvador said.

"We have his last known address, as well as business locations in the United States and in the Emirates, sir," Arnold responded while eyeing his small agenda.

"Send him through," Salvador ordered, with Arnold giving him an immediate yes. "Maybe..." Salvador had a thought.

"Cesar, tell me about Kelly," Salvador said, instantly switching the topic. "Is she all clear, besides the pregnancy?" He asked Baraga.

"She is one of our best, as clean as they can be." Baraga expressed. He went on to tell Salvador about her vitals and blood group.

"Arnold, call Simon." Salvador began delegating tasks, as he continued thinking about how best to bring everything together that very evening. Arnold walked away from everyone to make the call in private. "Bring her to my office." Salvador looked at Baraga as he also asked to be taken back to the main office. Baraga dismissed himself from the group, just as they took an elevator, which led to the third level of the property.

A very large and well-appointed room was divided into several sections where those who operated the place had all of the commodities and amenities they desired. Salvador's office was at the end of the room, a place with no windows, and only he and Indio, the chief of security, had the code to the numeric key. Inside there is a hidden safe under the floor near Salvador's desk, and only Salvador had the combination to open it. The safe was set up to open every single day at a particular time, for Indio to deposit the large sums of money being generated by Salvador's businesses.

Salvador walked ahead of everyone, while meticulously observing every single corner of the place. As he walked towards his private office, he asked everyone else to stay outside. He walked at a slow pace, looking at everything with caution. He made it a point to remember where everything was supposed to be and how.

Even though he rarely went there, he asked for the modernly decorated place to be kept totally clean and secured.

He took several steps towards a well-stocked bar to the right side of the office and after preparing two drinks, in two different glasses, he sat down at the executive chair behind his desk. He picked up a remote control from the drawer to his left and looked at a monitor above on the right side of the wall. He stared ahead for a moment, before pressing the power button on the remote control. The monitor turned on, Salvador could see images of the different rooms within the complex, as well as the outside. Someone knocked on the door, Salvador watched as the monitor displayed who it was.

"Come in." Salvador stared at the door as it was slowly opened. Kelly walked in by herself. She remained not too far from the door, as someone closed it behind her.

"Come closer," Salvador asked her. She did not seem shy or uncomfortable, just cautious.

"So, are you the main boss?" Kelly said, speaking American English while walking closer to Salvador. She seemed undistracted and more relaxed than before, as she walked towards Salvador staring right at him. Salvador saw the poise in her attitude, something which he always recognized in those eager to do for him what he needed to get done. He embraced those people and squeezed out all the juice he could squeeze, from each and every one of them.

"I've never liked the sound of that word when it has been directed towards my persona," Salvador told her, answering her in English, as he walked from behind his desk holding both glasses. He directed the one in his left hand towards Kelly. She eagerly took the drink and gulped it down.

"Can I have another?" She asked. "What is it?" She walked closer to Salvador to hand him the glass. Salvador did not take the glass, just placing the tips of his fingers over the edge, where Kelly's lips were printed.

"Dewar's," Salvador responded, just as he gave his glass to Kelly and took the empty one from her hand. "Where are you from originally?" He asked her.

"San Diego, California." Kelly's voice sounded calm as she replied, just before taking a sip from her new drink. This time she did it smoothly while closing her eyes, to get a better feel for the aroma and taste of the liquor.

"San Diego," Salvador repeated, walking closer to her while downing his newly poured drink in a quick gulp. "I love the outgoing attitude of the people there. I got to enjoy a baseball game while I was there. The Padres, you know?"

"My mom and dad took me and my little brother there to watch a game once,"

Kelly said. "They thought it would be a good opportunity to have a new beginning to our family relationship. It was the first time in months they didn't have a fight or slammed something at each other's heads." She chuckled.

"I know the feeling." Salvador was already behind Kelly. His hands were free and over her shoulders. "Come with me." He told her while holding her right hand with tenderness as he led the way towards a very large and comfortable looking sofa. Kelly stopped him three steps short of it and turned him around to face her.

"What is it that you want from me?" She asked. Salvador did not answer, nor said anything while Kelly began to remove his tie and unbutton his shirt.

"You are the boss. You have so many other beautiful women working for you, desiring to please you. You can have all of them if you want to. What is it that you want from me?"

"Your skin…" Salvador spoke softly and allowed Kelly to continue undressing him. "Your voice…" He continued. "Your breath, your eyes, your internal body, and whatever else you have to offer. I want it all."

∞

At the same time, at a secluded location north of Ciudad Juarez in Mexico, three Mexican men were opening a bottle of tequila. They were having a candid conversation in a clear field of a very large property. There were four shovels on the ground by their feet. The sound of soft moans were the only interruptions in the background. The area was intentionally kept very dark, with no light fixtures anywhere around. Only the light of the full moon was providing a soft glow over the land. The sky that night was partially cloudy and as the clouds continued to roll by, peeks of stars twinkling above could be seen.

Soon, the headlights of several vehicles were fast approaching from a short distance. When the vehicles finally came to a stop, a small group of men stepped out of the vehicles. They walked up to the others with flashlights in their hands. Those with the flashlights remained behind, while three other men stepped forward towards the men who had been drinking.

"How are we doing here?" Someone asked in Spanish, his face hidden under the shadows of the night. One of the three men put the tequila bottle down and straightened himself as he responded.

"Everything is good patrón, they are all in there, as you requested." The man answered the owner of the property, as the one next to him took the bottle from the back of his hand.

"Very good, take me to see." The patrón ordered.

"Yes patrón, this way please." They all walked towards where the moaning sounds were coming from. The patrón, still under the shadows, looked ahead into a ditch in the ground. There were five men covered with plastic wrap and tape all over their bodies. When they saw the man who ordered their demise, standing right above them, they moaned and cried softly as they trembled.

"All of them, correct?" The patrón asked.

"All of them patrón ..." Someone quickly replied.

"Okay, do it quickly." The patrón said. The three others hurriedly picked up their shovels and began covering the hole, pouring dirt over the men in it. The patrón walked away from them and into the large-sized house. It was dark since there was no electricity connection. He lit up a match to take a quick look inside. There were stacks of dollars covering the entire place from floor to ceiling, leaving no space to move anywhere.

The fire of the match was about to be extinguished in between the tips of his fingers. He dropped it to the floor near a large stack of money. He walked away and closed a fortified metal door behind him. But then, he paused and thought of something. He stopped, turned around, and pushed the door slightly and observed for a moment, until the light of the match was completely gone, leaving the place in total darkness once again. As the patrón walked back towards his vehicle under the cover of darkness, he could see the dead bodies of the men who had been the ones shoveling before. They were now being consumed by flames as he walked by them, while his men were pointing their flashlights towards the direction leading to their vehicle.

"Put them in the same hole." The patrón ordered the men holding the flashlights.

∞

Back in Costa Rica...

Two couples on vacation, took a stroll down the beach while laughing and enjoying the ocean breeze of the night. They could see the lights of the hotels adorning the coastline like a jeweled necklace. Barry hugged his wife Jenny, as Donald playfully ran after his girlfriend Stephanie. Stephanie laughed hysterically while falling on to the sand. Donald ran to her aid and Stephanie pulled him over to make him fall as well. They embraced each other while rolling over back and forth, splashed by the waves of the ocean.

"Can you believe what she just did to me?" Donald shouted out, laughing.

Four men dressed all in black, leaving only their eyes visible through the layers of fabric over their heads, loomed closer towards the couple. Donald looked up surprised. He screamed and stumbled, trying to grab Stephanie's hand to run away.

Two of the men already had Barry and Jenny seated on the sand, with knives pointed at them.

"What do you want? What do you want from us? We're not carrying any money with us." Barry said to the men. "We can go back to the hotel if you want and give you the money there." Barry was desperately trying to negotiate with the men but all he got in return was silence.

"Please don't hurt us!" Jenny pleaded. "We're just celebrating our second anniversary, please!"

"Don't be worried." One of the men whispered to Jenny in her ear, speaking English in a peculiar accent. "We are not here to do anything to you." The man added while walking towards Donald, who seemed very preoccupied and unwilling to sit down.

"You need to relax." The same man spoke to Donald.

Damn! Why didn't I bring the stupid kitchen knife like I wanted to? Donald thought while remembering a small argument with Stephanie when they left their room earlier. She argued against Donald carrying the knife with him. He had told her it was only for protection, just in case.

"You don't understand," Donald said to the man. "You cannot do this to us! We are tourists. We are under the protection of this government. The laws have changed in this country, they advertised this at our travel agency."

"I already told you," The same man spoke to Donald and his friends. "We are not here to harm you. You are just coming with us for a short moment, a very short moment."

Sometime after, Donald, Barry, Jenny, and Stephanie were thrown inside the back of a red trailer truck. They were scared and panicking. There were others inside the truck, all bound and gagged. Jenny looked at one of them, who appeared to be unconscious, laying on the floor of the truck. He was a man wearing a piece of black cloth around his belt; a Kris from a Gypsy village.

∞

At the same time...

Salvador had Kelly's bare body over his. The delicate skin of her neck was at the receiving end of the calm passion of his lips. At the same time, his hands traveled up, down, left and right, over the beautiful smooth skin of her back.

"It has always amazed me..." Kelly lifted her face up inches from Salvador's. She stared into his eyes while speaking. Her right hand rested over the left side of his chest; his heartbeat was nearly nonexistent.

"...How one can get so close to someone's soul, by the passionate and driven touch of our skins." Salvador remained silent as Kelly continued. "We lose ourselves into the moment and allow our skins and hands to do most of the talking. The longer that moment, the longer the true essence of our souls, is quietly released into this immediate world we are sharing. As we make love. Circumstances do not matter, social status does not matter, skin color, age... The only thing that matters at this moment, are the needs of the deepest parts of our souls. The needs of our flesh and our minds, our desires. I believe this is the true essence of what love may be. No matter how it ends, if we go our separate ways or if we stick around and continue seeing each other from time to time. Or if a relationship develops...

"I believe that once we share this moment in which our skins and our souls' touch, no matter how it was caused or under what circumstances, I believe a bond of love, no matter how small, a bond of love has been formed. And this is what would keep our emotions together in one way or another because we are all creatures of love. Even if we forget about each other the second we separate. Something will always remain of the moment. Sadly, only some of these moments will be truly memorable."

Kelly allowed the left side of her face to rest over Salvador's chest. His skin was still warm and mildly moist, and she embraced it with tenderness.

"And if the moment was bad and forgettable?" Salvador whispered. "If it was a moment you will want to forget with all of your heart? Then what would it be?"

Kelly allowed her face to rest more comfortably.

"Then that moment was meant just for that," Kelly replied. "To be forgotten."

"You are a special person," Salvador whispered into Kelly's ears. "I believe there is so much more you could be doing with your life."

"Like what?" Kelly asked.

"You have potential," Salvador said. "And you are smart. With the problems your dysfunctional parents posed over your young and untrained mind, you were able to sustain yourself. You went out there on your own, and you survived this far. But this life is not for you. You have so much more to offer. You are a kind person, and that kind heart of yours may not only do well for you but for others as well."

"Would you help me?" Kelly asked him. "Would you help me make it a better life? If there is someone in the world who can, that person might be you."
Salvador stared into her eyes, she stared into his, and there, Kelly saw something

which she had not seen in the many people she had dealt with in her young life.

"I believe I can," Salvador said to her.

Moments later, Salvador walked out of the office, there was no one else around. He walked alone momentarily and found the others sitting at a resting area in a different room. They were gathered around waiting for him.

"Arnold?" Salvador said.

"Simon sent someone," Arnold replied. "They will be here shortly."

"Cesar, Kelly will no longer be put to serve. We are moving her out of here." Salvador told Baraga while walking by him towards the exit. His vehicle was already waiting for him, Arnold walked by his side.

"Yes sir, as your order." Baraga quickly confirmed.

"Back to the casino, boss?" Arnold asked.

Salvador looked at him for a moment.

"Oh sorry." Arnold recanted, "Back to the casino, sir?"

"Yes," Salvador replied. "There are deals to be completed there."

At the casino, all around the roulette table, Gordon and his gang, surrounded by many others, were having the time of their lives. The drinks kept pouring over their glasses and all over the casino carpet as if it were water. They went over the line and inappropriately touched some of the casino waitresses as they walked by. Verdes kept a watchful eye over each of them, and at times his impulses were about to betray him, but he would remember these men were Salvador's personal guests and with a look of his eyes, everyone watching knew to stand fast and to keep the peace around them.

"Richard! Richard!" Kemp was shouting at the top of his lungs. "I'm taking the twenty-eight black this time! I got this fucking table now! Watch me."

They all yelled and shouted with excitement, while acting unruly and out of control. Verdes could see, second by second, how things were about to get worse. He was growing increasingly upset and his insides were about to boil over. Gordon had just won again and this time they all exploded in laughter, jumping around and dropping their glasses on the floor.

Verdes gave the order to his security personnel to calmly remove them from the area. Hector was the person in charge of security. Verdes spoke to Hector's ear, and he moved quickly to go ahead with the rest of his men. But as he turned around, he paused silently and gave Verdes a quick look.

Verdes turned to look the other way and saw Salvador standing twenty feet away from them. Verdes stared at Salvador for a few seconds before walking up to him. Salvador had a very serene look on his face. There was no particular display of any emotion noticeable in his demeanor. He just stared at the men he had brought there as his guests doing exactly what he had told them to do. Salvador had also noticed three men who he immediately recognized not belonging there. Their demeanor, the rigid way in which their bodies moved, their interactions, nothing in those men belonged to that particular moment, nor the ambiance. He realized one of the two men who had been standing in the back of the ambassador's mansion from earlier that night.

"What do we do with your guests?" Verdes stood next to Salvador, as his security personnel waited for orders. Salvador made a couple of body and hand gestures, which indicated that he was talking about his guests, while in reality, he was telling Verdes something totally different. Verdes did not make a fuss about anything and followed Salvador's lead.

"I came back to take the troubles away from you Adriano." Salvador padded Verdes over the shoulder and slowly walked over to Brenan, who was the one closest to him, while Verdes walked away in a very casual manner, with one of his men following him.

"Are you guys ready to take the party to the next level, gentlemen?" Salvador asked, with his presence sparking an even louder outpour of joy and happiness amongst his special guests.

"Now the real party will actually begin!" Kemp shouted out. While quickly walking closer to Salvador, he snatched a drink from the tray of one of the waitresses in order to land it in Salvador's hands, almost as if it was a pre-arranged move.

They all gathered around Salvador who had arrived like a magician, getting ready to perform magic tricks for them. Salvador drank and shared in the merriment, under Verdes's watchful and relaxed demeanor. Salvador looked at him from the corner of his eye, Verdes got the signal and calmly made his way out of the room, after giving a hand signal for the security personnel to follow Salvador's lead. Gordon was very excited as well but was able to keep his composure.

"Indeed, as Mr. Kemp just said." Salvador began to say to everyone. "The party has just begun, please follow me."

Salvador had his guests follow him away from the private gambling salon for VIP patrons, and into another area where two heavy-set security guards stood in front of two golden doors. They immediately opened the doors inwards for Salvador. Salvador walked ahead and guided his guests to walk ahead of him, were two strikingly beautiful women with platinum blonde hair and dressed in very tight red dresses, waited for them in front of a private elevator. This elevator would take them all to one of three penthouse suites.

"Vanessa, Indira." Salvador greeted both women, they replied with smiles and kisses.

As everyone walked into the large-sized elevator, Salvador patted Gordon over the shoulder.

"The house has prepared the Presidential treatment for you," Salvador said. "You can call it, a type of once in a lifetime kind of experience." Gordon's eyes gave away the excitement building inside him, but he wasn't the only one ready to experience what was planned next. Brenan could sense it in the air.

"I want to own her." He said greedily into Salvador's ears, not being able to take his eyes away from Indira. She was the taller of the two. Indira stared back at Brenan as well. She knew exactly what Brenan was thinking without any need to read his mind.

"You will have that and more," Salvador whispered in his ear, just a moment before the elevator door opened to reveal the Presidential penthouse. It was impressively large and luxuriously decorated. An awe-inspiring view of the ocean from all angles of the place lay before them. But that was the last thing everyone was paying attention to. As they walked in, they were all greeted by very young and very beautiful women of different ethnicities, dressed in bikinis, and having a party of their own.

At that moment, Bradford walked into the suite, followed by Verdes and two other men.

"What the hell are you doing Bob?!" Bradford shouted at Gordon. "You know you are not supposed to be here. For all you know, this could be a trap." Bradford walked closer to Gordon, looking extremely upset. "Let's go! Let's get out of here!" He ordered Kemp and the others. Verdes looked to Salvador as if asking him what to do about Bradford. Salvador looked back at him with a relaxed look on his face, as he walked up to Bradford.

"Mr. Bradford," Salvador said, "You are insulting not only me but your associates as well, by doubting their intellect and my intentions."

"And what are your intentions, Mr. Montero?" Bradford replied. Salvador did not like the way Bradford used his actual surname to address him. But he kept a calm demeanor. After a brief conversation, in which Gordon and Kemp gave their inputs that culminated in the Americans deciding to stay at the hotel, Bradford left the room. But not before giving a warning to Salvador and a reminder to his associates.

"We are here to attend to a very important diplomatic agreement," Bradford told Gordon and the others. "Do not allow yourselves to lose sight of that. And to you Mr. Montero, as long as these men are within this premises, they are your responsibility. I don't think I need to remind you that they are under diplomatic protection, which means the consequences will be swift and costly, if so much as a hair is harmed from their heads."

Bradford did not get an answer to his last words. Neither from Salvador, nor from his friends. He was escorted away by Verdes and his security detail. The giant doors of the penthouse closed behind him.

Immediately each man introduced themselves within the different groups of girls. It did not take long for them to begin to undress. Brenan was ushered away by Indira and another woman into a room. Kemp and the others assumed occupancy of a different area of the suite. But Gordon remained cautious, still thinking about the warning Bradford had given him and the others. Salvador noticed his hesitation and knew exactly how to handle that.

He asked Gordon to take a moment in one of the large balconies to enjoy a drink, a cigar, and good conversation, all while enjoying the view.

"You are a very interesting man, Mr. Salvador," Gordon said.

"You flatter me, Mr. Gordon," Salvador responded. "Please call me Sal, my friends, and close associates call me Sal."

Gordon lifted his glass to toast Salvador's gestures. Salvador lifted his glass as well.

"Can I ask you something personal Sal?" Gordon turned to look the other way as he heard a loud bang and then ensuing laughter.

"Sure," Salvador said.

"What do you think about your new president?" Gordon asked. Salvador finished the last drops of his drink and placed the glass on the floor. While considering his answer, he took a long drag from his cigar.

"He is a true patriot and the future of the new generation of this nation," Salvador answered. "He will be very good for this country. It is what the people need right now: young blood, smarts, and good connections to enable him to move the country into the future."

"That sounds about just what anyone would say at a public gathering of donors, very diplomatic," Gordon replied. "But, indulge me if you will. Tell me, what do you *really* think about the man? Not the politician." Salvador thought about his answer for a moment.

"As a president, he will be a good businessman." Salvador replied. "As a businessman, he is not yet fit to be a leader." Salvador looked at Gordon dead in the eyes as he phrased his words. Gordon took a moment to absorb from his cigar, as well as Salvador's words.

"I don't believe you are the type of man I should go around bullshitting, Sal," Gordon said.

"I will appreciate it very much if you didn't," Salvador replied, as the two men shared a laugh.

"I was warned about you, even before I got to meet you at the ambassador's house," Gordon said to Salvador, nearing a step closer to him, as he looked over his shoulder. Salvador stared at him in silence, allowing him to continue speaking.

"Everyone in this part of the world and some of us abroad, have a pretty good idea of who you are. Or, at least, what they want us to believe about you." Gordon continued.

"Tell me," Salvador said. "What did they tell you about me? If I'm not mistaken, I believe that right till this moment you have already made up your mind and decided not to adhere to whatever they told you. Including to stay away from me. Otherwise, we wouldn't be having this conversation, Mr. Gordon."

"You are correct," Gordon said. "But please call me Bob. And to be very honest with you Sal, you have shown me more true character than many of the people I have met in a while. You are a natural human being and you are who you are and are not afraid of being it. You are not shy about displaying your true colors Sal, I like people like you. Unapologetic, straight-forward. So far you have offered me much more than what I have been offered by many of my, so-called associates. You have offered me true openness, without reservations or protocol. I want to thank you for that."

"It takes one to know one Bob," Salvador told Gordon as they shook hands with a firm grip.

"Have you ever heard of Duarte, Sanchez and Mella, Bob?" Salvador asked Gordon.

"Not really, who are they?" Gordon asked.

"I'm going to tell you a little story and you can draw your own conclusion from it," Salvador said to Gordon.

"It is actually a historical account," Salvador added. "And I will need to start by reminding you of your own revolutionary past. During the time in which your founding fathers went to war against the British Empire, if it was not for the help of the French, you may have still be paying the Queen taxes. But thanks to their help, you guys have now enjoyed over 200 years of independence.

"The French took a gamble and heavy loses but they got your country out of the grasp of the British, the entire thing was, of course, self-serving for the French. They truly pulled a fast one on their bitter rivals while changing history. But history has a very funny way of teaching us lessons, even when we really don't want to learn any of them.

"Fast forward to February 27 1844, when a well-educated man known as Pedro Santana, observed from a safe location how a secret group called Los Trinitarios (The Trinity), spearheaded by three men: Duarte, Sanchez and Mella, chose El Conde, which was then known as "the gate of the count" in the old city walls of what is now known as Dominican Republic, as the rallying point for their insurrection against the government of Haiti, which actually controlled the entire island under the full support of the French Empire.

"The French saw their influence and territorial strength threatened by the regional acquisitions by the Crown of Spain. Spain saw no need for this, for they had already attained so much territory, they barely knew what to do with all of it. Hence, all the countries in this part of America speak Castellano, the king's language, the Spanish king.

"To continue, the French needed to send a strong message and they armed and secretly engaged in helping the people of Haiti take over control of the island of Hispaniola, now comprising of the Dominican Republic and Haiti. But on the morning of February the 24th of the year 1844, the Trinitarios openly challenged the Haitians and surprisingly gave them more than they could handle.

"The Trinitarios were successful and unstoppable, and for the next ten years, the Dominican men fought to preserve their country's independence from their Haitian neighbors. The French pushed Commander Faustin Soulouque to take the country back. They were in shock, not knowing how such a sudden undertaking was so successful. They offered men and weapons for the commander to organize Haitian soldiers to get back control of lost territory, but this effort was to no avail as the Dominicans, who everyone thought was underequipped and unprepared, fighting under the command of Pedro Santana, would decisively win, every single battle against the Haitians.

"History will tell us that the Dominicans fought with small arms and swords, and in this way, they were able to send the Haitians running away by all fronts. This same history will bring out the names of Duarte, Sanchez, and Mella, as the true heroes of a nearly impossible to accomplish revolution, and everyone will be satisfied by this happy ending in history. Right?

"On February 27th of 1844, one hundred Dominicans seized the fortress of Puerta

Del Conde in the city of Santo Domingo. The following day, the Haitians surrendered and evacuated towards the West side of the island, where they have remained ever since. Now, the French were not going to give up that easily, they continued investing in the Haitians, sending weapons, provisions, money, and secret convoys of manpower. But they always ended up being crushed by the Dominican forces.

"When everything was said and done, and after years of trying, the French finally gave up on the Haitian people, leaving them to fend for themselves, which they could not. The French held a grudge against the Spanish Crown, for a while. Did I mention Mr. Pedro Santana?"

"That was one of the first names you mentioned," Gordon replied, completely engrossed in the story.

"Pedro Santana came from a rich family." Salvador continued. "His grandfather, I believe his name was Manuel, I'm not completely sure of this, but he made his fortune by selling coffee. He was one of the first coffee exporters into the U.S.A and he made sure his children were well educated there. Pedro Santana grew up in the U.S., where he went to college he met and actually married an American woman, who happened to be the daughter of a very powerful Senator of the U.S. Now, as the story goes, this Senator was very influential and had the ear of the President of the United States and he may have been the one who sold the notion of not having any more foreign occupation in countries with tactical proximity to the U.S.

Hence, you've seen what they did to Puerto Rico? Commonwealth, my foot! Weapons, money, and even manpower to a certain extent was all said to have been funneled by the U.S. through Santana. To secretly help expel the foreign influence away from Hispaniola. Some portions of this information have been corroborated by a few Latin American governments, but they have never been willing to openly disclose it. Other parts came to light many years after everything was said and done, Bob. Some parts of it may be truer than others, but indeed, they are all part of history. The French came across parts of this by accident, or maybe divinity. The true facts would probably never be corroborated, but they gave some very powerful people in France things to think about, including the possibility, that they have been holding a grudge against the wrong country."

"What are you telling me?" Gordon asked Salvador, smiling and bringing his drink up to his lips.

"That there are people in this world," Salvador said, "to whom loyalty is only a statement of subjugation because, at the end of the day, they hold everyone as a playing card."

"Well, what about WWII?" Gordon asked. "The U.S. went through heavy losses to help the French there."

"France, alone?" Salvador automatically replied. "They did not go in there to help France, Bob. They had to get involved to save Churchill's ass. And the Queen, for that matter." Salvador placed his cigar in his mouth and looked out at the view. A serene look came over his face.

Salvador had given Gordon something to think about. Just then, Arnold walked into the place with two very special presents for him, courtesy of Salvador.

"Ah...!" Salvador turned and saw Arnold. "And this special treat is for you Bob. I want you to consider this a birthday present." Gordon allowed the hand holding his drink to go down slowly. "Let me introduce you to Amber and Tiffany!"

"But I am not the birthday boy, Sal," Gordon said softly to Salvador, as he placed his cigar slowly between his lips. There were no words for him to express to Salvador how pleased he was with the surprise, and Salvador needed none.

"I am one who believes, that it is only for foolish people to wait three hundred and sixty-four days out of the year, to go out and celebrate only one day," Salvador said to Gordon, smiling broadly.

"How far are you allowing them to go?" Arnold asked quietly, as they walked out of the room.

"Let Gordon decide on his own," Salvador replied.

"Is this the road which will get you to where you want to go?" Arnold was walking right behind Salvador while talking to him. Salvador did not look at him to answer the question.

"Yes, this is the second step," Salvador said. "From here on, the next steps will be like walking down the hill."

Moments later, Salvador and Arnold had gone down to a security room, where Verdes had been waiting for them. Salvador entered the room behind Arnold and the first thing he saw was the three men he had seen earlier, seated around a table having coffee. The men asked to speak with Salvador alone and Salvador agreed. He ordered Arnold, Verdes and the rest of his security team to leave the room.

"Go ahead, what is it that you want?" Salvador asked the men.

"We don't want anything," Parker said. He had a thick mustache, lots of hair on his head and was wearing a white shirt and dark gray linen pants. He was accompanied by two others.

"And we have absolutely no problem with you or your business Mr. Salvador."

Timber, another one of the men dressed in a tan linen suit, that suited his dark skin tone. He was cleanshaven except for a neat mustache.

"We just want to make sure that Mr. Gordon and the rest of his associates don't get into any trouble." Timber continued. "We hope you understand our position, Mr. Salvador. Mr. Gordon, as well as the rest of his friends, are the President's guests and we have been entrusted to make sure his guests get back to the ambassador's mansion without any inconveniences."

"I understand your position," Salvador said, being a man of few words when dealing with potential adversaries. "But I don't believe you have anything to be worried about."

Salvador went ahead and showed them video feed from one of the security cameras in the hallway outside the presidential suite and they could clearly see Gordon and the others being ushered into the suite in the most comfortable and secure conditions. Salvador assured the men that at the moment, his guests were having the best time he could possibly offer them, under the law.

Salvador was about to walk away from the men, but it was as if something caused his legs to take only two steps ahead. As he turned around to look at them again, he decided to break with his own rule of 'few words.'

"Gentleman, let me make this clear." Salvador said, "Mr. Gordon and his friends were where they were, by self-appointment and nothing else. In case you may believe anything else, I will tell you that I attempted to dismiss myself from the festivities at the mansion, as well as Mr. Gordon and company. But as it happened to be, Gordon and his friends, for reasons I'm yet to figure out, actually wanted to get to know more about me than what I like to reveal to people who I'd just met.

"I really don't have much time for frat parties at this time in my life, as you gentlemen probably have become aware of. But rest assured that Mr. Gordon and the rest of his men are experiencing the best hospitality money can buy, for absolutely free. This I believe will be of great benefit for the president. He is ultimately the one person with the most to gain, since the reviews these men will give about our warm hospitality and the relaxed and laid-back attitude of our facilities, to future investors from all over the world, will be very inviting.

"And now gentlemen…" Salvador then decided to dismiss the men and continue with his endeavors of the night. "If you will please excuse me, I am a very busy man, with very little time left in my hands to take care of the fine details of my retirement plan. Therefore, I ask you to continue enjoying the rest of the night here without me. I hope you gentlemen will not take it as any form of insult."

The men did not say much and without hesitation they left the room, knowing full well that Salvador not only sent a message to the Costa Rican President but to the American President as well. Verdes and Arnold went into the room after the men were gone.

"They are CIA," Salvador said to Verdes and Arnold.

There was a degree of sincerity in what Salvador had said to the CIA. And even though they were very aware of who he was, they were also aware of the fact that Salvador had nothing to gain from Gordon and the others. They were outside of his needs and business interests but nevertheless, Salvador was dangerous. And they needed to keep an eye on him, Gordon and his friends.

"It seems they decided not to take on your invitation," Arnold said to Salvador while observing the CIA agents exiting the hotel on the screen of one of the security monitors.

"Yes," Salvador said. "They are making sure we know they are leaving, but it is almost certain they will still be watching us. They are tasked with the safety and security of the billionaire's boy group. There's no way they'd just leave them here under our protection." Verdes and Arnold looked at Salvador understanding that he knew exactly what he was talking about. But they were wondering what his plan was, not understanding what he wanted to achieve with the handling of Gordon and his friends.

Indeed, the CIA had left a security team near the property and an asset inside the casino. It was in their best interest to make sure Gordon and the others were ushered back to the presidential mansion safe and sound. Gordon needed to conclude the talks with the Costa Rican President in order to satisfy the would-be American treaty, which was his main agenda in the country. The CIA was given a specific timeline to follow, which Gordon and his friends were unexpectedly prolonging.

At the same time, within the lavish walls of the penthouse suite, Gordon was engaged in a sadistic celebration with the young women. Gordon was enjoying their openness and the fact they did not say no to anything he wanted to do to them. He even bit some of the girls on their lips while kissing them. He splashed them with alcohol, and they appeared to love every moment of it. As one bled from her nose and mouth, Gordon couldn't tell if it was his blood or theirs, nor did he care. Kemp and the others got very distracted and very curious by the loud noises and screaming coming from Gordon's room and decided to join in on the action.

"Hey, brute!" Kemp shouted out as he walked in on Gordon. Kemp was in a momentary state of shock and so were the others, as they walked in the room. It took them a couple of seconds to understand the scenario.

"We want in!" But they did not hesitate to join. Seeing the blood and mess got them even more excited. Kemp jumped into the action, bringing in the rest of the men with them.

The two women dressed in red slowly walked out of the penthouse and ordered the men guarding the front door to leave. The men did not ask any questions and immediately followed the order. At that moment, Verdes relayed that information to Salvador when he was preparing to leave the hotel in a different vehicle, through the underground parking garage. He needed to be on his way to take care of the final leg of his very busy night.

"The SUV is already at the pick-up spot you designated before, sir," Arnold informed Salvador. The car in which they were traveling exited the hotel as part of a small group of vehicles, which were occupied by inebriated gamblers and other guests. The CIA team monitoring the hotel movements was not aware of Salvador exiting in one of the vehicles and they remained stationed where they were.

Sometime later, it was already 4 a.m. and Gordon, Kemp and the others were secretly escorted out of the hotel in a similar fashion in which Salvador had made his exit. Salvador was just arriving at a popular area near the center of the city. It was another modernized urban area complete with up and coming businesses and restaurants. Raffa advised Salvador about a street cleaning vehicle driving by, about a block away from where they were. Salvador ordered him to pull up near a pharmacy ahead to the right side of the street.

∞

The streets were nearly desolate, with not much visible traffic, and not many people around at this hour, just as Salvador preferred when conducting his operations. The other SUV part of Salvador's security detail was ordered to wait two blocks away. Salvador calmly exited his vehicle and walked towards a door right next to the pharmacy, where he went three steps down. A skinny man wearing reading glasses opened the door for Salvador.

"Good morning sir, happy to see you." He said as he greeted Salvador.

"Morning Mirno," Salvador said to the man, as he walked into a very dark hallway. Another door was opened for him by Mirno's twin brother, Aaron, wearing similar reading glasses as Mirno.

"Aaron," Salvador said.

"Sir, it is very good to see you," Aaron said greeting his boss. Salvador walked a few more steps until arriving at a room with a very sophisticated setting, where several men sat around a table searching through papers and documents. Everyone saw Salvador and saluted him with respect while continuing with their duties. Salvador looked at them as he walked a few more steps further into the room, where there were others occupied on cellphone conversations, speaking in Mandarin and Eastern European languages.

"Simon," Salvador said while extending his right hand to firmly shake the hand of the man he had in charge of the operation being conducted there. Simon was a well-dressed man of low stature and a big sized head, with a very serious face which inspired respect, the type of men Salvador was eager to keep in the position Simon had. Everyone was obliged to answer to Simon to stay in good terms with the man Simon needed to answer to - Salvador.

"Sir, I am very glad to see you were able to take the time to stop by," Simon replied, before tersely briefing Salvador about the details of numerous international business deals.

"Tell me about Kelly," Salvador asked Simon.

"She is in great condition." Simon instantly replied. "And she was a perfect match!"

"Show me," Salvador asked. Simon seemed monetarily confused but did not hesitate to accompany Salvador towards a secret room filled with monitors with many different views. The screens were showing some of the operations being conducted by Salvador's personnel and were being remotely monitored by a group of men and women who specialized in the medical field.

"Everyone leave the room," Simon ordered all in the room to exit, all except for a woman in her sixties named Esperanza. Salvador looked at them one by one as they walked out of the room facing the floor. They were not allowed to look at Salvador or Simon in the face. Esperanza was seated in front of a monitor where she was now observing how a team of three Chinese nationals, two men and one woman were about to perform surgery on Kelly. Kelly was completely sedated, laying on an operating table and the Chinese woman was about to cut open her abdomen.

"Wait one moment," Salvador said

"Hold it," Esperanza said, speaking Mandarin over a microphone which was connected to the operating room. Esperanza then looked at Salvador waiting for his next order, as did Simon. Salvador stared into the monitor in silence as some of those in the operating room stared into the camera. Salvador had set his sight on Kelly's face and for a moment his mind took him back to a road in San Diego, a road near a place where he could see mountains in the distance.

"Go on," Salvador said, without taking his eyes away from the monitor.

"Proceed." Esperanza worded into the microphone, to which those in the operating room were quick to react and Kelly's stomach was slowly opened by the Chinese woman while the two men assisted.

"Mr. Woo will be more than satisfied with the organs sir," Simon said to Salvador. Salvador did not answer, his eyes were still locked onto the monitor, observing how the surgery was being conducted, staring at Kelly's organs being slowly taken out of her body. Her kidneys, her lungs, her liver, her heart. One by one her internal organs were deposited into special medical transport cases under the supervision of Salvador, Simon, and Esperanza looking through the monitors and a few others at the operating room.

"Also, the Chinese have ancient knowledge from their history that they are now in the process of perfecting. You wouldn't believe how long they can keep the organs and tissues alive and pumping even after being brought out from the donor's body..." Simon continued telling Salvador, but he was only half-listening. He was already plotting his next move.

Salvador called Arnold's cellphone while taking a few steps back.

"Make the call," Salvador ordered Arnold. "Inform him that they will be ready to play ball."

"I'm on it," Arnold replied. Salvador ended the call and was ready to call someone else but he paused for a moment to look at the monitor one more time. At that moment he decided not to make the next call, and after gazing over at Esperanza concluding with her duties and Simon getting ready to walk out of the room, Salvador stared at Kelly's lifeless body alone on top of the operating table. He could see a glimpse of her insides until someone walked by and covered the body with a green color sheet.

Salvador's satellite phone rang. He was not expecting any calls at that particular time and hesitated to answer.

"Yes, who is this?" Salvador ended up answering the call.

"Mr. Salvador?" A man speaking in English with an accent asked.

"It is," Salvador replied.

"This is Edward Chao. I understand you wanted to speak with me." This was unexpected for Salvador, but he had gotten used to taking advantage of moments like this.

"Mr. Chao, it is my pleasure to hear from you."

"I've heard many good things about you, Mr. Salvador. What can I do for you?"

"For me, a very small favor, Mr. Chao. For you, a very lucrative deal."

"Go on, Mr. Salvador, I'm listening." Mr. Chao sounded interested in the potential of a good deal.

Meanwhile, Gordon and his friends had arrived at the ambassador's mansion, and the handlers assigned by the President, assisted in all they could to bring each of them into their bedrooms.

"Mr. Gordon are you alright? There's blood on your shirt. What happened, sir? We need to get you a doctor right away." Javier began fussing over Gordon. He was one of the local men hired by the CIA, upon the recommendation by the Costa Rican government in assisting Gordon with his needs. He had seen splatters of blood all over Gordon's shirt and pants and was about to get in contact with his superior. Gordon held his hand tightly, to prevent him from reaching the house phone.

"It's not my blood, Javier," Gordon said. Javier and Lucas, the other assistant with him, looked at each other with a preoccupation on their faces, but Gordon reassured him that nothing had happened to him, nor any of his friends. He insisted for them not to say a word about the blood to anyone. Javier and Lucas agreed with Gordon, and after putting the hush money he placed inside their pockets, they left him alone in his room. Three of the others assisting the rest of the guests, met up with Javier and his partner while walking down the stairs. One of them mentioned blood over someone's shirt but Javier was quick to tell everyone not to say anything. He noticed they had also been given hush money.

Although Javier made sure that the rest of the men understood they were paid to keep quiet about the blood situation, he quickly contacted one of the CIA handlers named Tony, to inform him about what he saw.

Javier told Tony that Gordon or maybe one of his associates may have done something really bad at the casino. Tony had an idea of what might have taken place and he ordered Javier not to mention the matter to anyone and to call only him if anything else develops. Tony was very direct in his orders and assured Javier that he and his partners would be paid very well and in dollars.

Tony had to pass the information along to the American consul Keith Premolars, who was also part of the operation being conducted.

"Do you have a handle on this?" Premolars asked Tony.

"Yes sir, I will put my asset on it to make sure he gets any trail left behind, cleaned up," Tony replied.

Premolars wasted no time in contacting the Costa Rican President, but he was sleeping at the Presidential vacation property and did not pick up his cellphone. Rachel Williams was next to him in the bed and she took the call. She spoke to Tony for a short time and gave them directions on what needed to be done.

"Who are you talking to Rachel?" Romalyn asked her. She replied that it was not for him.

"Good," Romalyn replied. "I was worried she may have tried to come back from her mother's house early."

"Don't worry." Rachel said. "She will not be back until tomorrow afternoon. I have someone watching her. Go back to sleep and rest. Tomorrow you have many deals to sign on."

"Good," Romalyn mumbled while resting his head back on his pillow. After watching him for a short time, Rachel then went on to make a call with her personal cellphone as she quietly walked into the bathroom. She glimpsed over at Romalyn, while quietly closing the bathroom door. He was snoring, and she did not want to be interrupted by the sound.

The phone rang twice and a man in a tuxedo traveling inside a limousine answered the call. It was Conan Sunderland, a man with a long trail of dirty deeds and suspicious international operations. Sunderland was in his late fifties, who styled his blonde hair into a neat mullet. He was the type of man the CIA contacted when they needed a clean bill of health for the maintenance of their op's.

"You are up early..." Sunderland said while answering the phone.

"And you are partying hard, I presume..." Rachel responded. "Are you inside your limo, barbarian child?" She teased Sunderland.

"One of us has to make the sacrifices my dear," Sunderland replied. He was accompanied by two other men in tuxedos, who were quietly listening to the conversation.

"Your sacrifices and the lengths you go, on behalf of your patriotism never surprises me, Conan." She added. Sunderland could not prevent others from listening to her sarcasm. One of them handed him a glass of champagne, as he continued his conversation with Rachel.

"Is this for something important, Rachel?" Sunderland asked. "I am on something important right now."

"I am not calling you at this time in the morning if I didn't have anything important to tell you." Rachel quickly replied, sensing Sunderland was probably in a hurry to get her off the phone. "Put the glass of champagne down, I don't want for you to miss the information I am giving you. Advise your friend in the Oval Office, that the bankers are a go, but there may be a slight hiccup which their handlers need to remain on top of. Salvador got to them and took them out of the guarding grounds of the ambassador's mansion. As of now, it does not appear anything was compromised. Nevertheless, we won't know until everything has been completed."

"Why wasn't I informed of this earlier?" Sunderland sounded agitated while putting the glass down in the cupholder. Rachel knew he was probably getting nervous about what she just told him. "Did you hear from Parker?" Sunderland asked.

"I haven't spoken to him yet but one of his men communicated to me what I just told you. I figured Parker must still be out there putting some links together and cutting loose others, just in case." Rachel was not finished with her words when Sunderland suddenly ended the call.

"Bitch," Rachel grumbled. She then sat on the toilet while lighting up a cigarette and a not too distant memory came back to her. She was at a black-tie fundraiser event and the president of the United States was in attendance. She was having a conversation with Sunderland as the president walked in their direction accompanied by three of his favorite Senators: Siegel, McNamara, and Pierce.

Rachel hated Siegel, his dirty jokes and how he liked to touch women inappropriately. She attempted to avoid one of his surprise attacks, by ending the conversation she was having with Sunderland speedily. Sunderland had just informed her about the trip she was about to take to Costa Rica and her mission to make sure the new Costa Rican President complied with everything which was about to be asked of him.

Sunderland explained to her that Salvador had the Costa Rican President in his hand, Gordon and his crew were part of the plan to loosen Salvador's grip on the country and the politicians they needed to be on board with. She then remembered listening to President Smith telling her in his own words, "He will tell you that he wants to help us but whatever needs to be done against Salvador, needs to be done with extreme finesse or Salvador could ruin everything for everyone. The son of a bitch shits in his pants by the mere mentioning of Salvador being nearby. Handle Romalyn with care, understood?"

"Where are you?" Rachel's thoughts ran back to where she was, as she heard Romalyn's voice calling her from the bed.

"I'm taking a shit. Be there soon." She said, her eyes gazing forward as she placed the cigarette back between her lips.

Chapter IX:

Misguidance

Later that day, it was three o'clock in the afternoon. Ramon was driving his truck to make a delivery at a warehouse, located an hour away east of the capital. Luis was tagging along for the day and Ramon appreciated the company. Luis was doing all the talking for the first leg of the trip. He had been entrusting Ramon with his inner deepest secrets, which included a tell-all story about Carmen, the love of his life. Luis wanted some advice from Ramon. Ramon did not want to be rude to him, but he really did not want to hear about it.

"Luis…" Ramon said. "I truly would like to be able to give you the right answers, for you to have a successful outcome to this situation with Carmen, but to be honest, my relationships have been few and I have nothing good to say or show for them."

"But at least you had a few of them." Luis countered. "Carmen has been my only real relationship, but she is more mature than me and there have been a few times in which I have felt embarrassed around her, by my stupid actions."

"It has happened to me too, don't worry." Ramon cut him off. "If you ask me, I believe that most women are more mature than us, but we don't want to tell them because we are afraid that they will use this to gain what they want from us."

"I never felt that way." Luis continued. "When I made mistakes or was insecure about anything and Carmen had the answers, I always gave her the credit for solving the case. Come to think of it, maybe this is the reason why we keep having problems. Maybe it went to her head that she is better than me or something."

"No Luis, that is not the case man," Ramon said. "Women go through rough times sometimes and when they are like that, it is best to let them be by themselves. Only they understand how and when whatever they are feeling is going to be fixed."

"How do you know when to reach back to them?" Luis then asked.

"No one knows Luis." Ramon gave an automatic reply. "Sometimes it may be a family thing, or they want to be more with their friends, or they don't feel cute. It could be anything, man. This is why I just told you, you have to let them be. Whenever they are back to normal, they will reach out to you."

"I think you are right." Luis thought for a moment. "You know what, she had mentioned something about us visiting with a family member and I didn't want to take the trip with her, I had a bad food experience the last time I went to their house. I think this was the cause of the problem, to begin with. This woman is very strict when it comes to her family matters. Shit, you see Ramon!" Luis patted Ramon over his right shoulder. "You see! You were able to give me advice man, and you didn't even try. I always told you that you're a natural. Remember, even your mother used to tell you that."

Luis quickly remembered that Ramon was still sensitive about his mother's death, he attempted to get a hasty switch on the subject, but it was too late. Ramon became quiet and began reminiscing about some of the thoughts he had been harboring for months.

"Sorry, Ramon." Upon seeing the sudden change on his face, Luis attempted to move the conversation to where it was before. Ramon asked him to take the wheel and drive for the next few miles so that he could take a nap. Ramon pulled up to the curb and switched places with Luis. Luis knew Ramon was still struggling after the sudden death of his mother, which happened only six months after the death of his only sister. Although Ramon did not say much about his feelings, the few people who kept regular contact with him knew he was affected very negatively by the loss of his family.

Luis looked at Ramon as he slept and could not help wondering that this was the reason why Ramon regularly frequented Barbara's house. Barbara was the local witch and she had a good reputation when it came to Santeria and supernatural things. Ramon wanted to find closure and understanding about the bad card his family had been dealt. Barbara has been the catalyst helping him make sense of his reality, by guiding him spiritually.

"Maybe I should go to see Barbara more often," Luis said to himself out loud.

"What did you say?" Ramon asked him, with his eyes closed. Luis quickly told him that he had said nothing, that he was just murmuring out loud. Ramon accepted his response while adjusting his body to continue with his nap.

"She has been able to bring me some peace," Ramon told Luis, speaking in a very quiet tone of voice while his eyes were still closed. "Whenever I want to feel my mother or my sister's presence or maybe get a message from them, Barbara helps me. I am very afraid of death Luis. I'm petrified of the thought of dying without doing something better or something bigger than what I have been doing with my life.

"When I was little, my father used to scare me by telling me ghost stories so that I would behave. Neither he, nor I knew it at the time, but it messed with my head. I also go to Barbara because she gives me things to protect myself from death, to safeguard my life from bad accidents or whatever. You know, stuff."

"Why are you so afraid of dying?" Luis suddenly asked. "From the moment we were born, this is the one thing that will certainly happen to us. We all have our date predestined, Ramon. If you come to terms with this truth, you will not be afraid to live in the now. You will live a happier life."

"Luis?" Ramon said. "Can you stop?" Luis laughed and continued driving while talking all the way towards their destination.

∞

A few hours later, Jeff was set to meet with his connection in the country. A longer time than what he was expecting had gone by. And he had begun to lose hope at some point that the meeting with the wanted drug lord would even happen. They had been waiting for weeks before finally hearing from Jeff's contact and things had been move. He and Clarence were near a popular street, a couple of miles away from their hotel. Jeff was very intrigued at the thought of going horseback riding after seeing a group of men riding their horses in the middle of the street, along the side of cars and trucks. They stopped for toasted butter sandwiches and hot chocolate from one of the local street vendors. A guy nicknamed Mickey Mouse, a nickname given thanks to his big ears and bulbous nose, walked fast and approached Jeff from behind.

"Give me your wallet gringo!" Mickey Mouse barked. Jeff quickly put his hands up into the air in surrender, while Clarence attempted to move on the unknown person.

"Shit man, don't you know I don't have a good heart to deal with shit like this?" Jeff said, while extending his hand towards Clarence to let him know that this was the person they had been waiting for.

"You not in Kansas anymore Jeff!" Mickey Mouse replied. "When you find yourself anywhere outside that big oasis you call home, you need to grow eyes in the back of your head and outside your ears because anyone can be a threat. You got this?"

"Yes, I got it," Jeff said.

At first, Mickey Mouse had some reservations about bringing Clarence with them and told Jeff about his boss's lack of enthusiasm for seeing too many new faces in a short period of time. But Jeff was able to convince him of the contrary, by explaining Clarence was his photographer, and that he was needed to document with quality pictures and sound the information his boss would be sending to the eyes and ears of the American public. Jeff explained that if he was able to produce an American quality interview, in the way he was envisioning it, his boss would hold Mickey Mouse in higher regard.

Mickey Mouse had time to think about it while eating a sandwich, which he was dipping into Jeff's hot chocolate. A short time after, they walked into a car Mickey Mouse had parked around the corner, where a quick conversation followed, via two-way radio. Mickey Mouse was told to bring them both. Clarence and Jeff were relieved. Moments later, they were being driven by five men in two Jeeps, into one of the deepest areas of the jungle. Their faces were covered by black sacks, preventing them from seeing the roads or anywhere they were traveling by.

"Hey! Gringos!" The driver said, speaking to Douglas and Jeff in broken English. "You need to consider yourselves very lucky that El Pesado (The Heavy One) is allowing you guys to do this interview with him. He normalmente doesn't like publicity but lately, he's feeling old and he's talking about his legacy and how people are going to see him or talk about him when he's dead. Mierda! Here you are, like sent by destino to give him the perfect shit to show himself to the world in the future. This shit is going to be funny. But don't tell him I said that, or I kill you both, okay?"

As Clarence and Jeff heard the driver, Jeff could not help to think that he sounded a bit disrespectful in the way he spoke about his boss and this aspect of the adventure was making him nervous but at the same time more curious about getting to know the true world in which the powerful, feared and wanted drug lord, governed.

Jeff knew the man behind one of the most powerful drugs and human trafficking organizations in the world must have some serious demons and issues surrounding him. He wanted to dig deeper into those issues and find out what exactly made him who he was.

"Here we are." The driver announced. Someone removed the sacks off Jeff and Clarence's heads. Jeff could see the lush and dense vegetation surrounding them. They had driven for a long time and now they were very high up, looking down at the tropical rain forest that seemed to go on forever. Several different types of birds could be heard echoing all around them. White-faced Capuchin monkeys swung from tree to tree over their heads. Clarence's patience was being put to the test. Helena was not the only thing occupying his mind anymore. Getting back to her in one piece was part of it as well.

As they got off the military model Jeep Wrangler, they could see armed men all over the place. Jeff was not surprised to see that El Pesado chose his compound to be near a waterfall which made it look more like a summer camp than the well-protected hideaway of a dangerous criminal organization. The men seemed relaxed as they were smoking and drinking outside the main compound. They even had beautiful women with them, to further amplify the ambiance.

"¿Esos, son ellos? Are those the reporters?" Asked El Pesado, whose real name was Manuel Guillermo Montero. He was a heavy-set man in his early fifties wearing designer sandals, shorts, and a white polo t-shirt and sat next to his most trusted advisor, a man named Garido. They were by a small fire pit, where a man was cooking goat on top of a makeshift grill. Montero was enjoying a fruit salad, with some of his heavily armed bodyguards sitting nearby, keeping steady eyes over the two strangers who clearly did not belong there.

Clarence and Jeff were ushered to where Montero sat. "Come closer. Sit here by me, gentlemen." Montero beckoned.

Someone crying not too far away caught their attention. Clarence and Jeff looked over to see what was causing such a commotion. Clarence immediately became petrified. Jeff was nauseated by the sight. Bodies had been chopped up into pieces and lay in a pile not far away. The man crying out in pain and begging for mercy had his arms tied around to a tree. Two men with machetes began hacking away at his body.

Jeff couldn't hold back any longer, he walked away to vomit near a tree. He felt like he was about to pass out. The sound of laughter jolted him back to where he was. He saw the man was hanging on to the tree by one of his arms, as the other had been completely severed from his body. One of the machete wielders was laughing as he picked up the arm and began hitting the crying man over the head with it.

"Please, just finish it." The man begged. Clarence could not stop watching the cruelty taking place in front of his eyes. He had never felt so helpless before. Montero stared at them, eating his salad as if this was part of his daily routine. The most sadistic torturer was a wiry, strong-looking young man with short hair. As he turned around to laugh and taunt his victim, Clarence saw he had a scar on the back of his neck. The torturer did not like the way Clarence was staring at him.

"Turn your damn face away, if you don't wanna be next." He ordered Clarence.

He turned around to continue slashing the man tied to the tree. The man cried and began praying. Clarence turned away but the look of deep hatred in the eyes of the torturer still resonated in his mind. It was the likes of which he had never seen before.

"Slow down Jason, you gonna kill him too fast. He's not going to suffer enough." One of the men said laughing. Clarence at that moment noticed that Jason was looking at him again. Jason's and Clarence's eyes kept contact momentarily.

Neither man knew at that moment, the hand that destiny would play them.

"Don't pay attention to that. Come and sit next to me." Montero instructed Clarence and Jeff, speaking to them in perfectly good English. "Come and ask me questions, come closer, come," Montero said to them. Jeff was the first to sit down on a wooden chair, right across from Montero. The man with a rifle, over his arms, hinted to Clarence to sit on a chair behind Jeff's.

Jeff shook hands with Montero very respectfully and told him how thankful he was for the opportunity he was given. Clarence sat right behind Jeff and asked Montero if he could take some pictures while pointing the camera towards the man who was being killed.

"I hope I don't have to remind you that you are here to take pictures of me and me only. The only other time that you are allowed to take pictures of anything else, is when I specifically tell you. No one likes a snitch. That is why that man is getting what he deserves." Montero spoke to him in a very serious tone of voice. One of Montero's men then walked up to Clarence and pointed a gun to his face.

"Erase that last picture you took."

Clarence did what he was told to do, and he showed the man how he did it. Satisfied, the man walked back to where he was standing before and began looking at Jeff.

"Okay, so let's proceed. Mickey tells me that you are a journalist for a very important news channel in America." Montero asked Jeff.

"Yes sir, that is my job." Jeff quickly replied. "I work for ABN news, the uh, American Broadcasting Network News."

"Oh, I know it!" Montero added. "Mr. Carl Thomas, the famous news anchor, I know, I used to watch the six o'clock news every day while I was in California. Just because I knew *everything* he said in the news, was the truth. That man is a very serious man. If he was a businessman, he would be the type of man I would do business with. You can tell in the expression of his face, the truthful sound of his voice, even the gestures of his body as he speaks." Montero said while showing some gestures of his own, imitating the mannerism of the news anchorman.

"Oh yes, all those things are true about Mr. Thomas. I'm sure he would love to meet you someday. A man of your stature, sure, yes, he would love to meet someone like you." Jeff did his best to say things Montero would probably like to hear. Montero was very flattered.

"Maybe you can arrange an interview with me and him next time, yeah?"

"Oh yes, the moment I get back to the States, I'll call up the station and see what his schedule is like," Jeff assured him. "If only we knew how you felt, you see my brother is actually one of the producers of the 6 o'clock news show. I'm sure we can arrange for something."

Hearing about a possible interview conducted by the famous Mr. Thomas was music to Montero's ears. That short conversation was exactly what Jeff needed to break the ice, make some sort of connection and have a successful interview. It also ensures his and Clarence's chances to get home alive.

"Very well then," Montero said while adjusting himself in his seat. "You may begin my interview now. What do you want to know? Ask me anything." Jeff wasted no time, pulled out his notepad and asked Montero if he would permit him to record the conversation. Montero acquiesced their request. Jeff then pulled out a small recording device from one of the pockets inside his jacket and placed it on a table near Montero.

Montero took the device and told Jeff that he was going to hold it so that his voice could be heard well. Clarence took several pictures of the crime boss, as three of his men posed by his side holding out their guns. Jeff began asking him questions.

"To what do you attribute the sudden emphasis of the United States government in capturing you, sir?" Jeff began.

Montero smiled and looked around at his men as if not sure about in which way to respond. "Oh, don't get me wrong." Jeff quickly added. "The alleged causes are there of course. You have been charged with drug trafficking, murderers, extortion and many other alleged crimes against the State. Those we are aware of sir. But there are many other wanted persons with similar crime stories, and they are not as popular as you are, nor achieved such fame as you have." Jeff was holding the pen right on top of the page and waited for the answer to the question.

Meanwhile, Montero stared at him for a moment. "Your problems..." Montero began. "No. The problem is that you Americans think that your bad habits are not problems at all. They are nothing but a good marketing strategy crafted by the very same people you elected to lead the country. You see, while the American population has become increasingly addicted to the drugs we have been providing, the benefits of that addiction is being utilized by your own government. This is to cover the deficit they created." Montero took a moment to ask one of his men to bring him a drink and Jeff asked him to be more specific about what he was saying and about the insinuations he proposed.

"It is very simple." Montero continued, while Jeff nodded his head, giving him a physical cue to continue.

"Your government has been involved in a game of dirty international gambling and it has not been going well for them. In fact, they've lost plenty. Two years ago, your newly elected president was lured, by the heads of several powerful corporations, into getting a group of top-secret CIA operatives to take part in a very wicked project, which was to yield billions of dollars for the benefit of those who got in at the right time.

"Part of this secret project consisted of the sale of weapons of war to a list of various South American countries in order for those countries to defend their borders and political capital from hostile attacks. The problem was that the countries cited in the list were not at the moment involved in any serious political conflict and that was where the pivotal part of the CIA came about."

Jeff looked very excited about the entire story Montero was telling him about the government and besides recording it he also wrote everything out in detail.

"You see, it was they who created the necessary situations and climate, which resulted in the development of various conflicts, assassinations, international turmoil, and thereafter, the development of a couple of undesired armed conflicts."

"For the record, are you trying to say that the guerilla conflicts affecting this part of South America have been caused by the United States Government?" Jeff asked, leaning closer to the recorder.

"Not only the conflicts! They also are the ones responsible for the so-called drug epidemic which you are enjoying at the moment. Your president had the CIA contact me and request my assistance into bringing as much drugs as I could into your country. Of course, they charged me some taxes, but the business was very fruitful for both of us while it lasted. My money was supposed to be secure, but I was robbed.

"Now that the deal is off, your country has made me public enemy number one so that they could keep what they took from me and increase your taxes to fight this so-called *drug epidemic at home* and use your tax payer's money to cover some of their losses, get payouts and at the same time, look good in front of the international community." Montero paused to take a few sips of his drink.

"Sir, if the deal you had with the American government was so lucrative for both parties, why did it end?" Jeff asked him.

Montero laughed and took another sip of his drink. "Luis, pasame un tabaco." Montero ordered one of his men to bring him a marijuana joint. It was already rolled for him and Luis lit it up before handing it to Montero.

"It turned out that your government and those corporate executives were outsmarted by a smarter player, a player who didn't make noise and took all the loot and quickly ran from the burning house."

"Who?" Jeff asked.

"The Russians of course," Montero replied. "They saw the opportunity where your government created chaos. For years they have been trying to bring their shit to this part of the world, do you know why? They have stockpiles of weapons and ammunition that they are not really using. They have been waiting for the right time to get back at you Americans for what you did in Afghanistan. You went in there uninvited, getting into other peoples' business, as usual.

"You basically drank the booze and slept with the other man's wife and then ran away. You understand? No one likes to get fucked over when they're not looking. The Russians are no exception. You Americans like fucking with everybody and don't clean up your mess after you are done. That's why the world is getting the way it's getting. You are actually teaching everyone your dirty tricks and see what's happening now? We are all using them against you, but you don't like it when those tricks are used on you.

"Your government went in and ruined the Russians' plans. The Russians took it on the chin, but they were not going to just take it sitting down. This was the perfect opportunity to get revenge and they got it. Now, the deal your government made with me is finished because they don't want to pay me what they owe me. They stole a couple of billion dollars from me and to prevent me from getting my money back, they are trying to kill me and that is why they declared war against me. By doing this, they kill two birds with one shot. They keep my money, they keep some of the taxpayer's money and while at it, they cover their asses with the weapons blunder. And I am also sure they will figure something out to get back at the Russians at some point."

Jeff was speechless. What Montero was revealing to him was almost unbelievable but at the same time, if it was all true, it would make perfect sense. Montero asked him to take a look at the recording device to make sure it was recording everything he said. Jeff took it from his hands and assured him that it had recorded every single word he had said till that moment.

"Good," Montero mumbled, just before he took the device again and while keeping it close to his face, he continued to reveal even more details to Jeff for another hour.

"And I will tell you this last thing, Mr. Jeffery," Montero added, before concluding the interview. "When your government gets in trouble again, they will do it again. And those secret monetary back channels controlled by the four banks I told you about, will come running to put money on the table to help create a conflict in whatever part of the world they have the opportunity to create. The more bullets are used, the more money everyone will make."

Montero was finally done with what he needed to get off his chest. He handed Jeff a heavy stack of papers tied together, along with a large stack of cash."

"I will not give you the originals but don't worry. This is enough to back up much of what I told you, and remember what I said before, keep it in your head. If there is nothing out there for the people I told you about to benefit from, they will find a place to create a conflict."

Montero also told Jeff and Clarence not to leave the country yet, until they were advised to do so. Jeff was not told the reason why, but Montero only told him enough for him to understand that it would not take too long for Mickey to give him the green light to go back to the U.S.

Clarence could not wait to be put on the jeep and looked forward to being blindfolded so that he could leave that place, never to come back again. As he and Jeff were being ushered towards the jeep, another vehicle was approaching. Jeff was exchanging last-minute notes with Montero, who did not see the need to give him additional supporting evidence to back up his story. Montero assumed Jeff already had enough to go on.

Clarence was already on the jeep but did not dare to call out to his friend to hurry up. He instead asked one of the guys who walked with him to put the sack on his head. The guy had a smile on his face and told Clarence that he knew he could not wait to leave. Clarence just smiled nervously as they guy put the black sack over his head. The other vehicle arrived and parked right next to the jeep. Clarence could not see anything but felt relieved to hear Jeff's voice approaching. Suddenly he heard Jason's voice near him. His heart began to beat faster. *What the hell does this guy want now?* Clarence thought to himself.

"Come over here bitch." Clarence heard Jason hollering at someone. "You kept me waiting for too long and I am going to give it to you just the way you don't like. You're not gonna be able to walk tomorrow." He told a woman who was dismounting from the jeep that had arrived.

"No baby, please don't do it too hard today." She said to Jason in a very sexy and enticing tone of voice. Clarence could not believe what he heard. His head tilted to the right as he focused on the voices.

"Come, let's go. I got a few things I've been thinking of doing to you. You know how I love seeing you in those short shorts, you slut." Jason told the woman while giving her rear end a hard slap. At that moment, Clarence pulled the sack off his head and saw that Jeff was sitting next to him.

"What are you doing?" Jeff asked him flustered. Clarence turned his head towards the other side and there he saw Helena kissing Jason passionately; in the same way she was kissing him the day before.

Helena was moving her face away from Jason's, but she still had his bottom lip in between her lips. She moved her eyes past Jason, to look at the men being blindfolded where she saw Clarence staring right at her in disbelief.

Helena's eyes opened wide; she was completely shocked. But she pretended she did not even see him and pulled Jason by the hand so that they could go to Jason's place within the compound. She walked away with him as Clarence watched the woman he was in love with, walking away with a man he thought of as a despicable sadistic lowlife, knowing fully well what she was about to do with him.

"Hey asshole! Get that damn sack back on your head." One of the men screamed at Clarence. Jeff already had his covering his head.

"What are you looking at?" The same man asked. "I hope you're not looking at Jason's girlfriend. Yeah, she looks good." He continued saying while walking closer to Clarence. "Listen, Gringo, if you value your life, don't ever look at that woman again. Not even if you pass by her in the street. Now put that shit back on your head."

"Is there something wrong?" Jeff asked Clarence as Clarence continued to stare at Helena as she walked away with Jason. He watched her with great pain. The sack over his head was pulled down abruptly, covering his eyes.

As they were being driven away, Montero's men started casually talking about the men who were being killed earlier. Clarence could not stop thinking about Helena, while Jeff paid close attention to the conversation taking place in the vehicle. The jeep stopped abruptly, and Clarence could hear the sound of sheep and men herding them along.

One of Montero's men made a comment about the sheep headers. Jeff then heard the men with the sheep talking to Montero's men, immediately noticing their Eastern European accents. He then heard the men saying that the sheep belongs to the new Gypsies who arrived in town. They began complaining and saying how uncomfortable they felt with them around. However, they were not to be touched because Montero said they were under his brother's protection.

This captured Clarence's attention as well. He heard one of the men telling a story about someone he knew.

"This guy was approached by a little Gypsy boy and the little boy brought the guy up to an old woman. She told him she could tell his fortune and help him if it was a bad one. The guy said that the lady told him about a problem he was having with two other guys near the shipyard. The old lady told him that the problem was because one of the guys dated the woman he was with and he found out that the woman broke up with the port guy, to be with him."

The other men began laughing at the story. "Man, your story is full of shit!"

"No, it's really true! Listen to this... The Gypsy lady had given him three numbers to play at the local lottery. I played the *same* numbers with him and guess what? We won! And then we went out gambling on the same night!"

"Damn, I want to meet that lady too," Jeff commented, while his friend went back to think about Helena. He became conflicted with the question of what to do about his feelings for her, knowing what he now knows.

∞

In the meantime, Montero was given another satellite phone to make a call. He let the phone ring three times and he then hung up and waited ten seconds to call again. This time the person he was calling picked up the line immediately.

"I completed the interview," Montero told the person on the other line. "I will make some other moves to get the journalist out of the country very soon so that he can push forth what I told him over the American media. That will give us the leverage we need to get a grip on President Smith.

"If he decides that giving us our money back will be better for him than have me giving more interviews, then we win. And if he keeps attempting to come after us, we win as well because now we have a means of putting our voices out there and they will be put under the scrutiny of their own people. Even if half the public doesn't believe what I said in the interview, the president's every move would be looked under a magnifying glass by journalists and the media, while we continue to make ours in the dark."

Montero then listened to what the person on the other line had to say and he agreed to everything he heard. At that moment, Montero watched one of his men walk closer to him to inform him that his transport was ready.

"My ride is here, I'm gonna call you when I get to Mexico," Montero said. "I don't know how long it's going to take to get there this time because of all the military exercises the Americans are conducting in the region. My driver told me that we are going to have to make some extra stops to prevent the vehicle from being picked up by radar. So, I've decided to stop by Colombia to go and oversee personally how Hector is doing with our last transaction. Good luck to you."

"Good luck to you too, dear brother," Salvador told Montero before hanging up. He took several steps towards the window of his home office and calmly stared outside. He watched the many people working for him- the gardeners arranging new flowers, his heavily armed security personnel walking around and above his property and several women carrying clean sheets and laundry towards a back house near the kitchen entrance. He then lifted the satellite phone and dialed a number, the phone rang once and an American person, picked up the other line, speaking English.

"Yes, do you have any news for me?" The American asked Salvador.

"You have a green light to take him out," Salvador told the American.

"Very good, we appreciate the gesture, Mr. Salvador." The American answered back smiling. "Rest assured, knowing that you have finally decided to be a fully integrated part of our close circle of beneficiaries in the region, I believe your decision to take this step will certainly be well received by my boss. I am very sure now that we will be able to help you with anything we can, whenever you require our services."

"I don't need your help," Salvador said dismissively. "But make sure you tell your boss, the future President, when he is placed in power as the present one is expelled, that one of these days I will come to get my money back." Salvador then hung up the phone and continued staring outside the window in silence.

∞

On the same day, it was 4 o'clock in the afternoon. Gordon, Kemp and the others were driven, under very tight security, to meet with a group of the most important financial operators in the country, at the well-guarded conference room of the central bank of Costa Rica. This was the one place in the country, Salvador had not been able to smear his hands all over.

President Romalyn had arrived secretly fifteen minutes earlier. He was the most important link within the deal about to be made and even the president of the U.S. was set to be in the room via telephone. Rachel Williams was also present. She had arrived with Mr. Javier Mendoza, the president of the central bank and the chief economic adviser to President Romalyn. Mendoza's ties to the U.S. went back years, something that started during his education at Yale University where he was first contacted by CIA operatives. He had been protected by them ever since, and therefore, out of the reach of Salvador's hands.

Everyone had been seated around the conference table and just as expected, the U.S. president was on the conference phone line. The documents were put in place and all the arrangements the U.S. government wanted were handled accordingly. President Romalyn was very pleased by the potential the continued flow of foreign investments into the country was about to create. Mendoza was able to put it all together in record time supposedly for the benefit of everyone, but in reality, it was mostly for his and Romalyn's personal gains. The President of Costa Rica saw Mendoza as more than his right-hand man. He saw him as the brother he never had. Rachel Williams and the rest of the CIA operatives liked it just that way.

Mendoza was a very loyal asset and he always knew that with the U.S. government protecting him, he was untouchable. At times, he felt almost more important than Romalyn himself. Gordon and his associates took care of everything that needed to get done regarding the international monetary parts of the deal, which involved top secret transactions between several banks in Switzerland.

Kemp and Brenan had tight relationships with the CEOs of various banking conglomerates in Dubai and the Emirates. These also added to the equation of the billions of dollars in deal-making that they had just completed, in record-breaking time. With the assistance of the United States government, as well as the support of the CIA operatives, the completion of this deal worth billions of dollars was established and put in motion in a matter of minutes. This will mean more high-end development, more investment into the country's infrastructure, more money for social services and entertainment as well as tourism, which will settle the final stage of terminating Salvador's stronghold on many important players within the country. The politicians within the social and political backbone of the country had been too afraid to confront Salvador in the past. This will completely change everything for him and what he knows as his way of life.

Those connected with the U.S government, have been wanting for years to achieve certain goals and make the moves that needed to be made, to make possible for the new beginning which till now, seemed impossible. The U.S President gave Romalyn a personal number where he could keep in touch, something which pleased Mendoza and everyone else. Rachel quickly and discreetly recommended for Gordon and his friends to leave the country at once.

"We have achieved something which has taken years of planning to pull it off the way we did." She explained to Gordon. "We completed it in a matter of minutes Mr. Gordon. I can understand that you may still have a certain level of interest for the exploration of the curiosities of this country, believe me, I do. But time is of the essence and it will be more prudent if you and your associates depart from this country as triumphant heroes and not as thrill-seeking tourists."

Gordon laughed out loud at the comment and so did Kemp, who was standing right behind Rachel. Rachel had already said what she needed to say. She turned around and winked at Kemp while walking towards Romalyn. Parker was allowed in the room at Rachel's request. Rachel saw him while turning her face, as she passed by him.

"Your luggage and all of your belongings are already in the waiting vehicle, Mr. Gordon," Parker said. Gordon was very comfortable with Parker, he had learned to trust him, and he understood that Parker was a man guided by a strong set of rules and boundaries. This is something which had helped him deal successfully with a variety of dangerous conflicts and situations, all around the world.

"Lead the way." Gordon said to Parker, just after patting him over the right shoulder." Parker looked at Kemp and Brenan, who were also ready to walk out, and after discreetly gazing at Margaret, he walked ahead of the billionaire's boys pack.

∞

At the same time, half a world away, a truck was reversing into a cargo pick-up ramp. After properly placing the truck container into the pickup gate, three heavily armed men went around the back and a fourth man opened the container door. Niema exited from the container accompanied by Vitaly and three others, Alexis, Dimitry, and Vladimir, who the armed men seemed very happy to see.

"What time?" Niema asked Alexis, one of the men who greeted him.

"Tonight at 1 a.m.," Alexis replied.

"Vitaly, move ahead with two of your men and scout the area until my arrival," Niema ordered. Vitaly wasted no time and took two of his men, to be at the appointed place, before Niema's arrival.

"The rest of you meet in an hour at the next location." Niema gave the last order for the moment but Alexis was worried about leaving him alone. Niema reiterated to him that this was the way he was going to conduct today's operation.

"Just do what I told you, Alexis," Niema told him. "I value your loyalty and your regard for my safety. You should value my way of doing things as well."

"I never doubt your strategies boss," Alexis replied. "It's just that..."

"Go on Alexis, everything will be okay." Niema interrupted. The others placed their attention on him and as Alexis walked away, they quickly followed behind.

Hours later, at 1 a.m., Niema found himself walking alone towards the location of the meeting. The place was a very popular underground club, where American and European gangster rap was blasting through speakers. 32-year-old Niema dressed as a young club-goer wearing a hoody over his head and his dark color pants tucked inside his boots, looking very inconspicuous as he made the line to get inside.

Vitaly was already inside with Dimitry and Vladimir, they were dressed for the occasion and gave an impression of modern individuals enjoying themselves. Vitaly was by himself at a corner of the bar while Dimitry and Vladimir were chatting up a couple of women not far from him. Niema walked by them and looked at Vladimir. Vitaly spotted him right away and quickly moved in his direction. Niema walked towards the bar and asked for a drink.

"White Russian." He told the bartender, a very sexy looking 28-year-old Asian American woman named Fei. She was facing the bar preparing someone else a drink. As she turned around, she seemed to ignore Niema. Vitaly was about to approach him but Niema discreetly waved his hand for him not to. Dimitry and Vladimir stood by the other side of the bar and watched Fei prepare the drink that Niema ordered.

She wrapped a napkin around the glass and placed it in front of him. Niema reached for the drink while placing a hundred dollar note over the counter as his hand slightly touched Fei's. She ignored it and turned her back towards him again.

Taking a short breath, she began setting up three glasses to begin preparing more drinks. Niema took the drink and walked away from the bar while giving Vitaly a quick signal with the index finger of his left hand. Dimitry and Vladimir got the signal as well. Niema had seen the napkin; Fei had written the word "Clear" on it.

Outside the club, Alexis was waiting at the driver's side of a sedan with bulletproof glass windows. There were three others with him that seemed nervous for the occasion.

Niema finished his drink in one gulp and calmly walked towards the restroom. It was small, with only two toilet stalls and two urinals, which were all occupied at the moment. Niema waited for the toilet to the right of the door to be accessible and he went in as soon a man came out. Vitaly and the others remained outside acting casual, Niema waited two minutes until the restroom was empty. Meanwhile, Vitaly and the others did not allow anyone else to enter.

"My friend is handling a female business in there," Vitaly said to two young guys who were about to walk into the restroom. The guys laughed and walked away. Niema then pressure pushed the toilet against the wall with his right foot. The toilet gave way to a doorway. He walked ten steps ahead until four well-dressed men met him.

"You only have three minutes." One of the men told him.

"I only need two," Niema replied while walking through the men and into the room they were guarding. As he walked in, there was an older looking heavy-set man, with white hair and a white beard, seated on a sofa at the end of the room, which was decorated in a 16th-century European style.

"She is the only reason I accepted this." The man said, speaking in Russian. He had a glass of brandy in his hand, Niema remained five feet away from him, staring at the man in silence.

"They are under the assumption you are still west-bound, and this is why you are here today. I love her as if she was my own daughter and I will curse myself if I put her in any peril ever again." The man said. "I warned her not to ever fall in love with a man if she would not be able to grow old with him, but I had to learn twice the hard truth of the illness of love and its irony. Women will never learn how to say no to their hearts, even if the same heart is stabbing her with a knife!"

"Mr. Bratislav, I…" Niema attempted to respond.

"Don't." Bratislav did not allow him to continue. "You don't have to explain anything to me. We create our own destiny from scratch, and we build it from whatever life hands to us. If we are able, we can make a living out of it. If we are intelligent, we can make a fortune for ourselves and for those who demonstrated their loyalty when we expected it. If we are wise, we are blessed to know not to have taken the path we have chosen with our opportunity, but we are not wise and have never been. We are all greedy and our greed has taken away our humanity and our lives. You are lucky to still have yours, although I wouldn't count on much more luck moving ahead."

"This is why I wanted to come personally Mr. Bratislav," Niema said. "I wanted to honor what you did for me. After this day, the options left around my world will be zero to none."

"I do not need to know anything else." Bratislav again was not eager to give Niema much of a chance to express himself. "The cost of your extra time is the least I could do for her. Don't waste more of it trying to explain anything to me."

Bratislav stood up after placing his glass over a table next to the sofa. He walked close to Niema staring at him into his eyes.

"The only thing that separated you from the rest, was the nobility of your heart," Bratislav said, standing in front of Niema, staring at his face. Niema displayed no emotions and remained firm.

"Sir, this…" Niema said.

"Not to me, I said," Bratislav replied. "Explain it to her, and then leave, never to show up in her life again." Bratislav walked away and as Niema looked ahead, Fei was standing at the end of the room.

Niema waited a few seconds before walking towards her. Fei met his gaze, and her eyes seemed filled with anger and a mix of other emotions. Emotions that Niema knew too well, will hurt her more than anything else.

"Why did you have to come back?" Fei asked him. "You should have just stayed where you were, where you had been declared dead."

"I am indebted to you, and to Mr. Bratislav for the chance, you both took on my behalf." Niema took three steps closer to Fei as he spoke with measured words.

"Cut the bullshit," Fei said sharply. "We made a promise to each other, you promised…"

"I know what I promised." Niema went on to say. "But I have also revealed something to you, which I have never told anyone else."

"What?" Fei seemed both surprised and angrier than before. "You mean to tell me that this is about the ghost story you told me that day?"

"Yes," Niema replied. His face emotionless, his eyes staring coldly. Fei stared into his eyes, she did not know what to say or do. She did not know what to think.

"Did you tell him?" She asked.

"I have only told you," Niema replied.

Almost an hour later, Niema was driven by his men to the outside of the city where a private seaplane was waiting for him. Niema got out of the black sedan, that Alexis was still driving. Vitaly and Vladimir got out with him.

"The transport is only for you." A very tall African man, dressed all in black and wearing a turban, advised Niema. He turned and looked at his men standing right behind him.

"Do what I told you," Niema told Vitaly. "We will meet at Marseille."

"Good luck, boss." Vitaly and Vladimir said. Niema turned around and the man standing in his way allowed him to go board the airplane.

Chapter X:

Foe's Whisper

In the meantime, Pete Basset, one of U.S. President Smith's go-to men, had just stepped out of an airplane at Toronto Pearson International Airport in Canada. Basset was an average looking man, very pale skin, round face, out of shape, not much of a dresser and had a bald spot getting ever larger over his head. He traveled light, only a small carry on and a backpack, which made him blend in perfectly with the rest of the population at any part of the world.

It did not take him long to get out of the terminal and hop on a taxi which transported him to a five-star hotel at the center of the city. Once he got to his room, he began a transition ritual, which involved taking a long shower, applying sunless tanning lotion all over his face, tops of his hands and upper body. He then began putting on a dark blue three-piece suit with a burgundy tie, and a well-fitted hairpiece that he glued over his bald spot. In a matter of minutes, Basset had transformed himself from an average Joe into a totally different man.

The suit made him look slimmer and taller, the fake tan gave him a more rested and sophisticated appearance and the hairpiece gave him a more youthful look. He looked at himself in the bathroom mirror to finish his transformation by spraying cologne and wearing a pair of thin-framed reading glasses, which made his face look sharper.

"Shit," Basset said out loud while admiring himself in the mirror. "I should do this more often." He displayed a very confident smile and headed out of his room. He made his way to the hotel's private parking, at the rear, where he got into a late model Lexus. He then drove for thirty minutes until arriving at the front of an elegant but low-key restaurant called La Pearl. After parking the car across the street, and looking everywhere, Basset got out and walked into the restaurant. He was about to approach the host but there was no need, for the restaurant manager happened to be walking by and recognized him. They spoke for a few seconds and the manager himself walked him to his reserved table.

The place was dimly illuminated on purpose, and the chatting of the patrons gave it a buzz like atmosphere, which Basset felt comfortable with. He ordered a beer which was brought to him in a tall glass. Eight minutes later, as Basset was ready to order a second round, Wendy Millsap an attractive and svelte woman in her 40's, walked into the place wearing a dark-colored coat. Basset and Millsap saw each other, and she walked up to the table while removing a scarf off her neck in a way in which Basset considered very sexy, as she revealed the below the ear's length of her hair and more of her pale skin.

"Hi, I'm sorry I am a bit late." She said, speaking with a British accent as Basset got on his feet to pull out a chair for her.

"Oh, no worries Wendy..." Basset said. "I arrived a few minutes too early if you ask me." He then sat down just as Kev, his waiter, walked up to the table to greet Millsap. Basset wasted no time and ordered her a dirty martini. It did not take long for Kev to come back with the martini and another beer for Basset.

"Thank you, darling, that was very efficient," Wendy said to Kev.

"Not a problem, I will give you a few minutes to decide what you want to have for dinner," Kev replied.

"That will do, Kev," Basset said, trying to get rid of the waiter.

"How is the office?" He then asked Wendy, who was having another sip of her drink at the moment.

"Chaotic." She replied. "Someone has been snooping around our winter files and management believes it to be the Germans."

"Winter files?" Basset questioned. "I was under the assumption MI5 did not keep winter files any longer."

"MI6 was under heavy pressure by the budget inducted by the new PM and the bloody a-hole had them dump some of their load on us," Wendy answered.

"Shit, that must be very irritating," Basset said, empathizing.

"Very…" Wendy agreed.

"Are you hungry?" Basset asked.

"I can go for some fish." Wendy hinted, smiling.

"Ah, we can order the Chilean sea bass over pineapples soaked in an apple cider vinegar sauce and grilled spinach with garlic and mashed potatoes," Basset recommended to Wendy.

"That is a mouth full, but I like the way it sounds." Wendy was instantly sold on Basset's recommendation. She did not have to hear more, Basset smiled and waved at their waiter.

Basset went ahead with the fish for Wendy and the Peruvian chicken dish for himself, which Basset seemed very curious about. An additional bottle of wine was ordered by Wendy and in between the food, jokes and much laughter, they both had a wonderful evening. Basset then decided to make a complete deal and decided to order a decadent chocolate dessert cake for them to share.

"Why not?" Wendy was more than eager to go the extra mile with the cake addition, which they both finished in a matter of seconds, sparking a momentary debate on who had eaten more cake.

Basset asked Kev for the check and while he went ahead to prepare it, Basset asked Wendy to walk with him out to the small patio at the back of the place. It was a chilly night, but a few heat lamps set out all around provided for a temperature adjustment which could be enjoyed momentarily.

"Peter, we should do this more often," Wendy said while smoking a cigarette, which she then shared with Basset.

"I certainly second that motion." Basset joyfully replied.

"So, do you want to hear what I've got for you?" Wendy said to him while taking the cigarette from his lips to place it in between hers.

"Oh shit, work…" Basset replied smiling. "Sure, thanks for reminding me, yeah why not." Both Wendy and Basset laughed for a moment. Basset got another cigarette and allowed Wendy to keep the one she took from his lips.

"Timoshenko is losing ground as we speak." Wendy began. "There was a second vote of no confidence against him at Parliament last week."

"We heard about it," Basset said, agreeing.

"It did not transpire publicly. You have a good asset in there." Wendy almost sounded impressed. "Very good. Now take this into consideration, Timoshenko is pushing to try to make a final move to regain the trust of the few Comrades who switch positions. He is very close to getting the support he needs to organize an operation to recover the territory lost to the rebels, between Tajikistan and Afghanistan.

Those still loyal to Timoshenko are well aware of your government arming the rebels but they are being cautious about supporting his strategy, they feel they had already given him too much. Kirov Bakunin has all but denied a vote and there are three other major players set to be supporting this hot newcomer who has been placing fresh new ideas, for a more upbeat and modernized stronger country, in their heads. His name is Borya Vyacheslav. Old schooled by the true hardliners but educated in Oxford by the new wave."

"Another newcomer with ideas bigger than their capabilities." Basset inserted.

"No, you should look out for this guy Peter." Wendy quickly responded. "I've heard he walks around with a hard-on, aimed at your country."

"What has he done to deserve so much critical acclamation anyways?" Basset asked. "Especially by the oligarch."

"All," Wendy said. "Left and right from Stalin's book of tricks, he learned what he needed. At a young age, he made lucrative deals with both the Vory V Zakone, the VOR and the Bratva, Russian brotherhood. Selling them weapons from the private stocks of the Oligarch, ensuring the easy flow of South American drugs, making lots of money for everyone who hired him, becoming the darling of both Political and criminal worlds. He is a self-made man, with glorious Nationalist ambitions, and we believe he will soon have the means to push his agenda forward."

Wendy paused and walked closer to Basset while dropping her cigarette and stepping on it to put it out.

"We have already begun preparing for him," Wendy told Bassett. "I believe it would be wise if you guys do as well."

"I'm pretty sure the white house is already on him," Basset said, not wanting to entertain too much of the focus on a prospect to which his government already had the upper hand, as well as a victory against.

"How about the other matter?" He asked Wendy.

"It is a done deal," Wendy said. "My people set him up with a small group of venture capitalists from France. They like putting their hands on everything and we use them for situations in which we want to keep a reachable distance, just in case. As we speak, he is under the assumption that he will get preferential treatment under the sponsorship of a well-connected businessman with ties to the House of Lords.

"He does not understand the big heads could care less about his kind. They are only interested in the potential investment to be collected from people like him-immigrants with an illusion of dressing in the proper attire, while learning how to spit out certain words with a proper English accent, poor soul. He may wake up one day with a big headache and absolutely no rights, even over his own toothbrush. And we'll say, 'if you don't like our ways, then leave.' But he will have to leave empty-handed.

"He believes that by helping this businessman with the migratory situation of a tribe of undesirables, he will, in turn, acquire enough support to prevent a potential extradition process, should he need it. I also made an assumption of my own. I believe this man is totally infatuated with my country, thinking he belongs there, boosted by his own ego and self-centered sense of supremacy. Regardless, Salvador will cease to be a potential problem for your President very soon. He is counting on his retirement over at the Queen's country. Your people should have an easier time picking him up across the pond."

"This certainly will be much appreciated by my government." Basset agreed. "Indeed, Gabriel Montero has made himself into the most uncomfortable headache for the President. I believe he will be very happy to hear the news."

"I'm quite aware of a few things your government could do for mine." Wendy hinted as she held Basset's hand.

"Ask and you shall receive," Basset added a joking tone with his reply. Wendy brought her body closer to his while her eyes said things, which Basset was very eager to reciprocate.

"Are you staying at the same hotel?" Wendy asked him.

"Yes," Basset responded.

"Let us go and indulge in adultery for a few hours." Wendy held his hand and led the way.

A day later, in South America. Susan was at the local outdoor market getting groceries with her children. David was trying to make Lora play with him. She was a little withdrawn since she had nightmares the night before and she was still upset about them. Susan was also trying to cheer up Lora by offering her some candies that Lora rarely declined. She was unaware that she and the children were being closely followed by someone. This person had his eyes mostly on Lora as he unnoticeably moved through the crowd of people in the small crowded market.

Susan asked Lora if she wanted to be carried and held her hand as she spoke to her. David was playing by himself as Susan spoke to Lora.

"I just want to stay outside and go to the playground," Lora said. "And mommy, when is daddy coming home?"

Susan looked down at her daughter. She did not really know what to answer.

David looked up at his mother, he was also curious to know when his father was coming back, so he waited to hear what she was going to say. Susan looked at him and then looked at Lora again.

"He will be back from work very soon, sooner than you guys are expecting." Susan then quickly told the children that she was going to cook their special favorite meal today and that got them both excited.

Suddenly, a tall fat man was standing right next to Susan with a chocolate bar in his hand. He was offering it to Lora, trying to beckon her to him. Susan had a very bad feeling in her stomach that made her take a step back. She stood in front of her children.

"Who are you and what is it that you want?" Susan cried out to the fat man. She noticed another man right behind them, the one who had been following them the entire time. Then another man suddenly showed up. This one was eating an orange with the peel still on, and it looked as though he hadn't bathed in months. The tops of his hands were covered with hair and seemed very dirty. Susan recognized him. A look of deep fear took over her face.

"Hello again." The man said to Susan. Susan attempted to move around and away from the men, but they forced their way around her and blocked her from getting away.

"What do you want from me?" Susan said while holding her children close to her. Her eyes desperately searched for someone who would notice she was in trouble and might come to her rescue.

"Shhhhh. Don't you worry," the fat man said. "We're not here to hurt you."

"Well... Not yet anyway..." The one eating the orange added while looking at Lora with malicious eyes.

"We want an answer to what we asked you some time ago and we need that answer right here, right now." The fat man demanded as he took a step closer to her.

"I told you, my husband is the one who has the final say in this," Susan said. "That property was given to him by his mother and he promised her that he would keep it in the family and fix it for his own children and grandchildren. I told you I cannot convince him to give it up. He will not sell it." Even though she was afraid, Susan was assertive in what she told the fat man.

"Wrong answer!" The man eating the orange snapped at Susan, after tossing away what was left of the orange onto the floor and walking closer to the children.

"Lucas!" The fat man said to the other man, making him stop just a step away from grabbing Lora. Lucas looked at the fat man upset.

"Let's take them now, what else do we need?" Lucas said angrily through his teeth.

The fat man walked slowly towards Susan, as she stepped back.

"Time is running out for you. And your decision not to cooperate is going to cost you, my dear." He said to her breathing heavily. "Make sure you let your husband know of our little chat. I hope he will be more reasonable than you."

Susan and her children were visibly very shaken up. She did not know where the men had come from or who they were working for. Worse yet, Susan did not know what to do. Communication with her husband was very difficult since he was out at sea. Even if she would resolve to give in to the demands of whoever wanted to buy their house, the property was still under her husband's name and only her husband had the authority to sell it.

"Hey! Miss Susan..." Shouted one of the vendors in the market. He approached Susan and the children after seeing how these strange looking men were harassing them.

"Hey..." The vendor called out. At that moment the men moved away from Susan and the children while noticing the vendor walking in their direction. Susan quickly grabbed the children's hands and pushed her way through the men.

"Carlos!" Susan said as she continued walking fast causing the vendor to follow her and the children. He took a quick look back at the men. The men were staring at Susan, completely ignoring the vendor.

Carlos then walked back to his own stand, where Susan was waiting for him.

"What happened? Why were those strange men surrounding you and the children like that?" he asked Susan.

"Someone wants to buy our property and they won't take no for an answer. My husband is away working as you know. All kinds of strange things are happening around us all of a sudden. And even though I sent a telegram to Marcus explaining our situation, I have no idea when he will even receive it. I am just trying to stall for time until I hear from him."

"You better stay away from those guys. I really don't like the looks of them." Carlos advised Susan.

"I've no idea about who they are and why they're after my house so badly. Have you ever seen those guys around here before?" Susan asked Carlos.

"Not really, but they seem to work for someone bad. These types have no respect for anyone's life." Carlos said to her. "If there's somewhere you can go hide, I would suggest you go do that instead of staying where you are. Since it's your property they're after, you're not really safe there. I'll come by in the evening to say hello. Maybe if they see people visiting you, they'll feel less inclined to do something rash."

At that moment Susan found herself in a very bad predicament, not knowing what to do next, and not knowing when her husband would come home for certain. She looked at her children and attempted to control her emotions. She could not hold back anymore and burst out in tears. Carlos was trying to be helpful and comforted her as much as he could.

"Don't worry Susan. I will stop by after the market closes to check on your guys. I'll help you guys to put on some extra locks, just in case, and see what else needs securing."

"Thank you, Carlos. That would be really helpful." Susan was very grateful. She wiped away her tears and felt a lot calmer.

Later that evening, Carlos followed through with his promise. He arrived at Susan's house with an extra lock for the door and some candy for her children. He noticed someone staring at him from a window across the street and as he turned his head to look around, he could actually see others peeking from behind curtains and cracks in their blinds. He ignored them all and went inside the house when Susan opened the door for him.

The children were happy to have Carlos as their guest for the evening and Susan was as well. They rarely had people over at their house, something which Susan's husband did not like Susan to do while he was away working. Carlos played with Lora and David on the living room floor. Carlos was a lot younger than Susan and the kids felt very comfortable around him. It was really relaxing for Susan to see. At that moment, for a short time, she forgot how worried she had been. Susan even smiled and laughed to herself as she watched them run and play in the tiny living room.

Susan decided to cook something special and asked Carlos to stay and have dinner with her and the children. Carlos accepted the invitation and as Susan cooked, he installed the extra lock on the front door and replaced a couple of rusty screws on the door hinges.

Amidst the happy evening, neither Susan, the children, nor Carlos realized that one of the men who had confronted Susan earlier at the market took a short stroll by the front of the house. He peeked in through the cracks on the front door and window shutters.

∞

In another part of South America, misty rain was falling throughout the mountains and the dense forest areas of a guerrilla-controlled part of the Nicaraguan jungle. The U.S government had put a hold to diplomatic talks with the Nicaraguans and Colombians, under the assumption that powerful drug lords were under their protection in exchange for large monetary payouts. A mission was organized to develop tactical information, which could be useful to dismantle their relationship, as well as the stronghold guerrilla forces had over the territory.

Several pickup trucks and a Hummer SUV traveling in between them, carrying armed men, were approaching a large compound comprised of several properties, which could be seen at a cleared area at the center of the forest. A group of men positioned around various parts of the compound prepared themselves as if something big was about to go down. They all had their weapons pointed at the oncoming vehicles.

"I think he's here." A Spanish speaking Colombian man, carrying a machine gun, told another one standing in front of a big wooden door.

"Very well, go and gather Hector and the others and guide him towards the rear. I will let the boss know." The man in front of the door told the man carrying the machine gun. He quickly walked away to follow the order, while the other man knocked on the door.
"Boss!" The man called out while placing his ear against the door.

"Come in." Someone behind the door said. The man pushed open the door and walked into the room, where several other men were having a meeting. They all sat comfortably on large sofas around a couple of coffee tables, while smoking cigars, drinking liquor and engaging in conversations about their respective business dealings. Meanwhile, three others silently conducted their operations in front of computers, which had been placed behind a wall near an open space. It led to a back porch a couple of feet away from them.

"He has arrived, I told Pedro to call Hector and the others and bring him by the rear as you ordered." The man said speaking in English, as he entered the room. He was standing next to a tall and very elegant man with short dark hair and fair skin. The fair-skinned man didn't respond to what the other man told him and simply walked ahead to where the others were. He walked up behind another light-skinned man who was seated at the center of everyone, with a cigar in his left hand and a beer in his right. He approached his ear to speak to him very quietly. The man then walked back up to the one who had just entered the room and signaled him to leave with a gesture of his right hand.

Outside, the pickup trucks and the Hummer were already by the front entrance of the compound and some of the men inside were getting off, still carrying their weapons in hand. A man with long black hair and dressed completely in white walked out of the rear right passenger door of the Hummer and was respectfully greeted by Hector and several other individuals with him.

Hector was a tall Colombian man with a high sense of style and fashion, which one can tell by the very expensive suit he was wearing and the expensive limited-edition watch that adorned his wrist, not for telling time but rather his taste and income. The men around Hector were heavily armed as well, and even though he and the man dressed in white seemed to be very good friends by the way they greeted each other, everyone around them appeared to be on the edge and neither group seemed to trust the other.

"How are you, Hector?" The man dressed in white said as he and Hector hugged each other.

"Very well Laurence, and now I feel much better seeing you here to complete our deal," Hector replied.

"Yes Hector, it's been a long time coming. I believe we have waited too long dealing with nonsense and trivialities, which has cost us a great deal." Laurence said.

"You are absolutely correct. Too long indeed..." Hector concurred. "Pooling our resources together should have been the first priority but the stubbornness and childish behavior of our youth prevented us from understanding it early on."

Laurence could feel Hector's sincerity in his tone of voice. "I understand now and I'm here because you requested my presence to do a proper introduction of the new merchandise and to make sure we begin to do things the right way. So, let us begin doing exactly that. I strongly believe that the fact that I was in the country visiting my associate was more than good timing but perhaps divine intervention Hector."

With a gesture of his right hand, Hector gave a signal to his men.

"I trust you understand that I am a businessman still and my time here will be very short, therefore..." Laurence announced.

"I understand Laurence, I know your time is very valuable. I'm very grateful that you were able to make this trip on such short notice. Please follow me."

Hector immediately led the way towards the rear of the property with Laurence and four of his men walking next to him along the side of a small group of Hector's people. The two groups of men let their guard down somewhat and became more at ease for the moment.

"How is everything going around here?" Laurence asked Hector.

"It is the same all the time. The only thing that changes is the people and some of the politicians we have on our payroll." Hector replied, laughing at his own joke. "Everything is changing faster than usual, from what I've seen so far," Laurence added, causing Hector to chuckle shortly before he continued speaking. "I will tell you this. Based on what I've seen throughout the places I've visited, people usually are the key factor in changing the face and the classification of places Hector." "I'm a believer of that as well," Hector replied. "I know a developer who used to say 'if you have poor and uneducated people living in an area of any city in the world, they will call that area a ghetto, a place where adding investment and infrastructure will only be a waste of money and resources. Take the same area and add a few educated and better-dressed people and they will call it a middle-class neighborhood and I fucking believe him because he followed the model in his construction projects.

"The son of a bitch will not sell to ugly people no matter how much money they had. He used to say 'if I have ugly people living in my property, more ugly people will come with them- ugly men and women who will make some ugly kids. What the fuck am I going to do with so many ugly people? The place will lose its value.' He wouldn't sell to anyone who didn't look like a damn movie star or some very important person. If they were at least presentable looking, dressed right and had the money to get in, he would look past their education and background. He did business with them. And that vain son of a bitch has had a very successful run in his endeavors. I can tell you that."

Laurence nodded in agreement while laughing.

"Everyone was banging down his door to get into that part of the neighborhood with all the gorgeous people. Because that meant they were cool and beautiful too. This just drove up the prices and he got to charge whatever the fuck he wanted."

Laurence and Hector laughed together as they walked towards where the others were waiting.

"Who do you think that is?" A low tone whispering voice asked while observing through binoculars from a distance.

"I don't know, I don't think I have ever seen him around here, but he looks very important. It may well be one of their main clients or maybe an important weapons supplier."

"Yes, I think you're right. The meeting they have going on in there was not on the schedule and now that I think about it, there are a couple of big birds in there as well. The likes of which don't come out of their nests often."

"Yes, roger that. Those who arrived inside the three armored vehicles... I think we should call it in, just in case. They may want to see his face or at least find out who this guy is."

The conversation continued for a short time by two camouflaged Marines who were hidden under the cover of dense bushes and tree branches several miles away from the compound.

The Marines had camouflage sniper rifles that blended perfectly with the jungle surroundings and as one of them continued observing the movements around the compound with oversized binoculars, the other one operated a military issued minicomputer.

"What was that?" The Marine holding the binoculars asked.

"What was what?" The one handling the computer quickly asked, while slowly reaching for his rifle as he saw his partner reaching for his without making a sound. Their faces were covered by specially designed gas masks, which were part of their camouflaged suits and their voices were only heard by one another through their communication devices built into their masks.

"Check the perimeter."

The Marine handling the computer quickly proceeded to observe the status of the security devices they had scattered all around their perimeter. They also continued looking at live feed from hidden cameras they had positioned in key places around where they were and near the vicinity of the compound.

They saw nothing that could jeopardize their safety or their position. Not even the jungle animals bothered them. They kept their guard up for several more minutes and they re-observed the area around them five more times before they went back to their previous work.

"What did you hear, Trevor?" One of the Marines asked.
"I don't know Sam, to tell you the truth," Trevor replied. He had gone back to observing what was taking place at the compound through the binoculars.

"Maybe it was some kind of animal and the sound were brought by an echo," Sam suggested.

"Echoes, sounds of the wilderness, I've been in this fucking jungle for too long already. While those fucking drug dealers and arms dealers are out there enjoying themselves, eating delicious meals, fucking gorgeous women and living the life. I'm beginning to wonder whose job is better." Trevor said in a frustrated tone of voice.

Sam noticed Trevor's demeanor and did not like what his partner had to say.

"What the fuck are you trying to say? Tell me if I heard correctly soldier? Because I don't want to even think that I heard my best man and the only one I would trust with my life, begin to turn his back on his country."

Trevor put the binoculars down slowly and closed his eyes beneath the mask for a moment before he spoke. "It's not about doubts, Sam, it's just..." Trevor began to explain himself.

"Let's focus on our job soldier, in what we need to do for our families and your children's future, not to mention the country which is counting on us," Sam said, cutting him off. He had placed his hand on Trevor's shoulder. Trevor looked at him and saw that Sam had the part of his mask, which covered the area around the eyes, up and he could see his eyes, despite being covered all around by dark face paint, staring at him very seriously. Trevor knew all too well that look and could not look back at Sam's face as much as he would have wanted to.

"I don't want to disappoint you, Sam. It's just that I'm beginning to feel the weight of everything on me." Trevor said.

"Take a break and get some sleep soldier," Sam told him. "I understand the feeling all too well. I'm no stranger to it and that is why I'm ordering you to erase it from your head. Don't let it take over the best of you, because you are stronger than it." Sam paused for a moment.

"I already called it. The drone will be in the air soon enough. Go on and get some sleep, I will take care of the rest." Sam said. Trevor then passed the binoculars to Sam and slowly crawled back up to a narrow space they had made to position their bodies to rest. Sam looked at him for a moment before taking his position to observe the compound again.

Trevor accommodated himself in a fetal position and took his mask off and placed it next to his head. He reached inside one of the pockets of the upper part of his camouflage suit and pulled out a bar of hard dark chocolate that was specially designed for missions like this.

He looked at the chocolate bar for a couple of seconds and after closing his eyes and opening them again he broke it into two pieces and placed one half back inside the pocket. He then pulled out a thin plastic bag filled with yellow liquid protein and placed it on his chest to drink it after he ate the chocolate bar. A few quick flashbacks of memories with his children, mother, sisters, and brothers, and a girlfriend he loved dearly, back in his town, went through his mind. A smile came to his face, as he thought about all the fun times from the past.

He then looked at Sam for a moment, and he saw that he was submerged in his observation of the compound. He stared at his friend and comrade for a couple of minutes wondering how he could do it. How he could be the way he is? How he could forget about those whom he loved? How was he able to mold himself into someone who has nothing to lose for the sake of the mission at hand? He knew he could never be like him even though Sam had categorized him as his best man, but he was too tired to reflect more on his thoughts and his eyes closed for what he thought would be a couple of minutes, even forgetting to drink his protein.

Suddenly, Trevor felt a rough shaking on his chest. It was Sam's hand, shaking him to wake him up. Trevor was drowsy and couldn't immediately hear Sam's voice quite well. But he shook himself awake and quickly placed his mask on and pulled himself together.

"Shit Trevor, they are killing each other down there!"

As Trevor heard him, he immediately moved to position himself near Sam. Sam had placed the binoculars down and was trying to establish contact with the rest of his support team, but something was blocking his signal. He was trying over and over, but he just couldn't gain access.

"What the fuck is going on out there?" Trevor asked.

Sam didn't say anything as he continued trying to establish contact. Trevor continued observing the compound. The sounds of gunfire were getting closer to where they were and with it, came along the smell of gun powder and blood.

"Sam, what the hell is happening? What happened? What did I miss?" Trevor asked.

Sam ignored him for a moment. He had stopped trying to establish contact with the support team and instead went back to verify the security system around them. He was also attempting to figure out if the drone was already nearby. The night would soon fall. The sun was about to disappear behind the mountains and for the first time in many years of combat missions, Trevor was seeing Sam momentarily confused.

"For our good luck, the night will provide us with cover for our retreat," Sam said.

Retreat? Trevor thought.

"If I had to take a wild guess, the new guy might've had something else in mind at the meeting. He probably caused what's happening down there right now. If it's so, and he had the audacity of bringing himself in there to do this, the extra back up is probably not far. So, we have to move with caution just in case." Sam said while he was able to gain access to his security devices and that alone gave him a renewed sense of confidence.

"Why would this individual try to take on these guys in their own territory, putting himself in there to do so?" Trevor asked, keeping his head low.
"I believe it might have been a trap for the one in white," Sam said, making his own speculations about what was taking place at the compound. "But we cannot be sure just yet."

"It could be." Trevor then said. "Considering that they had to have more to gain from taking out our guy in white. Because to be able to do this, they had to have more money to give to Campo Azul than what they were getting before. We just don't know yet who this 'white' player was. We don't even know if he had the weight and power to be of Campo Azul's benefit for this to be happening."

Sam meanwhile worked away on his gadgets.

"Shit Sam, we've got to get out of here!" Trevor was growing more anxious.
 Sam didn't offer a response to that. He was able to make sure their escape way was clear. He moved towards Trevor, still holding the computer close to him. The gunfire was still echoing in the distance. Sam and Trevor speculated about what could have caused the sudden gunfight, but their speculations, in reality, were not even close to the real reasons behind the sudden eruption of violence and the massacre occurring in the compound.

A short time later, it was already pitch dark. To adorn the darkness of the night with their sounds, the animals from the jungle began their nocturnal recitation of a colorful rhythm. Sam and Trevor were running very fast and cautiously, already miles away from the compound. The two Marines already knew the road ahead of them like the back of their hands and as they ran through the bushes and trees, they made a momentary stop to make sure they weren't being followed. Trevor got down on one knee facing towards the rear and Sam was facing forward, both with their weapons positioned in front of their faces and ready to shoot.

"Clear," Trevor said.

"Clear," Sam replied. As soon as Sam spoke, Trevor got up and continued running behind him. Sam took a quick look at his florescent compass, which he could see with the night vision lenses of his mask, to make sure they were still going the right way. He took his eyes off from the road for an instant.

"600 yards ahead," Sam said.

"We're already there." Trevor jokingly replied, allowing himself a quick smile as he felt they were finally approaching safer grounds.

"Shhhhh…."

Sam heard a very low whispering, which made him stop cold and get down on his right knee to assume a guarding position with his weapon.

"Sam, what is it?" Trevor asked. He was already on his position, giving his back to Sam. The barrel of his rifle was moving left to right very slowly as Trevor looked everywhere without missing an inch of the immediate terrain around them.

"I heard something," Sam said. He remained in silence observing his surroundings and Trevor, but his night vision lenses were only allowing him to see the glare of the eyes of some of the animals lurking in their path. The nocturnal predators were in search of their nightly meals. Then suddenly, something made those same animals abruptly flee the terrain as if they were escaping a much larger predator.

"Sam?" Trevor again asked Sam remained in silence, still combing the area with his eyes and the barrel of his weapon.

"Three O'clock," Sam whispered. Trevor quickly positioned himself by Sam's side with his weapon ahead. He also had night vision lenses but when he looked at the direction Sam had indicated; he couldn't see anything beyond the trees and the bushes ahead.

"Where, Sam? I don't see anything." Trevor asked feeling nervous.

"I saw something there, right by the side of those trees. It moved very fast." Sam said. Trevor continued to stare at the direction. Sam took a couple of steps forward and Trevor followed him closely towards where he had seen movement.

"Couldn't it have been a wolf or a coyote?" Trevor said. "Let's go, Sam, let's move soon."

Sam didn't answer. He remained silent and observing the direction he pointed out to Trevor. Trevor was nervous but ready and eager to move. His trigger finger kept on fidgeting, moving back and forth.

"Get down," Sam whispered. Trevor slowly got down on his chest following Sam's order. Sam had done the same and he and Trevor disappeared under the long bushes, which were being gently moved by the wind.

The clouds in the sky moved with the speed of that same wind. From time to time, it covered the moon, which had just appeared on the far sky to illuminate the night momentarily and then as soon as the wind made possible for some illumination, clouds took over one more time and covered the moon completely.

"… Ssshhhhhh…"

The same whispering sounded again, and this time Trevor heard it as well.

"Sam…" Trevor started to say something.

"I heard it too." Sam quickly replied. They were still moving very slowly and quietly propelling their bodies with their legs while they kept their weapons pointing ahead and their heads slightly lifted.

"Where did it come from?" Trevor asked.
"I don't know but stay silent," Sam replied.

"Aaaaaaaahhhhh!"

"Trevor! Trevor!"

Sam heard Trevor screaming and got up immediately. He couldn't see him and grew flustered. He began to move around in every direction calling out for Trevor. But Trevor didn't answer. Sam was cautious not to shoot his weapon in fear of hitting his partner.

"Trevor, where are you? Shit! Trevor answer me!" Sam continued speaking into his mic. Then suddenly, he saw Trevor being tossed ten feet in the air, hitting his right shoulder against a tree as he landed.

"Sam… I'm here," Trevor said weakly. Sam knew that his partner was badly hurt.

"Trevor!" Sam quickly moved towards Trevor and without putting his guard down, he touched Trevor's neck to check his pulse and quickly patted him on the shoulder to wake him up. Trevor reacted to his touch.

"What happened to you, are you alright? Can you walk?" Sam asked. His attention was still on the surroundings and his weapon was moving with him as he asked Trevor about his physical condition.

"I don't know Sam. I can't feel my arm; I might've broken something." Trevor said, while slowly getting back on his feet. Sam noticed in his voice he didn't sound like he was very good, and he figured that there was something wrong with his communication device.

"Adjust your frequency selector, your voice sounds distorted," Sam said. Trevor then touched a section of his mask behind the left ear to try to solve the problem by adjusting the device.

"Where's your weapon?" Sam then asked.

"Where is it? I had it with me." Trevor replied as he began searching around for his weapon. Sam kept guard to protect Trevor as he searched for it. He suddenly saw something moving not far from where they were, immediately catching his attention.

"Twelve o'clock, contact, contact, contact," Sam said. Trevor heard his voice still with distortion, but he already had his weapon in hand and immediately assumed his position. Sam was already firing his weapon towards the position he saw movement. Trevor didn't hesitate and did the same while limping a step to assume a good position. They both fired their weapons for a short time and then Sam got closer to Trevor and touched his arm to signal to him that it was time to move. They began to make a run for it while turning around, in a synchronized fashion and firing at their rear.

"Do you think they made us?" Trevor asked. Sam remained quiet as he ran ahead of him and he didn't answer Trevor. Not until he made sure there was no danger coming from the opposite direction.

"I don't believe they made us," Sam answered. "But I really don't know who's after us."

Sam was going to continue speaking but then became silent again. He turned to look at Trevor. Trevor wasn't looking at him at that moment and Sam just began to move ahead running again.

"Let's move fast," Sam said as Trevor began to follow him. Suddenly Sam felt strong gusts of wind blowing from within the dense parts of the jungle, almost pushing him backward.

"What the hell?" Sam whispered as he saw a blurry image of something charging right towards them. He attempted to fire his weapon. But everything happened in the blink of an eye, just a second before everything went completely dark for him.

Two days later, Doctor Patricia Wryly walked the hallways of a military hospital ship accompanied by two female nurses. The vessel was located near the coast of Brazil, supporting military exercises that were taking place between the United States, Argentina, and Brazil.

Doctor Wryly had a chart with several pages in her hands, which she was surveying as the two nurses accompanying her walked by her side. One of the nurses was pushing a cart carrying several small containers filled with medicines for patients. The other nurse was carrying a chart as well as some medical supplies.

"Here we are. I hope he's doing better tonight." Nurse Brown commented as she was about to open the door to a room to visit their next patient.

"Yes, I know what you mean." Doctor Wryly said. "He will be doing much better tonight."

"I don't even think he slept at all last night, he had the worst nightmares he has gotten since his time here." Nurse Brown replied.

"Major Gray, Samuel Gray." Doctor Wryly said reading his chart, right before she entered the room with the nurses.

"Is this what they had on?" Army General Edgar Mulligan asked Donald Burton, a civilian who was in charge of the handling of private affairs. They were accompanied by three other members of the military as well as by two more civilians inside a restricted area. They had the weapons, camouflage uniform, gear and various other instruments that belonged to the two Marines, Sam and Trevor, including the laptop Sam was using to communicate with the rest of the operations team.

"Yes, sir," Burton replied while holding one of the masks the marines had on at the Nicaraguan jungle.

"As you well know, this is the standard military issued communication equipment, battle protective face gear and the rest of the standard issued attire," Burton said as he walked around the platform table where the Marines' equipment was being displayed. General Mulligan picked up one of the weapons and looked at it for a few seconds before putting it back on the platform so that the other two civilians, who remained very quiet in the background, could also take a closer look.

"Is Major Gray already good enough to be debriefed, Mr. Burton?" General Mulligan asked Burton.

"Well…" Burton said as he thought about what to say next and that caused General Mulligan to push on with the pressure.

"We need to talk to him and get every single bit of information he could possibly provide us with, about what happened in the compound, and we needed to know it a long time ago Mr. Burton. So, I will ask you again. Is he ready to be debriefed now?" General Mulligan demanded while squinting his eyes into a frown.

Burton understood that the need to get the information from Sam was enough to go ahead with their debriefing at that time even if the Major's health wasn't optimal.

"I suppose that your interest in obtaining whatever you can get from Major Gray represents a good deal for the safety of our national security General Mulligan, so I guess it will be best if we do go ahead with Major Gray's debriefing at once," Burton said to General Mulligan. Mulligan looked very pleased with Burton's decision. As he looked at the civilians with him, it seemed as if they were anxious as well to hear what Sam had to say.

"Lead the way, Mr. Burton." General Mulligan said.

"I will give the order to the nurses in charge to bring Major Samuel Gray to a place more suitable for what you want to do General. It'll take only a couple of minutes to arrange." Burton replied.

"Very well then Mr. Burton."

"Please follow my assistant and I will take care of the rest."

General Mulligan, the other military men with him and the civilians were guided by one of Burton's personal assistants outside the room while he remained behind, taking one last look at the weapons and instruments that belonged to the Marines. He began placing a call through his cell phone. Another man walked into the room and stood next to the door as Burton made his call. Burton looked at him and the man gave him a positive sign while remaining standing where he was.

"A considerable amount of Cyclic Optotomic Radiation was found all around Garrison's body." The man by the door advised Burton. "They were definitively attacked by one of *them*."

A half-hour later, General Mulligan and those others with him, gathered inside a different room where Sam had just been transferred into. They observed as Doctor Wryly and Nurse Brown pushed the Major's bed inside the room. Sam was awake and seemed very aware of everything around him. He immediately attempted to salute General Mulligan as soon as he saw the uniform even before the face.

"At ease son, don't worry about formalities right now." General Mulligan told Sam, as Doctor wryly and Nurse Brown adjusted the devices of his bed to the connections in the wall.

"Whatever you have to ask the soldier has to be done quickly, gentlemen." Doctor Wryly said. "He's still under the effects of the medication we gave him to prevent infection and to control the effects of the trauma. Therefore, I will ask you not to put pressure on him and not to make him try to remember things that are not clear in his mind yet. We don't want to get him too excited."

Doctor Wryly was assuming almost a mother-like tone of voice to address the people interested in speaking with Sam.

"Don't you worry Doctor, he'll be all right." General Mulligan said. "We just want to ask Major Gray a few things, nothing too complicated or confusing. Remember that he is a Marine and a very well trained one." General Mulligan assured Doctor Wryly, walking near her side as she and Nurse Brown left the room.

"Sir, don't worry," Sam said. "I'm okay, you can ask me anything you want but I would like to know about Major Garrison before anything. I haven't seen him since we were brought out of the jungle. How is he doing sir?"

The General looked in Sam's direction without making eye contact. He then turned to look at the other military men with him. Burton looked at Mulligan and then, from the corner of his eyes, he looked at the two civilians near him.

"Mr. Burton, this is the part in which I will ask you to allow us a moment of privacy." General Mulligan told Burton.

"Sure, I understand," Burton replied. He and the others silently left the room.

"Son..." General Mulligan addressed Sam, while slowly walking close to the side of his bed.

"You and Major Garrison have done plenty of service on behalf of your country and I want you to know that your country and your fellow soldiers will never forget the sacrifices made by the two of you." General Mulligan began to say.

Sam didn't like the type of speech Mulligan was giving him. That way of talking was all too familiar to him and he immediately sensed that something was wrong. His heart sank, knowing what the end of the speech would sound like.

"Sir, what I did for my country I did it from my heart, you don't need to give me the speech. I don't need to be thanked for something which is part of my duties to my family, my fellow soldiers and my country, Sir." Sam said, speaking like a true soldier. "Just be honest with me and tell me if something happened to Trevor."

General Mulligan wasn't surprised by Sam's attitude. He knew Sam was a combat soldier and the type of man whom he had to be straight forward and to the point with.

"Major Garrison didn't make it son." General Mulligan broke the news to Sam. He looked at him right in the eyes as he did. Sam's eyes remained fixed on the General for some time, until he let his head down and closed his eyes tightly.

"He died shortly after the rescue team extracted you both from the pickup location... I'm sorry, son. I know he was like a brother to you."

General Mulligan tried to be as compassionate as he could while breaking the news to Sam. After he spoke, he decided to give him a moment and walked away from the bed and stood by the door.

"He was my brother..." Sam mumbled his words in a way that could only be heard by him.

"The day had gone by normally," Sam said. His voice sounded distant and as he spoke, he used one of the fingers of his left hand to wipe a tear from his left eye. As he began speaking, one of the two civilians behind Burton opened the door to a crack and requested to be allowed in the room. Mulligan agreed but signaled for them to remain silent. Burton followed the men into the room and stood quietly by a corner. One of the other men moved a chair to sit closer to the bed.

"Early in the afternoon, we noticed that preparations were being made around the compound. We didn't really know what it was for. The day began like any other, it was supposed to be just a regular day in the lives of the drug kingpins of the La Corona Real cartel, but I guess it turned out to be their last."

Sam began recounting the story of everything that took place on the day he and Trevor were forced to abandon their post by the sudden attack against the compound controlled by the Corona Real drug cartel. His memory was a bit sketchy, but he did his best to give accurate details to the General and the rest of the people in the room with him. The two civilians that came with General Mulligan were paying close attention to every single word he was saying.

"So that sound, the sound you heard as Major Garrison was reaching for his weapon, was it the same sound he heard when you were near the compound post?" General Mulligan asked Sam.

"I can't quite describe what sound Trevor heard or if it was the same sound that I heard, sir." Sam continued. "He couldn't describe it himself. He just said it was like a whispering but nothing else."

"Was it a whispering sound or maybe a whispering voice that you heard Major?" General Mulligan asked Sam. Soon after, the civilian seated close to Sam's bed signaled him with a look of his eyes.

"To be honest with you sir, I don't really remember what it was. The only thing I can tell you is that afterward, I felt a strange sensation and I thought I saw something coming at me. I couldn't tell if it was hostile or not and with the situation at hand, I couldn't jeopardize my life or the life of my partner, therefore, I opened fire."

"Did Major Garrison follow through as well?" General Mulligan asked Sam, interrupting him briefly.

"Yes sir," Sam replied.

"He positioned himself two steps behind me, an arm away to my right and engaged the possible threat as soon as he heard me."

"Did he get to mention if he saw the threat also?" General Mulligan again asked, interrupting Sam.

"Sir, after we engaged the enemy there was no time for comment or analysis, everything happened very fast and swiftly. The last thing I can remember clearly is the moment I saw Major Garrison move in front and away from me and suddenly, he was flung away into the air and fell almost 40 feet away from where I was. I didn't know how, or who did that to him. All I can tell you is that a moment after, the same thing happened to me."

Sam took a moment to decompress. He was upset, almost irritated at his own recollection of the events, thinking about what he could have done right or differently to save Trevor's life. Something, which the civilians with General Mulligan took into consideration as they analyzed his demeanor and the way he described the events.

"I don't even know how we made it to the extraction site, sir," Sam said shaking his head.

"Search and rescue extracted you and Major Garrison half a mile away from the pickup sector," Mulligan mentioned. "The camouflaged clothing detectors indicated that your position was not changing for an extended period of time, and you were presumed to be in trouble at that particular location. You were located first and then it took a couple more minutes to retrieve Major Garrison due to high winds. Major Garrison was declared dead on arrival."

After General Mulligan's final words, silence took over the room for a moment, as if that moment of silence was in honor of Major Garrison. The two civilians with General Mulligan looked at each other discreetly and then the one seated close to Sam looked at General Mulligan. Mulligan picked up the signal and gave the man a positive sign by tilting his head.

"Major Gray, my name is Norman Vaughn." The civilian sitting close to Sam introduced himself while pulling out a very thin, sleek video player from his jacket pocket and brought it close to Sam's view. Sam greeted Vaughn while looking at the video device with curiosity. He had not been aware of the technology he was being exposed to.

"I would like you to look at this footage one of our agents was able to capture from the compound's various security cameras. It's a little grainy, but we were able to collect some details out of them, which we managed to piece together."

Vaughn brought the device closer to Sam and he could immediately see that the footage was recorded sometime after the gunfight. Sam's eyes opened wider as he saw several burned bodies right by the front entrance of the compound. At that moment, he had a flashback of a memory which made him remember the sound of an explosion he heard as he and Trevor were running towards the extraction point.

"I remember I heard an explosion," Sam commented.

"Yes, that is good. Continue watching the video and maybe your memory will get clearer Major Gray." General Mulligan said. Sam continued watching the video and the person filming it didn't appear to be part of the military group of Special Forces doing the observation in and around the compound. He noticed the highly advanced gear the person recording was equipped with, as he saw the reflection of the person on a wall mirror, while the person walked by, collecting footage. It was military fatigue that Sam had never seen before. Sam was not too concerned about the person filming the video as he was looking at the brutal and horrible death that met all of those men inside the compound.

There were random body parts everywhere, small fires still burning in some areas of the compound, men who had been violently pushed through walls. The entire vicinity was a one-sided massacre. Since the smell of blood and burning flesh could be smelled all over the jungle for miles, it forced some of the men from the Special Forces inspecting the place, to cover their mouth and nose with cloths in their hands.

"Were we able to determine who attacked them, sir?" Sam asked General Mulligan.

"That is why we are showing you this footage, Major," Mulligan replied. "We were able to analyze the footage recorded by two of your surveillance cameras and the footage collected by the cameras mounted on your camouflage suits, which gave us the perspective of your point of view. The video you are watching is the sum of the footage collected by yours, Major Garrison's and our cameras."

Sam stared at him for a moment before he continued watching the video in the mini-player, which at that time was showing some of the video recorded by one of the cameras Sam and Trevor had positioned to record the movements near the borders of the compound.

"That is from the angle of one of my surveillance cameras, correct?" Sam asked Vaughn.

"That is correct Major, the camera positioned on the North West corner from your position," Vaughn answered.

"As you can see in this footage, we deduced that those men firing frenetically in every direction were part of the security personnel in charge of protecting Mr. Hector Ernesto Obregon, the leader of Corona Real. If you look now in this edited portion, we added for the better understanding of what we are contemplating, you may see that the individual wearing the black suit and blue shirt coming out of the compound to receive one of Mr. Obregon's guest, is the same one leading this group firing into that direction."

Vaughn asked Sam to look at the specific footage of the video, the image switched back to the images captured by the camera's position by the other corner of the compound and then to the camera mounted on the camouflage suits. Sam immediately recognized the footage because he remembered seeing what he was watching now in the video. He continued looking at the footage for a couple of minutes and the footage then switched to the video collected from the other surveillance camera recording the northeast corner of the compound.

"Look over there," Vaughn said, as the images of the area the men were firing at, appeared one more time in the video.

"This is the angle captured by the other surveillance camera you and Major Garrison mounted around the compound, and as you can clearly see, bullets are hitting everywhere around the bushes in that particular spot. Those bullets are being fired by the men you saw in the previous images. As you can see in the clock, the time frame is the same, but if you pay attention closely, there's no one at the receiving end of the bullets' barrage.

"We can even see that those men are not being fired upon. Now the question we ask ourselves is, who or what were those men firing their weapons at, in such a desperate way? The research team collected almost 98% of the bullets that were fired into that area, which means those bullets hit nothing! Again, we have to ask, who were they firing upon? What would warrant that kind of firepower?"

Vaughn paused and stared at Sam in a discreetly inquisitive manner. General Mulligan was also staring at Sam waiting to see if the video would trigger his memory to remember more details of what took place at the compound. Sam continued to watch the footage being played in the video while at the same time trying to force his mind to remember any other particular detail about the events. A momentary flash of something passed through his mind, it was similar to the image of an unexpected attack. An attack by something which he could not describe.

"There was something else," Sam said.

"What is it Major, what can you recall?" General Mulligan asked.

"Major Garrison. I remember now, at that moment when I was firing my weapon to where I thought a threat was coming from. I think I remember hearing him say a couple last words, but what's stuck in my mind was something he said like 'it's a ghost Sam.' I think that was what he said, 'it's a ghost'."

Sam closed his eyes again as if he was trying to dig deeper inside his mind.

"Now I believe I understand what he meant with those words, I didn't see anything and the only thing I heard was a whisper, the same thing that happened to those men, happened to us… We were firing at the air hitting nothing and yet, the air was striking us, and we were hurt bad. We didn't know what we were up against sir, we never even saw it coming but it got us. It got us."

Sam let his head down and tears began to roll down his face. At that moment, Vaughn looked at General Mulligan, who was already staring at him, as if waiting for a sign. Vaughn gave him a calm and positive gesture by nodding his head affirmatively. Burton looked at Vaughn in agreement.

"Don't worry son." General Mulligan told Sam.

"Everything will be okay now. Everything will be okay, and we will make sure Major Garrison did not sacrifice his life in vain. You have my word son."

"Thank you, sir..." Sam said to General Mulligan.

"These gentlemen would like to have a word with you, son. I would recommend you hear what they have to offer with a very open mind but most of all, with your heart."

Mulligan excused himself from the room and Vaughn then took a couple of steps closer to Sam's bed and pulled out a black envelope from a briefcase his associate Burton had given him.

"What I am about to show you is highly classified and it comes accompanied with an offer, which General Mulligan has given us permission to present to you." Vaughn presented to Sam.

"Major Gray, whether you understand your present situation or not, you have been marked for death, and you are one in a group of privileged individuals who have stared at its face and survived it... And that is not the end of it. From now on, you cannot be part of the world you used to know because if you do, you will not be only putting yourself in the path of death once more, but also anyone else around you.

"Known or unknown to you... This is why we have been entrusted to present to you the opportunity of a lifetime and the only opportunity you will ever have, to keep those you love safe. And, have a chance to avenge the death of your fellow soldier, your brother. We will allow you to extend the career you chose, the career of protecting your country, with the only difference being that this time, you will not be only protecting your country. You will be entrusted with protecting the entire world, Major Gray."

Sam did not yet understand what Vaughn was talking about, but he did not need to hear anything else. He wanted in and he wanted in no matter what the cost would be.

"Major Gray, we will offer you the opportunity to do this by allowing you to become part of the most sacred pact man has crafted to fight against the forces of evil..."

"I'm in sir," Sam answered. There was no regret, fear, nor hesitation in his voice and Vaughn knew at that moment that Sam was one of those men he had always been in search of and had desperately needed to find. Those like him, who will make up the most critical part of World's Alliance Last Line - WALL.

In a very short period of time, Sam was exposed to things he would not have been able to comprehend if they were revealed to him in another case scenario. He was a combat soldier, strong and capable, but Vaughn advised him that neither his strength nor his military skills were full insurance against the world he was about to become part of. Fighting against the forces of evil was not conventional warfare. He would no longer be sent into battle against bullets or rockets but against something much worse and he had already gotten a taste of it.

"Major Gray," Burton said, "We will make arrangements for you to be transported to a different facility, where you will become better acquainted with what we have just presented to you."

Chapter XI:

Unearthing Pain

The next day, late in the evening, Susan and her children had just finished their dinner. Lora and David were playing on the floor. Their old black and white television was tuned in to a variety show which Susan was watching as she finished cleaning the dishes. There was electricity in the neighborhood, something pleasantly surprising for that hour of the day. Susan could hear a larger than usual crowd walking the streets outside. Lora came up to her and told her that they were out of milk. Realizing that the children will need milk for breakfast the next morning, Susan decided to take advantage of the streetlights being on and take a quick trip to the nearest grocery store to get the milk and a loaf of bread.

The children wasted no time and slipped on their sandals. They did not worry about taking off their pajamas since they all wanted to go out fast to be able to come back home as quickly as possible, while the power was still on. The street was more alive than usual, with more people taking advantage of the electricity to run last-minute errands. This allowed Susan a little more breathing room.

Indeed, they rushed as fast as they could in and out of the grocery store. On the way out, Susan was stopped by a young woman who looked very sick and desperate. The woman asked Susan if she could spare some change so that she could get something to eat for the night. Susan attempted to ignore the woman but after taking a second look at her face, she recognized her. Susan remembered that she had been a vibrant and beautiful looking young woman a few years back.

Susan looked at her for a moment and a melancholy feeling took hold of her, the children watched as their mother whispered something.

"Mom..." David said to her, to try to get her attention. Susan then extended her hand to give the woman some money. She took the money from Susan's hand and quickly rushed away from her side to continue looking for anything else she could find on the streets.

The electricity suddenly went out. As the darkness engulfed them, the children and Susan could not see anything past their hands.

She took hold of Lora and David and quickly accelerated her steps on her way back to the house while hearing the low sounding voices of the drug deals being made and the nocturnal plans being arranged between cars and alleyways. "Thank you." Susan and the children were shaken when out of nowhere, they heard the voice of the woman Susan had just given money to. She had followed them, to thank Susan for her kindness.

"Sorry I didn't say it before." The woman added, just before running away from them. For the children, it was very scary, the way the woman appeared and disappeared out of nowhere.

As usual, Lora and David did not like walking in the neighborhood when it was so dark and uneasy feeling. They were anxious to make it back home. Susan continued walking at a fast pace as she looked around to make sure no one was coming too close to her and the children. David again looked at his right arm, not being able to shake off the weird sensation of something being over it as he walked.

Susan and the children finally made it back to the house, Susan took a moment to make sure no one was nearby before she opened the door. As she did, she saw the shadows of two eerie-looking individuals walking in her direction. She quickly pushed the children inside and rushed to close the door.

It was very dark inside the house, but Susan and the children had memorized where their furniture, candles, and matches were, so they were able to move around in the darkness without any worries. Susan told David to hold on to Lora's hand as she got the candles.

"Here they are." Susan lit up a match and was ready to light a candle with it, when she realized that only two candles were remaining and one of them was already half melted.

"Ahhh!" All of a sudden, a very hard knock was heard on the door, Lora and David screamed in fear, but they quickly hunkered down on the floor as they had been taught to do in case of emergencies. The sudden knocking shocked Susan and she dropped the candle and the matches on the floor. Everything became dark again.

"David, don't let go of Lora, ok?" Susan whispered to David, while she quickly went down on the floor to find the candle and the matches.

"Eeeeeeeehhh..!" Someone was shouting right outside the door and this made Susan and the children even more nervous.

"Mommy..." David whispered but Susan quickly him not to worry because she was about to find the candle. Then, the pounding against the door began again very hard, as if someone was trying to break it in.

"Got it." Susan had found the candle and the matches, and she quickly whispered for David and Lora to come her way as she prepared to light the candle once again. David answered but Lora was still in silence. Susan again called her name, but Lora still did not answer.

Susan lit up the candle and David now could see his mother. Susan moved the light towards Lora's face, and she could see that her eyes were wide open, aware of everything that was happening but in total silence.

Susan asked her if she was okay and told her to come near her, but Lora did not move or say anything. Lora just stared at Susan's face with her eyes wide open without making any moves or gestures.

"What's wrong, baby?" Susan again asked Lora, while bringing the illumination of the candle closer to her when she saw a very hairy and dirty looking hand slowly moving over Lora's right shoulder.

Susan screamed, and a quick draft of air blew out the candle's light. Susan fumbled to quickly light it up again.

Susan again screamed out of the top of her lungs as she could see Lora's tears coming down her eyes not able to make a sound due to the very heavy looking hand covering her mouth. She also saw the stare of a skinny and strange-looking man with curly hair and dark eyes that seemed almost too big for the size of his face standing near Lora.

Susan's body was trembling as she looked on, without being able to do anything, how the skinny man caressed Lora's left shoulder with the fingers of his right hand.

"Please, Please..." Susan whispered. "I'm begging you, don't do anything to my children. Please tell me, what do you want from us? We have no money or valuables but take anything you want from the house, but please leave my children alone!"

Susan was trembling and almost at the point of losing her voice. She stared into Lora's eyes while ignoring the heat of the melted candle wax on her finger. She held it straight up with a strong grip to be able to keep the illumination over Lora's face.

"Come to me..." The man behind Lora told Susan while indicating what he wanted. "Come closer to me, I want to tell you something, yes?"

Suddenly little David picked up a cup from the table close to him and hit the man holding Lora over the hand he had on her shoulder. He then kicked the man several times while screaming at him to let go of his little sister. The man holding Lora stumbled, without losing his grip on the little girl.

Susan moved slightly but could not do anything else as another man, heavier looking than the other two, emerged from the darkness behind her. He grabbed David by the hair and pushed him onto the floor. Susan again screamed and pleaded for the safety of her children. The man who had just hit David turned around and looked at her. His hair was long, reaching up to his shoulders. He had a lot of hair that was visible underneath the tank top he was wearing. David looked up to him from the floor, seeing his cotton pants, black shoes, and the large scar on his hand.

"Mommy..." David was crying in pain while lying on the floor holding the back of his head with his hands. The man who pushed him took a couple of slow steps past Susan and towards the one holding Lora. The light of the flame allowed Susan to see the very ominous look in his eyes.

"Little, little girl..." The man said, letting his voice sound in a very low tone. He looked at Susan. She was still petrified and unable to move a muscle, retaining only the strength to keep her arm up as she held the candle.

"Do you want to come with me...?" The skinny man with big eyes asked Susan, staring at her maliciously. Susan's eyes remained only on Lora and David, who was still in pain, crying on the floor. The man with the big eyes then walked a few steps closer to Susan. The larger man with the tank top placed both hands over Lora's shoulders and held them tight. The man with the heavy big hands, who was still unseen, walked around towards Susan was. Lora's eyes opened wider and Susan did not take her sight away from her. She could hear David and see him from the corner of her eyes, but she did not stop looking into Lora's eyes as if she was trying to give her strength.

Then, the man behind Lora began to move his hand around her neck. The unseen man was now standing next to Susan. Susan attempted to move towards her daughter, but she was quickly restrained by the third man. He grabbed Susan's neck with his right hand, and he did it with such strength that she was starting to lose the feeling in her hands. The man holding her neck grabbed her wrist and held it up. The candle was almost about finished, the hot wax melting over her fingers.

Oh God… Susan began to sob, she felt utterly helpless.

"I'll get her, you take the girl, and you kill the boy." The man holding Lora said to the one choking Susan and the other man near David. The man near David held up a lit candle to see better.

The hairy man slowly released the grip around Lora's neck, while eyeing Susan's neck. Susan looked into Lora's eyes, but Lora was not looking at her anymore. Susan's eyes moved, trying to figure out what was it that Lora was looking at. The man who was behind her now was right in front of Susan and he placed his other hand around her neck as he began to strangle her.

"There is nothing you can do now." The man said to Susan while squeezing her neck tighter. "We told you to release this property and you wanted to play hard, and now we will play very, very hard on you and your little children, you stupid bitch!"

"Mom…" Lora said softly. The man strangling Susan turned his face to look at her when he heard her voice.

Susan attempted to look at Lora and as she was able to catch a glimpse of her, she could see her looking, not at her, but in the direction behind the man who was holding her.

"Don't worry, I will take her out of here and you will not have to hear her voice anymore." The man behind Lora told the other strangling Susan. The man with the big eyes was ready to handle David.

"Don't forget about me." He told his associates. All three men shared a quick laugh, as they prepared to conclude what they were there to do.

My babies please, just close your eyes. Susan thought in her mind to her children. She could not speak, she felt herself fading.

"Mom." Little Lora's voice now resounded commandingly, in a sound not her own, and in a manner that called everyone's attention. At that moment everyone in the room looked at her in surprise.

"Close your eyes," Lora said. Suddenly, a gust of wind extinguished the flame of the candle, causing pitch-black darkness to consume all.

"Aaaaahhh!" There was a loud and sudden crying, followed by the sounds of a hard and violent struggle within the confinements of Susan's two-room house.

Outside, under the silent darkness of the night, the homeless woman to whom Susan gave some money to earlier, was walking and carefully moving near the walls of the thresholds with her head facing down trying to find anything of value that anyone may have dropped.

"Hmmm..." Something was shining just a few steps ahead of her and she quickly lunged towards it and threw herself on the floor to get whatever it was.

"Come now, what, what is it?" It turned out to be just a piece of aluminum foil when she picked it up. She dropped it back on the floor as soon as she saw a cigarette butt near the edge of the wall to her right. That wall belonged to Susan's house.

Not thinking twice, the woman placed the cigarette in her mouth and desperately searched for a match within her undergarments to light it up. There were some sounds which captured her attention momentarily but the desire to feel the smoke seeping down her throat and into her lungs were stronger than her curiosity.

"Oh, God..." The portion of the cigarette was very small and as she held it with the tips of her fingers it was almost burning her, but nonetheless, it was a pleasure she desperately needed to feel at that moment.

Then, the window shutters of Susan's house burst open right behind the woman's back, pushing her towards the floor face down. She screamed as she hit the floor startled. But she quickly turned around to see who pushed her from behind. Out of nowhere, she saw a man being flung out through the open window and right above her.

The woman screamed, rolled over and covered her face with her hands. She then heard loud screaming coming from inside the house, prompting the curiosity of some of the neighbors of the adjacent properties. The neighbors discreetly peeped through their windows to see if they could watch what was happening while trying not to make it too obvious. No one cared enough to put themselves in harm's way on behalf of anyone else, there would not be any attempts made to help anyone in need. That was the law of such neighborhoods: No one for anyone.

Silence followed the sound of a very hard and heavy impact. The homeless woman lifted her head up very slowly. She was afraid for her own safety, but she also wanted to know what was going on. She looked around her immediate close space and then checked her body everywhere and realized nothing had happened to her. Now it was time to stand up and see what else took place, and she was very careful to do so. She could still hear certain sounds which she could not understand, nor figure out where exactly they were coming from.

She took several steps away from the wall, while never taking her eyes away from

Susan's house and from the window that was now wide open. Momentarily, the dense clouds covering the entire sky gave way to a glimpse of the moon. Its illumination allowed the woman to see the bloodied bodies of two of the men who had been inside Susan's house, lying dead on the ground only steps away from her feet.

The homeless woman couldn't believe what she was seeing, she was shaking uncontrollably and even more frightened now than before. She quickly placed both of her hands over her mouth to prevent herself from screaming as she got a closer look at the dead bodies. One of them was the skinny man with big eyes, and the other was the one in the tank top.

"Oh, God..." She murmured, realizing that she actually recognized one of the dead men.

Then, another loud impact made the woman fall backward on the floor. She screamed even louder this time and rolled over and away from the dead men as fast as she could. She crawled up against a wall across from Susan's house, which stopped her from moving back any further. Again, she looked everywhere checking every part of her body to make sure nothing had happened to her. Her back was against the wall of a house which was divided into three different rooms. There was a window right above her head and someone could be seen blowing a candle out, then shutting closed the curtains and the shutters abruptly.

It was very dark once more. The homeless woman was breathing hard and her hands and knees were shaking. Her eyes were wide open and deadlocked on Susan's window.

"I… I've got to get the hell out of here… I have to…" The homeless woman was attempting to propel herself up and out of there, but her body was not responding, and she could not force herself to move a muscle.

She looked up to peer inside the house from where she was sitting. She did her best to close her trembling lips tightly as she held her breath. It was pitch-black, and she could not see anything into the window but from within its darkness someone was looking straight at her and she could not avoid the sensation of being watched.

She felt it. She felt a heavy stare all over her skin. She felt as if someone was right in front of her, breathing over her head. Her eyes were tightly shut now and only when she heard the screeching sound of the window closing slowly, she was able to open them again. She couldn't understand what she was seeing. Shadowy dark hands were pulling the window shutters in. Hands that were too big to be human.

"What the hell is happening inside this house…?" She asked herself. She was frightened to her core and was still hearing the echoing sounds which she could not figure out. Something suddenly jolted her to stand up and run away from there as fast as her legs could take her.

∞

The next morning, at a border town close to Los Chiles, located to the south of Nicaragua and to the north of San Jose in Costa Rica, the 9:30 a.m. bus arrived on time at the bus station, which served as the major connection to other cities and towns to the east and west. The day was bright and sunny, and the area was packed with local merchants and a variety of stores providing goods and services. The hundreds of travelers who passed through the station from near and faraway places daily relied on these merchants.

The local government and the individuals in charge of managing it had been provided with some much-needed funds by some members of the cabinet, working for the newly elected President Romalyn. With their assistance and observations made by presidential envoys, local mayors were able to improve the area for tourism and this gave a boost to the local economy. There was a renewed charge of energy to that once-forgotten part of the country. The energy which was being channeled not only by the local merchants but also by international interests from neighboring countries.

Thirty-year-old Clayton Barns had just gotten out of the nine-thirty bus. Although he was an unassuming man, he had a notion that to the locals, he was not from around there. He looked like just another tourist. He was already expecting for the vendors to approach with the usual traps they use to entice tourists into spending their money on useless items. Nevertheless, he looked around trying to blend in and not attention calling. But his crew cut, good physical shape, his demeanor, and clothes placed a barrier between himself and the actual tourists passing by the place. He was wearing a light blue dress shirt, black pants, black shoes and dark shades which allowed him to observe people without anyone noticing it. He was carrying a light briefcase in his left hand and a folded map in between the fingers of his right hand. Barns took a moment to appreciate the view provided by the mountains behind the land he had just traveled through. He removed his sunglasses to look at the view in the distance, revealing his blue eyes and a small scar above his nose.

Several of the taxi drivers stationed in the area approached Barns offering their services but he just continued walking, politely ignoring them. He was quietly observing the surroundings as he made sure he had a fair assessment of everything taking place around him.

After walking towards the corner of the street, Barns then saw something that captured his attention. He walked across towards a small cigarette store with a wooden sign hanging over the door, which appeared as if it had recently been polished and painted. There was a man seated inside a parked car reading an international newspaper printed in English, just outside the store. The man looked like a local, there was nothing special about him. Cheap silver-framed sunglasses, white shirt with sleeves rolled up and a thin gold chain with a very small cross. His black hair was lacking a haircut. A mustache that covered a small portion of his upper lip. Hairy arms and lightly tanned skin. Barns stopped at a short distance away from the car and looked at the driver momentarily, while many of the bus passengers who had just arrived as well, walked in and out of the store after getting their last-minute drinks, snacks, newspapers, and smokes.

"This place is much more crowded than I was expecting." Barns said to the man seated inside the car. Barns began placing the map near the car's window so that the driver could see it.

"Believe it or not my friend, you arrived here on a very slow day." The man inside the car smiled slyly, while gently taking the map from Barns' hand to place it inside the newspaper he was reading.

Barns then pulled out a cigarette and placed it in between his lips before pulling out a small box of matches from his left pants pocket. After lighting up the cigarette and releasing a long cloud of smoke, Barns looked back at the other side of the street and in a discreet manner, studied it from end to end.

The driver then invited him to come inside the car, but Barns took a moment to meticulously observe every single detail of everything and everyone across the street one last time. He then took one more drag from his cigarette and walked towards the passenger side door while releasing the smoke into the air and then dropping the cigarette on the ground. As soon as Barns got inside the car, the driver smoothly drove away from the area of the bus station, under the curious eyes of some of the regular taxi drivers stationed there.

"Barns." Barns said introducing himself.

"Jenkins." The driver replied.

"How long have you been here?" Barns asked the driver while placing another cigarette in between his lips.

"Around three weeks, but I didn't travel here directly," Jenkins replied. "I met with a handler in Venezuela and I stayed there for two days waiting for additional information about the logistics concerning the target's location. The handler was told that the target had informers everywhere and they must proceed with extreme caution. He provided me with a solid alias, and additional info so that I would not look out of place in this part of the world. There was also a theatrical introduction to my character.

"Me being chased by a jealous ex-girlfriend back in Venezuela, getting arrested when I got into town and I'm now out on bail until the woman, who is accusing me of abuse, gets to this country to proceed with the court process. Etc." He then looked at Barns.

"That was quite an introduction to your character, as you said." Barns commented.

"It was a joke," Jenkins replied, laughing as he was searching for a cigarette inside his shirt pocket.

"You were convincing, I have to give it to you!" Barns laughed as well.

"I came to this country to get married to someone I met a few months ago." The driver continued. "This is the real story. During a night of wild pre-wedding celebration, we got into a brawl and we ended up arrested. She was released the next morning, while I spent two more nights in jail. I am from Venezuela and I have problems with the government there. My wife-to-be paid off the chief of police and three of the cops at the station, to get me out of there without much questioning. I got out, and now I have a bad reputation. My woman and I have to fight disorderly conduct charges, which will be thrown out anyway."

"So, this is the actual alibi?" Barns asked. He stared at the driver, partially confused by the story.

"Yea, it had to be done. My performance created the perfect alibi for you and our other partner arriving in two days. My old friends are coming to see me to offer me moral support. And one of them is an attorney! And he offered to help me by giving me some advice on how to beat the charges."

"And you actually believe that they will buy that here?" Barns asked, with doubt in his voice.

"I am here, you are here," Jenkins replied. "Let us wait for our third party. If we're still alive and operational after that, then it worked. We all entered the country through unconventional routes, and this government does not have any reliable intelligence agencies. I am more afraid of the regional drug cartels. They are in fact, able to collect more intel if and when they need to. They are the ones we need to be careful with."

"That is exactly what I'm afraid of." Barns said.

"In this case," Jenkins replied, "the false intel they were able to acquire from one of their sources, was regarding their rivals." Barns stared at Jenkins as he spoke. "They will be momentarily distracted by that. It will buy us enough time to get our job done." Jenkins kept his eyes on the road.

"Let us hope that it will." Barns commented, keeping his arm outside the window while enjoying the view of the open road Jenkins had taken to drive to their next destination.

"By the way," Jenkins asked, "how's your Spanish?"

Barns looked at him and smiled. "¿Qué piensas tú?"

∞

Elsewhere, the strange homeless man was lurking by the side of a tree on a hill that was surrounded by a dense forest. His long dark hair was covering the sides of his face. A volcano could be seen miles away in the background. As he slowly hunched down till his knees were near his chest, he wrapped his arms around his legs. His eyes were wide open, revealing a dark and eerie glare, staring out into the distance.

In the valley far away, the final group of new arrivals of a Gypsy clan was being welcomed by those who were already settled. Their lengthy voyage had originated from Eastern Europe and had been arranged by an unknown benefactor. The benefactor till this time, had been sponsoring them and putting things together to grant them safe passage into their new country.

The newcomers were only passing by this particular village, their final dwelling place had already been prearranged elsewhere in another part of the forest. Some of those walking became surprised and their faces filled up with happiness. They spotted an unexpected person who had come to greet them. Senuca, the *Phuri Dai*, the leader of the clan, walked out from amongst a group of very intimidating looking Gypsy men. Those men who walked very close to her were keeping her under their protection.

Senuca was a lady in her late fifties but very well maintained. She was wearing a dark color gown with a scarf the same color over her shoulders. Another scarf covered part of her hair. Her skin was tanned, her eyebrows were thick and dark, just like her jet-black hair. Her eyes were dark green and spellbinding. She was rigid looking, strengthened by time. Senuca embraced one of the youngest children and kissed her forehead as the rest of the Gypsies gathered around, greeting her with reverence.

"And where is Adamo? I have been waiting to see how big he has gotten." Senuca spoke in her native Romany language to address Irina, who was the apprentice of the leader of the group that had just arrived. She was a young and vibrant looking woman, with dark eyes and her light brown hair set in a ponytail. She was wearing a long green skirt and a black t-shirt. Irina had taken several steps closer to Senuca, with her eyes down, in reverence to the Phuri Dai.

"Thank you for arriving to greet us personally my Phuri Dai," Irina said to Senuca while greeting her with the utmost respect, bending down on one knee and kissing her right hand.

"Adamo is so big and handsome now. You would not recognize him anymore." Irina said. "He has become a Gadjo Kris now my Phuri Dai, very responsible.

Madame Ina decided to allow him to guide some of the elite young warriors ahead of time, due to the skills and level-headedness he has displayed with his duties on previous occasions."

"Wise decision." Senuca commentated. "But I was still expecting to see him leading the protective party at Ina's arrival."

"Yes, my Phuri Dai, he takes his responsibilities with more seriousness than everyone else. As soon as we set foot on this solid ground, he headed out to inspect with Rhodri and his men. They wanted to go into town and scout the areas to see how things will be, but Adamo opted for meeting with the leaders of the Krisatora at the village, to begin preparations for Madame Ina's state. He told his men, 'the town will not go anywhere, and there will be time to study it at a later moment'." Irina then became silent, realizing maybe she had said too much about the son of Senuca's younger sister, Ina.

Senuca did not say anything to Irina, but she had a thought before she took several steps to welcome the rest of the people of her clan. Irina also had a thought after seeing the Phuri Dai's reaction. She knew too well how possessive Senuca was with those who fell into her goodwill, and for this reason, she was not completely sure of whether to trust her or not. Adamo was one of those who shared her favoritism. She loved him as if he was her own son and this reason alone made Irina worry. She knew too well that Senuca and Ina did not see eye to eye, with Senuca always asserting her stamp on the final word of all the clans' affairs, just so that she can always keep her power over her younger sister, who also happened to love Adamo like the son she never had.

From the distance, the homeless man was watching every one of them. His vision allowed him to view them as if he was seeing them from only a few feet away. He looked everywhere but he could not find what he was actually searching for within the group of new arrivals.

He allowed his eyes to close and after revisiting several memories, he settled on one where a man with long black hair and a silver streak, was snatching a young girl in a violent struggle and leaping out from the window of a castle. He slowly transported his mind into another occasion, where he was seated inside a car with his eyes closed. His head was down, and his long hair was trickling down moisture over his clothes. The sound of heavy rain falling over the top of the car, and rowdy drunk people running about, were part of the ambient background belonging to the unsettling night.

The car was parked in a very dark alleyway, behind a big truck and some people could be seen walking back and forth running to seek cover from the rain, going inside the place across the street. That place happened to be a very popular restaurant bar, that was frequented by dangerous people and those in search of a good time, cheap drinks and easy women.

Inside the place, the scene was very noisy and festive with everything out in the open- music played loudly, cigarette smoke filled the air, barely dressed women walked around the bar and cruised back and forth in the arms of their potential clients. While others drank and reveled in the momentary happiness. It was what took place behind the secret closed doors, by the back entrance next to the kitchen, that gave real importance to the place. At that moment, a lucrative deal was about to be finalized between a very influential politician, Manuel Solano and the feared 'El Salvador.'

Salvador was about to make a payment to Solano to guarantee arrangements for the proper migratory status of a group of illegal foreigners, including a substantial number of Gypsies, which at that time were yet to arrive in the country. The transport vessel bringing them had been delayed due to unknown circumstances. Solano was well connected and was at that time in charge of the office of interior, immigration, and all foreign affairs matters, making him the go-to man for what Salvador needed.

Solano was very corrupt, easily swayed and more than willing to put himself at the service of a man like Salvador. At that moment, Solano was being kissed on his ear by an attractive woman in a short, tight pink dress sitting on his lap. He let Salvador know that for the right price, everything could be arranged.

"Very well Mr. Solano," Salvador said, speaking in Spanish with a very refined accent while looking at some of his men in the room. "I don't yet fully know you, but you come well recommended. Now we will do business." One of his many men in the room poured more Champagne into Solano's glass at Salvador's request. Solano was being entertained, kissing the woman by his side, smelling her hair while enjoying his drink. Salvador observed him calmly and collectively. He was just analyzing Solano's behavior before deciding to make a toast.

"To our new partnership, with the distinguished members of our government. Salud!" Salvador said, raising his glass in the air.

Everyone cheered, and Solano gleefully agreed with Salvador, fully aware that with this opportunity, he was going to finally be able to acquire the wealth and real influence that he had been yearning for.

"I want to tell you, Mr. Salvador." Solano began saying. "That it makes me incredibly happy. And it gives me great satisfaction that a man of your reputation and caliber, has taken the steps to join forces with me. With my position in the present establishment, I guarantee that you will not be disappointed in putting this investment in my hands." Solano then happily gulped down his drink.

"I have great hopes for you Mr. Solano," Salvador replied, taking a sip from his champagne. Solano went on to promise to personally be at the helm of any operation that required the assistance of his cabinet. "I will personally guarantee your total satisfaction and success in utilizing this country's borders and anything else you wish for me to place at your disposal."

Solano's words were the type of words Salvador always liked to hear from the people he was about to put inside his pocket. Salvador was wearing dark glasses and Solano could not clearly see the expression of his eyes, but he saw that Salvador was smiling and Solano did not hesitate to drink his entire glass of Champagne and then ask for more. He began kissing the woman by his side as he told her how much he desired her at that moment and all of the things he wanted to do with her.

"Very well then…" Salvador commented, just before calling on one of his men.

"José!"

José was one of Salvador's three trusted handlers. He was a short and intimidating looking man, a little overweight, sporting a curly afro with lots of hair products in it. As he heard his name, he opened a door behind him, and three other men walked into the room each carrying a brown box.

Salvador began walking away from Solano, while politely asking the women to leave the room for a while.

"Sir…" José said, speaking to Salvador in Spanish. At that moment Salvador put his glass down on a table close to him and took off his sunglasses and handed them to a man standing by his right side.

The men then placed the boxes next to each other on the table. José pulled out a small knife from his back pocket and slit open the top of all three. Then he slowly walked backward, while keeping his eyes on Solano.

At that moment Solano stopped smiling, he noticed the weird manner in which José looked at him as he walked back, and he could not help getting a strange feeling. The man by Salvador's right gave a signal to the woman under Solano's arm and she hurriedly walked out of the room.

"Mr. Salvador, what is going on?" Solano asked Salvador, as he saw him walking behind him. Salvador placed his left hand over Solano's left shoulder. Solano took one last sip of his drink before putting it down on the table without turning around to face Salvador.

"Mr. Salvador…?" Solano again asked nervously but he still got no one to answer and Salvador continued standing behind him with his hand still over his shoulder.

Salvador then moved towards Solano's right side and slowly opened the top of one of the boxes closer to him.

"Manuel, Manuel, Manuel…" Salvador commented while taking two steps away from him.

Solano looked over at Salvador nervously and after a few seconds that began to feel like years, he finally looked at the box Salvador had just opened.

"Mr. Salvador...?" Solano's voice trembled. Sweat was beginning to drip down the sides of his face.

"I have seen the likes of many good men die in very wrong ways and for various wrong reasons." Salvador began to say to Solano. "When I think about some of those men Manuel, it upsets me. It upsets me to know that their fate was subject to the stupidity of a few, or for someone's material gain."

Salvador took a couple of steps and with his back turned against Solano, he continued speaking.

"From the time I was very young, I have been surrounded by death, Manuel. I have seen women and children being slaughtered like cattle, their bodies cut into pieces and given to the pigs or the dogs or even birds. Human beings lost due to the circumstances of being in places in which they did not belong, vanished never to be heard from again. Some people I know attribute such cases as pure bad luck, 'being in the wrong place at the wrong time,' my father used to say that. Others... others would argue differently. In any case, Manuel, whoever is dead, is dead, end of it. End of their chapter, end to the problem they represented."

Solano's face grew more worried after each word Salvador said. Salvador then pulled out a black bag from the box he had opened and walked closer to Solano with it. He then signaled one of his men, who then ushered Solano to sit on a couch, as Salvador placed the bag on a coffee table in front of the couch. He remained standing right where he was, just staring at Solano, completely expressionless.

Solano was very worried, but he did not know exactly what was happening and what was the point Salvador was attempting to convey. His fear and lack of experience in situations such as the one he was in, took the best of him to the point in which he could not even speak, out of fear of saying something wrong.

"Manuel, if there is one thing in life that I hate more than having a bad dream, is a traitor," Salvador said.

"My father once gave me advice, it was the only one he ever gave me, and I believe it was because he knew it was the only advice I would ever need in my life. He said, '*Son, every good man knows this from birth. Always surround yourself with thieves, murderers, alcoholics, prostitutes and wise men. But never be near liars. Words will sometimes cause more damage than actual actions.*'"

Salvador then motioned to Solano to look inside the black bag.

"Mr…" Solano attempted to speak. But Salvador quickly placed the index finger of his left hand over his own lips and with his right hand he ordered Solano to go ahead and open the bag.

"Mr. Salvador I…" Solano attempted to speak again but this time Salvador was not as friendly as before and in a slightly aggressive tone of voice, ordered Solano to open the bag.

Solano's skin was already beginning to turn pale, drops of sweat were trickling down from the hairline of his forehead and his throat had become completely dry. And without anything else that could have possibly been done at that particular moment, he proceeded to open the black bag in front of him.

Solano's hands were shaky and sweaty, his head was turned the other way as a pungent odor began seeping out from within the bag. He was only looking at the bag from the corner of his right eye, which was now only partially open. After a few seconds, he finally gathered his courage and opened the bag and quickly retrieved his hands away from it. He did not even attempt to look at what was inside.

Salvador extended his right hand and was quickly given a glass of Champagne which he began drinking while staring at Solano. Solano's eyes were still closed, and his body was still shivering as Salvador ordered Solano's glass to be refilled as well. At that moment Solano opened up only his right eye and observed as the Champagne began filling up his glass all the way from the bottom till it reached the top. The man filling Solano's glass placed the bottle right next to the glass and began to step away.

"Salud!" Salvador told Solano while lifting his glass up. Solano looked at Salvador not knowing what to do but noticing Salvador was waiting for him to pick up his glass as well. Solano went ahead and in a very slow manner, picked up the glass and slowly stood up as Salvador looked him in the eyes.

"Mr. Salvador… I, I don't understand." Solano muttered he was about to put the glass up to his lips when all of a sudden, he placed it back on the table and with his other hand he reached towards the black bag and slightly moved it.

His eyes opened widely, and his mouth dropped as he was both surprised and taken back. A surreal sense of relief took over his body as he plopped back down to the couch and picked up his glass and drank it till it was empty. Solano then placed it back on the table before picking up the bottle and bringing it over his open mouth to pour the Champagne all over himself until the bottle was empty.

"Mr. Salvador, why would you do this?" Solano asked, while looking at the bag and what was inside of it. At that moment, preparations were being made for Salvador's departure and he was getting ready to walk out of the room after giving his glass to one of his men.

"You are now a part of us," Salvador told Solano. "This gesture doesn't mean you are indebted to me. Your problems are now our problems and our problems are yours. Anything or anyone in your way will cease being a problem. I expect that all our matters are dealt with swiftly and with proper due diligence so that from now on, our mutual interests always go hand in hand Manuel. In the other two boxes are the rest of the heads of your enemies. Continue enjoying your evening now Manuel."

Salvador then signaled one of his men who went ahead and allowed several others to come inside the room with more boxes, while three others picked up the black bag and the boxes, which were brought into the room before, and took them elsewhere to be disposed of.

"Did you ever imagine that you would become an instant millionaire on a night like tonight Mr. Solano?" Arnold said, adjusting his glasses. He stayed behind to finalize the details Salvador needed to get done. He asked Solano if he was feeling well, while Solano looked at a large amount of the money he had just received as payment. He remained sitting with eyes of disbelief. Arnold pulled up a chair to sit right next to him.

Outside, the rain was slowing but the water was still trickling down from rooftops. Four heavily armed men came out of an SUV parked by a dark alley at the back of the nightspot. Two other SUV's were positioned not far, with more armed men inside.

One of the men who was nicknamed Chaparro was smoking a cigarette. The man standing next to him asked him to move away from the truck before the boss got back. The boss was very strict about people smoking around him or anyone he knew, he suffered from asthma and his tolerance for smokers was very short, even though he himself was a smoker and enjoyed a good cigar from time to time.

Chaparro quickly walked away from the truck, while holding his machine gun with his left hand and the smoke inside his mouth so it would not be lingering in the air near the vehicles and bother Salvador.

The homeless man was not inside the car anymore. The four men around the SUV's did not know but he was standing right by their side, staring at them in silence. He was leaning against a wall with his head down, water dripping down from his hair, covered by the shadows.

Then, the sound of a two-way radio was heard and one of the men carrying the radio quickly answered. The man was told that Salvador was already exiting and would be there very soon. The man told the others and they all assumed their positions to wait for their boss.

"Chaparro I told you to take the cigarette away from here, the boss is coming out and you damn well know he does not like anybody smoking near him. Chaparro!" Chaparro was being reprimanded by his partner. He could not see Chaparro from where he was but could see the smoke coming his way from where Chaparro was standing.

"Okay Miguel, I'm done," Chaparro shouted out to Miguel, without revealing the reason why he did not answer sooner.

He had been watching how the smoke exhaling from his mouth was moving in the air. He blew the smoke right ahead of his face but as it exited his mouth it was deviating from a straight line and was dividing into two directions, left and right as if he was blowing it at an invisible wall or something right in front of him.

He waved his arm left and right, but he could not feel anything. "Que estrano. How strange." He commented.

Salvador exited from the secret back entrance accompanied by his small army. He was ushered into one of the SUV's at the center, and after the rest of the men assumed their positions in the other vehicles, they went on their way.

The vehicle going at the back of the convoy had several men operating jamming devices, which they were using to tap into the satellite feeds of the local television networks, to make sure the satellite phones Salvador utilized to communicate with his associates, were not being spied on by the Americans and to keep Salvador secure and protected from his enemies.

At the same time, a mysterious dark mist was traveling at the same speed the vehicles moved, right on top of the main SUV carrying Salvador, undisturbed by the wind that was blowing against its direction.

Sometime later on the same night, all the SUV's were engulfed in flames and all around were the dead bodies of Salvador's men. A mansion, hidden deep within a forest area was also burning and shots, explosions, and loud shouting could be heard well into the distance.

The homeless man was walking away from the entrance of the mansion unbothered by the shots and explosions around him. He was dragging a very large and heavy-looking sack with his right hand and carrying another one, just like it but larger than him, over his left shoulder. He slowly paced over to where there was a flatbed truck, which had at one point, been driven into one of the walls of the house. He lifted both sacks into the air as if they were filled with just feathers and flipped them over the back of the truck.

The loud sound of a man crying and running from within the house, firing his machine gun frenetically in every direction, did not faze him. As he stood next to the truck, the man ran right to his face while still firing his weapon. Bullets went everywhere, passing by the homeless man's head. The man shooting was still shouting very loudly but it was as if he was not even seeing the homeless man standing right in his face. He looked inside the driver side of the truck, while shooting at it and turned around without taking his finger off the trigger.

He continued shooting everywhere erratically, while the homeless man stood motionless right behind him. Then, in a very calm manner, the homeless man slowly extended his left arm until his left hand reached the back of the man shooting. His hand was half closed and as he allowed his fingers to extend to full length, the head of the man popped like a balloon, splashing blood and brains all over the place where he was standing. His lifeless body dropped down to the ground.

The homeless man then closed his eyes and his gaze reached another place far from where he was. He saw two others, with long hair and strange looking just like him. They were searching inside a cave and suddenly, he saw a third one and this one was staring right at him. At that moment he quickly opened his eyes and wondered momentarily, while a light blue glow calmly covered his body like a moving wave.

"Time is shortening…" He thought, just before jumping onto the driver side of the truck and pulling it away from the wall to drive it into the denseness of the forest. In the meantime, Chaparro was shaking, his lips were quivering, and he could help but urinate all over himself.

He and Salvador were the only survivors of the massacre and were attempting to figure out where whatever or whoever it was that attacked them was hiding now. They searched the entire house by looking into all the monitors of the cameras they had covering the property.

At the moment of the assault, Chaparro was about to be reprimanded by Salvador. Because of him smoking, he left his post outside of the nightspot and all hell broke loose and every one of the men began to get killed.

Not knowing the magnitude of the attack but understanding that it had been a major one, Salvador armed himself and alone with Chaparro protecting him by his side, they made a run towards the panic room Salvador had prepared for the worst-case scenario. A solid metal box surrounded by thirty inches of concrete, from where he could maintain control of the cameras and lock himself from the inside.

As they ran for it, Salvador and Chaparro were able to see several of the men being killed by only the air around them. Salvador's eyes opened widely as he saw one of his men shooting at the front entrance next to three others when he saw the lower part of his body just lift into the air while his upper torso broke in the other direction, as if he was a toy.

When Chaparro saw another man being torn in half by thin air, he dropped his weapon to the ground and ran faster than he never had in his life. He ran to get into the panic room where Salvador was already closing the door. He made it just in the nick of time, nearly losing a hand while entering, as Salvador would not slow down the door to wait for him.

Chaparro and Salvador took their time looking into all the monitors. Some of them were completely disabled and others had been shot down by his own men. Chaparro was able to find one which was still operational and he quickly rewinded the video that had been recorded.

"Oh my God!" Chaparro exclaimed upon seeing what happened to the man who was killed last. They were in shock and completely horrified. Salvador was in silence, carefully watching the video. The two men could not believe what their eyes were telling them and yet they were seeing it.

The video showed the man shooting everywhere and all the time, there was what appeared to be a translucent cloud of dark fog, almost resembling the shape of a person. It was hovering right near him, but the video feed became unstable from time to time, making it difficult for them to figure out what exactly they were looking at.

The man shooting did not seem to see it, even though he appeared to be firing right into it. Then they watched as the man turned his head away from the foggy figure and a strange hand extended from within the fog and the resemblance of someone's face could be seen as well. Just like before, the mysterious figure caused the man's head to explode and his lifeless body then dropped to the ground.

Chaparro was nearly losing his mind as he began crying. Salvador's face neared closer to the monitor. He wanted to get a clearer look at what he believed he was looking at. What they thought was the face emanating from the mysterious mist, appeared to turn over to where the camera was and stared at it. They could clearly see it mumbling the words, '*Salvador, you will be next*'. The video then went dark when a sudden electric charge erupted all over the property.

Chaparro was petrified and still unable to utter a word, he saw what he saw, and he knew that Salvador saw it too. Now, the one thing in his mind was finding a way of staying as far away as possible from the man he had once sworn to protect with his own life.

Salvador was still looking at the TV monitor. He did not take his eyes away from it. Almost as if expecting to see something else, but there was no image and no feed from the camera whatsoever. Chaparro looked at him.

"Boss..?" He asked. Salvador did not look at him, nor answer. He remained staring at the monitor and thinking. After a few minutes, Salvador finally looked at Chaparro. He had something in his mind as he walked around and wondered while thinking it through.

"It was him…" Salvador murmured.

The homeless man opened his eyes again and observed as the new arrivals of Gypsies began dispersing to continue making their way to the other village. He observed as Senuca was being ushered to a pathway back towards her quarters when she made a sudden stop. The Kris around her did as well. She stayed where she was, looking down to the ground, motionless for a moment. She then lifted her head and slowly turned to stare towards where the homeless man had been staring at her from.

He then turned his head toward the opposite direction, and he could see someone turning their head around to look at him from a great distance, across an ocean. But he could not see the face, nor the resemblances of who it was.

At that moment, a gentle light blue glow surrounded his entire body. He vanished from where he was, just as Senuca's sight was set upon the direction of the hill he had been observing her from. She saw nothing but the trees.

Senuca remained motionless, in silence. Romano, her most trusted Kris took it upon himself to ask her if she needed for him to go and scout those hills, but she did not answer. Instead, she ordered everyone to leave her.

All her Kris dispersed but remained not too far from her proximity to ensure her safety, even from the unlikely scenario of a domestic assault. Romano watched her until she was already near the entrance of her quarters. He saw as she placed her right hand over the curtain which covered the entrance of her tent but hesitated for a second to open it and walk inside. Romano then looked at the direction of the hills and signaled two of his men to accompany him, while with another signal of his head, letting the others know to stay close to Senuca's tent.

Sometime later, Romano and his men went to scout the hill that Senuca had been gazing at earlier in the day. Romano found himself standing at the same place the homeless man had been standing before. He looked around and told his men to move farther and make sure the entire area was clear before they came back to him. He looked at two others, they looked at him, almost signaling that they were having the same thought.

"There is no clear sight of our village from here." Romano thought out loud to himself. "What could she have been staring at?"

Chapter XII:

Searching Thoughts

Four days later, back in Costa Rica...

It was a bright and sunny morning. Karina had accompanied Luludja, one of the village elders, to take a walk to one of the local markets of a nearby town. Luludja was in her 80's. She had a very mild manner to her personality, which was enhanced by the steady gaze of her deep black eyes. Her skin was dark brown, and her hair was long and gray which she had wrapped under a long green scarf. The scarf was the same color as the long skirt she was wearing, with a long-sleeve dark blue blouse.

Their traditional attire set them apart from everyone in the area. Karina was in her early twenties and much taller than the elder. She wore a long flower printed dress, with flowy sleeves and a blue scarf wrapped around her waist. She also wore a brown pearl necklace and kept her hair in a long ponytail, just as Roberta. Roberta who was thirteen years old with a very thin nose, dark eyes, and rosy cheeks. She was wearing bell-bottom pants, with a dark purple blouse and an old pair of leather sandals that day.

Roberta was busy walking with nine-year-old Clara. Clara had jet-black hair which was uncombed and all over the place. Her eyes were dark green, and she kept covering them from the sun. Her suntan made her appear a lot darker. Her ears were slightly too big for someone her size. She was wearing blue capri pants, white sneakers, and a long beige t-shirt.

Clara and Roberta were allowed to tag along with the elder, after requesting permission from their Phuri Dai. Some looked at them with curious eyes, assuming they may be the Gypsies, who have come into their town recently. Clara was the daughter of Antonio, one of the Gadjo Kris from Ina's village, but Karina had known her since she was born. Clara gave Karina an excuse to go and visit Ina's village from time to time, and she would go to bring Clara to visit Senuca's village. Karina also uses the opportunity to catch glimpses of Adamo, which had not gone unnoticed by Marloft; something she was unaware of.

Their clan of Gypsies were known to be very good farmers and had prided themselves in the true art of preserving their well-regarded spices to unbelievable flavors. But on this day, Luludja, a superior farmer herself, had the rare desire to step out of the confines of the village and walk around the gorgers (non-Gypsies) and see for herself what they have to offer in their markets.

Roberta was a very conservative youth who made it a priority keeping Clara very close to her, to keep her in line with her clan's rules. Clara was curious and energetic and enjoyed investigating and getting to the bottom of things as soon as she could. Luludja had brought Roberta over to walk with her near an area where the people selling their goods, specialized mostly in different types of spices. Clara walked ahead playfully, touching, smelling and inquiring about the stages of ripeness of some of the vegetables, spices, and fruits being sold. For her young age, she was very good at the art of farming, earning much respect from the other youth and as well as the elders. Clara saw something which she wanted to feel up close, and she skipped away from Roberta.

"Clara, can you not please?" Roberta yelled at her, shouting in Romani. But Clara waved her hand, letting her know she will not go far. Some of the people around heard Roberta speak and reacted in a certain manner. They did not recognize the foreign-sounding language and it sounded strange to them. Karina saw how agitated Roberta was becoming and approached her, as Luludja examined and smelled some of the spices close to her.

"Roberta, try not to stress yourself with her too much," Karina told her. "You have to understand that she is at that age, where she's becoming aware of things, more than before. You were once there, not too long ago."

"No Karina," Roberta said, walking ahead to reach after Clara. "I was not as rowdy and out of control as she is." Roberta took big fast steps to catch up to Clara, but Clara was too excited, running all over the place, even stealing some fruits by hiding them under her t-shirt. Runner, the little boy, was working in one of the small areas, helping one of the farmers to sell his vegetables. He noticed Clara stealing the fruits and Clara in return saw him watching her as she did. They both smiled and dismissed each other as if nothing had happened.

In no time, Roberta had lost track of Clara. She became upset and went back to Karina and Luludja to complain about it. Karina had noticed how upset Roberta was and insisted on Karina going after Clara with her.

"Luludja, give me your permission if you can," Karina asked the elder. She had to let her know ahead of time because she was in charge of the elder's care, not Roberta.

"Go on child, look around. Breathe as well." Luludja said smiling.

Karina asked Roberta to stay calm beside the elder, as she went ahead to find Clara. She began looking around the market, noticing how the men stared at her with curiosity and the women, with indifference. She paid them no mind, she looked at her clothing for a moment and laughed at how much she must stick out in the crowd. *I should have picked out the green skirt and the white blouse.* She thought to herself with a smile on her face.

In the meantime, Clara was enjoying an apple while Runner ate an orange. They were seated on the ground behind the worn-out wooden walls of the market, next to a small mountain of weeds and cardboard boxes and other things.

"¿Cómo te llamas?" Runner asked Clara her name, speaking to her in Spanish.

"Clara, es mi nombre." Clara replied in Spanish.

Runner had orange pulp all over his face, and Clara laughed at him as she got closer to him, to give him a piece of cloth.

"Here, clean up your mouth." She said. Runner took the cloth and wiped his face and mouth. Karina walked nearby where they were and spotted them. She watched them momentarily before she decided to go get Clara, but someone suddenly grabbed her hand and yanked her to the side. Karina reacted swiftly by grabbing the arm of the person pulling her and she was able to turn the tables around in a second. She placed her left leg behind the person's leg and knocked the person to the ground. It was a man that she saw falling to the ground. Clara saw Karina fighting and reacted quickly by pulling a small knife from the back of her pants, running to Karina's aid. Runner saw Clara run and was stunned by how feisty she was.

"Who the hell do you think you are?" Karina shouted at the man, while also pulling out a small knife hidden behind her back.

"It's me!" The man was shocked by Karina's reaction.

"Adamo?" Karina was surprised. Upon hearing his voice, she lowered her guard and retrieved the blade of her knife from the man's direction. Clara got to her side quickly and was ready to attack. Karina had to restrain her, she knew Clara was very aggressive and protective of those she loved. Runner also made it to their side, very alarmed, yet curious.

"Who are they?" Runner asked Clara. Karina kept her hand over Clara's chest, to keep her behind. She did not want to let her see Adamo. Adamo got up to his feet, dusting the grass and dirt off his clothes. He had on dark jeans that were slightly bell-bottomed, dark brown boots and a black shirt with his sleeves slightly rolled up. His Middle Eastern looks made him stand out from everyone else in the area. He had thick, dark, wavy hair, a sharp nose and deep-set eyes with a gaze that always seemed to look out into the horizon.

"You are getting better and stronger than before. I like it." Adamo said before taking a quick peek at Clara, whose mean stare gave him the impression of a warrior. Runner looked nervous.

Clara looked at Adamo, head to toes, immediately recognizing him. She knew her father was under his command. She recognized his status, by the purple cloth wrapped around his belt over his right hip, that indicated he was a *Gadjo Kris*, a high-ranking warrior amongst the Gypsies.

"Karina?" Clara said hinting to Karina, seeking for her to answer what she already believed she knew.

"Yes. He is." Karina responded to Clara, while staring into Adamo's eyes, as he did into hers. "I need to have a short conversation with Adamo." Runner did not understand what they said, but the scene was very interesting to him. "Can you go and stay where you have been, where I can see you and your new friend?"

"Ven conmigo," Clara said to Runner, taking him away with her.

"What are you doing here?" Karina asked Adamo.

Adamo took a step closer to her. She retreated, taking two steps back. "You are aware that you and your sect are not allowed to venture into this part of this town."

"This land, as well as the other lands we have been received into, does not belong to us. And we don't want to belong to them. And yet, we are creating borders and rules around us, which we so hate. It was fate that I ventured around these parts on this day Karina. Look at what surprise the Divine has offered me... Your presence."

"Are you alone?" Karina asked, as she looked around. She saw Clara staring at her, Runner as well.

"Others are with me," Adamo replied. "They did not see you, and the youths, nor the elder. I sent them in the other direction, so I can come after you and have this moment." Adamo stared at Karina. "I like what you're wearing." Sparking instant laughter from Karina.

"Do I have something on my face?" Adamo asked her, becoming contaminated by Karina, and began laughing as well.

"I look horrible." Karina said, "are you joking with me?"

"No!" Adamo replied, "I like the way the dress falls over your hips. I'm doing what you asked of me, years back."

"What was that?" Carina asked.

"Tsk, tsk, you have forgotten," Adamo said. "Your memory has never been as good as mine."

"You mock me and then insult me as well?" Karina was about to walk away. But Adamo walked closer to her and held her hand. Karina looked at Clara and then at Adamo's hand. Clara continued staring at them, as did Runner.

"When we were little, when we were just Clara's age," Adamo said. "You said to me, to always be truthful about my feelings. And respect the feelings of others. You said, 'if the person is not truthful with the other person, they will never share true friendship between them.' You said if I was your true friend forever, I will always tell you my true feelings, and what lingers in my head, even if it was offensive to you. This is the fourth time I remind you of this because it always escapes your memory and you become very upset with me."

"As the time when you stole a kiss from me?" Karina commented, not looking at Adamo when she did.
"As the time I stole the kiss, you wanted me to steal," Adamo replied, allowing the grip of his hand over Karina's to become loose, as Karina began to walk away from him. "Fate will put us together again, with more time to spare."

Karina looked back at him. "You have allowed your hair to become long again Adamo, it suits you well." Adamo smiled.

"If fate does not, I will," Adamo said to himself, watching Karina walk away, with Clara looking back at him. Runner had already gone back to his work.

Luludja and Roberta had been waiting for Karina near the outskirts of the market. Karina apologized to Roberta and the Elder for the long wait.

"You understand that our *Phuri Dai* has plans for you?" Luludja offered some words for Karina. They had been walking for a couple of minutes, in direction to the pick-up point where a driver was set to pick them up and drive them back to their village.

"I know this elder," Karina replied.

"This has been dictated from before the death of your mother." Luludja continued. "Marloft has become very fond of you. Our Phuri Dai knows this and believes it to be sooner than what she had foreseen. For she believes the time is not yet bestowing. She has a sense that you have not developed for him, what Marloft has for you."

Karina did not say anything. Roberta and Clara walked by her side, Luludja trusted their sense of understanding enough to talk about this delicate matter in their presence.

"It is for your benefit," Luludja continued. "That our Phuri Dai has yet to become aware of your feelings for Adamo. But if she becomes informed of this, it will cause a very unproductive conflict of interest for all."

Roberta did not look at Karina, but through her silence, she understood how Karina may have been feeling. Clara stared at her and decided to hold her hand tightly. Karina looked at Clara and held her closer to her. Clara could see her tears.

∞

Later that afternoon, Arnold was being driven by Franco, his personal driver, towards the back of a café in one of the newly revitalized areas of the city, known as Perla Street. This is where the new economy of the country was the most noticeable in the affluence of the new bourgeoisie who were catapulting into the upper-middle class at an astoundingly fast rate.

Arnold had come to meet with Solano, who had appointed people to the *Residence, Land Documentation, and Ownership office*. A man named Alejandro came along with Solano, they were seated in the back of Solano's car. He was of mixed race, slender looking with short brown hair and clear eyes. The driver was told to pull up next to Arnold's vehicle. Arnold quickly jumped out of his car, and into the front passenger seat of Solano's.

Arnold and Solano greeted each other like old friends. They had conducted lucrative deals in the recent past and for Alejandro's luck, Solano was offering an opportunity to make a name for himself within Salvador's circle of people who were fast money-makers.

"You always want to get a call from this man." Solano started explaining to Alejandro. "And when you get the call, do not answer. Just go and be where you need to be, to meet with him and do what he needs to get done." Solano and Arnold shared a short laugh. Alejandro seemed eager to get started with his very promising gig. After a short q & a by Arnold, Alejandro expressed his willingness to get his first assignment on the record. Arnold could see in him his willingness and easy to control behavior that he reflected. Alejandro explained to Arnold that he needed to put his family in a better position and he also needed to take care of some extracurricular affairs. Arnold handed him an envelope with his first payment. He told Alejandro it was the equivalent of what he will earn in two years. There was a very big smile on Alejandro's face which incited him to get straight to business. Arnold realized that he was the right puppet to be placed in a useful position.

"Tell me what I need to do, and I will get it done in a minute," Alejandro said, looking at both Arnold and Solano.

Solano also received an envelope, which he placed inside his jacket pocket without any comments. Solano remained silent while Arnold explained the situation his boss was having with Susan's property. Alejandro heard Arnold say how important this deal was for him due to the pressures his boss was getting from his European associates. Solano watched Alejandro as he nodded in agreement. He understood the urgency of the situation and the money he had just received compelled him to help Arnold, and Salvador, for that matter. He had been told about the potential construction of the new energy plant in the region. And he had also heard about the obstacle those inhabiting the area represented, which was the reason why Salvador was recommended by the government to deal with a situation they would not be able to deal with. But there were other obstacles.

Solano told Arnold that due to the way the new President was conducting things throughout the country, thanks in part to the pressure added by the Americans, new personnel were being hired to clear out corruption and unwanted scandals at all branches of the government. This had the potential of putting Salvador and his modus operandi out of the present equation regarding the displacement matter. Salvador may not have been aware of this, but Solano was there to give Arnold the hint.

"Some of my old friends are still holding good positions," Solano said. Alejandro agreed with him.

"But they are holding all of their deals back until further notice. The President has allowed various international monitors to observe the handling of the administration and give him their opinion about any changes necessary to satisfy the international community. He was given a lot of money by the IMF, and he is still trying to get more. I don't believe the people the IMF assigned to help him with the revitalization of the country will allow anything to go wrong. This means zero corrupt officials and zero handouts."

"Yes, I heard," Arnold commented.

"Exactly..." Solano added. "I am very lucky to still have my job. I don't need it for monetary purposes anymore, but the influence and power that comes with it is necessary for everyday living. Although I don't think the President wants to keep old-schoolers like me around for much longer. We may be dangerous for his image, therefore I'm sure my days are numbered, but I will not allow the Americans to have their way with me. This is why I brought Alejandro around. If they kick my ass out of office, he will be our link in there. Just got to keep him clean in everyone's eyes."

"Well thought out Manuel," Arnold said. He was sure Solano was making the right move but exactly for whom? He asked himself. "Romalyn believes the Americans will be the key to his success. He will be their best buddy in the region. He is only fooling himself, not anyone else. The Americans will use him and wipe their ass with his hands when they are through with whatever they are trying to pull around here. I can see them exploiting our resources, the tourism economy and anything else they can put their hands in. The same way they were trying to do with Salvador. You remember how the Americans were conducting deals with us not too long ago? Our drugs, their weapons, and our money. Everything was good. Now they want to clean shit they dropped, and they are using Bolivar as their toilet paper, by blaming him for the entire drug trafficking and their drug epidemic and all of their bullshit. When we know damn well, they actually created the problem for their own agenda.

"But enough of that," Arnold took a moment to focus his attention from Solano to Alejandro. "Is there anything that you can do to help me expedite this situation within the next few days?" Arnold asked. "My boss made a promise to his associates and you know how El Salvador is. He is a man of his word and we wouldn't want for him to fail on it, when we have all benefited so substantially from him. That would not be good for any of us, Alejandro." Arnold looked at Solano, Solano looked at Alejandro.

Alejandro understood exactly what Arnold was telling him. He knew Salvador had a lot of dirt on a lot of people. He knew Solano was one of them. Solano had been on his payroll for a long time, Alexander knew that if Solano did not push the extra mile for Salvador, he would be in other types of problems, which he knew Solano did not want to deal with. Going against Salvador's tide was risky and futile. And Solano had seen the results of that with his own eyes. Nevertheless, Alejandro understood he would be putting himself in the same situation Solano was. He did not care at all. He had just gotten paid a salary he had not even worked for and he knew there was much more to come.

Alejandro asked Solano's driver to get out and buy some coffees for them. "I tell you what." Alejandro began, as the driver left the car. "If for some reason this woman and her children were to disappear, and we could not find them to authenticate or verify their ownership in the matter of the property we are talking about, the town's affairs administrator, by that I mean me, could easily assume responsibility and or ownership of the property and use it as best fit for the benefit of the community and the growth of the local economy, and responsibly, clearly."

Solano smiled; Arnold understood perfectly what was needed to be done. They had been trying to get it done. He explained that they had already taken some steps to get the woman to give up the property, but she was relentless and there was also the matter of her husband who was abroad.

"If he also happens to disappear, it would make it even better for the resolution of the matter and that way, there will be less paperwork to deal with, Arnold," Alejandro concluded.

"Arnold," Solano said, "Do you believe that after all the time I have been dealing with you, on behalf of your boss, I have earned the right to speak freely to you, without making you feel disrespected?"

"You can," Arnold replied.

"What is happening Arnold?" Solano asked. "You have dealt with tougher people than a woman and her children. You have brought the heads of my enemies inside plastic bags, just to give initiation to our business affairs. You command Salvador's most lethal team of assassins. The feared long-nail crew. My question is, are you guys getting old? Why don't you just take it upon yourself and take care of this inconvenience for Salvador once and for all? I strongly believe he will not be disappointed, and you will further cement your value in his eyes."

Arnold smiled at the persuasion instigated by Solano. He was not insulted by the comments, but they gave him something to think about. After a moment of contemplation, Arnold decided to make a confession to Solano. He went on to tell him that his boss has been kind of slow in these types of matters lately. He said that he felt that Salvador had other affairs occupying his mind and time, but he did not know why he was reacting in the way he has been for the past few months.

"All I can think is that after the night he was attacked in his own mansion, he has been really meticulous about every single thing he does. I cannot quite put my finger on it, but I know it's not fear." Arnold again became silent and thought about something while momentarily submerged in thought. He appeared to have remembered something just then. Solano placed his right hand over his left shoulder while edging towards him.

"Arnold," Solano said. "You seriously need to be worried about that. The Americans have moved into the region and they are pushing everything they did not like, out of the country. And I believe Salvador is one of those things they will not allow to stick around for long. IF you do not want to be the dust under the broom, you need to start making your own arrangements."

Arnold agreed with Solano and gave him a handshake. Just before they parted ways and Arnold stepped out of the car, Alejandro telling Arnold to keep him informed about everything else he needed.

"Please Mr. Garcia, remember to give me at least a week's notice," Alejandro said. Arnold nodded his head positively, agreeing with Alejandro's request.

Not long after entering the SUV, Arnold receives a phone call from Salvador.

"Yes sir, I already spoke to Solano and his new guy and I have good news for you," Arnold said, after making signaling to Franco to make a right turn on a corner, three blocks away from where he had met with Solano. They stopped at a cigar shop with a white and very old looking wooden door, with two artificial mini palm trees on each side of the door. There was a sign reading *Original Cigars*, hanging almost sideways by the door.

"Go and get the special handmade ones," Arnold instructed his driver.
"You will give me the news later," Salvador tells him. "I want you to make the call to the bankers now. Do exactly as I told you and do not leave any detail out."

"Don't worry sir. I am on it as soon as you hang up." Arnold said. Arnold did not want to waste any time after receiving the new orders. He got out of the SUV and went into the cigar shop to get his driver.

"Good, go on then." Salvador ended the call, confident that Arnold was already following his order. He rested his head back momentarily. The vast portion of the city could be seen from the tenth-floor condominium he was calling home at the moment. Luxurious furniture, expensive paintings, and crystal chandeliers filled the place. High ceiling and marble floors gave the place a decadent feel. There was a wide dark glass window in front of him. He sat on a white rocking chair that looked like a relic from another time. A white robe covered his body. He looked out and around below, where most of the properties belonged to him. Some he had purchased, others he had built. Now, everyone living in them enjoyed a rent-free dwelling on his behalf.

Salvador stood up from the chair and after staring out the window for a moment, he decided to make another phone call. But he was going to use a different cellular phone. He placed the one he used to call Arnold to his right and dialed a number with a phone he already had in his left hand. The phone rang twice, and Salvador hung up. As he did, he placed that phone inside a brown leather bag and just as he was closing it, another phone within the same bag, began ringing.

At the same time, Arnold was making a call on his own cellular phone. Just as Salvador had done, Arnold allowed his phone to ring twice, before hanging up and putting the phone away inside a leather bag. And just as in Salvador's case, another phone inside the bag began to ring.

"Mr. Mikael?" Arnold said, using a subtle and at the same time query tone of voice.

"Yes." Mr. Mikael replied, with a heavy Russian accent.

"May we share a cup of coffee?" Arnold asked, moving his phone from his right ear to his left, "I would like to ask you about a personal matter."

"Sure," Mikael said, ending the call without saying anything more. Arnold then ordered Franco to go to Mikael's place. Franco already knew the address and changed the direction he was going upon receiving the new destination.

"We will be there in twenty minutes," Franco told Arnold.

"Make it in eight," Arnold ordered him, causing Franco to drive as fast as he could and without any regard for traffic laws.

Ten minutes later, Arnold took an elevator up to the fourth floor of a well-appointed private building. Arnold exited the elevator and walked over a carpeted floor, till he reached the door at the end of the hallway. As he got to the door, Mikael opened ahead of him knocking on it. Mikael was seventy years old, short, hairy and inconspicuous looking. He looked like the type of man, whom people would not even acknowledge on the street and that was exactly how he liked it.

"Hello again, Arnold..." Mikael greeted Arnold in a very pleasant manner and with a firm handshake.

"Mr. Mikael..." Arnold said.

"What are we doing today?" Mikael asked while pulling a notebook page out of the front left pocket of his Bermuda shorts, which he combined with a dark color chakabana (Cuban four-pocket shirt).

"The phone calls..." Arnold replied.

"Very well, let us go into the studio," Mikael says to Arnold, as they take a short walk towards the bathroom. Arnold took notice of the modest and colorless decoration of Mikael's apartment and asked him what the reason was that he did not get better furniture to match the setting of the apartment and the rest of the building.

"I really don't have any guests coming to visit," Mikael replied. "Therefore, I do not need to have any expensive furniture." A cat walked by Arnold's feet as he entered the bathroom following Mikael.

"It is just me and the cat." Mikael continued. "And before you ask about my choice of color as well, it is very simple. A neutral color allows me to see a clear contrast throughout all the spaces in my apartment. I understand where everything is, positions, shapes, shadows, etc. It is important to understand these factors when you are a former spy. You never know who may try to catch up with you when you are least expecting. You never know. Everything basically the same color will be self-advisory if there is anything else inserted within my recognizable setup."

Arnold did not ask anything else. Once both men were inside the bathroom together, Mikael asked him to close the door behind him. Arnold turned around and closed the door and by the time he turned around, Mikael was already walking into a secret room behind the shower. Arnold needed to go into the tub to be able to enter into the secret room, which was extremely different in contrast with the rest of the apartment. Mikael owned a very sophisticated setting inside the secret room with custom made computers, surveillance monitors and other particular gadgets, which he used to conduct his work for Salvador's organization.

"Very well, let us begin..." Mikael said to Arnold. "The same numbers I have in the list, names, and locations, correct?"

"Correct," Arnold replied.

"Any changes or additions in the schedule?" Mikael asked.

"No, the calls will be conducted in the same order the boss requested," Arnold said, while Mikael went to work with the preparation of the satellite phones, and some other additional devices he would be utilizing during the short operation he was about to conduct. Arnold remained on his feet while Mikael sat on a chair facing a large table with all his devices positioned in a well-organized and well-coordinated lineup. Mikael knew exactly where every single device and small gadgets were located, to the point where it was not necessary to look in any direction when he needed to reach for anything.

"See that chair behind you?" Mikael said to Arnold. "Bring it closer and take a seat next to me." While Arnold sat down, Mikael made a phone call to a building operated by social services in London. An Eastern European lady in her late eighties heard the phone ringing inside a brown box. She looked at it on her way to the kitchen and continued walking as Boris, her grandson, walked out of the bathroom with a towel around his waist.

"Da." Boris answered speaking in Russian.

"It's me," Mikael responded.

"Okay, give me a moment." Boris held the phone in his left hand while holding on to the towel, as he ran back to his bedroom, where he had a setup of various satellite phones connected to wires and hooked up to a computer.

"Grandma please don't disturb me for the next forty minutes!" Boris shouted out to his grandmother, closing and locking his bedroom door. "I'm ready now." He then told Mikael.

"We are ready," Mikael told Arnold.

Right about the same time, in New York City, Bob Gordon had just finished playing Tennis at the New York Racquet Club of 50th street and Madison Avenue. He was accompanied by one of his subordinates, an Italian American man named Vito. Vito's job was handling high profile investments in the European accounts belonging to Gordon's investment banks. They laughed and chatted as they walked into the locker room together. Gordon had a towel over his shoulders, while Vito was drying his face with his.

"I will meet you at the lounge in about thirty," Gordon said to Vito. As he was about to open his locker, his cell phone rang, he quickly answered. Simultaneously, Kemp, Brenan, and Miller situated in different areas of the country were also receiving phone calls.

"Hello?" Gordon answered.

"Mr. Gordon, this is Arnold." Arnold was seated in the same chair speaking to a microphone set over the table, while Mikael was occupied monitoring the rest of the devices.

"Arnold?" Gordon asked. "Salvador's right-hand man. Correct?" At that exact moment, Gordon, as well as Kemp and the others, were handed small parcels which they did not have to sign for. Kemp was seated in his car, accompanied by a lady friend, who was clearly not his wife. He attempted to question the delivery man who handed him the parcel, but the man waved him off before taking off into a waiting car. The vehicle sped off.

"Mr. Kemp, Mr. Gordon, Mr. Brenan and finally, Mr. Miller," Arnold mentioned the names of each and every one of Gordon's associates to make sure he got their attention. They all acknowledged they were listening, and Arnold went ahead with phase one of his duty.

"Each of you please open the parcels, which had just been delivered to you." Arnold begins instructing them. Mikael continued working while listening to the conversation, as was Boris.

"What is the meaning of this?" Kemp questioned. "Why are you calling us? What's with the packages?" He asked straight out, while the others were also intrigued.

"Mr. Kemp, follow my guide and you, as well as the rest of your associates, will soon be totally aware of what you need to know," Arnold explained to Kemp.

"Arnold, what is going on?" Gordon wanted to know also.

"Open up your parcels." Arnold again said in a serious tone. At that moment, Gordon and the others began opening the small boxes. Kemp was the first one to fully open his box.

"What is this?" He asked, while one by one, the others also saw what was inside.

"Arnold, can you explain this?" Gordon asked, after bringing a mini video player out of his box.

"Each of you gentlemen, have received a mini video cassette player." Arnold began explaining. "Underneath, inside a white envelope, you will also find a videotape which will fit in the player. Please go ahead, gentlemen and insert the videotape into your players."

Each of the men went ahead and inserted their videotapes inside their players. Kemp was the first one doing it and did not wait for any more instructions to press the play button. The video began to play on the five-inch screen of the video player. Kemp's lady friend wanted to peek at what he was looking at, but he quickly moved the video player away from her sight and exited the car.

She asked him if there was a problem, but he did not answer back. A preoccupied expression displayed over his face, as he took several slow steps farther away from the vehicle.

"What the hell is this?" Kemp asked, as did the others.

"What is this Arnold? Why am I watching this?!" Gordon shouted at Arnold, as he watched a mature looking man dressed like a doctor, wearing a surgical mask over his nose taking blood samples from Amber and Tiffany. The doctor was assisted by a man and a woman, both covering their faces with surgical masks as well. The other man wrote Amber's and Tiffany's names over the tubes containing their blood samples along with the date, which was five days before his arrival to Costa Rica.

"At this particular moment..." Arnold told everyone. "You are watching a portion of a recording that was taken five days before the party at the ambassador's mansion, as you just watched the nurse writing on the tube samples. If you will press the fast forward button for 30 seconds." Kemp as well as the others quickly complied with the order and pressed the fast forward button aggressively.

"You may stop now," Arnold advised them. At that moment, the video image was showing the same doctor and the others assisting him in a different room with Amber and Tiffany, both seated next to each other on a luxurious sofa while sipping wine. It was a different room, on the date of the party. The woman assisting the doctor is heard telling them that everything came out very well and they can follow her to another room. Both Tiffany and Amber seemed as if they were under the influence of narcotics, as they stood up to follow the woman. They ended up requiring the assistance of two other nurses to be able to walk straight.

The doctor and the man assisting him remained behind in the room and the doctor went ahead and displayed a copy of the New York Times to the camera filming the video. The doctor then asked the man to hand him two medical folders with the logo of a well-known Hospital located in Manhattan, New York. The folders had been dated from a day earlier. The doctor went ahead and opened Tiffany's folder, he pulled out a paper that he made sure the person filming the video had a very good close-up of. Kemp's eyes opened wide with horror while reading what was written at the top of the document.

"Arnold, what the fuck is this?" Gordon asked angrily.

"What is the meaning of all these theatrics?" Brenan shouted into the phone.

Kemp's lady friend was about to get out of the car, and he screamed at her from the top of his lungs. She was freaked out by this sudden change in demeanor. She quickly sat back inside the car and shut the door, nearly in tears.

"Within the box, you may also find a copy of the document, as well as a sample of your blood gentlemen, in the case you need to confirm the information you have just been given," Arnold told them. "As you may have become aware, you have all been infected with the HIV virus, and you have, while in the most brutal and sadistic way, killed two young girls."

"Are you out of your damn mind?" Gordon screamed out, prompting someone walking by him to speedily move away from his direction.

"Is this some kind of a sick joke!?" Miller shouted out.

"Keep calm gentlemen…" Arnold told them. "This situation will not have to escalate any further as long as you gentlemen comply with what will be requested from each of you."

"You cannot do this, this is extortion!" Kemp again shouted. "We are being framed; we were entrapped."

"Gentlemen…" Arnold said. "Regardless of how you feel at this moment, there is absolutely nothing you can do to change the outcome of your actions. Your main concern at this time should be your family, your reputation, and your future and considering the circumstances, I will suggest for you to start thinking real fast about the last thing I mentioned before. Now, gentlemen, we are not trying to ruin your lives and as long as you help us, we will help you. On the other hand, if you decide to go the other way and contact the FBI or CIA or whomever, you will soon see yourself dealing with the consequences of an international scandal, which will not only affect your business but also your private lives as well as the lives of each and every one of your family members. This gentlemen, has already been pre-arranged and we are ready to set it in motion in the blink of an eye."

"What is it that you want from us?" Gordon asked. He was nervous and confused, as well as unaware of the circumstances involving the actions taken by Salvador's men. "How the hell do you expect any of us to agree to do what you want if we really have been infected with HIV. This thing is a death sentence, if we are going to die from this shit, what do we have to lose?" Gordon sounded like a man who had suddenly been confronted with the loss of all his priceless possessions. The others were in shock and could barely speak for themselves.

"HIV, we can help you with that," Arnold replied. "The Chinese have a treatment for it, a cocktail of different medicines which helps to prevent the proliferation of the virus in your blood and throughout your body. The pharmaceutical community in America does not want to utilize this treatment yet. The reason escapes my understanding. The murders we can keep secret, this event does not have to get into the ears of others unless infamy is your desire. Your CIA handlers are not aware of any of this and I strongly advise for it to remain this way. If by any chance, if any one of you decides to be the smart partner of the crew and inform them of our deal, this would only mean death for all of you, and for them as well. And gentlemen let me assure you, if we wanted them or Ms. Rachel Williams dead, we would have killed them all already.

If you gentlemen are in accordance with us, each of you will receive ten years' worth of the treatment necessary to slow down the effects of the HIV virus and keep you alive, this on a timely basis, to make sure you continue honoring your part of the deal."

"But this is a contagious virus, what about our wives?" Kemp asked in a very agitated tone of voice.

"Your wives and mistresses are your problems to deal with Mr. Kemp, not ours," Arnold responded coldly. "You will receive instructions with the details of what we need from each of you very soon. In the meantime, act as if it's business as usual. Each of you can go to your private doctors if you feel so inclined to confirm what I've just told you. But keep this in mind, from this day forward we will be watching your every move. We will be aware of everything you do or say and with whom you speak with and do business with. We will contact you again in two days with instructions." Arnold looked at Mikael, it was time to finish. Mikael pressed a button that ended the call.

∞

An hour later...

Marsha, the homeless woman who had witnessed the two assailants being thrown out of the window from Susan's house, was telling her version of what happened to Salvador. Salvador was used to using Marsha as his informant. Through her, he would become aware of the deals and affairs happening throughout the neighborhoods and towns under his control. With Marsha, Salvador was assured to know what was going to happen even before it did.

Marsha was having a meal and drinking milk as if she hadn't eaten in weeks. Salvador observed how Marsha ate as he was sitting in a chair two feet away from her, legs crossed and hands over his right knee, one over the other.

Marsha would turn around to look at Salvador from time to time. She may have been somewhat embarrassed in the way Salvador looked at her. Marsha attempted to speak to him while eating, but Salvador simply raised his hand and insisted she finish her meal in peace. One of Salvador's servants came forward to inform him that Arnold had arrived. Salvador instructed his servant to have Arnold wait in his office. Salvador wanted details of what Marsha had to say and he knew the best way Marsha would give him those details is if she were completely sober and well-fed.

Marsha cleaned her plate completely of all the food. Nothing was spared. She sat on the floor and reclined against the wall. She patted her stomach and exhaled with satisfaction.

"Speak now," Salvador instructed her. He stood up and looked outside his window to see a small army of gardeners toiling away at his garden.

"Sal," Marsha said, "I swear, I was not drunk, I was not high, I was completely sober when I saw this." She wiped away food crumbs from her face with her hand. She pulled out a purple silk pouch that was hidden inside her bra. She opened the zipper and pulled out a white silk handkerchief that she used to clean the rest of her face. She gently and secretively folded the handkerchief back into its pouch and put it back where it was, without allowing Salvador to see it.

"Yes, I was really hungry," Marsha explained, "So I was anxious, I was looking for some of my clients to see if I could get some money for food. I was really hungry. I didn't want to get high."

Salvador turned around abruptly. "Tell me already!" He didn't want to hear her personal stories. For him, knowing that her dependency on getting high was a portal into her out-of-control mind and because of this, he knew he always had a loyal informant in his pocket.

"That woman, Susan..." Marsha said as she crawled closer to Salvador's feet.

"Yes, her house is the only house that I'm yet to own on that street. Everyone else has agreed to pack and leave."

"Maybe the reason you don't have that house is that she is protected." Marsha slowly began to hold onto Salvador's legs to touch him while she began to calmly get on her feet.

Salvador's eyes opened with curiosity as he looked at Marsha's face. At that moment, an old memory flooded his mind, back when Marsha was a young beautiful woman who he was very close to. She was his favorite. He took her everywhere with him. To trips overseas, expensive shopping sprees and his companion when he was making deals with other powerful drug kingpins. But he was also the one who set her up on the path to perdition where she became hooked deep into drugs, alcohol and mental struggles. For the most part, to satisfy Salvador's own desires.

"That woman is not protected by anyone," Salvador said dismissively. "She and her children have only been very lucky so far. Her husband has been lucky because he's abroad and that's what's kept them alive. But soon they will come begging and pleading for me to give them whatever I feel like giving in exchange for that stupid eyesore that's blocking me from completing my project."

Salvador pushed Marsha's hands away from his groin area. "No, you are wrong," Marsha said, standing up while adjusting her bra and smoothing her red hair. She stood very close to Salvador and whispered into his ears. "You have to listen to me, my love."

Salvador listened to her voice and a flashback of a memory passed through his mind. It was a time when he used to enjoy the taste of her body, under blue satin sheets and she would say those exact words to get his undivided attention.

"What then?! Tell me!" Salvador barked at Marsha.

"That woman." Marsha got even closer. "That woman has a *Baeka* around her and her children!"

Salvador turned around and moved away from Marsha in discontent. "What are you talking about? Have you completely lost your mind? Did you get high before coming to see me? What have I told you about that?!" Salvador was furious.

Marsha followed behind Salvador pleading for him to listen to her. "A *Baeka* is a mythical black magic creature with evil powers. You expect me to believe this? You got high that night and the drugs took over your senses completely." Salvador was trying to put distance between her and himself, but she was poised to get close to him and make him believe her.

"You have to believe me, my love," Marsha said.

"Stop saying that!" Salvador put his hand up to her face and pushed her away from him.

Marsha's eyes began to flood with tears. "You have to know I'm loyal to you and would protect you any way that I can." Marsha sat down on the floor and cried.

Salvador began to pace the floor of the room. He took out a two-way radio from his pocket. "Is everything ok out there?" He looked outside to make sure that his well-armed guards were positioned accordingly around the vicinity.

"Yes, Sir. All is clear." Sergio responded.

Salvador then looked at Marsha one more time as she cried. The images of a memory invaded his mind again.

He was inside the bunker with his man Chaparro. Chaparro was crying frantically. "What are you going to do? This ghost is going to come for you next!"

Salvador stared at Chaparro in silence and took a quick look at the monitor.

"I'm done. I'm done. I want to leave!" Chaparro was screaming. "Nobody is going to work for you! There's a ghost after you!"

Salvador considered for a second what to say to calm him down.

He then calmly looked back at Chaparro and quietly took out his gun while Chaparro had his back to Salvador. Without a word, Salvador pulled the trigger point-blank into the back of Chaparro's head. This way, Chaparro won't be saying a word to anyone.

Salvador found himself staring at Marsha. He decided he didn't want to listen to her voice anymore and started to leave but stopped short of opening the door. With his hand on top of the doorknob, he said, "One minute, that's all I'll give you." His back was still towards Marsha.

Marsh stood up, but this time she kept her distance and her composure. She spoke in a very serene tone of voice.

"I know those were your men that broke into that woman's house. I know because I recognized one of them. I have seen him once before. I remember him. I remember when you took me to your mansion at the Mexican location. He was leaving as we were arriving. I remember the burn scar on his right hand as he opened the door for us."

Salvador remained motionless and continued listening to Marsha.

"What I'm telling you is the truth. I would not lie to you because I still love you. And you know this. While I was standing across the woman's house, I saw something on the floor. I bent down to pick it up. Then I heard voices coming out from the crack of an open window. You see, I was aware you were having problems with that property. I have also seen those people that live there and the whispering I heard, were not the voices of that woman and her children.

"I approached the window and before I even got to peek through it, that man with the scar on his hand, flew out of it violently, smashing his head on the neighbor's wall. I got so scared! I ducked down and covered my head, fearing for my life. Afterward, I opened my eyes and looked at him. His head was split open! He was dead! Another man was thrown out just like the one before and landed just a few feet away from me! Dead! They were both dead! I was so scared, I couldn't move. Suddenly I felt a weird sensation like someone breathing behind my neck.

"I felt terrified, I felt as if there was someone right behind me. I was shivering and just shut my eyes closed. That's all I could do at that moment. I felt death was hovering all around me. I was able to open my eyes and somehow found the courage to turn my head around and look into the window and it was slightly open." Marsha covered her face with her hands, reliving the sensation like she was there again. "Oh my God..."

"Speak woman!" Salvador demanded. "Who did you see?"

Marsha composed herself. She wanted to finish her story. She wanted Salvador to believe her. "I told you what I saw."

"You idiot!" Salvador walked up to her and pushed her against the wall.

Marsha was very afraid of what he could do to her. "You have to believe me!"

"You're a good-for-nothing junkie!" Salvador cursed at her.

She fell to the ground sobbing. "I hate you! I hate you for what you've made me. I hate you, I hate you, I hate... But I can't stand it if something were to happen to you. You need to listen to me." There was a moment of silence for both Salvador, who was intrigued about what Marsha knew and Marsha, who was trying to find a way of making him understand that his life was in immediate danger.

"When I looked up to the window, I saw something pulling the window closed. I was petrified. I tried to stand up and run but I couldn't feel my legs. I was staring at the window and I saw a glare. And then, I don't know, but I felt something there. I felt it in my bones. A chill went down my spine. It was as if something was staring right at me. I was terrified. And then I heard a voice beckoning me by my name. I was forced to walk closer to the window, against my own will. The voice then told me, "Stay away from Salvador. Run away... Hell is coming for him."

Marsha threw her arms around Salvador and sobbed against his chest. Salvador stood motionless and stared ahead. The past seeped into his mind once again.

"Have you told this to anyone?" Salvador asked Marsha, not allowing his eyes to set upon her.

"No!" Marsha replied. "I've been wandering around for hours. I didn't know if you were going to be here."

Arnold and a few of Salvador's men came running. "Is everything ok sir?"

"Go back to your jobs. I need a few more minutes here." Salvador told him.

"Tell me again. Did you tell this story to anyone before coming to see me?" Salvador looked down into Marsha's face.

"No, I swear no one knows anything. No one even knows that I came to see you. I was worried something might happen to you. I still love you. I hope one day you can fall in love with me again. I know that's impossible but let me have this dream."

"I believe everything you said," Salvador whispered to her. He slowly embraced Marsha while staring at her face. At that moment, inside Salvador's arms, Marsha felt as she had felt once before. She couldn't believe he was holding her as he once did. Just for that moment, the warmth of his arms, the beating of his heart next to her face, just for that moment, Marsha felt a sensation she had long forgotten. She felt loved.

"I believe that you care about me. I believe that you still love me, that you've always loved me. You didn't run away to try to save yourself. You came here to warn me. I will never be able to repay you for that."

Marsha could see the emotions in his eyes. It filled her up and she was content. It was so long ago that Salvador held her lovingly. She couldn't remember seeing his eyes this way.

Salvador slowly moved away from her. His hands gently caressed her arms and then her shoulders and then they cupped her face. He looked into her eyes and Marsha looked into his.

"You were the most beautiful woman I have ever enjoyed," Salvador said to Marsha. "The moment I saw you walking in the room at that party, I said to myself that you were mine and mine alone. You knew your worth and that attracted me to you even more. You were not going to be anyone's toy. You knew what you wanted, you knew you could get it, and you knew how to pose a challenge for a man like me. That drove me to the brink of madness and desire for you, and it kept me wanting more... At one point, you let yourself too loose. I tried to bring you back, but you parted too far away from me.

"You did and gave everything I asked from you. That pleased me very much, but for a man like me, pleasing alone is not enough. Doing everything I want is not enough. I never wanted to see you as my equal, but I wanted to have someone next to me who could keep up and last.

"You succumbed to my desires, fantasies, and orders, but you were not able to keep up and you lost yourself into the weakness of the mind. Your mind was never strong enough, you just acted as if it was and when I put you to the test, failure was the result. For that, I hated myself."

Salvador continued staring into Marsha's eyes. She stared into his, seeing something in his eyes she had never seen before. His eyes had become moist with tears.

"But I did everything I did just for you, I've become what you wanted me to become. I did the drugs; I did every single sadistic thing you asked me to do. I degraded myself to the lowest I could lower myself into, just to please you and satisfy your darkest fantasies and desires. I did it all for you!" Marsha cried as she poured out everything she had inside.

"You did. You did, I still love those memories." He commented, causing a momentary flash of happiness on Marsha's face.

"But today I see what you have become thanks to that, but that was the challenge. That was the purpose of testing the strength of your will… You should have thought it through, at one point, you should have stopped yourself from destroying yourself, just to satisfy me. I gave you to the seductive desires of other women, I shared your body with other men, we shared them together as well, we shared the drugs and alcohol and the thrills.

"We took away lives together. I did it to show you the fragility of it, to show you how easily you could lose it all in an instant, in the blink of an eye. And yet you did not realize I was training you; you did not assimilate the training and gave yourself up to becoming just one more drop of fecal matter into the wasteland of the unworthy. You failed a simple test."

At that moment, Salvador's hands slid lower, going from Marsha's face and stopping right over her neck. His grip became tighter and tighter. The happiness in Marsha's face had turned into fear and shock. She tried to free herself from Salvador's grip. Her frail body was too weak and the feeble attempts to push and scratch her way out of Salvador's strong clutch were unsuccessful.

"If this is any consolation, you will be in a better place soon," Salvador spoke softly and slowly while staring into Marsha's eyes. "Understand that this is the only way I can prove that I once cared deeply for you." Salvador watched as the life escaped from Marsha's eyes and her body slowly gave up. Having finished, he released his grip and let her body fall slowly to the floor in front of him. He walked over her to open the door.

"Arnold!" Salvador shouted.

Arnold walked up to him with quick steps. "Yes, sir."

"Did you do it?" Salvador asked.

"Yes, sir," Arnold replied. "Everything went as you predicted. They all bit the bullet and the video was the magic touch to make sure they wouldn't even consider contacting their CIA handlers. I told them they will get instructions in about two days."

"Well done," Salvador told Arnold while placing his right hand over his left shoulder, as he moved slightly away from him. Arnold looked at Marsha, dead on the floor. Salvador looked at her again before looking at Arnold.

"Have Raffa and Pablo help you clean up this room, and then come join me in my studio," Salvador ordered Arnold.

"I will handle it," Arnold said to Salvador, watching him walking away in a very somber manner.

A short time had passed when Arnold walked into Salvador's studio. Salvador asked him if he had spoken with Solano about the situation with Susan's house.

"Things have become more complicated with Solano. He is in a challenging position at the moment. The things he was able to do before, may be more difficult for him now to get done now." Arnold said.

"And?" Salvador asked Arnold to continue.

"He is being scrutinized by the new government," Arnold said. "He told me that things cannot be dealt with in the same ways they had been in the past. I believe he is correct. He advised me to move in a way we see fit, to finish this quickly and he will take care of the paperwork. He introduced me to his new guy, Alejandro. He will take over for Solano."

"Very well then..." Salvador confirmed. "What about the other thing?"

"Yes," Arnold answered. "You were right, Solano is moving to betray you. He made his move on me. I was not expecting it, in the way he did, he caught me by surprise. You called it sir. And you were right. You said the moment things become tight, he will seek to free himself from any commitment with you and will try to hold onto the easiest target with a thirst for power to safeguard his own skin."

"Yeah," Salvador said. "That day at our first business meeting, I looked at his face and he struck me as the type of person who will go that route."

"What are you planning to do with him?" Arnold asked.

"We've got the upper hand on him," Salvador answered. "*He* approached you, leaving himself open. We know something he doesn't. Let's let him run as he wants to. He's not important to me at the moment."

"What about the woman and her children?" Arnold asked.

"Give the *Nails* the task."

"They are already on it," Arnold replied. "I have them watching the house from the property across the street. We kicked out the person who used to live there yesterday so that we could have a better vantage point. But they informed me no one is at the house and that they may not even be around. They also told me they saw heavy machinery and industrial equipment being kept two miles away from the area."

"I have heard about the machinery. But the family - where are they?!" Salvador exclaimed. "Don't waste time with this situation and find them. Get rid of them! All of them, quickly! I need to make sure I have all my cards over the table, should I need to use any of them."

"It will be done, sir," Arnold answered confidently. After a short pause, he continued, "There is also the matter of the four Gypsies that got away from the truck of bodies we were going to sell to those scientists from the Canadian pharmaceutical corporation."

"What about them?" Salvador asked.

"If the Gypsy leader gets to find out that it was us who abducted those men, we may have a situation with her. I've heard she is not an easy fist to deal with and neither are her assassins. What should we do about that case, sir?"

"The pharmaceuticals can handle the heat," Salvador told Arnold, almost disregarding the possibility of a much more difficult conflict. "They are well connected and have much more cash than I thought. The trail will not get to us, don't worry. Corpa..."

Salvador then had a thought. "These people are going to be the last piece I need, to complete the puzzle for my exile. Get out of this shit hole of a country, with all of these vermin, which makes me want to spit when I smell the air around them. I don't care about the people of this country Arnold. For that matter, these Gypsies. We will leave them here to rot with the rest of the garbage and the politicians when they get cleaned out by the Americans. I did what I needed to do for them, I got paid what I needed in intellectual capital, and I will use that capital to advance my final agenda with the Chinese Triad. If Corpa wants bodies to advance their drug tests, I will give them all the bodies they need, dead or alive."

Salvador went silent for a moment. There was something in his eyes, which spelled a bad omen but also opportunity. He then quickly changed the subject.

"Tell me about James," Salvador said to Arnold.

James had been the only survivor from Susan's house. Salvador's eyes were still glaring. He was contemplating the potential of his future outside of the present world he was dealing with, and into the glamorous, high society glare, with potential connections that he was aiming to acquire to enhance the pedigree of his persona up to another level.

"I went by to check on him, sir. He is still in a coma. The doctors don't know how long it will take for him to make progress, if any at all."

Salvador again kept silent for a moment and walked away from Arnold. "Okay, tomorrow give Mikael the rest of the instructions to give to the bankers. Let him focus on that, he is more than qualified to handle it. But tell him not to do anything until you give him the green light, Ok?"

"Certainly, I'll do it first thing tomorrow." Salvador began walking away from Arnold again.

"Oh, and Arnold, keep someone there at the hospital in case James recovers."

"I already have someone there, sir." Arnold quickly replied. "As soon as he opens his eyes, he will close them again."

Salvador was content with all of the actions his right-hand man had taken. Arnold had done everything he needed to get done, almost to the letter, but Salvador did not mention it to him.

Arnold remained where he was standing, waiting to see if his boss wanted to recommend anything else as he saw him still immersed in his thoughts.

Arnold then dared to ask Salvador what the problem with Marsha was. Salvador asked him to leave. Arnold then walked out of the studio and Salvador walked after him and made sure the door was locked. He then opened a secret door behind the bookshelf. He climbed down a narrow staircase which led to a bunker similar to the one he had at his other location. After making sure no one saw him, he walked inside and closed the door behind him. There was a black satchel resting over a table in the left side of the room. This one was larger than the one he normally carried around with him.

"You think I'm afraid of you? You are very wrong. And you will pay again for getting in my way." Salvador was talking out loud to himself. He was removing several cinder blocks from the floor, a few steps away from the entrance, until there was soil. He put his hands into the soil and dug out what appeared to be a ball of flesh in the shape of an egg. It was the size of a large papaya.

"You actually think I would not be ready for you this time, you son of a bitch. Come, come and get me... We will be waiting for you, and this time I will send you straight to hell!" Salvador was holding the flesh egg between his hands. Salvador's eyes opened up wide, almost to the point of displaying madness. But he had not gone mad, he was angry and eager to kill.

∞

On the other side of the world...

Noida, a city southeast of New Delhi the capital of India. Two men dressed in dark clothing and turbans were seen walking away from a cemetery and getting inside an awaiting small silver vehicle in the middle of the night.

The following day, a woman cried frantically on her knees by an open grave. At the center of the cemetery, she was screaming, trying to get the attention of a nearby crowd.

"I saw him, I saw him again. Oh, God! He spoke to me, but he left. I saw him! I saw him alive!" The woman sobbed. Tears streamed down her face and she was not able to control her emotions, even as the people she was yelling for approached her. When the people finally got closer to her, she was sitting down on the ground next to an empty wooden box, which was halfway out of the grave. The burial shrouds were tossed about.

"Adeela, what happened? An elderly man in the crowd asked the young lady crying by the empty grave. While bending closer to her to console her and help her up, but her words made no sense to those who came to assist her.

One day later, under the influence of grief and confusion, Adeela decided to take a trip to her parent's hometown, Rajasthan to the north of the country. She traveled light, with only a blue backpack where she packed some clothes. As she arrived at her destination and got off the bus, an old friend was waiting for her.

"Hi Adeela, I'm glad you came to visit," Julius said. Julius was the son of Adeela's father's best friend, and both families had known each other for a long time, at a point, even considering a union between Adeela and Julius.

"I'm so happy to see you..." Adeela told Julius as she approached him to give him a hug.

"Come. Let's get you out of here. Your parents are very anxious to see you."

Julius picked up Adeela's backpack for her and walked up the block to get his car. Julius made a quick stop and purchased a mango Popsicle for Adeela to cheer her up a little. She loved it and smiled as he came back into the car with it.

"I'm sorry about your friend Adeela..." Julius said. She did not say anything and stared at the streets and the people, while putting her hand out of the window, feeling the dry air move as they drove.

"How are you doing?" Adeela asked Julius. "I'm doing well. School is tough but I'm almost finished and then I'm planning to travel abroad." Julius consumed half of his mango Popsicle and placed the rest inside a plastic bag he had located by his left leg.

"Oh..." Adeela commented. "You're still so clean, you will never change. That is so good, the way you are." She told Julius.

"I cannot help it Adeela," Julius said. "It is impossible for me to see things out of place and not do anything about it."

"I know," Adeela said. "That is one of your best qualities, whoever marries you, will be the happiest woman in the world."

They laughed and joked around as Julius drove, and by the time they arrived at Adeela's parents' house, she was looking and feeling much better than when she first arrived. Her parents were not surprised. They came out of the house to welcome her, acting as if they knew Julius was going to be able to work his magic with her, and he did.

Everyone was happy to have her in the house, her grandmother the most. Adeela's room was exactly as she left it when she moved to the city with her aunt and brother, who was abroad in school at the time.

"Ammi, thank you for keeping my room this way," Adeela told her mother. Her mother embraced her and asked her to come and sit to drink tea and have some snacks.

"You must be so tired after the long bus ride. Come relax a bit." Her father said.

Adeela's mother and father were very thankful to Julius and asked him to stay for tea but he had to go to work and promised them he would come back the next day. As Julius was about to leave the house, several children ran by while crying.

"What is wrong with those kids? Did something happen?" he asked Adeela's parents.

"Do not say anything to Adeela about this." Adeela's father warned.

"What? Why?" Julius was a little confused.

Adeela's father accompanied him to the front of the house and told him about something very strange that was happening lately near one of the outer villages.

He told Julius that some of the children have been talking about seeing a child-eating monster around the outskirts of the village. Julius became very curious and even surprised. He had not heard about any rumors about a monster before and he found it very amusing.

"It is not a joke. Three children have gone missing. There is a rumor that someone's maid may have known about the monster but did not warn anyone." Adeela's father said very sternly.

"How could that be?" Julius asked. "Did the police corroborate that information?"

"The police are investigating as usual, but they don't really believe in supernatural beings. I think they are seeing this as a waste of time, and they do not want to do overtime searching for some monster. They feel, as some others do, that it is a kidnapping case."

"The three children missing, that is enough to obligate them to do their jobs," Julius said, sounding upset. "They must get to the bottom of this whether it is truly a flesh-eating beast or a child kidnapper. A crime has happened, and it must be solved."

Hours later, Adeela was in bed next to her mother, while her father was sleeping in the guest room. The grandmother was discreetly placing a plate with some food and sweets close to the fence behind the house garden. She looked everywhere to make sure no one saw her, and she quickly made her way back inside the house.

A short time went by, not a sound was heard besides the barking of some dogs in the neighborhood, which then went strangely quiet. The bushes in the area near the fence began to move agitatedly and then they were calm again. suddenly, a dark hand with two-inch-long nails and skin that seemed burnt, erupted from within the bushes and grabbed the plate the grandmother had placed on the ground. A short moment passes. The same hand reaches back but this time, it leaves behind a book in place of where the food was.

Chapter XIII:

Hand of Ujat

Twenty-four hours after, people stood by and observed with preoccupation, as three men from the next-door property helped a small group of policemen carry the body of Kali out of his small dwelling.

"They must have used a silencer." One of the mechanics from the auto shop whispered under his breath to one of his co-workers. They stood amongst other bystanders, who were also observing the scene. "No one heard anything. Whoever did this, was not an amateur." The same man continued saying.

"Did they steal anything from the place?" Another co-worker asked.

"We don't know yet." The man who spoke first replied. "The police are not letting anyone look inside."

∞

Two days later, in a neighborhood at the center of the border between the towns of Tolyatti and Astrakhan to the south of Moscow, Kliment, a young man in his late twenties, urbanely dressed but with a serious character, was making his way out of a grocery store. He was carrying a small bottle of vodka inside a folded paper bag and after taking a few steps, he waved hello to a few others walking towards him from across the street.

"What's up, where have you been Kliment?" One of the young guys shouted, saying parts of his words in English and the rest in Russian.

"Hi guys," Kliment greeted them, approaching them calmly.

"So…" Lyosha one of Kliment's friends said, looking sad as he walked closer to him. "Herman is gone, I still can't believe it, man."

"Yeah, I know what you mean. He was such a great guy. What a loss." Ilya, another one of the friends, said. "Last time I spoke to him he seemed very well, and he told me he had never felt so good about himself and about what he was accomplishing. He said he was working on several projects that were keeping him very busy."

"Yes," Pavel said agreeing. He was the youngest of Kliment's friends. "I think he was working for an international ecological company, some sort of *saving the earth* watch group, which strangely got taken over by a pharmaceutical company, in a very aggressive way."

The young men walked and talked together as they made their way to Herman's mother's house, where a wake was being held for her son. Pavel took the first step into Herman's house, where a small group of people was gathered to say their final goodbyes to the deceased. Herman's body was laid inside a casket, surrounded by bouquets of flowers, at the center of the living room in the small and modest-looking house.

"Hello Lyosha, how are you?" Polina, Herman's stepsister greeted the group. She walked up to them holding a small tray with cups of coffee for the attendants.

"I'm so sorry for your loss Polina. How are you and your mother doing?" Lyosha replied, as Kliment, Pavel, and Ilya also walked up to greet her. As Lyosha and the rest spoke to Polina, Kliment could see Herman's mother from where he was standing, and he could see how her grief had completely overtaken her. He watched as she sat in silence praying with her head down. A black veil covered her head and a crucifix rested in between the fingers of her hands.

"Your mother, how is she?" Kliment asked Polina. She looked at her for a moment and then she looked at Kliment again but didn't say anything.

"Can I go and express my condolences?" Kliment asked.

"Yes, go ahead, she'll appreciate it," Polina responded. "I have to go greet the others. I'll catch up with your guys in a bit." Lyosha was able to see some of the rest of Herman's friends, a group he hadn't particularly been fond of because of the way they usually carried themselves. Drugs, alcohol, and problems usually followed them wherever they went.

"Hey," Lyosha said to the other group as they walked past her.

"What are they doing here?" Kliment asked.

"They are just here because they probably didn't have anything else to do," Lyosha said.

"You are right about that, and also the free food," Ilya added, just as Petya, one of the guys from Herman's other group of friends approached his coffin with two other guys next to him. Kliment could see as they gathered around Herman's body and remained in silence. Petya looked at Kliment as he walked away from Herman's coffin and stared at him in a way Kliment didn't like. The others stared at Kliment in the same way, but he decided to just ignore them. Kliment began making his way to Herman's mother.

"Kliment, Kliment..." Herman's mother wailed. "My son is gone, Kliment. Why is he gone before me, why? He was so young and full of life, such a good boy, ohhhh... He had so many dreams. There was so much he wanted to do..." She hung her head as she sobbed for some time.

"I remember you were one of the only friends who always gave him good advice Kliment, thank you for that." She extended her arms to embrace Kliment. He held her as she cried.

"It's okay Mrs. Sokolova. You can be sure Herman was a kind soul and he is surely in a better place now. It would probably pain him to know how sad his mother is right now."

Kliment's words gave a mild sense of peace to Mrs. Sokolova and as the words began to sink in, her sobbing stopped for a moment. She looked at her son's face as Kliment continued to hold her in his arms.

"Would anyone else like some coffee?" Polina asked, as she was ready to walk towards a hallway that connected to the kitchen. Several people in the room lifted their hands and Polina began counting the people. Some of the other family members in the meantime were busy preparing food and more coffee.

Moments later, Polina got back from the kitchen with a serving tray and again asked for the people in the room that wanted coffee to lift their hands. To her surprise, some people jumped out of their seats and started nervously running away from the room. It seemed like Herman also was raising his hand out of the coffin.

"What's going on? What happened?" Polina asked while looking everywhere trying to figure out what was making everyone suddenly run away. Kliment, who became aware of what was happening, let go of Herman's mother and walked towards the living room. Lyosha also wanted to see what was creating the commotion in the room.

"What is happening? What is happening Polina?" Herman's mother asked, walking out of the kitchen.

"Mom don't, stay where you are. Don't move, Stay in your chair." Polina yelled out to her mother. But her mother was too worried about her son's coffin and didn't listen to her as she walked towards the living room to make sure it was fine.

"Oh my God! Herman!" Mrs. Sokolova couldn't believe what she was looking at. She couldn't speak anymore as she began to walk very slowly toward the coffin.

"Mom…" Polina started to say.

"Oh no..." Kliment said as he saw Petya and the rest of his friends walk away from the room grinning, trying to hold back their laughter.

"Oh my God..." Polina said.

"Herman?" Polina's mother whispered her son's name. She couldn't believe what she was seeing but she wanted to really believe that she was actually looking at Herman's hand slowly going down after it had been raised up.

"Do you want coffee, my son?" Herman's mother asked softly. "You always did like my coffee. Polina, bring a cup of coffee for your brother. He wants coffee, and, and he never left the house without drinking coffee before…" Herman's mother was shaking as she spoke.

Kliment walked over and stood right in front of Herman's mother, as Lyosha walked up to the coffin to see that Herman's arm had a string tied to his wrist, which was used to pull his hand up by Petya and his friends.

"Unbelievable! You miserable people, don't you have any shame?" Lyosha said, staring in the direction in which Petya and the rest of his buddies with him had gone.

"We thought they were going to feel good about the joke." One of them said.

"Let me see him, is he awake? Let me see him." Herman's mother said. Kliment stayed in front of her, embracing her and preventing her from walking closer to the coffin.

"Let me see my son, Kliment!" She said.

"No, please stay here. Herman did not wake up. It's just a mistake." Kliment told her but she couldn't be reasoned with. She could clearly see the right arm of her son still halfway up, resting on the side of the coffin.

"Petya…" Polina mumbled shaking her head. "I cannot believe what these guys have done, I can't believe it."

As she got closer to the coffin, she saw the trick used to make everyone in the room believe that the dead body was moving on its own. Polina quickly removed the string from around her brother's wrist and very gently placed the arm back in the position it was previously arranged. She then turned around and looked at her mother staring at her with great sadness in her eyes.

She had seen how Polina removed the string from her son's wrist and she quickly understood what had happened. Her head slowly fell on Kliment's chest and her sobbing made him even more upset at Petya. Lyosha looked at Kliment and then looked at Herman's mother and he stared as Kliment walked her away from the room. They were walking through some of the people that were returning after word spread what had really happened.

"You're going to pay for what you did," Kliment said. He looked at Lyosha with his eyes glaring. Lyosha understood, nodding his head in agreement.

Hours later, Kliment and the rest of Herman's friends and family began to go their separate ways after Herman's body was laid to rest at a cemetery a few miles from his mother's house.

∞

A day had gone by, and a mild drizzle was covering the town. The undertaker could be seen walking back towards the store house at the center of the cemetery grounds. He turned back and looked around while pushing the door open with his left hand and holding a small metal flask with his right hand.

Herman's grave had dozens of fresh flowers by the side of his tombstone. It read his name but no dates. Instead, there was a short passage from a book of poems he used to like reading:

Never treat me as another addition in the universe, as the count of those in it, takes place. Nor by adding a number, after every year of my passage. Just embrace me as who I am, who I was, even if I am recognized by my ideals alone. None more important than another, but an important part of it all. Too pivotal to be only a number dictated by the passage of time.

The undertaker picked up a shovel and placed it in a wheelbarrow inside his storage shed. Two men emerged through a broken portion of the fence by the far end of the cemetery. They walked slowly, unbothered by the drizzle. They were dressed in black hooded sweaters, black pants, and combat boots. Both had long beards covering their faces. One had darker skin tone than the other. They calmly walked in silence towards the storage house, where the undertaker was just beginning to dismount his equipment to put everything in its proper place and to call it a night. He poured himself a drink in a tin cup and placed it over a counter, with the flask not far from it.

"I see it." One of the men walking on the cemetery grounds pointed out.

"Let's proceed after we take care of the other." The other man responded.

"Very well then…" The first man added. He was carrying something similar to a pouch, held in his left hand. At that moment, the undertaker heard a sound outside of the door. His back had been towards it and his nose twitched as he smelled something in the air, and he had to sneeze. He slowly turned around to look outside. It was very dark; he could not really see anything. The undertaker picked up a flashlight that was next to him on top of an old table.

"Is anyone out there?" He called out but saw no one outside as he pointed the flashlight towards his left and right. He began taking a few steps away from the door. While turning to go back inside, the undertaker saw a glimpse of something which immediately got his attention.

"Who's out there?" He again asked, using a sterner tone of voice this time, while pointing the flashlight at the direction of Herman's grave. As he walked towards it, he saw what appeared to be a man digging a hole in the ground with his bare hands.

"What do you think you are…?" The undertaker was about to address the individual when suddenly, the other man stood by his side and waved his left hand in front of his face. The undertaker fell to the floor unconscious.

"Do you have him?" The man standing by the undertaker asked.

"Yes, I'm reaching it." The one digging the hole responded.

Close by, a group of people had just pulled up in a small clunker van right outside the entrance of the cemetery. They were very rowdy and drunk as they began getting off the van shouting obscenities and taking turns urinating by the cemetery grounds.

"Screw it! Forget it!" Someone shouted while holding a bottle of 100% proof brand-less vodka up in the air.

"Tonight, tonight I want to sleep with a woman that doesn't make noise, or complain, or talk back. Tonight, I want to do a dead woman." The leader of the group shouted, making all his friends, except his girlfriend, laugh out loud.

"What is your God damn problem, you jerk? Why do you have to speak like that in front of me?" The young man's girlfriend said as she squatted down to urinate. "Are you drunk out of your mind talking like that? I'm right here you idiot!"

"You are damn right! I am drunk out of my damn mind." The young man replied laughing hysterically while disregarding his girlfriend's complaints. In a very casual manner, he walked into the cemetery, while pouring vodka all over his mouth and the front of his shirt, still laughing loudly.

"Don't you understand woman, that's the reason why I want to get laid with a dead one tonight. And there are a few fresh ones that were just buried yesterday. Hahahaha! Anti! Bring the God damn shovel! I'm so damn tired of your nagging and complaining and moaning all the damn time. If I knew you wouldn't take that tape off your mouth, I would have put it on you every time."

The young man continued to rant very loudly, causing everyone to keep laughing. Some even fell to the floor hollering with laughter, making his girlfriend even more upset and almost sober from the humiliation she felt.

"Watch me, watch me!" The young man exclaimed. "A dead woman won't say anything while I'm doing her. It is the best. I don't even need to cover her mouth and face to keep her quiet until I'm done. It is the best feeling in the world! Wooooh!"

Everyone continued laughing and drinking as they made their way towards the center of cemetery. Meanwhile, the undertaker was still asleep on the ground near the store house. Whispering voices could be heard having a conversation around him.

"Then I guess it's safe to assume that the Canadian pharmaceuticals had some kind of knowledge about the negative side effects of the drug." One of the voices said.

"They knew about the side effects long before the preliminary testing." Another voice answered.

"The scientists in the other two laboratories in Zimbabwe and Nicaragua also had knowledge of this situation. Even prior to stage five testing of the initial formula." The same voice added.

"Corpa came up in the picture again." The voice of the man who spoke first was heard saying.

"The British company had run tests prior to the sharing of the chemicals, which conformed the new drug's main compound and they knew the devastating outcome of the side effects soon after the incubation period had begun.

"It is obvious that they knew what they were doing by hiding the findings of the test results from the American government's inquiry team. And I believe it was due to much more than to prevent bad publicity hitting the media, affecting their stocks. They have been planning these moves very carefully for decades and they have been getting better at it. I believe it is only a matter of time now before they find what they've been looking for, Adomer." The same voice finished saying.

"Corpa Pharmaceuticals..." Adomer said, standing looking towards the storage house. "They've been based in the United States for the past forty-eight years, but their true headquarters and center of operations have been based in the UK and right under the noses of the upper and lower parliament, as well as the House of Lords. They have been acquitted of more than seven different cases involving deadly side effects caused by some of their drugs. I believe these were slip ups made by low-clearance individuals working for the face branches of their local proxies of their international branches. The company had three different secret subsidiaries prior to WWII and way after the 1950's and besides the seven cases recently, they had an impeccable record as far as what we have been able to find."

"Till this point, we were able to locate only one of them, a company from Malaysia, which used to transfer funds to their laboratories in North Africa and here in Russia. This is the best lead we had gotten so far. At this point, we must capitalize on it before they put the operation in full motion somewhere else.

"I guess Iterdo was right about them, yet again. They don't have exactly what they want yet, and that is why we assume the leadership has remained in the UK, where they have everything under their control. In this way, they don't have to take chances dealing with other international institutions which may or may not have the same easy-going hand with their operations." Adomer concluded.

"Then I guess that is the real reason why they have been staying around the UK even with the heat they have acquired recently." The other voice said.

"They feel comfortable where they are because they feel no one can touch them. There must be someone in the inside they are very well-connected with, to be able to keep everything steady thus far. And the same connection is also moving negative information against the competitors who strangely suffered casualties after raising questions about the products being put out by Corpa. This is only helping them to enhance their growth and expand the reach of their products when everyone's attention gets distracted by Corpa's competitors.

"And this is what worried Iterdo the most, and I have to agree with him. Till this point, we have been only speculating that they don't have what they want just yet. But given the records we were able to tap into, where we have seen the horrors caused by their atrocious experiments, we must be very concerned about the question of *what is it exactly that they are after?*

"There are several names, Sacku, which must be inspected before any other steps are taken with Sir Lawrence McDowell being the one at the top of the list. Some, which are connected with some of the deceased and others that have somewhat of a direct link with the face company connected to Corpa." The unknown voice added.

"I agree, it will be the prudent thing to do before proceeding with the next part of the inquiry," Sacku replied.

"I would also like to add that if indeed they are being kept in safety by someone very powerful and influential, they are either gaining a great deal, or they owe the leaders of the pharmaceuticals even more than what they are paying for. Perhaps they are sharing mutual interests. Nevertheless, I believe we must also look deeply into the closest candidates in the House of Lords and pinpoint the source. It would be very dangerous if this situation gets to affect WALL's operations since we are aware that several members of the House of Lords are part of their inner infrastructure."

"I believe we should present this as part of our recommendations when the Ushers gathers next," Sack added, right before standing up and looking at the direction where the voices of the people were coming from. Sacku looked down for a moment and over at Adomer while observing the group of people coming in their direction.

"What would you like to do?" Sacku asked. "Do you want to come with us, or do you want to go back and rest for a while before war begins, Jeuras? Or should I call you *Herman?*"

Herman looked at him in silence, still deciding what will be his next course of action.

"You actually grew to like the life this assumed character was living…" Saku mused.

Herman was seated halfway out of his coffin, looking very much alive. His skin was pale but quickly regaining color as blood once again rushed through his veins. His body still remained weak. He continued squeezing his hands, tightening the grip of his fists, summoning the spiritual strength from within his inner being. Mentally propelling himself to once again be able to regain the ability to control his *kium.*

"I felt well where I was for the past few days, although I cannot bring my thoughts to describe what it was that I actually experienced. I have to assume I was only consciously aware of my impending return to this quabis, therefore my kium was relentlessly retaining my inner ability to move forward towards other realms." Herman said. "There are still many things that have to be done here. I will like to be able to continue with my task as part of my preparation until war arrives. It will be interesting to see the faces of those who killed me when they are able to see me again and realize that they couldn't keep me quiet as they had intended.

"But most importantly, I would like to have the chance to help Mrs. Sokolova to understand. I believe it will ease her pain, and yes Sacku, I grew into this character as you mentioned before. And I grew into him because of the depth of his conviction, as he fought against those who wanted to harm the innocent, with only the strength of a regular man. Those who loved him never really got to know who he truly was, especially his mother."

Herman's words were immediately followed by the extended arm of Adomer standing by his side, carrying the strange looking pouch in his left hand.

"S'ykel has informed the Ushers that Nenet has also been reawakened. She will join you and Iterdo in Malaysia. My understanding is that she has ominous news, which can only mean that Ara's prediction has manifested sooner than what we anticipated. And this time, war is almost certainly inevitable."

"S'ykel…?" Herman seemed surprised. "The last time I heard from him, he was considering his position within the Answer. He had been very vocal about the negative way in which, he believed, the very people we have been attempting to help have been leaning towards. He complained about them being undeserving of our gestures to protect them. He said that in reality they are worthless, and they should be put to test instead of being kept blissfully ignorant."

Herman did not really know what to think about S'ykel at that moment. There have been questions hovering through his mind from an incident they were both involved in, where innocent lives were lost.

"I understand, I have been dormant during several of his outbursts against the population, but to be honest, there were times in which he made perfect sense in everything he said. I grew to worry about the reality he had presented to my eyes for I was beginning to see as he saw." Sacku said as Herman adjusted himself to his feet.

"Oh my God!" Petya exclaimed, hugging his bottle of Vodka tightly to his chest. "What in the name of the Devil?" The high pitch of Petya's shouting startled everyone around him.

Sacku looked up, attempting to figure out who was the source of the shouting. He saw Petya and the rest of the people walking towards them. Petya's friends were screaming as well. They couldn't believe their eyes and at that moment they could not tell if what they were looking at was real or a hallucination caused by the drugs and alcohol they had in their system.

"Oh God! Herman! Herman! I can't believe it's Herman! He's... he's alive, he's alive! Oh my God...." Petya was stammering on and on while trembling. His friends, however, had some mixed reactions. Some dropped to their knees as they thought they were witnessing a miracle, while others ran away thinking they were living out a real-life zombie scenario. As if in a trance, Petya took slow steps towards Herman's grave. The bottle of Vodka he had been holding on to dearly, slowly slid away from of his grasp without him noticing.

"But you were dead Herman. How can you be alive? I saw your dead body at the wake." Petya said.

Adomer and Sacku just observed in silence as he walked up to Herman. Adomer moved to the side to allow Petya to get closer to Herman. Petya had not even noticed the other two men accompanying Herman. Sacku moved away and slowly walked over towards the others.

"Petya," Herman said. "What you did to Mrs. Sokolova was unforgivable. You caused her to suffer in such a way, at her weakest moment. How could you have been so cruel to her and the rest of the people there paying their last respects to her dead son?"

"But...how? You were dead Herman. You were dead and we were just... fooling around."

Petya was trying to wrap his mind around everything but no matter how many times he went backwards and forward in his memories, he could not make sense of what was happening. He was still in shock and mostly too stoned to understand what he was in the presence of.

"You are a very lost soul Petya," Herman said. "I feel very sorry for your mother to have a son the likes of you. And after she is gone, and there is no one left to run to in your time of need, what do you think will happen with you? In what is left of your life, what remains for you to see in this world... You will never experience peace and happiness in your life.

"You will end up living a life of misery. A misery, which you will never be able to comprehend. And you will not know where it came from or for how long it will be there. But it will be there, surrounding your soul, haunting you wherever you go.

"It will be caused only by the doings of your own hands and it will always be by your side. You will not only experience it within you but all around you, and it will eat you to your bones Petya. And when you see yourself in my place, when you are here, your soul will not even be able to rest. Only then perhaps, you will see all you have done wrong."

Herman began to take steps forward out of the coffin. He looked at his feet and then moved his neck around as he was getting back the feeling of proper control all over his body. He adjusted the suit that he was wearing from his funeral. Herman looked at Adomer, who was standing right next to Petya, who at the moment was crying and mumbling to himself. He could see as Sacku was walking back towards them. Sacku took a moment to look at Petya as he got closer to him.

Herman was speaking as he was walking closer to Petya. Petya's eyes were wide open but his body was in a heap of sweat and tears. Sacku at that moment waved his hand a few inches away from Petya's face and he instantly lost the strength to hold on to his body and began falling to the ground. Herman whispered some final words into his ears, the words he said caused Petya's eyes to momentarily open wider than before, in shock, right before his head hit the ground.

"Jeuras," Adomer called out.

Herman was looking at Petya at that moment and he then looked at the undertaker as they both lay unconscious on the ground. He observed them momentarily with a look of sadness and pity in his eyes. He stared wondering if there is still any hope for them.

Sacku stood by the side of Adomer and waited for Herman. Herman then turned and walked with them. The three men vanished into the woods under the veil of clouds, mist, and drizzle, leaving behind many unanswered questions in the minds of those around, including the undertaker who at that moment began to regain his senses. Petya with the rest of his friends, as if under a spell, were left lying on the grounds of the cemetery.

Kliment and Lyosha, accompanied by a few other guys had just walked into the cemetery following news that Petya was once again up to no good, doing one of his favorite things. Kliment and his group were ready for anything as they stormed into the cemetery, looking to give Petya some payback for what he had done before. What they were not ready for, was finding Petya and his friends knocked out over the cemetery grounds. A very confused undertaker was just waking up to find a group of strangers lying down all over the place and an angry bunch, ready for trouble.

Kliment looked down at Herman's grave. It was intact. He bent down to rearrange some of the flowers that appeared to have been knocked down by the wind.

∞

On that night, hundreds of miles away in the middle of the Atlantic Ocean, Marcus received a message via telegram, which had taken extra time to reach him. The communication devices on the ship had been disabled for some time and were in the process of being repaired. The crew members in charge of repairs had been having a difficult time fixing them.

The message was from Susan and his children. In the telegram, Susan pleaded for him to return quickly and explained to him the problems that she was having with the people who wanted their property. Marcus's mother gave him the house when she was in her death bed and she asked him to keep it in the family, no matter what happened.

He never knew the source of the attachment his mother had with that place, but he could not go back on the promise he made to her before she died. He never forgot her words. *"The destiny of our family's legacy rest in the hands of our generations staying in this house... Until the time comes, and the answer requests our presence. You must never relinquish this property, no matter the circumstances."*

Now things are different. He has a wife and two children. He had been working very hard to take them away from that part of town and give them a better life. He had been planning to keep the house in order to fix it and rent it out, to satisfy his mother request to an extent, but the events which had occurred while he was away made him change his mind and his future plans.

He was now more worried than ever about the safety of his family with this threatening situation that was quickly getting out of hand. He went first thing in the morning to ask the captain of the ship for permission to finish only half of his contract for now, due to the situation developing back at home.

The captain was more than willing to help him but first, they needed to arrive at their next seaport destination in order for him to get dropped off. Marcus was very worried and sent a telegram back, telling Susan to take the children to his cousin's house, which was out in the countryside, miles away from their house in the city.

∞

Simultaneously, Avraham had been provided with many assets, including a private jet, to help in the operation of finding and capturing, or if all else failed, eliminating the Prophet. The silver colored jet arrived at Heathrow airport in London. He was welcomed by two men and a woman, all elegantly dressed in suits and ties. Avraham was ushered into a white van by one of the men, whom he had seen before in a meeting. Avraham was wearing a regular shirt under his usual green military vest, dark colored pants and shoes. This was not a pleasure trip, and this was not a pleasurable time. He was beginning to assess all of the individuals from various lists he had put together, as well as the lists provided by other members of the task force. The operation was already in motion, but Avraham still had to bring a few more strings together to feel in true control of what he was doing.

Sometime later, Avraham was dropped off at a safe house. It was a brownstone in the middle of a very quiet street at the center of the Soho district, but he told by the woman that he will be picked up in one hour.

One hour went by and Avraham was called at his room and asked to come down at the back of the building, which he did. As Avraham went through the back of kitchen area in the first floor, he was surprised to see that no one was waiting for him. He was expecting a vehicle to be waiting for him. Perhaps a car, or van. But the area was completely isolated and empty. He looked at his wristwatch. It was 12:00 a.m. He took several steps as he paced around, thinking as he waited.

He looked up and noticed that the lights of the adjacent buildings were all turned on. *I don't like this feeling.* Avraham commented to himself. *Like I'm being watched, and I don't know by who.*

There was a garbage truck, making collection stops, about 400 feet from Avraham. Avraham looked at it and decided to move closer to the entrance he had come out from. The truck made two more stops, picking up garbage and containers. There were two men operating the truck. One was the driver and the other man was riding on the step, at the back of the truck. The truck made a stop right near Avraham and Avraham never took his eyes off it, while squeezing something inside the left side pocket of his pants. He was also trying to see the faces of the men working and calmly assumed a guarded posture, as he saw the driver of the truck was walking towards him.

"Hello, Mr. Azra. It is an honor to meet you." The truck driver greeted Avraham.

"I know you!" Avraham replied. "You were in one of the lists Mr. Vasiliev put together for the task force." Avraham noticed the man was Easter European, skinny and mild mannered.

"Yes sir, I am." The driver replied. Avraham looked at him for a moment, before looking inside the truck, where he saw someone sitting in the passenger seat. "I attempted to bring you into the assignment, but you were declined."

"That is because I was already in their system sir." The driver replied. It is nothing to be concerned about, I do appreciate the thought you put on me, sir. You may go into the truck now, sit on the driver's side please."

Avraham looked at the man sitting in the passenger side of the truck one more time, before walking towards the driver's side. As he got inside the truck, the door automatically locked, a red light turned on inside, while the windshield and side window glass became foggy.

Avraham looked at the person sitting next to him. The person was already staring at him from the moment he got inside the truck. Avraham couldn't see the person's face. He had on a black hat on and was wearing a George Washington mask.

"Your reputation is impeccable Mr. Azra." The person said. Avraham put emphasis on his voice: controlled and educated, as well as measured and deep sounding. But he could not figure out his accent, although he thought the voice had a particular undertone, from a dialect spoken in a village in Malta, Italy.

"Who are you?" Avraham asked the person. "The only reason I came inside this truck is because I know that man. I also know those who came to pick me up at the airport. So far, everyone has been clean. This is why I should ask you, why the need to conceal your identity?"

"To be honest with you Mr. Azra," The person said, "I myself see no need to conceal my identity. However, this is a measure taken for your own safety."

"I see," Avraham replied. "You must represent one of the powers."

"Indeed, I do, Mr. Azra." The man replied. "You may address me as Gerard, no last name required."

"My pleasure, Mr. Gerard."

"The pleasure is all mine," Gerard replied.

"What is the reason for this brief meeting?"

"In the condition of my position within our small membership," Gerard replied, "I am the one who supposed to personally assess, as the person who you are."

"You are giving me a final inspection, I presume," Avraham commented.

"I would not call this an inspection Mr. Azra. It is just for the sake of saying 'I have already done as requested.'"

"We are all very aware that you are the only person capable of undertaking what you have signed up to undertake. If you ask me, I just wanted to meet you personally. It's been my honor to do so."

"How many others did you consider before me? If you don't mind me asking." Avraham asked.

"You are the only person we had in mind, Mr. Azra." Gerard's answer did not need any other explanation.

"I see..." Avraham mumbled while a thought crossed his mind.

"Your impeccable reputation and your record are second to none. The decision was unanimous."

"I must thank you all, for the vote of confidence that you all have placed on me, to solve this matter," Avraham said.

"You don't have to Mr. Azra," Gerard replied, just before looking at his wristwatch. "Well, I do not believe there should be any conventionalism amongst us, at this time Mr. Azra. Therefore..." Gerard went ahead and took his mask. Avraham was surprised by the gesture of trust. But he contained his reaction inside.

"I thought it was not prudent for me to know your true identity," Avraham said.

"You still don't, Mr. Azra," Gerard replied while staring at Avraham in the most profound of manners. Gerard was a man in his late fifties. His blonde hair was combed in a sleek way. He had a thin nose, almost nonexistent lips and a mole near his left cheekbone. Avraham could not help but to feel concern about the yellowish color of the sclera of his eyes. Gerard stared back at him, almost as if allowing Avraham to study his appearance.

"I will not take up much more of your time, Mr. Azra." Gerard bid farewell to Avraham and as Avraham got out of the truck, he heard a few last words from his new fan. "I trust you are fully aware; failure is not an option Mr. Azra."

"I am," Avraham replied, without turning around to look at Gerard. The other two men walked back towards the truck and assumed their previous position, as Avraham walked back towards the back entrance of the safehouse. There was a sedan parked right outside the door. Avraham walked towards it and saw four familiar faces. There were four American men he had worked with in the past. Elite CIA spies he had worked with in the past that he trusted very much: Danny was in his early thirties, Clark and Ron who were in their early forties, and Benny who was in his mid-thirties. Avraham had personally asked President Smith to allow them in the task force.

"What took you so long?" Avraham asked the men inside the car, while one of them opened the rear passenger side door for him.

"Benny," Avraham said to the passenger next to him.

"How are you?" Benny asked Avraham.

"We were told to wait an extra five minutes Avraham," Ron said, who was the driver of the vehicle. Avraham was not really concerned about the delay. But he gave a thought to the calculation made, to make that possible.

"Let's go to the other side of town and meet with the British list," Avraham said to Ron after Clark handed him several folders with additional lists which had just been prepared for him.

"Where are the ex-navy seals?" Avraham asked Benny.

"It's waiting for you at the other safehouse Avraham," Danny answered, who was sitting up front. The sedan slowly entered into the city traffic of one of the main avenues.

Chapter XIV:

Warning

One day later, near a shipyard in the province of Samut Prakan in Thailand, three black luxury sedans were discreetly parked behind the back of a conglomerate of warehouses. Everything was shut down for the evening, and night had already begun to fall over the city.

After his failure to take care of the Niema matter, Sao Li had been ordered by Matsuda's people to give the logistical support to the person who had been now designated with the duty of eliminating Niema. Sao Li had also been informed of the person chosen for the assignment. He was not surprised to hear it was Bo Chin. Although he did not personally know him, he had grown to hate him more and more for earning such high regard within the leadership of Hun, an honor Sao Li had yet to earn. He had heard about Bo Chin at various other times in the past and had grown curious as to how all the operations this one person was assigned to, had a perfect level of success, thus catapulting him to the top ranks within the families in unprecedented time. Something which Li had been working very hard for, with lackluster success.

A single dark vehicle was approaching the warehouses, the headlights blinked three times. Sao Li, seated at the front passenger seat, ordered his driver, Jae 'Hwa, to do the same. It was an old black 1983 Mercedes sedan and it slowly pulled up right by the center of the other three vehicles, in front of Sao Li's.

Jae 'Hwa got out of the car, while Sao Li and the two others with him remained inside. One man came out of the Mercedes. Both Jae 'Hwa and the other man bowed respectfully and after a brief conversation, they each walked back towards their respective vehicles.

The man walking towards the Mercedes suddenly turned and walked towards Sao Li's car. Sao Li remained inside the car, just watching as the man walked towards him. The glare from the headlights of the Mercedes did not allow him to see the man's face nor make out his appearance. Sao Li only saw he was wearing a long black trench coat, but his curiosity was not enough to make him come out of his vehicle and greet the man. The man walked all the way until he was by Sao Li's side of the door. He stood right where he was without saying or doing anything. He just stared at Sao Li, and Sao Li stared at him from the neck down, while keeping the window of his car rolled up and his door locked.

The man then took several steps back and began to walk back towards his own vehicle. Sao Li's men looked at each other in all three cars and one of them shouted out to the man.

"Hey! What are you doing? Show some respect!"

Jae 'Hwa looked confused. He had done his part and acted respectfully by approaching Bo Chin to greet him, in the way he was supposed to. Which in actuality, it was supposed to be Sao Li's duty.

"Sajangnim (Boss), what's the problem? Why didn't you get out of the car to talk to Bo Chin? You were entrusted to give him the information yourself."

Sao Li put his window half-way down. He spat outside before giving his driver a loud slap on the face, which his men in the other vehicles heard.

"Never question me again!" Sao Li said through gritted teeth.

At the same time, the Mercedes slowly drove forward before speedily driving away from there. Sao Li hesitated a moment. He did not say anything. He remained in silence and thought for a moment before ordering his men to go after the Mercedes.

"Who the hell does this guy think he is?" Sao Li said, perspiring.

All three vehicles drove very fast and quickly caught up with the Benz. The driver of the Benz noticed as the three vehicles began driving erratically around him. The driver of the Benz continued driving as if nothing out of the ordinary was happening. Instead of slowing down, he pressed the gas to go even faster as the cars were all approaching a ramp to get onto the Bhumibol bridge, which will take them to the other side of the city.

The other cars were trying to cut off the Benz but each time Sao Li's men thought they had him cornered, the Benz made it out somehow, leaving a curtain of dust and smoke behind. The chase became faster and faster, swerving, cutting off other cars, causing accidents and creating havoc all around them. When the roads were cut off, the Benz drove onto the sidewalk. Panicked bystanders dodged for cover. No matter how the Benz driver tried to shake off the pursuers, at least one remained and was quickly joined by the others.

The Benz drove into a dark alley with a dead end ahead, where it finally stopped. The other three cars pulled up right behind him and Sao Li ordered his men to get out and surround it, under the doubtful gaze of his driver. One of Li's men banged on the heavily tinted glass of the Mercedes and ordered everyone in it to get out, but no one did. He looked all around the car, attempting to get a glimpse inside. Not knowing what else to do, he turned and looked at Sao Li for answers.

Frustrated, Sao Li himself got out of his car and ordered his men to take everyone out of the car by force if they won't comply. Jae 'Hwa was the only one who hesitated and asked his boss to reconsider how he was acting.

"This man was sent by Matsuda San; we cannot treat them this way. It means disrespecting Matsuda San himself." Jae 'Hwa begged his boss.

Sao Li then pulled out his gun and pointed at his driver's face. "So, you wish to die right here on behalf of this dog, do you?" Sao Li shouted angrily. The driver put his face down and asked Sao Li to please reconsider his actions.

"I mean no disrespect boss. I am only trying to help by preventing a misunderstanding turning into something worse. They are not like us, you know this. They may do things in a different way. I mean no disrespect boss. I am on your side, remember? I'm only thinking about your best."

"Get them all out!" Sao Li ordered his men, with great irritation in the sound of his voice. They went ahead and attempted to pry open the doors. But this time, they were able to open all four doors of the Benz easily.

"It is said, that those who learn to listen before acting, are the inheritors of wisdom when it is passed along to them." Someone standing behind Sao Li, whispered. Jae 'Hwa looked at the person who was standing right behind Sao Li. It was Bo Chin, the same person who he had greeted back at the warehouse and the only person who had been inside the Mercedes all along.

The other men watched as Bo Chin grabbed Sao Li by his shirt with one hand and lifted him a few inches off the ground. Only Sao Li felt the restraint of the strength exerted by the man holding him.

"You are a fool. And this reason alone is why you have not moved up the ranks, not because of your arrogance, although that as well has been noticed." Bo Chin spoke in Korean to Sao Li, while Sao Li's men quietly stared, not wanting to make a move which might endanger their boss.

"I already have what I needed from you." Bo Chin said, while still holding Sao Li off the ground. "I have no more use for you. So, tell me... What do you do when you have no further use for something outdated and useless? Do you drop it in the garbage? Do you drop it in the river? Or do you burn it? Tell me Sao Li, what should I do with you?"

"Mr. Bo Chin please..." Jae 'Hwa pleaded, just as the rest of Sao Li's men pointed their guns at Bo Chin. The driver's eyes captured the real danger his boss was facing. When he saw Sao Li's feet in the air, he struggled to get the rest of his words out.

"I believe this has just been a great misunderstanding," Jae 'Hwa stammered. "An unfortunate one. I am pleading for your better judgment to excuse our wrongful introduction and allow us to try again if possible. We all have the same goals and duties to our organizations, and I believe that we shall place those, even in front of our own."

Bo Chin looked at the driver and then his eyes turned back at Sao Li. He took a couple of seconds, but finally opted for placing Sao Li down again.

Sao Li looked at Jae 'Hwa with anger, and Jae 'Hwa respectfully thanked Bo Chin for his understanding. Bo Chin then ordered Sao Li's men to move their vehicles out of the way while he got in the Benz. Sao Li did not say anything else, but he was furious. He quietly sat down in the back seat of his car while the rest of his men got into their cars.

Bo Chin drove away in the Benz, undisturbed by anything else and watched how some police vehicles drove by the other side of the street, still searching for the culprits involved in the car chase, which moments before had left a trail of accidents all over the streets.

"Boss, what do we do?" Asked one of Sao Li's men. Sao Li did not want to speak. He was furious and felt humiliated by what Bo Chin did to him in front of his men.

His driver looked at him, but his eyes seemed to be lost inside the dark clouds of his mind.

That strength... Sao Li wondered in silence. *It does not belong to any mortal man.*

"Boss, I will drive back to the hotel, if that's ok with you." His driver proposed,

Sao Li did not answer and Jae 'Hwa took the initiative and drove away, followed by the rest of the vehicles. Although he decided not to mention anything, nor what he had seen happen to Sao Li. Jae 'Hwa could not erase the impression Bo Chin had left on him. At that moment, he was the only one in Sao Li's inner circle understanding the very imminent threat Bo Chin represented to his boss's future and the future of all the men in his chapter.

At the same time, with all the information he needed in his head, Bo Chin pulled out a satellite phone and placed a call to one of his men. "We're going to Istanbul." Bo Chin informed him.

"We'll start making preparations immediately." The man quickly replied.

Bo Chin then hung up and placed another call to a man in London. The man was a former FBI agent who had been part of a group charged with aiding the ITG (Illicit Transaction Group.) It had been their mission to detect and neutralize individuals from international organizations, who made deals with stolen ancient artifacts to facilitate money laundering transactions and weapons purchases, in and out of the United States or any other countries.

"I found a very good lead to help in your search. I just need your monetary assistance to set things in motion." The man informed Bo Chin.

"What you found Thompson, do you believe one hundred percent that it is genuine?" Bo Chin asked the man.

"I am very positive about what I've said."

Thompson's new development caused Bo Chin to temporarily change his plans to go and personally inspect what the Ex-FBI agent claims to have found. Bo Chin told the man he would be there by the afternoon the next day and after ending the conversation with him, he called one of his men and ordered him to have his private plane ready at once.

Bo Chin closed the line. While the steering wheel continued steering the vehicle towards its destination, he extended his right hand and spread his fingers wide. A fading light blue illumination appeared around his hand. As it continued losing its density, he felt it becoming weaker when it flowed all around his body.

"She has to move fast. She has to find it for me before they locate me again." Bo Chin murmured to himself.

A few hours had passed, and he arrived at a very crowded street. There were street vendors, people drinking and a party atmosphere going on everywhere, making driving almost impossible. Bo Chin parked his car in an underground garage, where it was isolated behind closed doors.

Bo Chin then took a private elevator, with walls covered in rare ceramic tiles. He took the private elevator all the way up to the top floor, where only that elevator had access to. One of his men was standing guard right outside the elevator door and bowed his head to greet his boss as he walked in.

"Leave." Bo Chin ordered. The man quickly followed the order and opened a door, which led to a place two floors below. There were five other men observing monitors with views and images of everywhere in the nearby area, except Bo Chin's private quarters.

Bo Chin walked up to the end of the main salon and pressed a code into a digital keypad. The heavy iron door slid open to the left side and as Bo Chin walked in, the door closed behind him.

"You have come..." A weak female voice said, speaking softly in French.

"I have come to see you. I've missed you so much, Monica." Bo Chin responded gently, speaking in French as well.

"Please come closer... so that I can see your beautiful face." The woman asked him. Bo Chin did not move from where he was. He stood in silence, just looking at the 360-degree-view offered by the glass windows of the place. From the outside, the windows were pitch black and had a special layer which reflected all light away from the inside view, including the light of the moon, which was just beginning to show.

"Where are you?" The woman asked in a frail voice.

"I am walking closer to you now. Can you feel me?" Bo Chin whispered. Even though the woman heard his voice near her side, he had never moved from where was standing. He then slowly turned his head to look at her and watched her in silence. His long hair covered the profile of his face and he did not appear to breathe as he stood motionless. He had a streak of silver hair that fell to the side. He was now dressed in a traditional black Chinese *changshan* grown that reached all the way to his feet.

"I feel you so near me. I missed the feeling of this closeness you give me, and it makes me feel really good. As if I could fly in the air, just as the first time you came to me."

Bo Chin listened and continued staring at her without moving a muscle of his body. She, however, had the feeling and the impression he was standing right by her side, caressing her face. She was laying on a double king size bed with many pillows, which appeared to move on their own all around her. She was covered by a very thick cloth with small tiles woven into it, made from the same ceramic that was on the walls of the elevator.

"You have been so wonderful to me Monica." Bo Chi said.

"And you to me..." Monica gently replied. At that moment, the cloth covering her began to slowly slide away from her, revealing a very old, fragile body that seemed to belong to a 100-year-old woman but also that of a small child. There was a physical, living organism that looked like a large pillow underneath her neck, with symbiotic tubes, that seemed like veins transporting plasma, blood, and liquids to and from her body. The pillow made gentle motions as fluids waved inside of it. As Bo Chin lifted his right arm in a very slow manner, the pillow's motion decreased.

"I can feel you caressing me..." Monica whispered, just as a light blue glow floated all around her fragile small body. Unknown to her, her body began to shiver.

The intensity of the glow began to decrease around her body, but it began to increase all around Bo Chin's. Then, the motion of the pillow became agitated and suddenly, Bo Chin also became slightly agitated as well.

He realized Monica's life was being extinguished and so he rushed to gather more of her special ability from her faster than he'd ever done before. But Monica began to experience something very painful and her body started trembling and she could not control it as a very loud hollering exited from within her while making the bed and the room itself tremble.

Bo Chin looked worried and took a step forward but did not dare to go any closer to her. He suddenly felt a sensation that, for a moment, someone else saw what he was doing and was going to head his way soon. In a matter of seconds, Monica's body disintegrated into a pool of flesh and fluids. Bo Chin could no longer harvest her energy.

"Damn it! That's not enough to get me by." He was very upset and unable to contain his frustration. He cried out, causing the entire room to begin shaking. The walls began to crumble, and the windows and floors began to show large cracks. The lights began to malfunction throughout the entire building, and then the security cameras began to go out one by one.

"Elder woman..." Bo Chin said, just before exiting the room almost in a rush. He drastically opened the door just with the power of his mind, not pressing the buttons on the keypad this time. As the door was closing behind him in the same way, he ignored the very loud and devastating explosion which occurred in the place where Monica's remains were.

The elevator doors opened up in front of Bo Chin and as they began to close again when he walked inside, he could see how the fire now began to take over the entire floor. He exited the building, not wanting to look back as another explosion took place, this time consuming the entire top half of the building with it.

∞

Later that night, Sao Li ordered Jae 'Hwa to drive him to the airport. Sao Li had things he needed to put into motion. And staying one more night in Thailand was not going to be productive for him. As they got closer to the proximity of the airport, Sao Li ordered his men to ditch the vehicles they had been driving. They had all been rental cars under fraudulent accounts anyway and he no longer had any use for them. They drove to an area near one of the runways, where they did not see much air traffic. Sao Li wanted to walk and accompanied his men to get rid of the cars. As they walked back to their terminal, An'kor, one of Sao Li's men, saw the black Mercedes pulling up to a hanger near the private airplanes.

"BOSS! Come look at this!" An'kor called out to Sao Li.

"What is it?" Sao Li asked, unenthused.

"Boss, it's the Mercedes!"

Sao Li became frantic, almost running up to An'kor.

"Where did you see it?!" He demanded.

An'kor pointed to the hanger. Just at that moment, Bo Chin could be seen walking into his private airplane. Three men – one European, and two Chinese, all dressed in black, welcomed Bo Chin into the plane. Right under Sao Li's prying eyes, eyes that did not miss a single detail about the color, model, and right down to the serial number of the plane.

"In'Jung!" Sao Li called on another one of his men. In'Jung ran to his boss, almost stumbling against Jae 'Hwa as he did.

"Yes, Boss!" In'Jung had a briefcase with him, which Sao Li hurriedly opened. He took out a satellite phone and placed a call back to Seoul, South Korea. Sao Li was able to give the plane's details to the person he was talking with. A woman named Min Seo, who happened to be Hangul Ssi's youngest niece. She was romantically involved with Sao Li and since their relationship had to remain a secret from her uncle, she kept several trusted people at her disposal who would help her and Sao Li in anything and everything they requested.

Sao Li had suddenly seen the road to his redemption, flying away from him, but he felt that the flight was taking off only momentarily to eventually land in the palm of his hand soon. In a matter of seconds, he and Min Seo created a plan, which he had not been able to put together before. Matsuda's orders were to be respected and followed to the letter. But with this new development, he could do things differently while keeping his hands clean. He had a pretty good idea of whose hands would be getting dirty on his behalf.

"Ok, I will wait for the call. I am at the airport now." Sao Li ended the call with Min Seo. He turned to his men. Jae 'Hwa and the rest of his men saw a drastic change in his demeanor. His attitude was suddenly upbeat. There was a great level of determination, even in the way he walked.

"Let's go! We have to change our flight plans." Sao Li said. Hearing the tone of his voice, energized his men. But his words only created preoccupation in Jae'Hwa's thoughts. And the source of this preoccupation will soon be manifested in the most unexpected manner.

Hours later, Sao Li and his men arrived at Heathrow Airport in London. It was early in the morning and there was a heavy fog that covered the city. They exited the airport separately, wearing hats that helped cover their faces. They had also changed their attire from the usual expensive dressy suits to casual jeans and sweaters. They were then received by another of Sao Li's men, In Tak, who had acquired potential whereabouts of Bo Chin from a source within Interpol.

In the meantime, Bo Chin had arrived at Cromwell Road. He walked calmly till he reached a wall at the back of the Victoria and Albert Museum. A man was seated on the bench across the street and he seemed to be looking for someone amongst the crowd nearby. He was a skinny man with light skin and thinning dark hair, dressed in a tan color trench coat and a baseball cap. A Bangladeshi vendor in his sixties inside a magazine stand looked at him with suspicion and curiosity. The magazine vendor had gray hair and a matching beard. He was dressed a little too warmly for the weather, in a short dark puffy jacket with a blue button-down shirt that was sticking out from underneath it.

The man sitting on the bench had not noticed Bo Chin walking across the street through oncoming traffic. The vehicles missed him by mere inches while Bo Chin walked as if he was alone on the street. In no time, he was standing next to the man on the bench, staring at him, without the man realizing it.

"Gregory..." Bo Chin's voice resounded like a drum inside the man's head.

"Shit, man!" The man on the bench jumped out of his seat startled. "Can you not do these things to me? Here I was, like I always do, getting here before you, to see if I can spot you before you find..."

"Stop these childish games, Thompson." Bo Chin was not amused. "Tell me, what do we have?"

"We need to go somewhere else to talk." Gregory looked around as he spoke. He did not want to be seen but he was still unaware of the man inside the magazine stand still watching his every move. "Let's go inside the museum." He proposed to Bo Chin, unaware of a sudden sensation of dizziness that was affecting Bo Chin.

Bo Chin stared at him momentarily, wondering about something. He had a feeling about the man inside the stand but did not react, nor mention anything about it. Gregory stared at him, waiting for his answer.

"You got injured." Bo Chin said to Gregory. Gregory thought about what to tell him but then did not bother to explain the cause.

"Let's go into the museum, I have to show you something." Gregory once again said. Bo Chin was already walking ahead of him. Indeed, Gregory had a limp. He wondered how Bo Chin had figured that out so fast since he had not even seen him walking.

Fifteen minutes later, they were inside the men's restroom. Gregory brought out a document from inside his jacket pocket. At the same time, outside on the street, the Bangladeshi man inside the magazine stand walked to a telephone booth and placed a call.

"Milbio, is it you?" The man asked, as he kept watch over his stand not far away while informing someone about Gregory walking into the museum.

"A map." Bo Chin already knew what the document was even as Gregory still held it folded in his hand. "Where does it lead?" He asked Gregory, pacing just a few feet away, with his back towards him. Gregory took a brief moment to look at him while unfolding the large, document in his hands. He wanted to place it against the wall, but Bo Chin advised him against it.

"Yes, it *is* a map." Gregory stretched his right hand, handing the document over to Bo Chin. "I took this picture from a document from the Vatican's library. The indication of the map itself is not important, and as of this point, I will not know where it will lead. It is only the illustration of a layout. The lands covered in it are the borders of a very important castle.

Bo Chin took only one look at the map and handed it back to Gregory. "This ground of rocks is where the foundation of Constantine's castle was laid upon." Bo Chin said. Gregory was not looking at him as he spoke, but he knew Bo Chin had knowledge of things which he and many others did not. Gregory was someone who had spent his entire life in search of things others did not care much about, and this was the cornerstone of the association between him and the very mysterious man, who funded his quest and research. Bo Chin was after something which, even with his vast knowledge and deep insight, he has yet to be able to find. Gregory was trying to help him find it and enjoying doing his dream job while at it.

"Yes," Bo Chin listened to Gregory's words as he kept his eyes over the wall ahead of him. "These are a portion of Constantine's land."

"Go on..." Bo Chin slowly turned around to look at him. Gregory attempted to walk closer to him, but Bo Chin lifted his right hand, to maintain a distance between them. Gregory took a step back while speaking. He had no reason to be afraid of Bo Chin, but he fully respected his strange mannerisms. Gregory did not notice as Bo Chin's left hand was wide open and extended over his head. As he took a moment to look down at the map in his hands, he did not see or feel anything. But Bo Chin released an invisible energy over him, that covered him starting from his head, all the way down to his feet.

"The map itself does not mean much," Gregory placed the map back inside his pocket. "Its importance to me is not of historical value, but of placement relevance. You see, there is a book, which was written centuries after the reign of King Constantine. And in this book, there is a descriptive drawing of the inside of a secret chamber, which may contain secrets, that the grandson of... "

"Arthur." Bo Chin looked at Gregory, calmly adding to what he was about to say.

"Yes. King Arthur was Constantine's grandson." Gregory replied, straightening himself up a bit. He paused to contemplate a thought before continuing. "A monk was handed a manuscript whose origins were never known. This monk was so taken by what he learned within the scriptures, that he decided never to utter a word ever again. He then decided to complete his penance by writing a book to pass some of the secrets he had learned, in the form of riddles, so that if one day, others manage to decipher them, they will be revealed with the truth. He wrote a book that took almost a decade to complete. This book has come to be known as *the book of the devil.*"

"The Gigas..." Bo Chin said, his voice almost in a whisper.

"The Codex Gigas," Gregory added. "I need you to get me that book, or at least get me near it. If I can take a picture of two of the pages, I may be able to put some links together. I strongly believe I may find a trail hidden within the information depicted in those pages, to coordinate them with what I have on this map. I came to this conclusion based on the scriptures of a previous document I came across."

"I will get you the book." Bo chin was ready to leave the restroom. Someone was outside trying to open the door, and Gregory became worried. But Bo Chin kept it locked by keeping his gaze on it.

"The book is at the national library..." Gregory spoke while attempting to follow Bo Chin.

"In Stockholm." Bo Chin said opening the door while contemplating the information Gregory was giving him. Two men entered the restroom in a rush. One of them eyed Gregory from behind his dark sunglasses.

"I will get you the book, be ready to do your part." Bo Chin told him. Gregory looked at the men's faces, who seemed angry. He had the feeling that they assumed he had locked the door on purpose.

"When are you going to get it?" Gregory followed Bo Chin outside the restroom.

"You will have it soon; I will meet you in Copenhagen by tomorrow." Bo Chin said, walking away from Gregory.

"I'll be on my way to Heathrow airport in an hour," Gregory replied. He was already walking outside the museum, thinking that Bo Chin was walking behind him. He looked back to say something, but Bo Chin was already gone.

At the same time, Sao Li and his men had reached the back of the museum. They had arrived in two different taxis and did not waste any time running inside the museum through the front entrance. A man stayed behind in each taxi to prevent the drivers from leaving, while Sao Li and the others went inside.

They did not make it in time. Gregory and Bo Chin were long gone. Sao Li was upset and greatly disappointed. As he walked out with the rest of his men, he received a message from Min Seo that she had gotten a call from a man named Milbio.

Sao Li quickly picked up his satellite phone and placed a call. The moment the other line was answered, he was told that Bo Chin's airplane was being prepared for departure. The call was abruptly cut off. Sao Li and his men ordered the taxi drivers to rush back to the airport. The drivers scrambled to get through traffic, Sao Li got upset due to their lack of driving skills. He yanked him away from behind the wheel and took his place. He accelerated through the streets of London, provoking some accidents in the process.

"Boss, they are calling you again." Jae 'Hwa said.

"Give me the phone!" Sao Li yanked the phone away from him while driving erratically. "Milbio!"

"It's me." A man with a French accent replied. "How far are you from the airport?"

"I don't know, fifteen, twenty minutes?" Sao Li replied.

"You're not going to make it," Milbio said definitively. "I have been told that the person fitting the description of the man you are after..."

"Bo Chin!" Sao Li shouted, interrupting what Milbio was about to tell him.

"They believe it's him," Milbio said. "The person is walking towards the same private jet that landed a few hours ago. The jet is being prepared for departure as we speak."

"Shit!" Sao Li was very angry and pressed on the gas to go even faster. He could not begin to understand how Bo Chin was able to make it back to Heathrow so fast. "Are you sure it's the same person?"

"It has just been confirmed," Milbio responded. "It's Bo Chin walking into the airplane. He's being accompanied by two others, the pilot and a woman dressed all in black with a big hat. Get to the airport. I will have the destination of the plane before you get there." Milbio ended the call.

"Tell the others not to slow down." Sao Li dropped the phone back into Jae 'Hwa's hand. But Jae 'Hwa did not have time to follow his order when the phone rang again.

"Give it to me!" Sao Li said. Jae 'Hwa instantly handed it back to him.

"He's going to Stockholm." It was Milbio again.

Stockholm? Sao Li thought before speaking. "Stockholm?" He then asked aloud. The taxi driver next to him looked at him fearing for his life.

"There's something else," Milbio added. "One of my informers told me that the person Bo Chin came to visit, is under FBI surveillance. And this investigation is being assisted in certain aspects, by Interpol."

"Can we use that to our advantage?" Sao Li asked.

"I'm already working on it," Milbio said. "By the time you get to Heathrow, I'll have something more concrete to tell you."

"Ok, make sure you call me back." Sao Li has now become very much excited. He was driven mostly to satisfy his desire of getting back at Bo Chin for the actions he believed caused him great disrespect in front of his men and his falling out of favor from Hangul Ssi.

Sometime later, Sao Li had Heathrow airport in his sight. After wrapping their hands and mouths with industrial tape, four of Sao Li's men put the taxi drivers inside the trunk of the cars. They took the vehicles and parked them in the long-term parking garage, and then went on to meet with their boss. Arrangements had been made for Sao Li and his men to have their tickets ready for the next flight to Stockholm.

"Boss, it's him." Jae 'Hwa gave the phone back to Sao Li.

Milbio was once again on the other line.

"What did you find out?" Sao Li asked Milbio.

"Listen carefully," Milbio said. Sao Li waved at Jae 'Hwa to go and prepare for the next flight. Jae 'Hwa also saw him holding the tip of the right shoulder of the black jacket he was wearing. Jae 'Hwa knew it was a signal for him to go and get new clothing. Bo Chin's contact, Milbio continued, "His name is Gregory Thompson, former FBI high-end crimes special agent. This information will cost you double the prices, Sao Li. This guy is very important for you."

"Why is he important for me?! I want Bo Chin!" Sao Li was furious.

"Because with him, you will get Bo Chin," Milbio replied. "The FBI is tailing him and wherever he goes, I will know about his whereabouts. And Bo Chin won't be far behind."

"Are you already on him?" Sao Li asked.

"I have someone in Stockholm, who will shadow him the moment he steps out of the plane," Milbio replied.

"Is he on his way to Stockholm too?" Sao Li asked, interrupting Milbio.

"Thompson?" Milbio asked. "I believe that he is the reason why Bo Chin is on his way there. The name of my man is Tarr. A fellow countryman of yours, but from the north."

"That is fine. Whether he is a defector or not, it's all the same to me."

"I feel the same," Milbio added. "He is in Espoo, in Finland at the moment. But that is only a one-hour flight from Stockholm. He has already boarded a plane and will land at Arlanda airport before Thompson does. Bo Chin's jet will get there before them. But Thompson will lead us to him. Tarr already knows your number, and I will give you his. Call him as soon as you land at Arlanda."

"And what about you?" Sao Li asked him. "Where are you going to be?"

"I will be in contact with all of you." Milbio ended the call, just as Jae 'Hwa was coming back with several shopping bags of new clothes that he purchased for his boss, himself and the others.

Hours later, Bo Chin's plane was about to land at the designated landing section of Arlanda airport for private planes. A man named Oscar in charge of operations of that section, was reviewing documents from the flight manifest belonging to the current timeline. Two men walked into his office, located near one of the hangers.

"What do you want?" Oscar asked them, seeing them walking into his office. He looked at them head to toe. One of the men named Liam was short, slightly overweight and bald. The other was Hugo who was slim, unshaven and had very unfriendly characteristics to his personality. They were both already wearing their work uniforms which were dark green jumpsuits.

"Carlson and Finn called out," Hugo said to Oscar. "The company sent us to take their spots for the rest of the week." Oscar was about to say something as he got up on his feet behind his desk while still staring at the two men. Before he had a chance to say anything, the phone rang.

"Stay there, don't go anywhere." He instructed the two men. The call was from the company his other two workers were hired from. The woman on the phone speaking to him confirmed that in fact, Hugo and Liam have been assigned to occupy the position of the other two operators. Oscar was informed that Carlsson and Finn had been suspended for drug use and that they would probably be permanently replaced. Oscar hung up the phone and asked Hugo and Liam if they knew what they needed to do. They both answered yes, and Oscar went ahead with his duties and told them to get to work.

There was a private plane that landed before Bo Chin's. It belonged to a wealthy Canadian businessman named William Gagnon, who was being accompanied by his entourage of six people. Three luxury vehicles were waiting for him, as well as three of his business associates.

Hugo and Liam and three others had already helped the passengers and their luggage out of Gagnon's plane. A small commotion occurred when a briefcase allegedly containing very important documents had gone missing. People could be seen scrambling in and out of the plane, searching for the missing briefcase.

Bo Chin's plane landed and made its way to the waiting area near the same hanger Gagnon's plane had been parked. Hugo and Liam were all set to help with the luggage, and as the plane stopped in its designated spot, they quickly went to work but kept their eyes on the people getting off the plane. As the door opened, Hugo seemed to be momentarily disoriented and then became confused. There was no luggage for him to carry out.

Liam walked next to him to help but Hugo informed him that there was nothing in the luggage compartment, while walking towards the side of the plane. The slender woman with the big black hat was just exiting the plane. The side of her face partially visible to those near her revealed pale skin and red lipstick. She was wearing a long black trench coat that matched the hat. Hugo and Liam remained standing just a few feet away from the plane. The other three workers were about to approach them, but Hugo waved his hand, signaling them to go back. One of the men saw them without any luggage in their hands. Realizing there weren't any, he turned around to tell the others that there was nothing to do. Hugo and Liam were scrambling around, acting as if they were still looking for luggage, meanwhile discretely staring at the woman as she walked down the short steps. From where they were, they watched as a black sedan drove up near the plane.

Two men with short hair and dark suits exited the sedan. One remained near the driver's side and the second opened the rear right side door for the woman. He and Liam waited to see if anyone else exited from the plane, but the sedan drove away and no one else disembarked the plane except one of the flight attendants. She was dressed in a black blouse and a black pencil skirt, with her hair tied back in a low bun. There was one other attendant, but she closed the door and stayed inside the plane with the pilot who never showed himself.

Hugo and Liam closed the cargo compartment and walked back to the small office. They looked at each other, wondering if they had missed something. They acted casual as they entered the office where their boss told them to take a break and wait for the next airplane to arrive, which would not be for another two hours. Hugo took the opportunity to look for a phone and placed a call.

"Nothing, we did not see the man you described." He said to the person he had called.

"Keep watch over the plane," Milbio ordered.

"We will," Hugo said, before Milbio ended the call.

∞

Late that evening, Sao Li and his men had made it to their hotel *Miss Clara* in Sveavägen, Stockholm. A hotel with a decent location, set within a walking distance to the center of town and central train stations nearby. They had already met with Tarr, who was assisting them with what they needed to know about the FBI investigation on Gregory. Tarr told Sao Li that Milbio was on their way to meet them, but not in Stockholm. But where Niema will soon be.

Sao Li did not understand the concept of the plan being proposed by Milbio, but Tarr had received specific instructions on what to tell Sao Li.

"Milbio has a video and three pictures," Tarr said. "Which will change the course of this situation to your favor, Mr. Sao Li." Tarr handed Sao Li a blue folder.

"In what way?" Sao Li asked while opening the folder.

"Take a look at the pictures for yourself." He said, pointing at the folder. "Milbio saw Niema, exiting from the establishment run by Mr. Bratislav. Niema's love interest, the woman named Fei is there, who also operates in the establishment as a bartender. In this way, she interacts with Bratislav's best clients without Bratislav himself having to conduct closed-door meetings with any of them." Sao Li carefully looked at the pictures as Tarr explained to him their meaning.

"Now, this is what Milbio requested for you to do, Mr. Sao Li. YOU and your men will assist in the takedown of Mr. Bratislav. He does not have to survive. But Fei does. Upon completion of this task, the woman will be taken to an undisclosed location in Marseille, France where she will be held as bait for Niema. This is where Niema will come to meet you personally and this is where the person known as Bo Chin will come to complete his job of executing Niema. You will have them both in the same place and under the same roof."

In the meantime, Bo Chin had ordered Gregory to stay put. He was resting and eating a sandwich at a local cafe located in a quiet mostly residential street. Cozy three and four-story buildings and small privately-owned shops filled the peaceful neighborhood. At the same time, three men were watching him from inside a dark blue van across the street. A pleasant young lady with blonde hair in a short ponytail, and wearing a dark green waitress uniform, walked up to Gregory and offered to refill his coffee. Gregory happily accepted and allowed the young lady to fill up his cup. She smiled briefly and went on to attend some of the other patrons in the tiny cafe. Gregory stared at the coffee cup momentarily, before bringing it up to his lips. He took one sip and as he brought the cup back to place it on the table, there was a brown sack, folded in front of him, over the table.

"What in the world?" Gregory said.

"This is the Gigas." Bo Chin was standing right beside him, startling Gregory as he became aware of him.

"You are going to kill me if you continue doing that," Gregory said.
"You will not die like this." Bo Chin replied. "This is what you requested from me to continue your work, but I must bring to your attention that this is not the true version of the Gigas."

"What do you mean?" Gregory was both concerned and confused. "I was under the assumption that there was only one copy of this book ever made."

"Indeed..." Bo Chin said. "But this particular version is not it. I believe there are two others. They were created due to the importance of the first version, to protect it from destruction and from allowing others to decipher its secret."

"If this copy is not the original, it may lack the elements I need to find what we are looking for," Gregory told Bo Chin.

"I understand this." Bo Chin agreed. "Nevertheless, I decided to bring you this for you to have a close look at it. You are good at what you do. You may be able to figure something out from it."

"But I may not..." Gregory began to protest.

"I may have an idea of where the true version may be." Bo Chin added. "But I cannot be certain for the time being. Therefore, I suggest you do the best you can with what I brought you."

"But why didn't you try to get the copy located at the museum?" Gregory asked. "That one is the original. If you could have at least borrowed it, I could have taken a few pictures and ..."

"This is the one from the museum." Bo Chin interrupted Gregory.

"The museum had a fake copy of the Codex Gigas?!" Gregory was baffled by what Bo Chin had told him. "All of these decades? They had a fake all this time?"

∞

At the same time elsewhere, Niema was standing by the side of a window at an undisclosed location. The room was ornamented in 16th-century style. After releasing the curtain that he had been holding to look outside, Niema took a seat on an antique chair. A butler entered the room holding a silver tray. The butler set down the tray on a table next to Niema and served him tea and biscuits on delicate china before leaving the room. A man entered the room after the butler had left. He entered through another door, at the opposite side of the room. He was slim, dressed sharply and had a small amount of hair left on his head.

"How are you, Leopold?" Niema asked, speaking in English.

"I am as well as the last time we saw each other." Leopold O'Murchadha replied. He was a gentleman in his late seventies, but with a much younger appearance.

"I was under the assumption that you were on your way out of town before I got here," Niema said. "My apologies if my arrival disturbed your schedule."

"No, don't be silly Victor," Leopold replied. "I am leaving later tomorrow morning. But, there is something which has come to my attention and I strongly believe it is not in your best interest for me to tell you. But I wouldn't be able to live the remaining years I have left of my life if I did not."

"What is it?" Niema asked. Leopold did not answer immediately. He walked slowly towards the same window Niema had been staring out from. Leopold took out his gold watch from the vest pocket of his three-piece suit. He quietly looked at the time and placed it back in its place. It was raining outside. Leopold silently stared at the drops of water falling against the glass. His eyes seemed to be trying to figure out their falling path. From the corner of his eye, he could also see several armed men watching over the property.

"It is such a strange thing..." Leopold said after a while. "The types of news that tend to fall on our laps during this type of weather.

"Leopold, tell me what it is that's bothering you." Niema got on his feet and walked over to Him. Leopold brought out a note from within his jacket pocket.

"I was given this information not long ago, Victor." Leopold handed the piece of paper to Niema. He took it from Leopold's hand and read it quickly. His eyes opened wide. His hands gripped the paper, barely able to contain his anger. He did not say anything to Leopold and walked away. Leopold watched his friend leave. He looked to the floor, second-guessing what he had just done.

"Did I just send him to his death?"

∞

At that particular moment, Bo Chin was about to walk away from Gregory when a strange sensation took over his attention. Gregory was about to say something to him, but Bo Chin was already gone. In a matter of seconds, Bo Chin was seated in the back of the black Mercedes Benz sedan. There was a dark skin man with a clean-shaven head and face, seated behind the wheel. There was a gray stone inside the palm of his left hand.

"Sire..." He said, after seeing Bo Chin appearing right behind him.

"What is it Amare?" Bo Chin asked him.

"Something has occurred," Amare said, speaking with an English accent. He handed Bo Chin a satellite phone.

"Yes, Mirela?" Bo Chin said.

"Sire, Niema has been summoned into a trap." Said Mirela, the woman dressed in all black, who had exited from Bo Chin's plane earlier. She spoke with an exotic accent and in a very calm tone of voice. "We believe this is the doing of Sao Li." She continued.

"Where?" Bo Chin asked. Amare looked at the rear-view mirror and noticed that Bo Chin was no longer inside the car. He did not make anything of it and turned the car on. He then began to drive away from behind a building from a somewhat crowded area of the city.

Elsewhere, Gregory was seated inside a taxi. He had the sack with the giant book over his lap with his hands folded over it. The taxi had stopped at a red light and Gregory was shaken to see that Bo Chin was standing next to his window. The window was already halfway down.

"Take a plane to France." Bo Chin instructed Gregory. "There is a document buried under the walls of an old church. A manifesto of hidden items, written by a witch. It may be of help to you. You shall combine it with what you can put together from the forgery I procured for you. Until I can provide you with the true version. But time is of the essence. I may not have too much of it left to share. I will need you to meet me in Marseille. I will give you the document there. Wait for me by the location near the hotel."

"The same place we met last year?" Gregory asked.

"The same..." Bo Chin answered. The taxi driver turned his head momentarily to look at Gregory. Gregory saw him but ignored him. He wanted to take a quick look at the traffic light. He wanted to make sure he had enough time to say something else to Bo Chin, but by the time he turned his face back to look at the window, Bo Chin was already gone. The traffic light had gone from red to green, and the car began to move again, just after the taxi driver took one more look at Gregory through the rear-view mirror. It was very easy for him to notice the concerned look on his face.

Earlier, Milbio had gone ahead and given the order to an associate to handle Bratislav. Le Varon, Milbio's associate, controlled all the gangsters involved in the drug trafficking and distribution throughout the entire north and part of the south of France. Their base of operation was located deep within the impoverished half of the city of Marseille. Milbio was set to acquire a very good share of the expansion of the gangsters' sales if they were able to take control of Bratislav's territory to add to theirs. All they needed was an excuse and an opportunity. Milbio provided both, in the form of Bratislav's association with Niema, who had become a persona non grata, thanks to his disavow by the umbrella of the syndicates under the control of the Royal Lotus, who went by different names in different countries.

Le Varon wasted no time and after taking out Bratislav and his men, he sent a message to his clients to inform them of the changes to come. It was simple: If they wanted the same merchandise or even better, and at a cheaper price, all they needed to do was accept the new conditions that were about to be introduced. The conditions were not set out to affect the way of operations of any of the clients but nevertheless, a few of them proclaimed their loyalty to Bratislav. Le Varon did not have a problem with them, as long as they did not interfere in the changes that would be in effect immediately. He gathered them all at a warehouse for a meeting, which had once belonged to Bratislav and personally addressed them. He spoke to them in English, which was the neutral language they all understood.

"If you want to be loyal to someone who cannot do anything for you any longer, be my guest. Your clients will stay with you, so long as you can provide them with whatever merchandise you have left. As soon as they find themselves starving, you will watch them go to someone else. Even your most loyal ones will abandon you. This is demand and supply. I will ask you to answer a question for me: When this happens, who is going to stay loyal to you? Not even your employees will hang around for long. They will need to eat and feed their families as well. And if you try to go to different suppliers, you will not get the quality. You will end up getting shit, which had already been handled by many hands before yours."

Le Varon did not have to do much explaining. This was the birth of a new Era. They all had to put the memory of Bratislav behind them in order to survive in the future. And so, they agreed to deal with Le Varon from that moment on and the new proposals being made. His first order of business was handling of the water property connections they each had.

Having used forged documents to travel, Niema arrived by air into France the next day. It was 3:30 in the afternoon, he knew he had to act fast. therefore, he put the wheels into motion with Vitaly and Ivan. Anatoly had traveled with him by self-appointment. As Niema and his men were about to catch a taxi outside the airport, they were approached by a panhandler. It was an old man who reeked badly of alcohol and tobacco. Vitaly quickly placed himself between Niema and the man. But it didn't stop the man from throwing a paper bag between Niema's legs before running away. Anatoly and Ivan pushed Niema away from the paper bag.

Vitaly brought a small knife out of his pocket and attempted to chase after the panhandler but Niema stopped him. They watched as he ran and got on the back of a scooter with another man. Niema's attention on the man was short-lived. He looked at the paper bag on the floor as he heard a ringing sound coming from it. Vitaly told him not to get close to it but Niema picked the paper bag up and opened it. There was a phone inside the bag. Everyone looked at one another as Niema answered it.

"Listen carefully..." Niema could not recognize the voice of the man talking on the phone, but he listened to what he had to say. The man also had a strange accent, which Niema was trying to figure out. He was given an address where he would have to go and await further instructions. The address he was given was that of the Hotel Intercontinental, a popular hotel right at the center of the most popular area of Marseille. Niema made it there in no time and Anatoly and Vitaly rented three different rooms, under different names.

"Boss, I don't think it's safe for you to stay in this place. I feel like a sitting duck." Vitaly was very out of place and impatient. Niema was calm and collected. He had the phone on top of a table, set against the wall near the bed. Anatoly and Ivan were staying separately in the other two rooms. They were both constantly looking out the window.

"Boss? Say something..." Vitaly said, feeling insecure about Niema's behavior. Suddenly, someone knocked on the door. Vitaly got startled and brought out his knife. Niema walked in front of him and placed his left hand over his shoulder. Vitaly looked at his boss, walking towards the door as if nothing was happening. "Boss, wait, don't go to the door," Vitaly warned him. Niema had never done that before.

"Relax, Vitaly. Everything will be okay." Niema said while walking towards the door, against Vitaly's advice.

"Who is it?" Niema stood by the side of the door without taking his eyes away from the small gap between the floor and the door. He was paying close attention to the shadow of the person outside the door. He could only see a very small percentage of it, just a dark line.

"I have a flower delivery for Marcelo." The person behind the door said. Niema seemed more relaxed upon hearing what the person said. It was a code Leopold used from their past endeavors. He carefully opened the door. There was a large rectangular wooden box which was left outside on the floor. The men each picked up one side and brought it inside the room. The person who had brought it was already gone. Niema did not bother to look for the person and quickly closed the door.

Niema opened the box and a smile displayed on his face. Vitaly looked into the box and smiled as well.

"Okay boss, I am feeling better already." Vitaly bent down and quickly pulled out a small, German-made, semi-automatic weapon from inside the box that was containing a nice collection of guns.

"Get Anatoly and Ivan," Niema said to Vitaly while collecting a handgun for himself. "But make sure no one sees you near their room."

"Yes, boss..." Vitaly was about to leave the room with the weapon in his hand.

"Vitaly..." Niema pointed it out to him. Vitaly looked at the weapon in his hands and smiled while walking back.

"This is the only way I feel safe boss, sorry." Niema chuckled as Vitaly handed over the weapon. He looked at Vitaly as he exited the room, a thought crossed his mind. But before he had the time to think about it carefully, the phone he was given began ringing.

At the same time, Gregory was inside a hotel room as well. He was just coming out of the bathroom with a towel in his hands. There were various documents over the bed, as well as a small burgundy travel bag. After putting on a pair of light blue jeans and a black shirt, he took a look outside his window. It was a sunny afternoon and the streets were populated by all kinds of people. Gregory looked at his wristwatch and realized that it was almost time to go where Bo Chin had told him he will meet him. He put on his hat and quickly stuffed all the rest of his belongings inside his travel bag before he exited the room. Already out in the lobby, Gregory decided to take the elevator down, but it was going up at the time. He was only on the fourth floor and decided to walk down the stairs. Someone was about to stumble against him as he was about to take his first step down.

"Sorry, buddy..." Gregory said to one of the men, who he saw walking up towards the fourth floor.

"Sorry, I was not looking," Anatoly replied to Gregory. Ivan was right behind him. Soon after, it did not take long for Gregory to make it out of the hotel. He had decided to catch a train and then a taxi, to get to the meeting place. He was walking towards a corner when a minivan pulled up next to him. Two men were walking on the sidewalk, wearing white polo shirts and khaki shorts. They suddenly pushed Gregory inside the back of the van and quickly got in it as well. Gregory tried to fight the men, but he was subdued and was persuaded into staying still since there was a gun pointed at his face.

"Who are you? What do you want from me?" Gregory said to the three men behind the back of the minivan with him. "You look American. Are you?" He asked them. One of them pulled out his wallet and showed his identification to him.

"FBI, Thompson." The man said, addressing Gregory by his last name. His name was Richard Anderton. He was a slender man in his late thirties, with salt and pepper hair and a mustache.

"What is this about?" Gregory asked Anderton.

"We know what you are about to do." The driver of the van said. Gregory turned his head to look at him, but Rick Handelman, who was next to him, turned as he spoke to him. Handelman had a familiar face and Gregory thought he may have known him from somewhere.

"We have been after you for a while Thompson," Handelman said. At the same time, Vitaly and the others were inside the room looking for Niema. He was not there, and Ivan gave Vitaly a note he had found over the table near the bed. Niema had left it for them to follow his instructions.

"Shit..." Vitaly said. "We have to get moving fast. Let's go get what you need, and then let's get going." Ivan and Anatoly gathered the weapons and ammunition they needed and prepared to follow Vitaly, who was already armed and ready to go.

"Where is the boss Vitaly?" Ivan asked, while only steps away from the door.

"He went ahead. We need to follow his instructions now." Vitaly replied.

In the meantime, the FBI men were searching Gregory's bag. They had all his belongings out, including the map and three other large documents like it.

"I believe you have the wrong man," Gregory said. Staring at Handelman who was reading a corner of one of the documents, where Gregory had written some of his personal notes.

"As Nick said," Anderton commented referring to the driver, "We have been watching your moves for some time now, Thompson. And today, it happens to be your lucky day." Anderton had a phone in his hands, which he tilted back and forth as he addressed Gregory. The phone was nearly identical to the one Niema had been given.

"Our intel says you're about to do one of those lucrative and illegal deals that you've been taking part in since you left the FBI," Handelman said. "We know you were on your way to Toulouse to finalize the deal, and we know your associate will be waiting for you to make the exchange."

"I don't have a clue as to what you are accusing me of, gentlemen." Gregory sounded sarcastic in the way he replied to the allegations from the FBI agents. Based on what they had told him, he knew they didn't really know what he was up to. But unfortunately for Gregory, what he did not know was that he had been entrapped by Sao Li and Milbio.

"You can stop playing Thompson," Kruger said, shaking his head. "We already know everything."

Kruger began thinking about something which happened minutes before Gregory had exited his hotel. Someone had thrown a rock against the window of the minivan the FBI agents were using to spy on him. Nick Kruger, Handelman, and Chuck Lumbar exited the van and Kruger were the first one to see the paper bag on the ground near the driver side door. He kicked it with his right foot, and it had suddenly started to ring. The men nearly jumped out of their socks.

Kruger hesitantly picked it up. The same man, who had spoken to Niema, spoke to Kruger now, providing him with a secret Interpol code, utilized by secret informants to communicate information to their handlers. He gave them valuable information regarding a deal which Gregory was in the process of finalizing with the next hour. The FBI agents came to the conclusion that it would be the perfect opportunity to get their hands on Gregory, as well as dismantling the crime organization he had been allegedly working for.

As Niema left the hotel, the FBI agents were told that he was Gregory's connection. They watched Niema walk. They were told that Niema was on his way to meet with a buyer who had been waiting in the city of Toulouse. They thought of following Niema but were told that there was no need for that. They were given the address where the meeting was to take place. They were given a list of items Gregory had asked his supplier for, including forty illegal elephant tusks and two recently stolen paintings from a famous auction house.

As Handelman continued interrogating Gregory, Nick was driving to the rendezvous point, the same place where Niema was headed. It was the underground level of a parking garage, at the center of Les Carmes, a popular part of Toulouse.

At the same time, Bo Chin was standing inside a dark dungeon. There was a mysterious glare in his eyes, which began to extinguish as he vanished into the dark entrance of a secret cave, leading to hidden catacombs. He was now standing deep under the ground of Le Louvre. There was no visibility as Bo Chin stood in front of a mud and brick wall, where bones were scattered all over the ground. He opened his hand and extended it forward. A brick began to move. It slowly hovered in the air, away from the wall. The brick remained in the air, as Bo Chin placed his hand inside the hole where the brick had been. He reached inside the hole and retrieved an old dusty document rolled up and stamped with the blood seal of a royal stamp. Bo Chin looked at it for a moment but then, something else demanded his immediate attention. A strange sensation filled him. And it was something he was going to have to take immediate attention upon.

A minute later, Vitaly was seen entering a store across the street from the parking garage. Niema had already walked into the garage location. There were only one elevator and a ramp which ended at the fourth level below ground. Niema had already walked deep into the place. It reached five levels underground, and there were cars, minivans, and scooters parked all over. The parking garage was filled almost to capacity. Niema had walked down to the third level. The person on the phone was telling him what to do and he was ordered not to take the elevator. He was complying with the orders but was also being careful and taking his time.

He paused for a moment between the third and fourth levels. As he looked around, he smelled the air. He went down into a push-up position to take a quick look under some of the various vehicles. There was liquid under some of the cars. Niema placed the index finger of his right hand over the liquid under the car in front of him and brought it close to his nose. He recognized the smell. His facial expression changed; it was suddenly not as relaxed as earlier.

As he got back on his feet, he could see the shapes and shadows of a couple of men. They were up ahead at the end of level four. There were parked vehicles around them, as well as two burned-out lightbulbs, keeping the area partially dark. The group of men walked up from behind the parked cars and made themselves visible to Niema. Three of the men were of dark skin color and two were white. The men were wearing dark hoodies that covered their heads and reflective sunglasses over their eyes.

Niema walked at the center of the driveway, where arrows painted on the ground pointed towards each direction, in and out of the garage. The only thing on his mind at the moment was Fei's wellbeing and her immediate whereabouts. He looked ahead at the men and then quickly looked around, trying to see if they had Fei with them. He then looked at the phone in his left hand. It had gone silent, and he was hoping for more instructions. He had stopped walking, but the group of men was slowly closing in on him. Two hundred feet separated them from him.

Then, he set his gaze past behind them, and he could see someone holding Fei and bringing her forward in his direction. It was a dark-skinned man also wearing a hooded sweater and sunglasses. There were two others next to him, dressed in the same manner, with hoodies and jeans. Fei seemed in good condition, given the situation. Her eyes were covered by a dark cloth, and her hands were tied behind her back. But Niema was also able to see something else, something which he could not describe. And it was moving behind a wall, away from the man who was holding Fei. He moved his eyes and his head to attempt to get a clearer assessment of what he was looking at. The men walking towards him saw what he was doing, and they became guarded while looking behind their backs, at those holding Fei.

What is that? Niema asked himself while taking several steps forward, after putting the phone inside the left back pocket of his black cargo pants.

"What's going on, what is he looking at?" Said one of the French-speaking men, near the man holding Fei. The man released the rope tying Fei's hands and allowed her to walk forward towards Niema. He wanted to walk closer to her, but one of the men walking ahead of the three behind was guiding Fei by telling her where to walk. She walked past them, touching two of them as she did. Her hands were wide open, and her arms extended forward.

"Keep walking, one foot in front of the other." The man who had been holding her before said.

"I'm here, it's me..." Niema said. Fei heard his voice and the expression on her face changed. She almost smiled but controlled herself as she calmly accelerated her steps towards Niema. He once again looked around as Fei drew closer to him. he spotted a few people seated inside cars to his left and to the right of Fei. He knew they were not there reading newspapers. But Niema was also trying to look for what he had seen behind the men who had been holding Fei. He was a little taken aback and tried to rub his eyes quickly with the back of his hands. But he still couldn't figure out if what he saw was just a shadow, or if his eyes had betrayed him. Then, the phone began to ring, just as Fei's arm was able to touch his left shoulder.

"Victor...?" Fei said.

"Yes..." Niema replied. "I am so sorry I dragged you into this. I am truly sorry Fei." He said to her. Fei then removed the blindfold and let it fall to the ground. The phone was ringing behind Niema's pocket but they both ignored the sound.

"I am not, Victor..." Fei replied. "I am sorry you did not bring me with you when I gave you the opportunity. When I looked into your eyes the last time we saw each other, I stared into yours, waiting for you to grab my hand and take me with you wherever you were going. I am sorry and upset that it had to be in this way that I was brought back to your side. By the doing of others, and not by you. I hate you for this." Fei's eyes began to fill up with tears as her lips quivered. Her hands were trembling. She looked back at the men who had held her captive. She then looked into Niema's eyes and slapped him with all her strength. He let her and then pulled her into his arms. As he held her, she cried with her face over his chest. Niema looked at her and then at the men staring at him and the woman he loved. The phone had not stopped ringing and he calmly took it out of his left pocket and placed it over his ear.

"What a beautiful scene Victor." Niema recognized the voice immediately. It was Sao Li. His eyes narrowed and his teeth clenched hard against each other.

"You do not seem surprised Victor. That makes me feel good." Sao Li continued. "It shows that you are giving me credit. It shows that indeed, you had thought in your head, that this could only be my doing."

"Is it?" Niema asked sarcastically. "Were you really able to come up with this surprise all on your own?" He paused for a moment and stared at the men, now slowly inching closer to him. Fei moved her face away from his chest and looked up at him. "For some reason, Sao Li, I am having a hard time believing that you put all this together on such short notice. I believe there is something else behind what you are doing. I don't believe this to be entirely about me. Otherwise, why take out Bratislav and his men? Don't tell me you wanted for me and Fei to be together without anyone between us. Are you becoming sentimental in your old age?" At that moment, Niema discreetly placed Fei's hand over a gun that was concealed on him.

"Maybe I am, Victor..." Sao Li said. "But I must admit that your perception is almost accurate. I am not impressed but I like knowing that you are not as simple as I had figured you will be. Indeed, it is not only about you."

At that moment, Niema saw as the men began to disperse and hide. He quickly placed Fei behind him as he looked around, contemplating the situation and how to get her out of it alive. They took several steps back towards the third level. He then heard someone calling on his name from the third level direction. Fei turned around and was the first one to see who it was.

"Victor Niema?" It was Handelman and Anderton, with Gregory walking in between them. They had their guns drawn and Handelman walked ahead to address Niema.

"Who are you, people? What are you doing here?" Niema asked him, while again moving Fei behind him. He could see that Gregory seemed to be very out of place and confused.

"We're FBI, Victor," Handelman announced.

"You are talking to the wrong man FBI," Niema said to Handelman while looking back at the direction where the men who had Fei, were hiding. "And it is also possible that you are also in the wrong place." Niema was weighing his options. He had calculated the chances of him leaving the garage without losing his life were set at 50/50. If he was able to do what he was there to do, Fei would walk out alive. But now, with the surprise addition of FBI agents, things could be moved slightly to his favor.

"You are going to have to come with us, Mr. Niema." Handelman walked ahead, getting closer to Niema and Fei. Fei was also looking around and preparing herself for the worst. She was holding the gun in her left hand, pointed down, placed between her and Niema's bodies. Fei noticed Handelman was keeping his close behind the back of the right hip.

"You don't understand mister whoever you are, FBI or not," Fei said. "You are actually in the wrong place. It would be better for you if you walked out of here while you still can."

"Miss, you will have to come with us as well," Handelman replied. "We have some questions for both of you." He looked back at Gregory. Alderton was standing behind him. He was also looking around but had not noticed that three men were walking down from the level above. Niema looked at the other side and saw the rest of the men walking out from behind the cars.

"Come with me." He told Fei, holding her hand tightly.

"Easy, Mr. Niema," Handelman said, extending his hand towards Niema while keeping his gun down. Suddenly, Niema saw the same shadow he had seen behind the men holding Fei moments ago. This time, it was near a wall behind the FBI agents.

"We need to get out of here fast," Niema said to Handelman while walking towards him. He was trying to figure out what was it that he was seeing. At that moment, the phone started ringing again. Niema answered right away.

"I will enjoy this moment very much Victor." It was Sao Li again. "It was nothing personal against you before, but it is now. I just wanted you to know that."

"Then why don't you just come over here and show your face?" Niema replied. At the same time, the black Mercedes slowly pulled up across the street from where the FBI minivan was parked but it was almost a block and a half away from it. Kroger was aware of all the vehicles driving by and pulling up close to the van, but he could not see the Benz parking from where he was.

"By this time, you must be aware that your contract was given to someone else." Sao Li said to Niema. "You, yourself mentioned to me when you had me in the palm of your hand, remember?" At that moment, all of the men in hoodies began walking towards Niema and the FBI agents. Anderton saw them, as did Handelman and Gregory.

Who are these guys? Handelman asked himself nervously, as he began taking a few steps back.

"You should have killed me when you had the chance." Sao Li continued. "But you didn't, and I will take full advantage of the opportunity you have given me. Thanks to you, I will regain my honor, and I will obtain the position I deserve within my people's movement. You know what Victor? It is good that you will finally be out for good. You were never really a part of it. Because you are not one of us."

Niema continued listening to Sao Li's words while watching how the strange shadow was still standing where it was. But then, someone walked from behind a wall. Niema saw the person calmly walking in his direction and knew who it was. The others walking from the third level saw the person as well and asked amongst themselves who it could be.

"What's going on here?" Anderton asked, immediately bringing a two-way radio out from under his polo shirt. "Nick, call it, we've got unexpected company." Kruger heard Anderton's call over the walkie talkie and quickly jumped into action.

"Shit!" He said while getting his gun ready as he got out of the van. "The cops are not going to get here in time," Kruger said, talking on the radio while he ran towards the garage, which was still one block away.

"Call it in Nick!" Anderton shouted back at him. Kruger heard his voice, accompanied by the loud and sudden sound of gunfire.

"Shit!" Kruger shouted while running as fast as he could towards the garage. "I called it! I called it!" He shouted out, as he ran down the garage driveway, he could hear the shouting and the gunfire all around. Three garage attendants ran away, as did several customers.

"Where are you?" Kruger asked, speaking over the two-way radio, while moving between car to car, taking cover, while running towards where his partners were. The gunfire continued non-stop. Kruger was sweaty and exasperated while concerned for the others. Several bullets hit a wall near him, sending him straight under a car, where he could see and smell the gasoline splashed underneath it. He was only steps away from the fourth level. Kruger was about to stand up and as he did, a man ran in his direction shooting oppositely. Kruger fired back and got him in the back of the head. The man dropped dead on the floor.

"Shit." He whispered, just as he slowly walked down. Bullets hit the wall two inches over his head, just missing him. Once again, he dropped to the floor. This time, a man was thrown flying over him. He could see the body and the man's face as he flew past. The man's head had been cut in half.

"Shit! Shit! Shit!" Kruger held his gun with both hands and crunched himself down against the side of the car. A crumbling sound was heard. It was as if cars were dropping on top of each other. Kruger fired his gun at someone who had seemed to be coming his way. He missed and shot the window glass of a couple of cars near him. He knew he could not stay where he was, and he needed to go and help his partners. The clock was ticking, and the barrage of bullets continued coming from everywhere.

As he stood up, a man was charging towards him. He was ready to shoot Kruger. He pointed his gun at him and pulled the trigger. The man's arm was yanked upwards and he was pushed against the wall behind him. Kruger screamed out loud and then looked at the man who was standing near him. It was Gregory. At that moment, Kruger saw a dark misty shadow moving from behind the car next to him and standing near Gregory.

"Agent Kruger, we've got to leave this place now!" Gregory said. He had bent down and was observing the driveway through the broken windows of a car.

"What the hell is going on?" Kruger asked Gregory. "Where are Anderton and Handelman? Where are they?!" Gregory looked at him and Kruger did not like what he saw in his eyes.

"We have to go, Kruger," Gregory said, ducking down to the floor right next to Kruger. An explosion on the wall near them broke a hole towards another area of the garage. Gregory's left leg was pulled away towards the hole. He did not know how or why, but as Kruger saw it happening, he did not think twice about running through the hole and away from the sounds of the bullets which were coming in his direction, now louder than before. Gregory had gotten on his feet after he crawled through the hole. Kruger was about to follow Gregory and his hand was touching the floor, when he saw Bo Chin standing near Gregory unfazed by the sounds of the explosions and mayhem.

"You there," Bo Chin stared at Kruger while addressing him. "Take him two blocks south if you want to leave this place with your life." Kruger looked at Bo Chin, feeling a sensation in his heart, which he had never felt before. "Where is the forgery?" Bo Chin was now addressing Gregory, Kruger heard his words and assumed that Bo Chin had something to do with Gregory's illicit deals. He also saw as Bo Chin handed Gregory a document that was rolled up, with a red seal on it.

"The Gigas is hidden," Gregory said to Bo Chin. "Is this what you said you will give me?" He asked him. Kruger had no clue as to what was happening between Bo Chin and Gregory, but he knew everything happening in the garage at the moment must have been their doing.

"Leave now." Bo Chin said. "Take him and you will live. Go now." He stared at Kruger deep into his eyes, while speaking very directly. When Kruger blinked his eyes, Bo Chin was already gone. He looked at Gregory in shock while Gregory got on his feet and looked at the rolled document he had been given.

"Kruger, let's get the hell out of here now!" Gregory said looking at Kruger. Kruger checked the ammo in his gun and started running away from the hole. Gregory followed him and just before they went through a door, Kruger took one last look back. What he saw caused him to get down to the floor.

"What the hell was that?" Kruger shouted at Gregory. Gregory followed his gaze and looked back, not seeing anything.

"What happened? Get up! Let's get out of here!" Gregory shouted at him. He paused only for a moment, before running ahead. After looking at the wall and the hole from where they had run away from, it took Kruger another second to get up and run after Gregory.

In the meantime, at the streets behind the garage, Anatoly was driving a car that had just broken through a wall. Niema and Fei were in the back seat looking through the rear broken windshield of the car.

"Go, boss, run!" Anatoly shouted to Niema.

"Get out, let's go!" Niema said to Anatoly. Something didn't seem right. Niema then looked at Anatoly closer and realized he had been shot several times in the chest. Anatoly looked back at Niema and smiled. Fei heard voices coming from behind them. She pointed the assault rifle she'd been carrying in that same direction.

"It's been a pleasure working by your side boss." Anatoly held Niema's hand. "Thanks to you, my family will live a very decent life. Much better than what they ever thought I would do for them. My father must be very disappointed though. I didn't turn out to be the loser he predicted." Anatoly and Niema laughed through their sadness. Niema looked at him with sincerity in the sorrow he was feeling.

"Go, boss, please go," Anatoly begged.

"Victor..." Fei said.

"You are one those rare friends a man never knew he had, until..." Niema did not finish what he had to say to Anatoly. Anatoly was gone. Niema let his hand go finally.

"Victor!" Fei shouted, just as several bullets hit the trunk of the car. Fei fired back, spraying bullets in every direction. Niema then grabbed her arm and they ran away through the back streets.

"This way!" Someone shouted. People could be seen running away and hiding. Black smoke billowed from the exit tunnels of the parking garage and the sound of emergency vehicles could be heard from around the corner. Two blocks away,

Niema had taken hold of the assault rifle as he and Fei ran on the sidewalk. Niema continued looking at the rooftops of the small buildings around the area.

"Where are we going, Victor?" Fei asked Niema. He did not answer. He was still looking up. Then Fei abruptly stopped running and dropped almost back to the floor, dragging Niema down with her. He got down on one knee and held the rifle ready to shoot anyone, Fei was looking ahead. She gasped as her eyes were wide open. Niema's attention was to the rear, to where they had heard the men following them.

"Get up!" Niema ordered. "On your feet Fei!" Fei did not move, nor say anything. Niema pulled her arm and she pulled his arm back. He looked at her, before looking towards the direction where she was looking. A soon as he looked in that direction, his reaction was instant. He turned his entire body away while pointing the rifle ahead, and without hesitation, he opened fire.

In a matter of seconds, Niema emptied the entire clip. The smoke was still flowing out of the barrel of the rifle when he tossed it away. Fei was already on her feet and ready to run. She had held on to Niema's arm, but he had other plans besides running away from what he knew, was the bottom of a situation, where the only way out was down. At that moment, Niema turned around to face Fei. She looked into his eyes without any idea of what he was about to do. He had pulled out a leather pouch from one of the right leg pockets of his cargo pants and without saying anything to Fei, he poured an oily textured green liquid from the pouch over Fei's head, arms, and body.

"Victor!" Fei cried out, not understanding why Niema pushed her away. She almost fell backward but stumbled against a car, while cleaning the liquid away from her eyes.

"Remember the ghost story I told you?" Niema looked at Fei with distraught eyes. "That's him! Run!" Niema shouted at her, practically pushing her to get away. It took a couple of seconds for her to accept what Niema was attempting to do, and she could not fully understand him. But nevertheless, she trusted him and decided to listen.

From the corner of his eyes, he watched as Fei ran away which gave him a small sense of comfort. Ahead of him, Bo Chin walked slowly in his direction. Niema had a difficult time believing how such a nonthreatening looking man could be feared by so many. Niema saw he was dressed strangely out of time and place. His clothes looked old fashioned, to say the least. Bo Chin had on a dark long robe with an open cross collar that looked very much like something out of ancient China.

"Victor Niema..." Bo Chin said while walking closer to Niema. The streets were still filling up with people running everywhere, while heavily armed policemen exited their emergency vehicles. Three officers had already arrived near the main entrance of the parking garage. There was thick dark smoke everywhere they looked, and vehicles engulfed in flames were blocking their sight. At the same time, Gregory and Kruger ran past the minivan the FBI had been using. And as they were about to turn the corner, the black Mercedes pulled up in front of them in the middle of the street. There was a man dressed as a ninja in the driver's seat, where only his eyes were visible. He signaled to Gregory and Kruger to get inside the car. Gregory was the first one to get in the back seat. Kruger hesitated to get in, finding the entire thing too strange.

"Get in already!" Gregory insisted for him to get in at once. But Kruger did not. The driver drove away, accelerating very fast, leaving the FBI agent confused and stranded in the middle of the street.

At the same time, Niema had poured the last remaining portion of the liquid over his hands and arms. Bo Chin had stopped walking and stared at him in silence.

"You have been a valiant warrior Victor Niema." Bo Chin said. "And for your valor, you will be given an honorable death." Niema looked behind Bo Chin. He also could see three men dressed as ninjas, holding long swords, and running in his direction. He turned his head around and saw two others coming from the opposite way.

"The only death I will find honorable will be dying by own choice and at my own time," Niema said to Bo Chin, just as he lifted his left hand in the air and allowed it to go down fast. At that moment, shots were fired at the two men running towards Niema from the rear. They were hit with explosive bullets, which caused their bodies from the torso and up, to blow up. Bo Chin saw as his men perished, their legs were still fidgeting and bleeding over the sidewalk. He seemed not to care.

Niema sought cover behind a car, observing as Bo Chin stared at him, motionless, unaffected by the bullets. The other three men ran past Bo Chin on their way to Niema. They seemed indifferent to the luck of their associates and carried their swords ready to strike. One of them, was only a foot away from Niema as he held his sword in his right hand up in the air.

Niema stood up holding his hunting knife in his left hand. The man running close to him was struck by a bullet in the right arm. His arm and his head were both taken off this body. What was left of his body, fell to the ground by Niema's feet. Niema put his attention towards the other two, who continued running in his direction. Even as the body of the one who had been hit, was trembling on the ground with his blood spilling all around. Bo Chin stood motionless, still staring at Niema. As another of his men was struck on the knees, that man fell to the ground and continued crawling towards Niema, with a sword in hand and without taking his eyes away off his target. His legs remained behind.

"Cease." The last man going after Niema and the one crawling on the floor heard Bo Chin's voice. They both looked back at Bo Chin, sheathing their swords behind their backs. They then looked back at Niema and at the others who had been killed.

"Sire," The man turned around and kneeled while facing Bo Chin. The other crawled back towards his leader but could not continue any further due to the heavy blood loss. The one on his knees looked at Bo Chin and then upon his dead associate. He turned and ran back in the same direction he had come from. Niema watched as the men ran away and switched his knife from his left to his right hand, to face Bo Chin. But he could no longer see him. Niema then heard a loud cry coming from the building across the street. He then saw Ivan drop down from a top floor window and hit the street headfirst.

"Shit..." Niema said. He looked ahead again, and Bo Chin was once again standing in the same place where he was before. At that moment, a truck turned the corner at a very high speed and crashed its way through every vehicle parked in the street, all the way to where Bo Chin was standing. Bo Chin did not turn around to look at the truck, which ultimately ended up half-way inside a store.

Niema stepped back but did not run away. Bo Chin was standing right in front of him, as a group of men exited from the truck, shooting their machine guns at both men. Bo Chin looked down to the ground and whistled, as Niema again lost sight of him, amidst a rain of bullets and explosions. There was crying and shouting. Smoke and dust flew everywhere. Niema had crunched down on the floor to take cover from the bullets but instead, heads and arms flew about in every direction. It did not take long for all the men to be disposed of by Bo Chin, who was now walking towards him from within the blinding smoke. Bo Chin stopped walking and rested by the side of the burning truck. Debris was still falling from the wall of the store's façade and above the small building.

"You have run out of surprises Victor Niema." Bo Chin said, this time calmly walking towards Niema. Niema was on his feet and for a moment, looked at his hands. They were still wet from the liquid that he poured on them. He then looked at Bo Chin, confidently walking towards him. And this inspired him to hold his knife with a tight grip and readied himself for a fight.

"I guess it will not be honorable after all, Victor Niema." Bo Chin said.

"Then bring it over..." Niema replied with anger in his voice. He was not finished speaking when he felt something pulling his right leg from behind, making him slide sideways and fall to the floor. Just at the same time, something flew past his head, barely missing him. It was like a ball of fire that sizzled past the side of his left cheekbone. The only thing he was able to see was a trail of black smoke spiraling towards the wall next to him, breaking a hole through it that was seven feet wide. Niema had fallen on his back but was able to get back on his feet with agility. He shook of debris and dust from his head and face.

But then, as soon as he did, he felt the crushing grip of a hand almost breaking his neck. He was quick to react and grabbed Bo Chin's arm with his left hand while bringing his knife up to stab him in the stomach. But Bo Chin released his neck before he even realized it. Niema looked at his left hand and saw drops of the oily liquid slithering down the side of his wrist. He then noticed Bo Chin was keeping a distance from him and was looking at his own right arm, which was giving out a strange pulsating dark glare.

It really works... Niema thought to himself while sliding the knife on the palm of his closed left hand to coat it with the liquid.

"Come and get me, you son of a bitch. What are you waiting for? I'm ready for you." Niema said, staring at Bo Chin, who was staring back at him. Bo Chin was slowly being covered by the smoke coming from the burning truck. He was about to strike back against Niema. Niema readied himself. But Bo Chin sensed something, which momentarily distracted him from Niema.

At the same time, Gregory was being escorted away in the black Mercedes, and was already far away from the vicinity, with the Codex Gigas and the secret documents from Bo Chin, next to him. Bo Chin then looked at Niema and before Niema could even move, Bo Chin was standing right behind him. Niema felt an overwhelming sensation and without even being touched by Bo Chin, he was slammed through the hole in the wall. He went right through it, dropping a few feet ahead inside. The knife had fallen away from where he was. His face was covered in blood, there were smoke and dust all around, accompanied by the blaring alarms sounding all around. Again, he quickly got back up on his feet, wasting no time, looking for his knife. Instead, he grabbed hold of a metal pipe that he held up like a baseball bat.

"Come! Come at me!" Niema shouted out. He was acting irrational and looked around everywhere. "I'm still here! Still alive! Come and try to take me like you did with Monica! Come and try it, you demon!"

"You give yourself too much importance Victor Niema." Bo Chin said. Niema looked for him through the thickness of the smoke and dust, attempting to figure out where the sound of his voice was coming from. "The value of the life of someone like your niece equates to more than one thousand of yours. You are an insect. Monica is out of your grasp. For now, live a few more days. As you have seen, I can find you, whenever I want to. Therefore, I must place my attention to where it is most required. I have more important events to handle. Perhaps I can put the life of an insect to some use."

"Your excuses don't matter to me!" Niema shouted out, while still looking for Bo Chin. He had gone back out into the street through the same hole in the wall. There were police cars, fire trucks and ambulances everywhere now. Half a dozen armed police officers were seen running towards him and shouting for him to get on the ground. Niema dropped the metal pipe on the ground and did as he was told by the police. There were no lapses in his mental judgment, he knew the fight was not yet over, but his fight was not with the police. As he lay on the ground, he could still see Ivan's dead body where he had fallen. He looked around while wondering about what Bo Chin had said. The officers were asking him questions regarding his identity while getting handcuffed. He did not answer.

Sometime later, during the early morning hours, Gregory was being ushered into a private luxury yacht in Marseille. He looked at the name on the side of the vessel, it read Le Xang. An elderly Asian man, dressed in an old-fashioned shenyi, welcomed him and asked him to make himself comfortable inside. Gregory was thankful to the man and asked if he could take a shower.

"Clearly you require one." The man said. "You will find fresh towels and soap in the resting quarters."
From a short distance to the harbor, the black Mercedes was driving away. Bo Chin was seated in the back seat, thinking quietly with his head down and his eyes closed. The vehicle was driving itself.

Back at the parking garage, Sao Li observed the commotion and the aftermath of the chaotic events a block away, from the fifth-floor window of a hotel room. Two of his men sat in the background as their boss wondered privately. He had a phone in his right hand and looked at it periodically.

How is it possible? He thought. *They both survived... How? Bo Chin could not kill Victor... The man could not eliminate Bo Chin...*

Sao Li turned and faced his men. They looked at him with attention. "How could they both live? They both escaped with their lives." They all looked at each other, wondering the same. Jae 'Hwa in particular, was very concerned with a thought in his mind. He wondered whether this failure had just been the beginning of a more chaotic time to come and if Sao Li was even ready to face the likes of what they just witnessed.

∞

A few days had passed, it was almost dawn. After staying hidden in a small space in the basement of a church, provided by a priest who knew Susan's mother-in-law, Susan and the children left for a safer place to stay until Marcus returned. They had just arrived at Carolina's house. Carolina, who was Marcus's distant cousin, lived in a small town behind the mountains, that was close to the ocean and away from the perils of the inner city. It was a small close-knit community where everyone knew each other by first and last name, where their neighbors worked, where their neighbors' kids went to school and what time everyone was expected to be home every single day.

This is where Susan knew her children would have a better sense of safety. Carolina lived in a nice house with ample space for everyone. Her husband was a known local fisherman and owned a seafood store, which he was planning to expand. They had four children- three girls and one boy. They were eleven, nine, eight, and the boy was six years old. Grace, Carolina's elder daughter, was very happy to see Susan and her cousins and she greeted everyone with big hugs.

All the children quickly ran to the backyard to play. Susan was about to go after them, but Carolina held her hand and asked her to stay with her in the kitchen. "Let the children play. You can help me prepare the feast I have planned for you all tonight." She said with a warm smile. Susan had a worried look on her face and Carolina noticed it.

"You can let go of that city life, Susan. You are safe here." Carolina assured her. "I don't know why you didn't think about coming to me any sooner." Susan embraced Carolina and began to cry in her arms. Carolina told her that she understood how she felt. She told her she knew how scared and overwhelmed Susan was in the city. Susan wanted to thank Carolina for receiving her and the children in the way she did, knowing the problems that followed them. But Carolina simply said not to be worried.

"It is alright. Just relax for once Susan." Carolina said.

Susan then noticed that Lora was near the door that was connected to the living room. She stood motionless staring at a dark corner and Susan ran towards her.

"Lora!" She cried out. Lora did not respond, and Susan quickly embraced her and carried her up into her arms.

Carolina ran after Susan. "What's wrong?"

She quickly turned on the light of the living room and to her surprise, Lora was staring at a little bird, that had escaped from its cage at the backyard patio.

"This little escape artist got out sometime yesterday, but it made its way back home after a wild night out on the town." Susan and Carolina shared a laugh at the expense of the little bird and walked back towards the kitchen while Susan placed Lora down.

"Lora, it's beautiful outside, go have fun with the rest of the kids," Carolina said. Lora was about to take a step forward when she saw the shape of someone standing right by the kitchen as Susan and Carolina walked towards it without looking ahead, while still laughing at the joke Carolina made about the bird.

"Mommy…" Lora said nervously. Susan looked at her and as Carolina got to the kitchen, there was no one there.

"Yes, dear?" Susan asked.

"Mommy, can you take me to the backyard?"

Susan told Carolina that she was going to be right back.

"Take your time," Carolina said as she began placing all the cooking ingredients on top of the kitchen counter. Lora continued to stare at whoever was standing motionless right near Carolina. Someone neither Carolina nor Susan could see.

Later in the evening, Carolina's husband, Albert, arrived from work and was very surprised to see that Susan and her children were visiting. Carolina did not have time to explain everything to him, but he went ahead and told Susan that he thought this would be a very good opportunity for her to connect with the type of life he and his family had.

"I've wanted to get out of that city for a long time, but the attachment Marcus has to that house and the promise he made his mother before she passed away, was what has kept us there all this time."

"I hope Marcus takes a chance and gets a fresh start away from all of the problems that come with living in the city," Albert said, while his wife nodded in agreement.

After an unusually festive dinner, they all went out to the back porch. They sat back while looking up at the stars and enjoyed some fresh lemonade, while the kids nibbled on some homemade pastries.

This is incredible... Susan's thoughts were all over the place. There had been a power outage in Carolina's town. It was the first time in a long time that she felt relaxed and not preoccupied with the weird noises she heard outside her door, during the dark moments of power outages at night. She was overcome with emotions and cried quietly. She placed her hand over her mouth, to keep anyone else from noticing. She was aware of how relaxed her children looked and how well they were interacting with their cousins.

Thank you, God. Thank you... This is incredible. She said to herself again, while actually allowing herself to recline back into her seat. She looked up at the stars just as Albert and Carolina were doing. She looked around one more time, and for that moment, all of the problems her family had been going through seemed to have vanished.

To be continued...

ABOUT THE AUTHOR

The author feels that this story was inside all their life but was only able to come out through a form of meditation. In this case, the meditation was taking a piece of paper and a pen and letting those thoughts out. Thus, the story was freed. It is now free to follow a path which will lead to those who may identify with its intended meaning. Its meaning is not only identified through the eyes of the reader, but also through the subconscious of their spirit.